Michaels

"Michaels has done it again....
Witty dialogue peppers a plot full of delectable details exposing the foibles and follies of the age."
—*Publishers Weekly,* starred review,
on *The Butler Did It*

"If you want emotion, humor and characters you can love, you want a story by Kasey Michaels."
—*New York Times* bestselling author Joan Hohl

"Kasey Michaels aims for the heart and never misses."
—*New York Times* bestselling author Nora Roberts

"Kasey Michaels creates characters who stick with you long after her wonderful stories are told."
—*New York Times* bestselling author Kay Hooper

"Michaels demonstrates her flair for creating likable protagonists who possess chemistry, charm and a penchant for getting into trouble. In addition, her dialogue and descriptions are full of humor."
—*Publishers Weekly* on *This Must Be Love*

Coming soon from Kasey Michaels and HQN BOOKS

A new Regency Trilogy
A GENTLEMAN BY ANY OTHER NAME
March 2006

THE DANGEROUS DEBUTANTE
April 2006

BEWARE OF VIRTUOUS WOMEN
May 2006

Also Available from HQN Books

THE BUTLER DID IT
SHALL WE DANCE?

Kasey Michaels

stuck in shangri-la

ISBN 0-373-77059-6

STUCK IN SHANGRI-LA

This edition published by arrangement with Harlequin Books S.A.

www.HQNBooks.com

Printed in U.S.A.

To Jean Herman, "Aunt Jean," friend and family member of forty years. Bet you and Mother are once again shopping at Leh's, sharing lunchtime stories over plates of spaghetti and meatballs, and giggling as you bring those poker machines to their knees.
We love you....

PROLOGUE

THE JUNE NIGHT SLIPPED softly over the edge of the horseshoe-shaped cliff marking the worked-out Pennsylvania slate quarry. Darkness crept on tiptoe across the lush, sweeping lawns that ran away from that cliff and settled around the large Victorian-era clapboard mansion...mercifully hiding from view the one-hundred-foot-long drive lined either side with three-foot-tall alternating ceramic flamingos and motion-detector frogs.

On the second floor of the three-story house, lights burned in the master bedroom as the grandfather clock in the downstairs foyer struck nine times, to mark the hour. The occupant of the room was up late tonight, as *Jeopardy* and *Wheel of Fortune* had been over for more than an hour.

But—hubba-hubba—it was Friday.

Date night.

Saturday night had been date night, before Hecuba Willikins had gotten cable, at which time he'd discovered a cable station that aired reruns of all the old *Perry Mason* episodes.

Adjustments had been made.

Hecuba stood in front of the full-length mirror, admiring the silk scarf he'd tucked into his burgundy satin robe, wondering if he had time to clip his toenails before…but no. No time for that.

He huffed into his cupped palms to check his breath, detecting only the scent of Polident, which was unavoidable. Then he gave the sash of his robe another tug around his wide, naked middle, and retired to the deep-green-velvet-hung four-poster, to take up his position there, the better to watch the door.

She entered from the bathroom, where she had hidden herself a half hour earlier, seductively dragging her pink peignoir along the carpet behind her as she went.

Taller than Hecuba by a good three inches, and thinner than he by a good seventy pounds, Lily Paige had brushed out her long, dark-brown hair, newly colored at the local Budget Classy Cuts, and had applied bright-red lipstick to her thin lips.

Her gaze never left the bed as she slinked seductively about the large chamber, clicking a battery-operated, gunlike gadget to fire up the dozens of fat white candles, turning off the lights even as she turned on the rotating disco ball that hung in the center of the room.

There was no wine. Wine was too relaxing for people of their ages. She poured sparkling apple juice into two champagne goblets, tossing back the contents of one, then slowly licking her lips as she presented the second glass to Hecuba.

"My own wicked temptress," Hecuba said, breathing in the intoxicating scent of her Jean Naté body splash. He watched with growing ardor as she opened the top drawer of the bedside table and brought out a dog-eared copy of *The Joy of Sex,* then joined him on the bed.

"All right, here I am. Which page this week, Horry?" Lily asked, removing her fuzzy bunny slippers, the ones with the sides cut out to leave room for her bunions.

Hecuba's blood roared in his ears. Those bunny slippers always turned him on. "You pick, my cruel wanton."

Lily bit back a sigh, as she was so often the one who had to choose. Couldn't Horry be more masterful? He certainly had no problem giving orders outside the bedroom. "Very well," she said, turning the pages until she'd found one that caught her attention. And shouldn't women naturally be on top? "This one?"

Hecuba, who had been reclining Roman–senatorlike against the pillows, pushed the book farther away so that he could focus his gaze on the page. "Afraid I'll crush you, are you, my delicate little Lily-pad? It's all your good cooking, you know."

But Lily was already busy lining up Hecuba's favorite props: his Lawrence of Arabia headscarf, his silken riding whip that he would hold but never use, the long-stemmed red silk rose he sometimes wanted her to clamp between her teeth.

Thirty years. They'd been together thirty years. They'd begun by playing Horry and the Housekeeper, and gone from there to Antony and Cleopatra, to the Lost Traveling Salesman and the Farmer's Daughter, even to Perry Mason and Della Street.

For six days a week they remained Mr. Willikins and Lily. But, oh, these Friday-night dates!

Hecuba picked up the remote control for his latest toy, pressed the Play button, and the sounds of Ravel's "Bolero" rushed from speakers placed in all four corners of the ceiling.

Candlelight reflected in the hundreds of small, square mirrors in the revolving disco ball.

Perfect. Everything was perfect.

"And *action*!" Hecuba called out, reaching for Lily.

There was huffing. There was puffing. There were two time-outs to rub down leg cramps. Lily found a moment to swat Lucky, Hecuba's big black cat, who only moved to the bottom of the bed for a while before padding back up to watch.

And then, only ninety minutes later, in what he privately considered a record for the new millennium, Hecuba roared like a bull for a second time as Lily rode him, astride; truly outdoing himself, his release a most beautiful, perfect thing, never to be matched. Soaring, driving, pumping away like he was thirty again. It was wonderful. He felt wonderful. More, more! Wonderful! On and on. Never stop! *Wonderful!* Wonder—

"Horry?" Lily said around the plastic stem still clamped between her teeth. "That's not fair. Horry, don't stop yet. Horry? Giddy-up!" She bounced up and down, urging him to keep moving. How dare he just lie there like some great lump? Sure, he'd had his satisfaction, twice! But what about her?

Lily removed the rose, tossing it to one side as she gave up, climbed off him, pulling her filmy nightgown down modestly as she sat back on her haunches and looked at him in disgust.

"Horry? That's not funny, Horry, and never was." She put a hand on his shoulder, to shake him. "Stop that, stop pretending to be—*Horry!*"

Lucky, who had been otherwise occupied watching the dancing lights from the rotating disco ball, as nothing was happening on the bed that hadn't happened before, slowly stretched, stood and walked across the pillows to look down at his master. And then the fur on his quickly arched back went up as his ears went down, he hissed and took off like a shot for the hallway.

Lily wasn't a stupid woman. She knew that cats *knew.* Cats always knew, Lucky knowing more than most, curse him. Not very hopeful, she still tried pounding on Hecuba's chest. She tried holding his nose and breathing into his mouth. She tried all of that, but nothing worked.

Then she removed the Lawrence of Arabia headdress and put it and the whip and the rose and the copy of *The Joy of Sex* back in the drawer.

And, a minimum of three times before she got dressed and called the police, she pushed at his cheeks with her fingers, trying in vain to remove the smile from Horry of Arabia's face....

CHAPTER ONE

DARCIE REED THANKED the secretary who'd informed her that Mr. Blackwell wished to see her in his office. She pulled the mirror from her bottom drawer and checked to make sure that her blond hair was still sleekly coiled into its French twist.

She stood up, ran her hands over the collar of her white, man-style blouse to be sure it lay flat over the top of her navy suit jacket, then smoothed down her below-the-knee matching navy skirt and picked up the file on the Hastings merger.

It was only ten o'clock, and a Monday, so she had not expected to be summoned to Mr. Blackwell's office, especially since the man had flown to Vegas for the weekend with his third wife. Bunny? Binny? Something with a B.

Maybe he was trying to catch her off her guard, asleep at the switch, whatever. Ha! Clive Blackwell would have to do more than ask for her work two days early to catch her off guard. Darcie ate, slept, drank, lived Blackwell Industries, and there was nothing she didn't know about the proposed Hastings merger.

Wednesday she would make her presentation, and

her recommendations. The board would review her findings, and by this time next week, hello, corner office!

Oh, yes. She was ready. Maybe she hadn't been born ready, and maybe she'd already had one false start, but, boy, she was ready now, if grim determination to succeed meant anything. After all, she had something to prove.

Head held high, her sensible two-inch navy pumps made no noise once she'd left the elevator on the forty-second floor and stepped onto the plush carpet of the executive suite. *Movin' on up, to the big time...*

Darcie concentrated on her breathing even as the receptionist (in line to be Mrs. Blackwell Number Four, if rumor was right) glared at her as if she was the enemy, then waved her into the big man's office before returning her attention to her nail file.

Darcie knocked with what she hoped was the correct mix of deference and assertion before opening the door. She paused with her hand on the crystal doorknob, looking around the large office furnished in Corinthian leather and real antiques, and blessed with one of the best views in Pittsburgh.

Someday, this would be hers. Someday, she'd have it all, everything she'd worked for so diligently all the way through college and grad school. Corner office, key to the executive bathroom, membership in the squash club—she could learn to play squash.

It was good to have goals. Even if she'd had to give up everything else in order to go for them.

"Darcie!"

"Mr. Blackwell. Good morning, sir," Darcie said, inclining her head slightly before advancing across a mile of Persian carpet to stand in front of the great man's immense desk.

Technically, professionally, she was Ms. Reed, but this guy was the CEO. Hardly professional, but she could make allowances for the CEO. She deposited the file on his desk. "I've brought the Hastings merger file with me. I finalized my findings over the weekend, and I'm prepared to brief you on the particulars before Wednesday's board meeting."

Clive Blackwell—who seemed to have entirely too much interest in watching Darcie tug on her skirt hem once she'd taken the seat he'd gestured toward—frowned for a moment, then his expression cleared.

"Oh, right, right. The Hastings merger. That's why I called you up here. I knew there was something I'd wanted to tell you before I left for Vegas, but I just remembered it this morning, when I happened to see you in the parking garage. Isn't going to happen. I was kind of caught up with Billie, you know, one last shot at getting it right? Dropped ten thousand at the tables and Billie's filing for divorce this morning. Yeah, well, that's life. No sense crying over spilt milk—Billie, I mean. Oh, and the merger, too, I guess."

"Sir?" Darcie asked, doing a quick mental recap of the hours she'd spent researching Hastings Industries. The hours, the days, the weeks of slogging through financial records and productivity reports and all that, to be truthful, pretty darn boring stuff.

This past weekend she'd never left her apartment,

never even gotten out of her pajamas; eaten Wheaties three meals a day because shopping would have taken too much time. And now this corporate idiot was saying the merger idea had been dropped? Dropped *last week*? No, that wasn't possible. "I'm afraid I—"

"Oh, no, no. Not to fret. I'm not upset. It was only a trial balloon, anyway. I never thought it would fly, personally, but we needed to give the new gal something to cut her teeth on, right? Ben Hastings backed out when he landed a juicy new contract with the government. Still, good practice, wasn't it?"

Darcie pictured all her work being fed into a shredder. Pictured Clive Blackwell being served up to that shredder as a chaser. She had to get away, go somewhere private and scream. A lot. She put her hands on the chair arms, figuring she'd need something to hold on to when she stood up. "I see. Then, sir, if you'll excuse me?"

He remained in his chair behind the desk, but smoothed back his thinning hair with both hands. "No, no. Sit. Stay a while, talk to me. Tell me how you like it here. You like it here? I have to tell you, I've been thinking about you a lot. Say, how about getting us some coffee while we talk awhile? I take two sugars. I like my coffee sweet. I like *everything* sweet."

No! Not a second time! What did she have to do—wear a sack over her head? Next career move, she'd only apply at female-run companies. "I'm sorry," Darcie said coolly as she got to her feet, "but I don't make coffee, Mr. Blackwell."

Clive Blackwell stood up, showing off his tummy

tuck and spray-on tan, and made his way around to the front of the desk.

Darcie recognized this as Step Two in Let's Seduce the New Girl. Step Three coming up—the one where she had to make a break for it.

"All right, sweetheart, no coffee. Do you want to let me chase you around the desk? That could be fun."

Darcie backed up two paces, ready to bolt for the door. "I—no, I—did you really just say what I thought you just said?"

Clive smiled. "Now, now, honey, don't get your knickers in a twist. Let's be reasonable here, all right? Let me make it up to you about this Hastings business, if you're that upset about it. How does dinner sound? You, me, a few bottles of champagne?"

And then he said those famous last words Darcie had already heard once in her short professional life: "Or do you really think I hired you for your brains?"

Darcie wasn't going to run. Not this time. She drew herself up straight, jutted out her chin, and said, "I have a master's in business, Mr. Blackwell."

"Exactly! Now you're getting it!" Clive crowed, moving closer even as Darcie retreated. "And that qualifies you to go after the master of this business." He swaggered where he stood. "That would be me."

"Why, you—"

"Mr. Blackwell? Excuse me, sir, but there's an emergency call for Ms. Reed."

"Tell them to leave a message. And, damn it, Mitzi, close the door."

Darcie picked up the Hastings file. "No, I'll take it in my office."

"I can have it transferred in here. I think."

"You can do that now, Mitzi?" Mr. Blackwell asked. "Don't get too smart, or you'll lose all your charm. Okay, transfer the call to my phone."

"No, really, I'd rather—"

But Mitzi had already raced back to her office on her four-inch heels, and while Darcie held the Hastings file protectively against her chest, the call was transferred.

Both she and Mr. Blackwell reached for the phone. He beat her, putting the call on the speaker.

"Clive Blackwell here with Ms. Reed. Who are you?"

Silence.

Darcie stepped closer to the phone. "Hello? Darcie Reed here."

The voice sounded hollow, as if the man was speaking through a tin can. "Ms. Reed? My name is Clark Humbolt. Attorney Clark Humbolt, your uncle Hecuba's attorney?"

Darcie kept one eye on the phone, the other on Clive Blackwell, who had begun circling her as if he was a hawk and she was a fuzzy yellow duckling. "Attorney Humbolt. Has something happened to my uncle?"

"I dislike being the bearer of bad news, Ms. Reed, but yes. Your uncle…unexpectedly expired Friday evening. As per his explicit instructions, he was cremated privately this morning."

Darcie reeled where she stood, which gave Clive the perfect excuse to catch her in his arms and pull her against his chest. "Oh, poor girl. There there," he said, rubbing her back, rubbing quite low on her back. "Humbolt? Clive Blackwell again. I'm certain dearest Darcie would like to know if it was a peaceful passing?"

Silence.

"Let…me…go," Darcie said, pushing herself free of Clive's clutches. "Attorney Humbolt? This…this is very much a shock to me. I don't think I'm taking it in. I had no idea Uncle Horry was ill. But you said unexpectedly?"

"He…um, that is…your uncle's passing was quite peaceful. He died in bed…sleeping. Ms. Reed, I know this is a bad time, but it is absolutely necessary for you to come to Cliff House as soon as possible for the reading of your uncle's will. Can you be here tomorrow?"

"Come to Shangri-La," Darcie said, using her uncle's name for the old house. "Yes, I can do that. I…I would have driven in this weekend, if you'd only called me."

"But I did, Ms. Reed, several times. You didn't get any of my messages?"

Darcie closed her eyes. She'd let the machine pick up all weekend, because she'd been working on the Hastings merger. She'd turned off the volume, and never so much as checked her messages, because she was working on the Hastings merger—and because she never got any calls anyway, not since…

"Oh, Attorney Humbolt, I'm so sorry. I would have been there for the services."

"No, no services. Your uncle didn't hold with such things, as you might know. He bought his urn years ago, and he'll be installed on the mantel in his study for the reading of the will. You will be here?"

"Yes. Yes, of course. Tomorrow, you said? I'm only six hours away. I'll drive in tonight and stay in a motel. I don't want to bother Lily. Oh, poor Lily. She must be devastated. She's been Uncle Horry's housekeeper forever."

"Yes, Ms. Reed, that she has. The reading will be tomorrow at eleven. Lily will then serve luncheon, although I'm afraid I have another engagement. Again, my sincere condolences. Hecuba Willikins was a…was an extraordinary man. And now, if you'll excuse me, I have another call to make concerning this matter."

Clive was advancing again, and Darcie took refuge behind the desk. "Who would you be calling, Mr. Humbolt?"

"He hung up," Clive said, pressing a button on the phone, then holding out his arms to her. "Poor little thing. Your uncle, dead. Although dying in bed isn't such a bad thing. Do you think he was alone?"

"He most certainly was—" Darcie had a flash of memory that had a lot to do with catching Uncle Horry pinching Lily's bottom when he thought no one was looking. "Thank you for the use of your office, Mr. Blackwell. My uncle lives—lived—just outside Philadelphia. I really must go there."

"Fine, fine, take all the time you need. And when you come back, I'll need you to accompany me on a business trip."

"A…a business trip?" Would the man just shut up and let her escape with at least some of her dignity intact? She still had to walk past Mitzi, for crying out loud.

"Yes, we definitely have some business to settle. Where shall it be, sweetheart? Paris? Rome? *Bimini?*"

Darcie threw the Hastings merger folder at him and took off for the door. "Pick a page, any page," she called over her shoulder, "and consider it my resignation, effective today!"

It was only as she gathered her personal belongings from her desk and headed for the parking lot that she at last gave in to grief over the loss of Uncle Horry, her dear, sweet, silly uncle Horry.

Combined with her anger and disappointment in yet another professional failure, that grief kept her weeping into a progression of tissues as she packed up everything in her furnished studio apartment. She'd been renting by the month until she was certain Pittsburgh would be her new home, so there was nothing more to do than turn in her key, ask for the security deposit she already knew she'd never see, and head her three-year-old car east.

CAMERON PIERCE IGNORED the meat loaf on his lunch plate as he tried to figure out how a nice boy like him got to be in trouble like this. Mrs. Merton, who'd been flirting with him ever since they'd ordered, now had her shoe off and was trailing her toes up and down his leg.

She'd been eyeing him up when he'd come to her Mainline, Philadelphia, mansion to listen to her husband's plans to add a two-story addition that would include a new master suite as well as an indoor pool and exercise room.

So, having already tagged her as a woman on the lookout for some...*diversion* in her life—what in hell had made him believe this invitation to lunch was to discuss the particulars of the project? Stupid. Stupid, stupid move. Now he had to pretend he didn't notice that she was initiating a game of footsie, and still play nice or else lose the commission.

Not that he and Doug needed the work. They were already pretty solidly booked into the next year. But an indoor pool? That could be a real fun project, something a little different, and he didn't want to blow his opportunity.

The foot moved up another few inches, and Cameron shifted slightly in his chair as he looked around the room. He spied their waiter, who was grinning widely as he watched, and the guy winked at him. Knock that tip back five percent.

"As...as I was saying, Mrs. Merton—"

"Sheila. Call me *Shee*-la," Mrs. Merton said, big toe sliding under his pants cuff.

"Sheila, of course, thank you. As I was saying, I believe the addition can be completed in ample time for you to be able to hold your annual Christmas—whoa!—that is, November first is our target—*umphff!*" He gave up. "Mrs. Merton, I really think you'd be happier with my partner."

She leaned forward in her chair, resting her chin on her hands. "I never met your partner. Doug, isn't it? Tell me about him. He as cute as you?"

"Oh, cuter. Definitely cuter," Cameron said, gently pushing Mrs. Merton's stockinged foot off his lap. How did the woman stretch that far and not slide out of her seat? "And he's a real…a real specialist in…in…excuse me, that's my cell phone. I'll be right back."

"Hurry," Sheila Merton said, and then she ran her tongue around her lips. "I'll be waiting."

"Cut off the lady's martinis. If that doesn't work, there's a fifty in it for you if you can figure out a way to dump some ice water in her lap," Cameron told the waiter as he headed for the exit, his cell phone already flipped open. "Cameron Pierce."

"Mr. Pierce, yes. I am Attorney Clark Humbolt. I hope you don't mind that I asked your office to give me this number after attempting to reach you earlier. I would have gotten in touch with you even sooner, but I was explicitly instructed not to notify you until the other concerned party had been contacted. That done, it is my sad duty to inform you that Hecuba Willikins expired last Friday evening."

"Horry?" Cameron stopped with his hand pushed against the half-open doorway to the street, earning himself a quick thank-you from a young woman who ducked under his arm and into the restaurant, tucking her business card into his suit jacket pocket as she went. He didn't notice. "Horry's dead? Christ—does Darcie…does Ms. Reed know?"

Cameron shook his head to clear it, then walked out onto the sidewalk, blinking in the sunlight. Darcie. Darcie was in Pittsburgh. Alone. Was she alone?

"Ms. Reed has been notified, yes. I have been instructed to have both you and Ms. Reed present at Cliff

House for the reading of the will as soon as possible. Shall we say tomorrow at eleven o'clock?"

"Me?" Cameron looked in through the large windows to see Sheila Merton pouting and waving to him. "Why me? I'm not a relative. Darcie's his only relative, right? Everything goes to her."

Everything, Cameron thought, wincing as he summoned a mental picture of Hecuba Willikins's Shangri-La. This attorney could call it Cliff House until the next millennium, and it would still be Horry's fantastical Shangri-La. *Frogs and flamingos and Lucky—oh my.*

"I fear I am constrained not to discuss the terms until the will is read, Mr. Pierce."

Turrets and pink siding and purple trim—oh my. "What? No, no of course you can't. Can you…can you tell me how he died?"

"Between us gentlemen, sir?"

Cameron frowned. "It's bad?"

"Not horrific, Mr. Pierce, although this information is only between the two of us, as you'll understand. You see, it could be considered an inopportune demise, as he was in bed, sir, and he was…he was not alone."

Cameron grinned. "That old dog. He was getting it on? Good for him! No, wait, excuse me, that was crude. He was…overexerting himself?"

"I am surmizing, from what the medical examiner told me, but it is rather clear, yes. He…went happily, Mr. Pierce. Now, you will tell me that you'll be present at Cliff House tomorrow?"

"Came and went," Cameron said to himself. "That

old dog. Oh! Yes, of course, Attorney Humbolt. I'll be there. And Ms. Reed?"

"That is confirmed, yes. And now, as I have no other information, until tomorrow, sir."

Cameron snapped the cell phone shut, breaking the connection, and wondered how Darcie had taken the news. She'd really loved that old guy.

She was probably on her way from Pittsburgh by now. Darcie moved fast when she moved, as he ought to know. He should probably go drive out to wait for her tonight at Shangri-La.

He rubbed at his forehead. "Oh, yeah. Swell. That'd go over big."

But he'd see her tomorrow.

"That'll go over even bigger," he told himself, heading back into the restaurant to excuse himself because there had been a death in the family. Not his family, but he'd take any family he could get, if it got him out of finishing lunch with Sheila Morton. Screw the indoor pool, it was time to introduce Sheila to Doug the Lady Killer.

Either that or start wearing a codpiece…

DARCIE USED the remote control still clipped to the sun visor to access the wrought-iron gates to Shangri-La and watched as they opened onto the long, curving drive lined with ceramic pink flamingos alternating with day-glo-green frogs.

She lowered the driver's-side window, the better to hear the frogs sing out *ribbit-ribbit* as their built-in sensors picked up her car passing by.

Uncle Horry had called the frogs his watch-frogs, and Darcie smiled even as tears threatened yet again.

The drive turned to the left and the house came into view, flamingo pink with purple trim. The colors hadn't been changed in three years, but Darcie was still trying to decide if the pink and purple was an improvement over the previous green and orange.

No matter what, she loved this immense old house with its late-Victorian style, its wonderful turrets and fanciful woodwork, its marvelous slate roof and wrap-around porches. So what if she'd teased Uncle Horry by chanting, "Gingerbread man, Gingerbread man," from time to time…it was a fabulous house.

She had spent a few summers here, before her parents died during her college years, and still visited often. Or she had, until last September. She hadn't even come east for Christmas, and a lot of her tears had to do with that inexcusable lapse. Especially since it had turned out to be Uncle Horry's last Christmas. Especially since she'd spent the day alone in her furnished studio apartment, crying into her wine cooler.

Darcie put the gearshift into Park and scrambled in her purse for yet another tissue as she thought about Christmas at Shangri-La. Every flat surface in the house seemed to be covered by singing Rudolphs and dancing Frostys and talking Christmas trees. Uncle Horry was a sucker for anything mechanical, and you could barely see the lawns for animated deer and waving Santas.

He'd arranged all of his outside ornamentation to face the house, not the street. The street, as he'd pointed out, was too far away for anyone to see the decorations, anyway, so why should he be looking at a herd of deer's backsides?

Today, however, Darcie saw as she finally left her car and walked up the wide, shallow steps to the front porch, Shangri-La was in mourning. The double front doors were draped with elaborate black crepe bunting, and all the drapes had been drawn tight over the windows.

Darcie knocked on the door, then tried the knob, which turned easily. Stepping inside the darkened foyer, she gasped as she saw that the black bunting must have been on sale, for it hung in deep folds over the grandfather clock, the large mirror and even wrapped round and round the long, curving staircase.

Putting down her overnight bag, the remainder of her luggage still hidden in the trunk, Darcie approached the staircase, to touch one of the fresh gardenias that broke up the black, sniffing at the heady fragrance of what she knew to have been her uncle's favorite flower.

"So, you're finally here."

Darcie jumped slightly and turned to see that Lily Paige had entered the foyer. The woman's tone was accusing, her outfit intimidating and yet comical, as she was dressed in unremitting black, except for the gardenia tucked behind her left ear.

"Lily," Darcie said, her bottom lip trembling. If only she could rush into the housekeeper's welcoming arms, to be comforted. But Lily Paige was not the welcoming arms "There, there, you just have a good cry, dearie" type.

In fact, as Darcie stood there, and Lily stood there,

Darcie had to bite back a hysterical giggle as, unwanted, Cameron's observation about the housekeeper ran through her mind: "You know what, Darc? Lily reminds me of Cloris Leachman in *Young Frankenstein.* Remember the night we watched that on video? Ramrod-straight posture, that tight bun, the way she has of looking at you down the sides of her nose? I keep waiting for her to say, 'Yes! He *vas* my boyfriend!'"

Okay, enough of that, because hysterical laughter would surely give way to hysterical weeping. "Um…the…the attorney told me Uncle Horry was cremated yesterday?"

Lily lifted her chin, threaded her fingers together at her waist. "There was an attempt made to contact you."

"Yes, I know. I…I was away on business. It was unavoidable. I stopped at a motel outside of Harrisburg last night, but I was hoping to stay here tonight before…um, before heading back to Pittsburgh." There was no way she was going to bare her soul to Frau Blücher, admit that she was, at least technically, homeless and jobless. "My usual room?"

Lily inclined her head slightly. "Mr. Willikins ordered it always kept ready for you, yes, even as you did not show up for Christmas or Easter. I suggest you go there now and wash your face."

Darcie was halfway up the stairs before it hit her. She was letting Lily order her around like some…some naughty child. Like Lily was now mistress of Shangri-La, and Darcie the unwelcome but temporarily necessary guest.

What did Lily know? Had Uncle Horry told her the provisions of his will? Was Lily Paige now the owner of Shangri-La?

"And what if she is?" Darcie asked herself as she walked down the hallway toward her room. "This place was Uncle Horry's, he could do whatever he wanted. Besides, it's not as if I want to move back here."

She opened the door to her room, to see black crepe hung over the mirror above the dresser, the heavy velvet drapes pulled tight over the windows. What on earth? This was a bedroom, not the Plant 'Em Deep Funeral Parlor.

"Oh, for pity's sake!" Darcie dropped her overnight case on the bed and went to the windows that overlooked the front of the house, pulling open the drapes just in time to see Cameron Pierce standing in the drive, looking up at the house he liked to call Turrets R Us.

She fought the insane urge to drop to her knees, out of sight, and just peek at him over the windowsill.

Did he have to be so drop-dead handsome? That sun-streaked tawny hair that he wore just a little too long. Those similarly tawny eyes, almost golden beneath expressive, winged brows, and always so full of amusement. That easy smile that had first attracted her to him. That long lean body, the one that looked equally perfect in cutoff shorts and a muscle shirt as it did in the impeccably tailored suit he was wearing now…and even more perfect without any clothes at all.

Why was he here? Had Attorney Humbolt put an obituary in the Philadelphia newspapers, and he'd come to pay his respects? And couldn't Cameron have just sent a card?

He looked up. He saw her. He smiled that easy smile. He waved.

Darcie pulled the drapes shut and stumbled over to the bed to sit down before she fell down.

The timing of his condolence visit couldn't be a coincidence, could it? No, it couldn't. So, could Cameron possibly be the other party involved, the other one that Attorney Humbolt had to notify about the reading of the will?

"Stupid question. Of course he is. Oh, Uncle Horry, what did you do? What on earth did you *do*?"

CAMERON'S SMILE WILTED as he watched the drapes fall shut. He'd smiled? He'd waved? Oh, that was classy, considering how the last time he'd seen Darcie, she'd thrown her engagement ring at him and told him where he could put the damn thing.

"Yeah, well," he muttered as he climbed the shallow wooden steps. "As my grandmother used to say, begin as you plan to go on. I'll be damned if I'll let her think she broke my heart. Jolly, jolly. Keep it light, and get the hell out of here as fast as you can, Cameron, old man. That's the ticket. And then get very drunk and talk to yourself some more."

He smiled wanly as he took in the ruffled black bunting over the doors, then lifted the brass knocker in the shape of a flamingo, hit it against the wood three times, then stood back to wait.

"Mr. Pierce, I'll assume? Just go in—it's nearly eleven."

Cameron turned around to see a tall, thin, deeply tanned man in his seventies climbing out of a BMW two-seater sports car he hadn't heard drive up, then reach back in to bring out a spiffy-looking leather attaché case.

The guy looked as if he was on his way either to or from the golf course, dressed in a bright yellow knit shirt and godawful orange-and-green-and-yellow plaid slacks, with a two-inch-wide white leather belt spanning the spreading waistline in between. His hair bore the imprint of a hat he wasn't wearing, and his left hand was a startling white up against his tan, as if he wore a golf glove more often than not.

"Attorney Humbolt?" Cameron asked, wondering why the hell he was in a black pinstripe suit and somber dark burgundy tie, while the attorney looked ready to party hearty. A two-inch-wide white belt? Didn't those die way back in the seventies or something? If they had, whoever had resurrected them should be taken out and shot.

"In the flesh," Humbolt said, extending his hand, squeezing Cameron's a shade more than heartily. "Excuse the clothes. Annual tournament, you understand. Benefits some charity. I tee off at one, so I appreciate your promptness."

"Of course," Cameron said as the front door opened and Lily the Terminator frowned out at the pair of them. "We could have done this tomorrow."

"No, not tomorrow. Hecuba was very firm on that. Everything done in three days, unless he kicked off over the weekend. Pay extra for everything on weekends, you understand. Lily," he said, inclining his head to the woman, who sniffed, then turned and headed back to her Bat Cave, or wherever the hell she hid whenever there were *men* in the house.

Attorney Humbolt stepped closer to Cameron. "Not a word, remember? But are you getting the same mental picture I've got?"

"Mental picture of what? Oh, wait a minute. You can't really mean that Horry was in bed with—oh, right, bad mental picture there. Definitely."

"Definitely definitely." Humbolt shook in a mock shiver. "She knows I know, you know, and she has to know that I put you in the know, so that you know now, too. What do you think? Hecuba blindfolded himself so he could get it up?"

"I...I have no answer for that one, sorry," Cameron said, trying to reconcile the official-sounding Attorney Humbolt on the phone yesterday with the dirty old man standing beside him now. Must be the plaid pants, he decided. Being serious in plaid pants would be like declaiming Shakespeare in a red clown nose and big, floppy shoes.

"Hello."

Cameron turned around quickly to see Darcie descending the stairs, trailing her fingertips along the bunting-hung banister, hesitating only a moment to glower at the gardenia her touch had loosened so it fell to the foyer floor. That had to burn her, since she was so obviously trying to make a big entrance.

"Hi, Darcie. Long time no see," he said, then inwardly winced. Too casual, way too casual. He might as well hang a sign around his neck saying that he was still nuts about her, and still mad as hell at her. He tried to recover. "I'm so sorry to hear about your uncle. He was a wonderful man."

"He was, yes, thank you," Darcie said, reaching the foyer and advancing toward the lawyer. "Attorney Humbolt? I'm Darcie Reed."

Oh, she most certainly was. Or at least she had been, when he'd caught a glimpse of her at the window, wearing something soft and flowery, her gorgeous blond hair hanging to her shoulders.

Now she'd morphed into the professional Darcie Reed, with her hair pulled back into what had to be a painful French twist, and wearing one of those ugly navy suits that fit her like a mitten, never a glove. He'd never been real crazy about the professional Darcie Reed.

"Slay any corporate dragons lately, Darc?" he asked, unable to control his tongue. "Guess those shoes are just the thing for climbing corporate ladders, too, huh? Nice and sturdy."

She didn't answer, but just glared at him with those icy green eyes before asking the lawyer if the will could be read now "... because I really must get back to Pittsburgh, and I'm sure Mr. Pierce is equally busy."

Mr. Pierce? He'd Mr. Pierce her. Wait until he got her alone and...

Humbolt glanced at his wristwatch. "Suits me. Shall we adjourn to Hecuba's study? I'll go flush out Lily to have her join us, and we'll be all set."

Darcie glared at Cameron once more, so he stepped back and bowed, flourishing one arm to indicate that she should precede him down the hallway toward the study.

She didn't move.

Waiting until Humbolt had gone, she whispered dangerously, "What are you doing here?"

Okay, this could be fun. He leaned closer and whispered right back at her, "I don't know."

"Stop that. Stop making fun of me, because I don't like it."

He leaned closer, whispered again, "I know."

"Oh!" she exclaimed, her hands drawn up into fists. "Do you know how much I didn't ever want to see you again?"

"Afraid you'd lose control and throw me down, rip off my clothes? Forget it, lady, I'm not that easy. Although that sack you're wearing? It's a real turn-on."

"Go to hell," she said, and all but ran down the hallway.

"Been there. Been there for nine damn long months," Cameron said quietly as he watched her go.

CHAPTER TWO

DARCIE SAT RAMROD STRAIGHT in the third chair of a trio of dining room chairs that had been brought into Uncle Horry's study and lined up in front of his desk, hoping Lily would sit down beside her.

Then again, she'd never been lucky.

Cameron entered the room next and sat down next to her, his hands folded in his lap as if he'd been called on the carpet to the principal's office and was secretly pleased about it. He was ignoring her now, so Darcie pretended to inspect the room she knew very well.

Uncle Horry had theme rooms—at least that's how Darcie thought about the Western Room, the India Room, the Florida Room. The study was his Gentlemen's Club Room.

The walls were a deep burgundy paint on stucco, what you could see of them, because he'd lined the walls with massive, mahogany bookshelves. There were also hunt prints behind glass in aged-looking frames, busts of old Greeks, an unabridged dictionary open on a mahogany stand. A massive Persian carpet covered much of the hardwood floor. His oversize desk sat in front of a truly marvelous bay window looking out over the lawns and cliff, into infinity. Well, as far as the opposite side of the huge slate quarry, anyway.

Uncle Horry had a rack of antique pipes, even though he'd never smoked any of them, rather like the books he had but did not read. There was an immense globe in one corner of the room, and huge leather wing chairs on either side of a campaign table placed in front of the fireplace.

A portrait of Benjamin Franklin hung over that fireplace—Uncle Horry's personal hero. And the rather gaudy golden urn that had sat on the mantel below that portrait for as long as Darcie could remember...well, she wouldn't look at that right now, knowing it was no longer empty.

And then there was the quilted burgundy velvet smoking jacket Uncle Horry had always worn when in this room. Darcie twisted in her chair to see the jacket still hanging over the mahogany silent butler next to the door.

She felt teary again, but still had to smile, as Uncle Horry's idea of a silent butler had been fairly literal, and what she was looking at was a wooden, potbellied and fully life-size, realistically painted tuxedo-clad butler with a smoking jacket folded over its outstretched arm. His name, she remembered, was Bupkus.

"Because Uncle Horry could talk to him all day long, and he never said bupkus," Darcie said, only realizing she'd spoken aloud when Cameron turned to look at her.

"Talking to me, Darcie? I sort of got the idea we weren't speaking."

"We're not."

Cameron grinned, and the tanned skin around his golden eyes crinkled. "Far be it from me to burst your little bubble, Darc, but yes. Yes, we are. See? I'm speaking to you right now."

"Then maybe, just this once, you're also *listening* to me. In which case, always hopeful, let me say—" No. This was neither the time nor the place. "Never mind."

Cameron cupped one hand to his ear. "Pardon?"

Darcie turned, eyes front once more, unsurprised that her vision now seemed suddenly red-tinged around the edges.

"Lily, please take the last seat," Attorney Humbolt said as he walked behind the desk and opened his attaché case, saving Darcie from making a fool of herself by growling at Cameron. "But first, it would seem that all your chairs are facing in the wrong direction. Please turn them about, to face the television."

Darcie couldn't help it; she looked at Cameron in question.

"Video will," he said out of the corner of his mouth. "We should have thought of it—it's right up old Horry's alley. Do you think he used his Daffy Duck voice?"

"That's not funny," Darcie said, but she had to bite back a smile. Uncle Horry's Daffy Duck voice had always been able to reduce her to giggles. She only wished Cameron hadn't remembered that.

"Ah, here we go," Humbolt said as he walked across the room, holding a DVD. "Hecuba showed me how this works when he first decided on a video will. Television on Channel Three, push this button until *Video One* shows on the screen, slip in the DVD, and—perfect."

"He's enjoying himself," Darcie said quietly. "And where did he find those horrible slacks?"

"That's twice," Cameron said, turning to grin at her. "You're definitely talking to me now. And I didn't even have to make an appointment with your personal assistant. I'm assuming you have a personal assistant?"

"Please, stop it, Cam," Darcie said, turning her pressed-together knees to the right, sitting as far away from him as possible without tumbling off the chair. "It would kill you to be serious?"

"Probably. You know, I've always hated your hair like that. It looks painful. I keep thinking you hold it together with thumbtacks."

Darcie had a sudden flash of the way the first thing Cameron would do when she walked through the door after work, was to kiss her…and begin unpinning her hair. He'd run his fingers through it, easing the tension that she'd brought home with her, and they'd sort of kiss their way into the bedroom, and…

No. She was not going to think about that. Not now. Later, when he was gone, and she could have a good cry. Crying had come easily since hearing about Uncle Horry's death.

Standing behind the desk once more, Humbolt picked up the remote control and hit Play, and the next thing Darcie saw was the old Loony Tunes bull's-eye with Bugs Bunny breaking through it, munching on a carrot while the familiar music played in the background.

"Oh my God…" she said, reaching into her pocket for a tissue. "It's…it's so Uncle Horry."

"Steady, Darc," Cameron said, putting a hand on her knee. "You'll get through this."

Darcie sniffed, bit back a sob and raised her gaze to the television screen once more…right after she pushed Cam's hand off her knee.

Fade to black, and then, suddenly, there was Uncle Horry, seated behind the desk that stood behind her now, smiling at an unseen camera.

Lily Paige sighed audibly.

"Hi, there, everyone. Darcie, Cameron. My little Lily-pad."

As Cameron suddenly seemed close to choking on his own tongue, Darcie leaned forward and looked to her left, to see Lily's thin cheeks going an unflattering purple.

But Uncle Horry was still talking.

"As you can see, I've got Clark Humbolt here with me. Oh, wait, you can't see that, can you, because he's holding the camera. Clark? Wave to the people."

A hand appeared, blocking out Uncle Horry's face for a moment, then disappeared again.

"There, that's nice and legal, right? Okay, let's get on with this. I, Hecuba Wallace Willikins, being as sound of mind and body as I'm ever expecting to get again, do hereby make this my last will and testament. Anything else, Clark?"

Clark Humbolt could be heard, instructing Uncle Horry to give the date and time.

"Good thinking, Clark. I don't want anybody saying I did this wrong. Today is January the second of two thousand aught four, and—what? Oh, my mistake. New year. Two thousand aught five. Happy now, Clark? Good. It's four o'clock in the afternoon and Lily's fixing us up a batch of pork and sauerkraut one day late for luck in the new year because she says she doesn't have to work on New Year's Day, and I'm getting hungry so I'm going to make this fast. Lucky, not now, baby. Get down."

The large black cat that had hopped up onto the desk, meowed what could have been feline-speak for "Who died and left you boss," and curled up on the ink blotter.

"Oh, well, it concerns him, too, doesn't it?" Uncle Horry laid one hand on the cat's sleek coat and narrowed his eyes as he looked at the camera. "Now get this straight boys and girls, I mean what I'm going to say and I'm not nuts, no screws loose here, let me tell you. So listen up."

Attorney Humbolt hit Pause, cleared his throat, and said, "He's right, you know. He was perfectly competent and everything is all perfectly legal. And, before you ask, yes, I did try to talk Hecuba out of it, but he was adamant. Now, to continue."

"Lily, my little Lily-pad, let's start with you, shall we? Lily, you've served me long and faithfully—"

There went Cameron again, choking. Darcie frowned. What *was* his problem?

"—seems only fair to reward you for these past thirty years. You will have a home at Shangri-La for as long as you want it, fifty thousand dollars on top of everything else you've managed to worm out of me over the years, including that annuity I'm still trying to figure out why I gave you. Maybe it was after that time when…oh, right, I remember now. I'm adding something here Clark. Lily also gets the custom-made barber pole in my bedroom. Personal memento and all that. Clark, for God's sake, hold the camera straight. You're waving it all around."

Cameron was now holding up one hand as he coughed and tried to apologize for coughing, and Lily stood up, shot him a look that should by rights have blown off the top of his head, then stomped out of the room.

"What am I missing here?" Darcie asked Humbolt, who had paused the DVD once more.

Cameron had slid down on his spine on the chair and was wiping tears from his eyes with a white handkerchief. "You…you don't…don't want to know," he managed to get out, laughing. "Trust me."

Darcie looked at the attorney, who wouldn't look at her, then at Cameron once more. And then, quickly, when she figured it out, looked at her toes. "Oh! I…I never knew…I, I mean I sometimes suspected that *maybe,* I mean, maybe years ago—a *barber pole?* What? How?"

Cameron patted her knee again. "Later, Darc. I'll draw you a diagram. *Ba-da-da-boom, ba-da-ba-bang.*"

Darcie glared at him, speechless, and Humbolt hit the Play button.

"So," Uncle Horry said, still petting the cat, "that's one down. Now for you other two. Sitting there, spitting fire at each other, I'll bet. I never saw two such pigheaded idiots in my entire life. Well, tough beans, kiddies, because here's the deal. What?"

Darcie watched as Uncle Horry seemed to be listening to something Humbolt was saying; then he nodded his approval. "Okay, back up, kiddies. First, a round ten thousand each to Saint Barnabas and the ASPCA. Gotta love the ASPCA, right, Lucky?"

The cat sat up, lifted one back paw over his head, and began licking his backside.

Uncle Horry laughed. "See that, kids? That's what Lucky thinks of the ASPCA. That's what he thinks of everybody. You gotta love cats, they don't give a good flying flip about anything. Heard a joke once about cats. About how, if they could only learn to use a can opener, they wouldn't need us humans at all. Yes, well, don't frown, Clark, I can say what I want. It's my will. Just be happy I'm not in the mood to tap dance."

This time it was Darcie who bit back a laugh. Uncle Horry did always have a "way" about him, and very little respect for the formalities.

"Anyway, back to you two. Darcie and Cameron. Humbolt here has already set up a fund or trust or something to take care of regular maintenance—paint, that sort of thing—for my little toys out front. That's 106 flamingos, 104 frogs. And you should be thanking me, because the frogs are on solar power. Those frogs could empty your pockets if they needed batteries. Still, paint, repairs—it adds up."

Darcie fought to keep still as she asked herself why she and Cameron both should be thankful for the flamingo-and-frog fund.

"You're probably asking yourselves, what should we

care about the old fool's flamingos and frogs." Uncle Horry leaned forward on the desk. "Well, I'm going to tell you. Besides the piddling amounts I just mentioned, everything else goes to...Lucky. He's good, might even be able to open cat food cans with his teeth, but I'm betting he can't run this whole place on his own."

Darcie blinked at the television screen. She was having some difficulty absorbing all of this information. Shangri-La had been left to Lucky? No...Uncle Horry had been eccentric, but he hadn't been crazy. Another shoe was going to drop, and she was already beginning to think she knew what size it was. Didn't Cameron wear a ten and a half?

Cameron was now sitting up very straight. "Lucky? He didn't even like that cat. Did he?"

"Uncle Horry loved that cat. I gave him that cat. *You're* the one who hates him," Darcie said, feeling the fragile calm of a condemned prisoner who still has hopes of a last-minute pardon, yet not really ready to believe the governor will grant one.

"Quiet, Horry's talking again. And I do not hate that cat. That cat hates everybody."

"What, Clark? Oh, right. Let me say that again, children. Everything—house, stocks, bonds, every last dime that's left after Lily and the church and the ASPCA—it all goes *in trust* for Lucky. For one month, during which, children, you two will have joint custody of Lucky. Wait, I'm going to read this. Clark wrote it all down for me and I want to get it right."

He pushed Lucky off the papers and adjusted his

reading glasses as he cleared his throat. "Ah, here it is. I hereby declare that the remainder of my estate is to be placed in trust for Lucky, one three-year-old tom cat, given to me by my dear niece, Darcie Reed, and now the property of her and her once beloved Cameron Pierce, with the provision—" he grinned at the camera "—I always said good wills should have provisions that drive their relatives nuts."

Cameron sighed. "'Once beloved,' the man says. Past tense. And here I always liked your uncle. Lucky and your uncle. I liked them both. I'm a good person that way. Even beloved...by some."

"Shhh," Darcie hissed. "Let's just get through this, okay? Then you can go somewhere and have yourself a pity party."

On the television screen, Uncle Horry was tapping the pages against the desk top. "All right, here we go again. With the *provision* that the aforementioned Darcie and Cameron cohabite Shangri-La for the period of that same one month, during which time they will be jointly responsible for the health and well-being of said Lucky. Cameron, take my room. You'll love it. Now, at the end of that month, the parties involved will have concluded between them which of the two of them will have permanent custody of Lucky, possession of Shangri-La and all my money. There's a lot of it, kiddies."

"Hit Pause, Humbolt," Cameron barked. "Freaking hit Pause." He stood up, wheeled to look at the attorney. "What does the other one get?"

"Hecuba addresses all of that in—"

"No! *You* address it. Now."

"Cameron, for God's sake," Darcie said, also getting to her feet. "What does it matter? This can't be legal."

"Actually, Miss Reed, it can be and it is. The wealthy are never incompetent, they are amusingly eccentric. In other words, this will hold up in court," Humbolt told her. "But to answer your question, Mr. Pierce, at the end of the month of cohabitation the party who does not assume custody of the animal gets Bupkus."

"You mean nothing," Cameron said, nodding.

"No, I mean Bupkus. He's over there, beside the door, if you'll remember. But that's all. One gets the inheritance, the other gets Bupkus. Hecuba, even while eccentric, did always possess a rather wry humor. We're talking millions of dollars here, sir, besides the house and land. The Willikins Widget was a very lucrative patent, remember. Horry was a reasonably wealthy man."

"And it wasn't even a widget, whatever a widget is, even if that's what Uncle Horry liked to call it," Darcie said, just trying to say anything she could to give Cameron time to calm down, because he looked ready to explode. "It was a precision-tooled spring mechanism that proved invaluable to the airline industry as well as many other—"

"I know what the Willikins Widget was—is. Damn it!" Cameron glared at Darcie. "Horry was your uncle. You take Lucky. Take the cat, take the land, take the house, take the freaking flamingos and frogs—take it all. We don't need a month to figure this out. But I will take Bupkus. Bupkus is cool."

Darcie narrowed her eyelids and glared right back at him. How dare he be the *nice* guy? "Oh, isn't that just *so* like you. You just love being the generous one, don't you?"

"Me? I'm the generous one? And what the hell does *that* mean?"

Darcie felt herself slipping over the edge, into Stupid Land, but she couldn't stop herself. "You should know. Last time I saw you, you were being very *generous*. With that…that *woman*."

"Oh, for crying out loud, Darc, I *told* you—"

"Again, if we could get back to your uncle's will, please? My tee time, remember?"

"Screw your tee time," Cameron said, turning on Humbolt, and the attorney backed up a few paces. "But you're right. Let's finish this. I don't want to be here any longer than I have to be, listening to her reciting some litany of my supposed sins."

"Oh, you poor baby," Darcie said. Sneered, actually. But he made her *so* mad. Next thing she knew, she'd be crying and he'd think she still cared whether or not he'd been kissing that tramp the morning after they'd had that huge fight about her career. Like she cared. She'd had a lucky escape, that's what she'd had. And now Uncle Horry was trying to get them together again? Not in this lifetime!

Humbolt clicked the remote one more time.

"Now listen up, children, because this is the important part. If either of you refuses to cohabit—I like that word, cohabit—if either of you is away from Shangri-La for more than twelve hours at a clip, or if anything happens to my Lucky, here—I mean like if he gets dead—then my half brother, Edwin Willikins, gets it all, lock, stock and flamingos. Get it right, children, or else that's—oh, wait, I'll let the little pink guy say it for me."

Uncle Horry spread his arms wide, smiled as the screen went black for a second before the Loony Toons target appeared once more. This time, Porky Pig stuck his head through the bull's-eye and said, "Tha-tha-tha-that's all folks!"

"HAVEN'T SEEN A ROOM clear out that fast since the last time we let you eat shrimp," Hecuba Willikins said, coming out from behind the draperies. Not that he actually *said* the words. He thought them. And not that he actually came out from behind the curtains. He came out *through* the curtains.

Lucky, who was now stretched out on the desk chair recently vacated by Clark Humbolt (Lucky liked warm leather), twitched one ear as if in answer.

"Out of my chair, hairball. Down!"

It came as no great surprise to Horry that Lucky ignored the command to vacate his supposed master's chair.

Horry knew a little about cats, but a lot about Lucky. He knew that cats come in all sizes. Lucky came in Double-X Extra Large. He knew that cats come in all colors. Lucky came in unremitting black, with green and yellow eyes (one of each), that had seemed downright cute when he was a kitten, but could look menacing and evil now that he had grown, had a wide, flat nose, and a head the size of a large man's clenched fist.

Lastly, but most important, Horry knew that cats also came in all personalities.

Lucky, bless his heart, came in Screw You.

But Horry loved Lucky, and had from the time Darcie had brought him from the ASPCA as a kitten and Lucky had taken one look at his new master…and bitten him.

So, knowledgeable about all things Lucky, Horry didn't push the cat to obey.

"All right, you stay there. I don't really need to sit, anyway. It's not like I'm going to get tired or anything, right? Well, maybe I could get *dead* tired," he said, then grinned. "Did you see my Lily-pad? I keep waiting for her to throw a black veil over her head. Poor kid, she's taking it hard. I was quite the lover, you know."

Lucky finally turned his head toward Horry and said, mind to mind, "I didn't realize you humans knew what we know, that all cats look gray in the dark. You two looked pretty pitiful, you know."

Uncle Horry lifted his chin. "Who asked you? And why doesn't your mouth move when you talk? I've been meaning to ask that since I first figured out that I'm dead but not gone."

Lucky yawned. "I'm a cat, old man. You want answers to the big questions, go find yourself a monkey. They do tricks. I hear they even have opposable thumbs."

"You're saying monkeys are smarter than cats?"

"Matter of opinion," Lucky said, stretching out his front paws as he raised his hind end in the air, stretched.

"Which one of us lets you humans keep us in cages? Oh, and it isn't going to work, you know."

"You mean Darcie and Cameron?" Horry perched on the edge of the desk. "Is too going to work. They love each other. They're just stubborn—need a little nudge. You'll see, it'll work."

"Nine to five it doesn't," Lucky said, then hopped down and headed for his favorite corner of the nearly priceless Persian carpet. He hadn't had a good claw sharpening in at least two hours.

CHAPTER THREE

DARCIE STOPPED in the foyer, turned around and held out her arms, hands raised like twin Stop signs. "Back off, Cameron. Just back off."

"Sure," Cameron said, coming to a halt. He could have caught up to her sooner, but he had been eager to get rid of Clark Humbolt before Darcie exploded, poor kid. And, speaking of explosions, maybe it was time to help Darcie along with that portion of the program. "Back off, you said? I'm pretty sure I know this one. This is the one where I try to help and you pack up and move to Pittsburgh."

"Help? Is that what you call getting what you want? Helping me? What about what I want? You do *not* do what I want. You've never understood what I want. And you want to know why? Because you don't *care* what I want. You never did. It's just what *you* want."

Okay, this was good. They were talking. "Right. And right now I want to give you sole custody of Lucky. Where's your problem?"

Darcie sort of growled, then slammed out of the house and down the steps, Cameron hard on her heels. She looked left, then right, before stomping off down the drive, stopping only when the first pair of sentry frogs began to *ribbit-ribbit* on either side of her.

Cameron waited, lips firmly stuck between his teeth, as she threw up her hands and turned around. "Nothing, Cam. Not a damn word!"

"Okay. How about a *ribbit*? Here a *ribbit*, there a *ribbit*, everywhere a *ribbit-ribbit*?"

There was that near growl again. Then she headed toward the cliff.

Naturally, he followed. He was going to go to hell for this, but he was actually enjoying himself. And wasn't it about time...after the way she'd dumped him? "Aren't you at least going to leave a note before you jump? After you climb the fence, of course. Can you climb in that skirt?"

She stopped. She sort of had to, he noticed, as her sensible heels were sinking into the grass with each step. "Okay, why not? I can be reasonable. We'll talk."

Cameron leaned against one of the hundred-year-old oak trees scattered here and there across the large lawn. "Good. For a minute there, I thought I was going to have to chase you all the way to Pittsburgh."

And what was this? He'd noticed this the first time. He said Pittsburgh and she shifted her eyes to the left, as if once more searching for somewhere to run? Wasn't she still knocking the business world on its heels in beautiful downtown Pittsburgh?

"You are still working in Pittsburgh?"

"I'm on family leave," she said, still not looking at him. "I have six weeks." Then her chin went up. "Mr.

Blackwell was with me. Well, I was with him. He's the CEO. I was in his office, reporting on a huge merger project I was in charge of costing out, when the call came about Uncle Horry, and he immediately offered me leave."

"Wow. I'm impressed, Darc. The CEO's office. Did this Blackwell guy notice—when you began to drool, I mean?"

"No, he didn't notice when—I did not drool! I have a very nice office of my own, thank you."

"Corner office? Great view? Those are two of your stupid goals, right?"

The chin went higher. "Can we please talk about Uncle Horry's ridiculous will?"

"No corner office, huh? Yeah, well, Darc, it's only been nine months. Don't be too hard on yourself."

"I am not hard on—oh! If you had your way I'd be barefoot and pregnant by now. I didn't spend half my life in school and then not want to use my education."

"Right. I'll admit it, I've come to understand that in the last nine months. Your general point, that is. But five years, Darc? I'm thirty-four—thirty-three when you hit me with this five-year-plan bunch of baloney. I turned thirty-four last month."

"Happy birthday," she said, almost spitting out the words. "And I'll be twenty-six next month. We have different priorities, Cam. You want to settle down, and I want to be where you were nine years ago."

"And I don't want to be pushing a walker and collecting Social Security when my youngest kid graduates high school."

She gave a dismissive wave of her hand. "Oh, like there's still going to be Social Security by then."

Cameron pushed himself away from the tree trunk. "Don't do that, either, Darc. Don't try to change the subject. Women can have jobs and still be married, have children."

"Jobs, yes they can. But careers? Not unless they've put in a good five years of slogging and working wild hours and giving all they've got to the job. *Then* they can be in a position where they can juggle all those balls and keep them all in the air. But not at entry level, Cam. It just doesn't happen. I have goals."

"Goals. Right. Now *that* argument sounds familiar. Here's my part. So I was supposed to play the fiancé for five years, on call when you had time for me, and then you'd be able to juggle your *career* to include a husband and kids? I was supposed to count on that?"

Darcie looked at him for long moments. "No, I suppose not. And it's not that I don't see your point, because I really do. I've thought about it, a lot. You want to be a father before your forties." She threw up her hands. "But it doesn't matter now, does it? We're just not suited for each other, that's all. You wanted what you wanted and I wanted what I wanted."

"And are you getting what you wanted, Darc? And if you are, do you still want it? That's the question that still bothers me."

"How you'd love it if I said no."

"Yes, but I'm not the sort to gloat. Go ahead, tell me you're miserable. I'd like to think I'm not alone."

Darcie snorted. "Oh, right, you're alone. You're never alone, Cam. Cam the babe magnet. Does it ever get boring—having to beat the willing women away with a stick?"

Cameron felt his jaw tightening. "I'm pretty much off women right now, Darc. You know what they say, once bitten, twice shy."

"How about I just pretend to believe that, and we can move on to what's really important. What are we going to do about Uncle Horry's will? I mean, you know what he's trying to do, don't you? He's trying to push us together so that we get back together."

Cameron grinned. "I didn't know him that long, but I always liked your Uncle Horry."

"Stop that. You know this is imbecilic. Uncle Horry was a silly, optimistic romantic."

"Like I said, I always liked your uncle Horry."

Cameron watched as Darcie's mouth moved and she didn't say anything. He watched as her cheeks went pink. He watched as her hands drew up into fists.

And then, just as he was about to do the smart thing and duck, he watched as she fought any homicidal urge she might have, and brought herself under control. It was like watching one of those cartoon characters go from calm to bug-eyed, hair standing on end, steam coming out of its ears, little %#&* marks floating over its head...and then smoothing back to calm again, without exploding.

Maybe it was the hairstyle. Or the suit. Or maybe even Pittsburgh. But this was not the same wildly screaming woman who had thrown his ring at him nine months ago.

Now to figure out if this was a good thing or a bad thing.

"Darc? Even if we decide to fight this will, we'll have to stay here while we're fighting, because if we lose, then you lose the whole estate, and we both know that's not what Uncle Horry had in mind. I mean—Lucky? Lucky's just his excuse to keep us here. So's this long-lost half brother. One's a hook to get us here, and the other is a threat to keep us here."

She rubbed at her forehead with both hands. She touched her cheeks and looked at him. She bent her head forward and pressed her hands over her ears. Took two deep breaths, looked at him again. "I know."

Wow. Maybe this new, calmer Darcie was a good thing. Except that he was still 99.9 percent sure she was holding back one hell of a frustrated scream.

"Okay, so we know. And we could fight it, except that would take longer than the month, so we might just as well make the best of this. You've got your family leave, I can certainly commute to Philly from here. It's a huge house, so we won't be on top of each other."

He hesitated, longing to say, "although we could be, if you wanted," then thought better of it. "Really, Darc, it could work. I'm not stupid, I know you don't want anything to do with me. And, frankly, much as I want you, I'm not ready to play the devoted boyfriend for another five years."

She blinked. Finally. "We just met each other at the wrong time, that's all. We're…we're at two different stages in our lives. And…and I really do need to prove myself, Cam. I really do."

"Prove yourself to whom, Darc? That's the part I can't figure out. To me? You don't have to prove yourself to me. To Uncle Horry? Your parents? Yourself? The world at large? Who, Darc?"

She turned, heading back toward the house, and he dropped into step beside her. "I'm good," she said quietly. "I know I'm good. But I've always been somebody's daughter, or niece, or the bright student with the right answers—in theory. I've never really been on my own, dependent solely on myself. To go straight from home and school to marriage? I've had no time to be *me*, find out who I am. Listen to…listen to what *I* want."

Nope. He was trying, but it wasn't computing. "I know who you are, Darc. You're the woman I fell in love with the day you nearly knocked me over with your umbrella on Market Street."

She smiled at him, but it wasn't a good smile. It was one of those "Oh? Really?" smiles, the kind that tell you you've really put your foot in it this time. "And six weeks later we were engaged. Well, we only were engaged for a week, but still engaged. Tell me, Cam. What's my favorite food?"

He answered without hesitation. "Pizza. With pepperoni."

"Wrong. That's your favorite food. I don't have a favorite food. I don't have a favorite style, not in clothes, not in art, not in furniture. I know nothing about me."

"So, because you don't have a favorite food, you decide to make yourself into this big career woman, and tell me to either come along on your terms or take a hike. Sure. That makes sense."

Darcie climbed the shallow steps to the front porch of Shangri-La and sat down in one of the wicker rockers. "It does, you know. I need some time in the real world, time to have some independence. I've lived at home, then lived in dorms. I had one apartment before we met, and it came already furnished. I've had two jobs in my entire life, Philly and now in Pittsburgh. Can I be great in business? I don't know. Do I want to be? I don't know. Can I cook? I don't know. Do I like modern or traditional? I don't *know!* And yes, I'll admit it, I don't know what I want. The…the business about my career was just an example for you, so you'd understand. It's not all of it. Once more, Cam, I need to learn my own potential, make my own way, not just go from home to dorm to marriage. Please tell me you understand that."

Cameron leaned back against one of the porch posts and cupped a hand behind his ear. "Wait. Yes…yes, I hear him off in the distance, but coming closer now. Frank Sinatra, singing "My Way." I think I'm getting all choked up here."

And still she didn't explode. Did she care so little for him that he couldn't even get her mad anymore?

Darcie began to rock in her chair. "Not funny. You are *so* not funny. I used to think you were, but you're not. You're…you're…ohmigosh, you're jealous!"

"Say what? *Jealous?*"

She looked up at him, her eyes wide. "Cam, that's

it—you're jealous! You can't bear to share me, even let me share me with myself. You want some dumb, doting, lives-for-only-you *doll.* You want to go out in the world all day, then come home to the little woman, who's waiting there with your pipe and slippers, like some faithful *dog*. House, wife, kids, picket fence. Me, doing what you want and expect. I just showed up when you decided it was time to get married. I could have been anyone."

"That's ridiculous." Did he say that too quickly? He might have said that too quickly. "I love—loved you for you."

"How could you, Cam? You don't know me. *I* don't know me. You fell in love with an idea, and I just happened to be there."

"I always knew Dr. Phil was a menace," Cameron muttered, pushing himself away from the post. "Okay, Darc, I get your point. I'm slime. There you were, fresh out of school, just starting to spread your wings in your first job, when I, selfish bastard that I am, came along and asked you to marry me. Damn, I should be horsewhipped."

Darcie jumped to her feet. "No, no! We both should be horsewhipped. Figuratively, I mean. Really, Cam. I take back what I said about you being jealous. Or selfish. We just went too fast. We rushed into everything without thinking, without weighing, without ever really knowing each other. And…and I panicked. I'll admit that, I panicked. I said I needed five years, because that was one way of stepping back, taking some time, figuring out if we were doing the right thing."

Cameron frowned. "I'm getting lost here, Darc. You pulled that number out of a hat? You don't really want a career?"

"Yes, yes, of course, at least for a while. I spent all those years in school, remember," she said, but she didn't sound so sure, at least he didn't think so.

"But five years, Darc. You said five years. That's not *a while*. After five years, you might never want to quit, and where does that leave me?"

"This isn't *about* you, Cam. It's about you *and* me. You wanted me to choose—marriage or career."

"Wrong," he said, advancing toward her. "I never said that. Okay, maybe I did. We were doing a lot of yelling that last night, as I remember it. I could have said that. You…you just took me by surprise, that's all. Caught me off guard. I wasn't expecting that one."

"Right. Because you didn't really know me. You had no idea that I had goals. Face it, Cam, we spent most of our time in bed. I don't know you any more than you know me."

"Back to pepperoni pizza, and being in love be damned," Cameron muttered under his breath. "All right. Here's the deal. We follow Uncle Horry's plans for us, because obviously he saw our problem much better than we did, than we do now. We move in, we get to know each other for the month, and then we see where we are. We don't talk about the past, never again. We start fresh, and we see where it goes, if it goes anywhere at all. The house, the inheritance, that's something else. This is you and me, starting over. Maybe starting over. Something."

She chewed on the inside of her cheek as she looked at him, appeared to consider his offer. "And no sex," she said at last.

"No—Ah, come on, Darc. Us? Under the same roof, and no sex?"

"No sex, Cam. We don't want anything to cloud our judgment. Are…were we really in love? Or was it really just physical? And no talking about the past, I agree, not even about how I found you kissing that woman when I came to your office to—well, never mind."

"I told you, I was angry. You'd just handed me that five-year ultimatum the night before, and when Blythe showed up at my office and came on to me like it was the good-ol' days, I—hey, I was stupid. Using an old girlfriend to take some revenge like a teenager. But it was just one kiss, it wasn't going anywhere."

"I thought we both just agreed we weren't going to talk about the past," Darcie reminded him. "But I'll forgive the kiss."

"Good. And I'll forgive the directions on where to put the engagement ring."

She dipped her head, but he still could see the color running into her cheeks. "Deal. I…I'll fly to Pittsburgh tonight, get myself some more clothes and be back here tomorrow by noon. Can you be here by then, ready to move in?"

"I can. So we have a deal. We spend this next month getting to know each other better."

"And getting to know ourselves better, don't forget," Darcie said, heading for the door. "And no sex."

"Right. Sure. You got it, Darc. No sex," Cameron said before the door closed behind Darcie. Then he walked down the steps to his car, tossing his car keys into the air and catching them again. "And rules were made to be broken."

DARCIE SAT ON THE EDGE of the motel bed and squashed the empty fast-food wrapper in one hand before tossing it in the general direction of the wastebasket.

Why was she here? Why hadn't she just moved into her old room at Shangri-La?

She let herself fall back on the mattress and looked up at the ceiling. "Because then he'd know."

So great. She'd lied to him. Almost lied to him. Lied by omission?

Whatever it had been, it hadn't been the truth—that she was no longer employed by Blackwell Industries. That she had not failed once now but twice.

Darcie blinked, and tears ran down the sides of her face.

It had all seemed so logical nine months ago…

Cameron had come home to his apartment to see her curled up in a small ball on his couch, sniffling into yet another tissue.

"Babe?" he asked, joining her on the couch. "What's wrong? Are you sick? Why didn't you call me? I thought you were supposed to be in New York for that meeting."

She threw her arms around him. "I was…but it wasn't going to be a meeting. I thought it was, but Mr. O'Donnell told me on the way to the station that he'd been waiting months to figure out a way to get me alone. Then he told me he'd reserved a one-bedroom suite for us."

Cameron stiffened inside her embrace. "That no-good son of a— Let go, Darc." He held on to her shoulders and looked deeply into her eyes. "Did he touch you? What happened?"

Darcie shook her head. "No, he didn't touch me. We were in a cab, Cameron, heading for the Amtrak station. I just sat there and smiled at him until we got to the station, then grabbed my suitcase and hailed another cab."

"Good. Although I wouldn't have minded if you'd given him a good kick before you took off. Okay. Tomorrow you get yourself right into the office and file a complaint against the bastard."

She sniffled again and shook her head. "Mr. O'Donnell wasn't just my boss, Cam, he's *the* boss. I'm out of a job."

"And he's out a couple of teeth, once I pay him a visit tomorrow."

"No, don't do that. Don't make things worse. And I thought I was doing so well. Two promotions in less than six months? And now nothing. I'm a failure. I failed, Cam. How could I have been so *stupid!*"

"Aw, honey," Cameron said, pulling her close, kissing her hair. "Don't worry about it—you know you were doing a good job. But, hey, now we can set a date, right? This living-in-sin business is nice, but I want to add a second ring to that hand. Then you won't have to worry about the O'Donnells of this world anymore. It's not like you weren't going to quit when we got married, right..."

Darcie sighed as she sat up on the motel bed and wiped at the tears that had been inelegantly running into her ears, tickling her, knowing that Cam's easy dismissal of her career hopes had been the beginning of a very hot, very nasty argument.

That's when she'd heard that five-year-plan idea leaving her mouth before her mind had fully processed what those words meant...and whether she'd really meant them at all.

She'd given up her month-to-month studio apartment right after Cameron had asked her to marry him, so once they'd yelled at each other until there was nothing left but a cold silence, they'd spent what was left of the night in separate bedrooms.

"And then I went to his office the next morning to apologize and found him kissing that old girlfriend of his," Darcie said out loud to the four uncaring walls of the motel room. "Talk about your lousy timing."

She'd run out of his office after telling him what he could do with his engagement ring, packed up her clothes and headed her car west, landing in Pittsburgh, to prove herself. To the world, to Cameron. To herself.

And found another Mr. O'Donnell in Clive Blackwell. And, darn it, she wasn't exactly Pamela Anderson. What was it with these men, anyway? Blond, not ugly, and they immediately decided she was eager for a good time?

So she'd spent nine long months alone, working just as hard as she knew how, so that when she had at last justified at least one part of her existence, she could return to Philadelphia and...and...and...

"Oh, God, I wanted to come back and show Cameron," Darcie admitted to herself at last. "I wanted to come back an equal, and tell him I believed him about that horrible woman, and that I know he really loves me and I really love him and—I don't *want* to learn how to play squash! God, I'm an *idiot!*"

Yet now, thanks to Uncle Horry, here she was, at the very worst moment, right after having to quit yet another job. Another failure. Coming back no more accomplished than she'd been when she'd run away. Yes, run away.

If she told Cameron she loved him and wanted to get married now, it would have to seem as if she couldn't cut it in the real world and now she was ready to play loving wife because it was safer. He'd feel like her second choice, her safe choice.

Because at least part of what she'd said to him this afternoon was still very true. He didn't know her all that well; he just thought he did. And she didn't know herself at all!

Sure, they could get married—but how long would it take before they both realized they'd married in haste and might well have the rest of their lives to repent in leisure?

She made a face. "I hate old sayings. A stitch in time saves nine. Better safe than sorry. Marry in haste, repent in leisure. But how do they get to be old sayings, unless they're right?" She closed her hands into tight fists. "Stop talking to yourself. Stop talking and start *thinking.*"

What did she love about Cameron? His looks? His looks were definitely the first thing that had attracted her to him. That thick, straight tawny hair that was always falling into his eyes. Those eyes. His smile. The way he took charge, taking her umbrella from her and holding it over her head as he directed her into that coffee shop...and then to dinner...and by the end of that week, into his bed.

Yes, there had been physical attraction. Immediate and obviously mutual.

She'd been so happy. A good job, her own apartment, a handsome, successful architect with his own business telling her he loved her. She was in Philadelphia, in the very center of life-after-college, and all the fairy tales were coming true, even the fairy-tale prince.

Uncle Horry had liked Cameron, a lot, and they'd visited there at least a half-dozen times for dinner, even for one entire weekend. Cameron had fallen in love with Shangri-La, itching to take it back to its former architectural glory, but he had also been indulgent of Uncle Horry's pink paint and flamingos and frogs.

But while Uncle Horry and Cameron always had something to talk about, Darcie, as always, had been rebuffed by Lily when she'd asked to be taught how to cook, offered to help with the care of Shangri-La's fourteen rooms. All Darcie had ended up doing during that long weekend was sunbathe, swim and sneak down the hall at midnight to sleep with Cameron.

Darcie picked up her hairbrush and began pulling it through her unbound hair as she watched herself in the mirror. “It’s going to be different this time. Life doesn’t just happen the way you want because you think it should.” She frowned at her reflection. “Who are you, Darcie Reed? What do you want? And why on earth would Cameron Pierce want anything to do with you?”

She carefully placed the hairbrush back on the dresser and headed for the bathroom, to shower, to get into her pajamas.

Tomorrow was the first day of the rest of her life. She should get some sleep.

“I’VE HAD LIVELIER drinking companions, you know,” Doug Llewellyn said, sitting back in his chair at the trendy pub situated around the corner from Architectural Design, Ltd. (restorations a specialty).

Cameron looked up from his glass. He’d been staring at its contents while his mind kept spinning, even as he wished the scotch could put the damn thing on Stun. “Sorry, Doug. Are you sure you’re okay with this?”

Doug, a handsome forty-year-old with thick, still-black hair and unusual-looking gray eyes, shrugged, then downed the last of his iced tea. “It’s a month, Cam. What can go wrong in a month? Be available if I need you, but call this a vacation, okay?”

He reached across the table and took Cam’s glass. “You don’t want this. A dedicated drinker would be on his fifth or sixth by now, and you’re still nursing your second. Between us, we’re a disgrace to the real drinkers in this bar.”

Cameron summoned a wan smile. “I was better at it in college, but drinking isn’t a sport anymore. Doug—

am I nuts? Why am I helping her? She threw my ring at me and left."

"You were kissing Blythe Harcourt, as I remember the story," Doug said, catching the eye of a barmaid and pointing to his glass of iced tea, then holding up two fingers. "You're lucky all Darcie did was throw your ring at you."

"Point taken," Cameron said, then sighed. "I should have gone after her, right then. But I was so pissed off, Doug. By the time I cooled down and went home, she was gone. It was three weeks before Uncle Horry would tell me where she was."

"So, you could have gone after her then, right?" Doug said as the barmaid placed two glasses of iced tea on the table.

Cameron began loading sugar into his glass. One, two, three, four...Doug turned his head, unable to watch.

"Horry advised against it. He said wait for Christmas, so I waited, but Darcie didn't come east. Then Horry said Easter, but she didn't come then, either. Nine months, Doug. Do you know it's been nine months?"

Doug laughed shortly. "Trust me, I know. And, while we're talking about this depressing aversion you seem to have developed toward women, thanks a lot for siccing Sheila Merton on me. I've seen less aggressive barracudas."

"No thanks necessary, Doug. It's a fantastic project and I know you'll do a great job. And, hey, fringe benefits."

"No thanks. I stopped out there before meeting you here, and Mr. Merton has quite a gun collection. Maybe

Sheila will latch on to one of the work crew. Women can't seem to resist a guy with low-slung jeans and a hammer."

"Depends on the size of the handle," Cameron said, but his heart wasn't in the old joke. "Seriously, Doug, what am I going to do? Horry said to give her to the Fourth of July, then go to Pittsburgh and make her listen to reason. Idiot that I am, I agreed. But now? Now Horry's dead and Darcie's got to believe I'd considered us quits until Horry's will got in the way. I mean, I told her I love her, I think I made it very clear to her, and she never said a word. Except to tell me I know nothing about her."

"Pepperoni pizza, I remember. You told me that one over the first scotch. Do you think she has a point?"

Cameron took a sip of iced tea, then added another sugar while Doug made a face. "She could. Damn it, she could. I met Darcie, Doug, and it was all systems go, you know? I wanted her, I went after her, I got her. When she hit me with that five-year-plan idea, I couldn't believe it. I thought she wanted what I wanted. House, kids, swing set in the backyard. Great sex."

"Far be it from me to break that particular bubble, old buddy, but it's my understanding that the kids and the swings in the backyard get a lot more time and attention than great sex. It's one of the reasons you don't see any ring through my nose. I like my women awake in bed, and smelling of perfume, not baby powder."

"You're going to die old and alone, you know," Cameron told his friend.

"And happily exhausted, with dozens of beautiful,

sobbing women at the funeral," Doug said, toasting Cameron with his glass. "But talking about my morally pointless but yet rewarding pursuit of the female of the species isn't settling your problem, is it?"

Cameron began bending his unopened straw into small, precise folds. "I think she still loves me."

"And you still love her. Excuse me, but I'm failing to see the problem here. Tell her, Cam. Sweep her off her feet. Take her to bed."

"Can't," Cameron said quietly. "She wants us to spend this month getting to know each other better. And no sex."

Doug spent a few moments wiping at his chin and the tabletop, cleaning up the sprayed iced tea. "No…no sex? And you agreed? I don't know who's crazier here, Darcie or you."

"I don't know. If she keeps wearing those ugly suits and shoes, and her hair all pulled back…but she isn't going to do that, is she? She'll be wearing shorts and those little tops she's got that don't quite cover her belly, and—I'm in real trouble here, Doug. I'd better come in to work every day, limit my time around her."

"That's one way, but when would you have this time you're supposed to have, to get to know each other better? I mean, haven't you ever heard of pillow talk?"

"You talk in bed?"

"Actually, I've never felt the need."

"No, you wouldn't. I've met your women, remember? But Darcie's right, Doug. I know I love her, but I don't know a lot about her. And, according to her, she knows less about her than I do."

Doug looked at his glass. "You think someone snuck some hard stuff into this? Because I don't think I'm hearing straight anymore. How old is Darcie?"

"Twenty-six."

"Oh, well, that explains it. Nobody knows themselves at twenty-six. You know yourself, and everything else, at sixteen, at eighteen, even at twenty-one. But twenty-six? That's when you begin to figure out that you don't know it all. I wouldn't be twenty-six again for the world."

"And yet you've never dated anyone older than about twenty-five," Cameron pointed out.

"Exactly. By twenty-eight, thirty, they want marriage. But in their early twenties? Hey, let's party."

"Darcie's not like that."

"No, Cam, she's not. But she is confused. You're nine years her senior. You know what you want. Darcie's still figuring it out, or at least she was when you two broke up. But it sounds like she's been doing some growing up over this past nine months or so. Hey, she's sure been running rings around you, right?"

"Life used to be a lot less complicated," Cameron said, pushing his glass away from him. "You met a woman, you fell in love, you got married, end of story. That's the way my parents did it. Mom graduated from Bryn Mawr, and she and Dad got married the next week."

Doug looked at Cameron out of the corners of those unusual gray eyes. "Ah, your parents. Good old Bill and Mary. How long have they been divorced now, Cam?"

"Shit," Cameron said, slipping down on his spine in the chair.

"My point exactly. Or Darcie's. No, I'm a man, I'll take the credit," Doug said, getting to his feet. "I think my work here is done. Give Darcie a kiss for me."

Cameron waved weakly and sat up once more, hunching himself over the table.

How big an idiot had be been? *Assuming* that Darcie wanted everything he wanted, when he wanted, how he wanted.

And he'd played the big hero, the protector, offering her marriage as an answer to her problems at work, like quitting was the answer to everything. Having a husband and children was the answer to everything. *Here, quick, I'll hide you, and all you have to do in return is wash my socks, raise my kids and warm my bed.*

No wonder she'd blown up at him. He'd seen quitting her job as taking them one step closer to what he wanted. He'd never wanted her to continue working once they were married. He was being honest with himself at last on that point.

"And I can't tell her," he said quietly. "We promised to keep the past in the past and start over."

"Right, on whatever you're talking to yourself about. And no sex." Doug appeared at the table once more, to drop several bills on the table. "I got the bill, and here's the tip. My treat. Have fun at Shangri-La, old buddy."

"Yeah. Right. See you," Cameron said. "Doug? I do love her, you know."

"I know, pal. Now go be your brilliant, charming self, and find out *why* you love her, and let her find out why she loves you. Because you're made for each other. You're both nuts."

Cameron grinned, feeling hopeful. "You're right. I always knew we had a lot in common."

CHAPTER FOUR

"NO! NO! NOT THE ROSE! You can't want to—well, that hurts," Uncle Horry said, slumping against the edge of the bed as Lily Paige bent the stem of the silk rose in half and shoved the whole thing into a large green garbage bag.

He'd been watching for a good quarter hour now—actually, a *bad* quarter hour now—as his Lily-pad systematically went about loading up thirty years of fond and often titillating memories for the trash.

His Lawrence of Arabia headdress. Gone. His riding whip. Gone. Oh, God, *The Joy of Sex.* Gone, gone, gone.

She'd poured the Jean Naté down the sink in the bathroom. She'd bunched up all the glorious negligees he'd bought her over the years and shoved them into the bag like so many unwanted rags. And there went their latest toy, along with an unopened package of size C batteries.

"Has the sentiment of a rock, that woman," Horry told Lucky, who was stretched out on the mattress, still a little high on the catnip mouse he'd played with, then gutted. "Who would have thought it?"

"Could have asked me. I would have told you," Lucky said, getting to his feet. "Watch."

Lucky walked to the edge of the bed, hopped down,

and began winding himself around Lily's skinny ankles, purring like a motorboat. Lily kicked him. "Get away from me, you miserable, mangy beast."

"See?" Lucky said, hopping up on the bed once more. "Oh, Horry, how I love Lucky. Oh, Horry, he's such a good companion for us, almost the child we never had. Yeah, right. I think she tried to poison me once."

"I...I never knew," Horry said, looking at Lily with some horror. "I thought she truly cared for me."

"You should have heard her late last night, cursing you for being a stupid, close-fisted cheapskate. Free housing in this old woodpile and a couple of bucks? Nice move, Horry. She thought she'd get it all, for services rendered. Cats are smarter. We take 'em, and then we leave 'em. You should have traded her in for two thirties a long time ago."

Horry looked at Lucky. "Nobody likes a smart-ass cat."

"You do. I'm adorable," Lucky said, rolling onto his back. "Scratch the belly again, Horry."

Horry got up and crossed the room, to watch as Lily struggled to free the thin, custom-made six-foot-high barber pole and then roll it out of the bedroom. It hadn't started life as a barber pole, but he hadn't expected Lily to take to a real stripper's pole, so he'd improvised.

"Ha! She can't move it. I've got it screwed into the floor, you know. Good! Hey, Lucky—watch this!" He leaned closer, and blew in Lily's ear. Once. Twice.

Lily froze in place, still with her arms wrapped around the pole. She then let go and rubbed at her left ear. She looked left, right, and then picked up the garbage bag and ran from the room, slamming the door behind her.

"Okay, genius, you're the big, bad, scary ghost. I'm all impressed. Now see if you can open the door, because, in case that steel-trap mind of yours hasn't figured it out yet, I'm locked in here," Lucky said, hopping to the floor once more.

"I don't know if I can," Horry said, looking at the door, then smiled hopefully. "I can walk through it."

"Bully for you, big boy. I can't."

"Good point." Horry put his hand on the knob. Gave it a twist. Nothing happened.

He'd had only a few days of this being-a-ghost business, so he was still learning what he could and could not do. He could go through walls, which was a kick. He could fly, a little. He could set off the frog sensors as he passed by. He could blow in Lily's ear. And, hey, he could scratch Lucky's belly.

If he could scratch, he could twist. It was simply a matter of concentrating.

So he tried again, his tongue stuck in one corner of his mouth as he grabbed and twisted, and this time it worked.

"Give that man a cigar," Lucky said, slipping out into the hall, then stopped to look up at Horry. "Now to go see Lily and make her wonder how I got out. You want to come along? You could open and slam some cabinet doors or something, and really get her wiggy."

"No, that's okay, Lucky. I mean, it sounds like fun, if I wasn't so depressed," Horry said, looking around his bedroom once more. "Wonder if she's going to come back with a ladder and take down the disco ball? I hope not. I think Cameron will get a kick out of it."

Lucky padded back into the bedroom. "You know what I think, Horry? I think we have to get rid of Lily."

"No, no. They'll need her. Darcie can't cook, for one thing. And Lily's a whiz at cleaning. I don't know what turned me on more, the Jean Naté or the Pine-Sol. I always told her all she had to do was dab a little of that behind each ear and I'd show her a few new tricks. Besides, where would she go? She's lived here for thirty years. Lucky?"

"What? Oh, right. I'm supposed to care, here? Sorry. All right, keep her around, no skin off this nose. It wasn't me she was robbing blind."

"Oh, she was not. Was she?"

Lucky looked up at Horry with his one green and one yellow eye. And then, Horry saw with horror, the cat winked at him.

"What do you know?" Horry asked him.

"Me? I'm a cat, Horry. I don't know anything but eating and crapping and sleeping and chasing. Quick, get a piece of string and watch me attack it. Ha-ha. Look at the little kitty, isn't he *cute*—now he's chasing his own tail! The depths you forced me to for some lousy shrimp. Not even jumbo."

Horry felt ashamed. "I…I never meant to embarrass you, Lucky."

"Right. A cat's got his feelings, you know. Of course, we've still got it better than dogs. Nobody asks us to roll over and play dead for a bone somebody else already chewed on. Now, come on, Horry, no sense staying here and feeling sorry for yourself."

"I never knew… I never realized how you felt. Gosh, Lucky, I wish we could have talked like this while I was still alive."

"You talked to me all the time, Horry, and I talked back. You just couldn't understand me until you croaked. Like, remember how I yowled at you when you got this crazy idea of putting me in your will?"

"You peed on the first draft," Horry said, remembering. "You didn't want to be in my will?"

"Hell, no. Not when you got to that business where if I croak everything goes to some relative of yours. I'm walking around here with a big target on my back for the next month, Horry. Never thought of that one, did you?"

"Edwin? You're talking about Edwin? Nobody even knows where he is. He could be dead, for all I know. I just used him to make sure Darcie and Cameron played by the rules. I could have said the ASPCA or the church, but I wanted something they'd really panic about, you know? Now come on, I think I heard a car door slam down there. Bet it's either Darcie or Cameron."

"Yippee," Lucky said flatly, slowly making his way into the hall. "It's showtime."

DARCIE UNLOADED the luggage she'd put into the trunk before leaving Pittsburgh, then stood and looked up at the house. Uncle Horry's house. Soon to be her house, unless she ran away again.

"No. No more running away. Today is the first day of the rest of— Oh, boy, this isn't going to work."

She picked up two suitcases and headed up the steps, onto the porch. She was just about to put down one suitcase to open the door when it swung on its hinges.

"Lily?" Darcie asked as she stepped into the empty foyer, then shrugged. "I'll have to have Cameron look at the lock."

She deposited the suitcases in the foyer, then returned to the car to get the rest, at which time Lily was in the foyer, glaring at the large pile.

"Hi, Lily," Darcie said with as much enthusiasm as she could muster, which wasn't much. "I see you took down the black crepe."

"He had enough mourning," the housekeeper said, motioning toward the suitcases. "You don't expect me to carry those upstairs, do you?"

"It was only a fleeting thought," Darcie said to Lily's departing back. "Jeez, what got into her? She was sniffling and crying yesterday."

Then it hit her. Sniffling and crying, yes, *before* the reading of the will. Darcie tipped her head to one side, considering Lily's reaction to the will. Embarrassment, yes, when Cameron started snorting and choking. But maybe a little anger, too? Maybe a *lot* of anger?

"Maybe she expected more, for services rendered," Darcie mused out loud, then wished away the unwelcome thought of Uncle Horry and Lily rolling around in bed together that immediately entered her head.

"Yeech! Won't catch me sleeping on that mattress. No way, no how. Oh, hello, Lucky."

She went down on her knees, to rub the cat behind the ears. "How's Mommy's sweet Lucky?"

Lucky purred, and lifted his chin, and she scratched him there too as his eyes squinted shut in an expression of near ecstasy…or at least she thought so, although common sense told her cats don't have expressions.

"Gathering allies?"

Lucky meowed and deserted Darcie to wrap himself around Cameron's ankles.

"Obviously not," Darcie said, quickly getting to her feet. "And, if I was, obviously not getting very far." She looked at Cameron, at how fairly edible he looked in khaki shorts and a darkest brown T-shirt that hugged his lean, broad-shouldered body. She was all in green, herself: lime-green knit belly shirt, short dark green skort. She'd dressed with care. Had he?

"Looks like we're going casual, huh?" she said, pushing her hair back behind her ears as Cameron dropped two soft-sided duffel bags on the floor. "I thought you were going to work, then sleep…er, stay here nights?"

"Nope. Doug told me to take the whole thirty days. He's going to a family wedding next month, one of those society bashes that goes on for a week, and figures he'll hit the wedding, then take off somewhere for the rest of the month. So we'll be even."

"Doug Llewellyn at a wedding," Darcie said, shaking her head. It seemed safe to talk about Doug

Llewellyn. "Isn't he afraid he'll break out in hives or something? I thought he was allergic."

"I know. I had to twist his arm to get him to agree to be my best man, and that was only because your pal Christine is already married. He said getting hit on by the maid of honor has never been part of his game plan at weddings."

"No, he probably goes for the junior bridesmaid. Oh! That was low, wasn't it? But he does rob the cradle."

"Not really, Darc. No younger than twenty-one, no older than twenty-five. The man has a system. And thanks for not jumping all over me when I mentioned the plans for our wedding. That broke the rules. Let's start over."

He stepped closer, holding out his right hand. "Hello, my name is Cameron Pierce. And you?"

Darcie looked at his hand, looked at his handsome, grinning face. "What do you think you're doing?"

He dropped his arm to his side. "I thought it was obvious. We're starting from scratch, just like this was our first meeting. I'm not exactly looking for another poke in the eye from your umbrella, but you get the point—no pun intended. So? Your name again?"

"Frustrated," Darcie said, picking up two suitcases. "My name is Frustrated. Keep going and it will be Homicidal. Now get out of my way."

"No," Cameron said, grinning at her in a way that made her want to punch him square in the nose, because he looked so adorable that, otherwise, she'd have to kiss him. "Not before you tell me you'll see me again.

I'm harmless, really. I'll even give you references. But I really do want to see you again."

Darcie blinked, remembering that those were the exact same words—the exact same line—he'd used on her the first time around. Beating down an urge to burst into tears and run for the hills, she said, "You can't be any more original than that?"

"Well, sure I can," Cameron said, and the next thing Darcie knew he had her face held between his hands and was kissing her. Rather ruthlessly.

Why she held onto the suitcases she'd never know, but she did. All through that long, probing kiss. Her eyes closed, her heart pounding, her knees turning to Silly Putty.

Only when he moved slightly away from her, her cheeks still cupped in his hands, and grinned like an idiot who'd just escaped his village did she open her hands.

"Ow! Damn it, Darc," Cameron yelped, hopping on one foot after her heavy suitcase landed on his sneakered foot. "What do you have in there—rocks?"

"Nope," she said, heading for the staircase, carrying only one suitcase and her purse. "Just my set of five-pound hand weights. I packed them right at the back of the suitcase, too, now that I think about it. You can bring the rest of the luggage up to my room later, Mr. Pierce, thank you. But hurry—it's almost lunchtime."

Once at the top of the stairs, she ran to her room and locked the door behind her before leaning back against the wood. "That can *not* happen again," she said, trying to regulate her breathing. "No running, no succumbing with nothing changing, nothing learned. This time we do it right!"

Then she went into the bathroom to splash cold water on her face. But not until she'd run her tongue around her lips, to savor the flavor of Cam's kiss one more time.

CAMERON FLEXED his toes inside his sneaker, then looked at Lucky, who had begun sharpening his claws on the rough tweed of one of Darcie's suitcases.

"How'd I do?" he asked the cat, who continued rhythmically digging his claws into the fabric. "That good, huh? Yeah, that's what I thought. But, hey, we're men, Lucky. We stick together, right?"

Lucky turned his head and looked at Cameron. Just looked at him.

Cameron moved back. It was an involuntary reaction, but one he was pretty sure made sense, a prudent defensive move.

"You gain another five pounds since I saw you last? What did you do—chase down and eat a Buick?" he asked the cat, who had to be twenty pounds if he was an ounce.

Cameron had seen smaller dogs. Maybe smaller horses. "Look, there's no reason we can't all get along here for the next month, right? Because she may have said no sex, but kisses are different. A man can do a lot with a few well-planned kisses. Watch and learn this month, Lucky. Not that it's going to take a month to bring Darcie to her senses."

Lucky's ears went flat against his head.

"You don't approve? All right, it won't take a month for *both* of us to come to our senses. Better?" Cameron added quickly. "Two-way street, definitely. I can be rational. But a month? No way. I mean, you did see the way she looked in that outfit? Her hair down? I'm good, but I'm no saint."

Lucky kept staring at him, but now he tipped his head to one side.

"Right. I'm talking strategy to a cat. Skip the rational part. But she did kiss me back," he said, picking up luggage, enough luggage to have him half staggering toward the steps. "Lucky? You coming upstairs with me? Us guys sticking together, and all of that?"

Lucky got to his feet and headed out onto the porch via the still-open door.

"Oh, damn," Cameron said, dropping the suitcases and charging after Lucky. "This isn't good. We're supposed to be in charge of your welfare, cat," he called out as Lucky broke into an easy lope that took him toward the far corner of the house. "Come on, come on back here, you stupid animal!"

By the time Cameron got to the corner of the house, Lucky had disappeared. Vanished. The lawn stretching from the house to the chain link fence lining the cliff was cat-free.

"Shit," Cameron swore quietly, poking in the shrubbery without success. "I just keep piling up the points, don't I?" He kept walking, still bent over, poking into the shrubbery, hoping against hope the damn cat would be sitting somewhere, laughing at him, waiting for him.

And then, to his shock and to the definite detriment of his back, Lucky came out of nowhere and landed on him, all twenty pounds of him, claws extended on all four paws, and Cameron was flat on his face in the grass.

He tried to sit up, Lucky still clinging to him, and attempted to reach behind him, get the cat off his back. God, this was a big cat. God, those were long claws. He'd probably need a transfusion. Stitches. Some time in a rest home.

"Hold still, I've got him," Darcie said from somewhere behind him, and Cameron obeyed immediately, since his efforts hadn't been working anyway.

"He's killing me here, Darc."

"Yes, yes, now stay still. I was on the porch when I heard you scream and—"

"I did *not* scream," Cameron said, with his teeth still clenched, and in considerable pain. "The damn thing jumped me. He could play tackle for the Eagles. Hell, anybody could play tackle for the Eagles. Ouch! Go slow, Darce. I think one of those claws is wrapped around a rib."

He could feel Darcie working at one paw at a time while crooning to Lucky, slowly convincing him to let go. "There," she said at last, and Cameron felt Lucky's back legs give one mighty push against him before the cat was off again, running toward the cliff.

"Stop him! He gets lost and you lose the house," he said as he got to his feet, pretty sure blood was trickling down his back.

"Lucky won't get lost. He's an outside cat, remember?"

Cameron stopped in the motion of trying to ease the material of his T-shirt away from his stinging, throbbing back. "He's an— You're kidding me, right?"

Darcie shook her head. "No. Lucky's always been an outside cat. Actually, he's always been a whatever he wants to be cat. Turn around, let me see your back."

"Don't touch it," Cameron warned, slowly turning around even as he took hold of the T-shirt at the shoulders, then bent over as he eased the thing over his head and threw it on the grass. "How bad is it?"

"It's, um, does it hurt?"

"Yes, it hurts. Is there any skin left?"

"How much do you need?"

"Ha. Ha." Cameron straightened, headed toward the house. "I'm going to go take a shower."

"Good idea," Darcie said, falling into step beside him, holding his ruined T-shirt. "But then come to me, because you'll need some antiseptic cream. And a bandage over at least one of those holes…er, scratches. How did Lucky get on your back? He's too big to jump that high."

"I was bending over, looking for him under the bushes. But you're right, that was a pretty good leap. Like he'd been shot out of a cannon."

"Well, I think it was very nice of you to go chasing him, thinking he'd get lost and I'd lose the house because I didn't take care of him."

"Yeah. I'm a real hero." He looked at her. "And a real jerk. I should have realized that glandular case of a cat can take care of himself."

"Uncle Horry told me Lucky once scared off a huge German shepherd that had wandered into Shangri-La. He said he'd never seen a dog run so fast with its tail stuck between its legs. Lucky's my hero."

"He's not mine. Not right now. He jumped me on purpose. Premeditated jumping. Leaping with malice aforethought."

"Oh, he did not." Darcie held open the front door. "Now go up to Uncle Horry's old room, take that shower, and I'll meet you in the study with some antiseptic cream and a couple of aspirin."

"And a cold beer. I deserve a cold beer."

"Big baby," Darcie said, watching him climb the stairs before turning, her expression one of mingled concern and horror at the way his back looked, to head for the kitchen.

LUCKY SAT ON THE FRONT PORCH while he licked one front paw several times, then rubbed it over his ear, an exertion such as he'd just had necessitated a complete body wash. He put his paw down and glared at Horry. "For your information, you old fart, cats don't fly. You do that again, mister, and I'm going to have to hurt you."

"I don't think you can, Lucky. I'm already dead. You should have gone back when I told you to. Cameron was scared he'd screwed up when you took off. He was worried about you, poor boy."

Lucky started on the other paw, the other ear. "Wrong. He was worried about your stupid will. I told you. You didn't give one thought to me when you came up with that cockamamie idea. Now you're throwing me on people? I do have my dignity. Cats, by nature, are very dignified, you know."

Uncle Horry looked at his pet. "Really? I suppose, Mr. Dignified, it's pointless to mention that you're now licking your own ass?"

CHAPTER FIVE

DARCIE LINED UP A TUBE of antiseptic cream, a roll of tape, some small gauze pads, a scissors and a bottle of beer on the desk in her uncle's study, then sat down behind the desk to sip on her own bottle of chilled beer and wait for Cameron to find her.

She didn't really like beer—it made her feel full immediately, and sort of sat in her mouth, with her unwilling to swallow it unless the beer was icy cold. But, then again, they were out of soda. She would just drink fast, before the beer got warm.

The study was located directly beneath Uncle Horry's old bedroom, so she could hear the shower running, could hear Cameron's footsteps once he was back in the bedroom proper.

She looked at the ceiling, imagining him walking around upstairs with just a towel wrapped at his waist.

His hair would still be wet and spiky where he'd rubbed at it with a hand towel. The lean, powerful-looking muscles in his arm and back would flex as he picked up one of his duffel bags and threw it on the bed.

He'd unzip it, rummage around inside for another pair of shorts, a shirt, his underwear, cursing under his breath because every blessed piece of clothing would be wrinkled.

"The man packs like he's stuffing a sausage," she said to herself, smiling weakly as she remembered their weekend trip to visit Uncle Horry and how Cameron had walked around looking like an unmade bed for two days.

Her smile faded. She did know some things about him. He liked casual dress. He couldn't pack a suitcase. His skin was a golden color, like the darker brown and gold hair on his head, the lighter golden hairs on his chest, his arms, his long straight legs.

He worked out three days a week at the gym a mile from his condo, running there, running home again, arriving all damp and breathing deeply and…yummy looking.

Sometimes she'd go with him, and he'd help her with the exercise machines, and they'd run home together, laughing as they fell into the condo, pulled off their workout clothes as they chased each other to the bathroom, ended up showering together.

Darcie heard more movement above her and imagined Cameron's damp towel falling to the floor as he stepped into his boxer shorts. Cutest little things, as he favored plaids, and in either soft knitted cotton or silk.

Because he left for work an hour earlier than she had, she used to lie propped up in bed, to watch him pull on those silk boxers…often coaxing him out of them a few minutes later.

Once, she remembered now, she'd accomplished that feat with her teeth.

She leaned forward until her forehead hit the desktop. "This isn't going to work. This is just not going to work. How can I get past the sexual attraction to find out about the real Cameron, the real me, if all I want to do is jump his bones?"

One thing was a complete no-brainer. They were wildly attracted to each other. Sexually compatible. Superficially compatible. If they never talked to each other, they'd probably get along just fine. After all, the one time they'd *really* talked to each other about anything even slightly important, the talk had gone swiftly to yelling, accusing...and her escape to Pittsburgh. Too bad they couldn't just spend their lives in bed together ...

"Darc?"

Darcie sat up, realizing she hadn't heard Cameron's footsteps as he left the bedroom. She'd gotten too hung up on the idea of him putting on his boxers, a thought that sent hot color into her cheeks.

"Oh," she said, getting to her feet, trying very hard not to look at him as he stood in front of her in hip-hugging black shorts and nothing else...unless she counted the glimpse of plaid silk waistband, and she couldn't afford to count that.

That's it, no more beer for her. Obviously, half a bottle was more than enough.

He tossed a knit shirt on the desktop as he padded toward her on bare feet, then grabbed his bottle of beer and took three long swallows.

She watched his throat move as he drank. Interesting. Ingest about half of one beer herself, and watching his throat work became a sensual experience. She was pitiful. Absolutely unsalvageable.

"I caught a glimpse of my back upstairs. I think, if you connect the dots, it'll show a rough rendering of the Phillies' new ball park. Ashburn Alley on my left shoulder, see?" He turned around. "What do you think?"

Her stomach lurched as she looked at the gouges in his back, the white welts around each gouge, the reddened skin around each welt. "Oh, Cam, it looks worse now than it did. I can't imagine what happened. Lucky must have been frightened."

"Yeah, that's it. I ran after him, and scared him. Poor Lucky. Remind me to apologize to the little bastard. I guess I'm just *lucky* he doesn't carry a .45 in one of his fat rolls, or I'd be a dead man."

Darcie pushed Cameron into a chair and picked up the antiseptic cream. "Um...you've had all your shots?"

"Better question," Cameron said, wincing as she used one of the gauze pads to dab ointment on the digs and scratches, "has Lucky had all his shots?"

"Probably. Uncle Horry took very good care of him." She made short work out of applying four gauze pads to his back, then handed him his shirt. "You'll live. And I am sorry, Cam. Really."

"Why? You didn't sneak up behind me and drop Lucky on my back, did you?" Cameron asked, pulling his shirt over his head, and Darcie threaded her hands together, to keep herself from reaching up to brush his hair out of his eyes. "But from now on? From now on, the care and feeding of Lucky is all yours. I'll find something else to occupy my time."

She screwed the top back on the antiseptic tube and gathered up the bandage wrappers. "Like what?"

He began tucking in his shirt, and when he reached for the button on his shorts, Darcie turned away, searching for a waste can. "Like, if you don't mind, buying some paint and painting the outside of this house, like I've been itching to do since the first time you brought me here. Or are you emotionally attached to the pink?"

"Not really, no. But you don't have to—"

"I know that. I want to. So, if you want, we can grab some lunch, then drive into town for some paint chips. A true Victorian can handle three colors. Basic house, major trim, minor trim—I'm using the technical terms here. We'll get into bargeboards and lintels and brackets later, and all that decorative work you insist on calling gingerbread. Do you have any special colors in mind?"

Darcie shook her head. "Burgundy? For the trim, I mean. Can I help?"

He finished off his beer. "I said you could, Darc. And burgundy's good, for some of the trim. Maybe use that, along with different shades of cream?"

"No, I don't mean just picking out the paint colors. I mean, can I help? I've never painted before, and it sounds like fun." And like something to do other than sit around here for a solid month, thinking about Cameron's plaid silk boxers, but she didn't say that.

Cameron's smile was a little slow in coming, and his tone a little too bright when he said, "Sure, why not."

"You don't think I can do it," Darcie said. "Never mind. There's plenty else I can do around here."

She brushed past him, heading for the door, and he followed her. "Come on, Darc, don't go off the rails. This is a big house. I don't want you up on a ladder. I've got it—you can paint the porches. Lots of porches, Darc. Lots of balustrades, railings, posts. You'd be a big help."

Darcie, as was her habit, tapped Bupkus on the nose as she left the study. "And I stay on the ground because I'm too dangerous on a ladder. Gee, thanks."

"Have you ever been on a ladder?"

She stopped, turned to glare at him. "No, and I never will be, if you have your way. It's all the same thing, Cam. I'll never know what I can do, if nobody lets me try."

He held up one hand. "Let me guess. We're talking about your career again, right? How'd we get there again?"

Darcie sighed. "I don't know. We're not supposed to. We had a deal. But, damn it, Cam, how am I ever going to know what I like, what I can do if I—let go! Where are we going?"

Cameron held on to her wrist as he pulled her down the hallway, through the foyer, out onto the porch, and down the steps to the gravel driveway. "Look up, Darc. Look all the way up. Three floors, Darc. Considering this house has twelve-foot ceilings and the whole thing is raised about six feet to accommodate the porches and a raised cellar? You're looking at being over forty feet in the air, hanging on to a ladder with one hand, slapping on paint with the other."

Darcie was a lot of things. She'd accused herself of being a lot of things. But she'd never believed she had a death wish. "Okay, okay, I paint the porches."

"Ah, a breakthrough. The woman understands that the man is only trying to protect her. Not *squelch* her."

She shook free of his hand. "I wouldn't go that far. And now I've got to worry about you hanging off a ladder way up there."

"Don't. I worked my way through school hanging from ladders. Painting, roofing, siding, basic construction, you name it."

Darcie turned to look at him. "You worked your way through college? I never knew that."

"You didn't?" Cameron raked his fingers through his hair. "I can't believe we never— You really didn't know? Cripes, Darc, what *did* we talk about?"

"And score one for the lady," Darcie crowed, then ran up the steps, because Lily was ringing the cowbell on the back porch, just the way Uncle Horry had always instructed her to call him for meals.

"TEMPTATION. That's ridiculous. How is anyone supposed to know what color temptation is?" Darcie said, handing Cameron the paint sample.

"Oh, I don't know, Darc," he said, lightly touching her mouth with the tip of his finger. "What color is your lipstick, anyway?"

She spoke to him from between clenched teeth. "Stop that. We're in a paint store, for crying out loud. Besides, it's against the rules."

Ah, here was his moment, and being in public when he told her about his small epiphany was probably safer than hitting her with it back at Shangri-La. "Wrong, Darcie. Sex is against the rules. Everything else is fair game. Flirting, courting. Canoodling."

"Canoo— What?"

"I'm not sure, so don't quote me, but I think that means petting. You know, Darc. First base, second base, third base? No home runs, I can live with that for a month if I have to, although you may hear me whimpering from time to time, so I wouldn't mind hitting a couple of triples."

She winced, looking to her left, her right, then whispered fiercely, "Could you lower your voice?"

"I could," he said, although that wasn't a part of his plan, and she had to know it. If she didn't, she'd know it in a minute. "I like your hair that way, Darc. All soft and swingy." He reached past her to pull out another paint sample. "Here, look, this almost matches. Silken Mist. Hey, am I good or am I good?"

"You're impossible," Darcie said, randomly grabbing at paint samples and then heading for the door. She opened it, then glared at him. "Now what? Why are you stopping?"

"Give me a minute, Darc," Cameron said, as an evil thought invaded his mind, followed by an even more evil chuckle. He reached for two cans of the bright red paint. *Oh yeah.* "Just let me get a couple of brushes and some other stuff, and I'll meet you at the car."

Darcie let go of the door and walked back over to

him. “Red paint? I don’t want the house to be red. Pink is bad enough. Besides, that’s really bright.”

“Yeah, fire-engine-red enamel, and for once the name fits the color,” Cameron said, gathering up a package of brushes and heading for the counter. He’d already checked out the freestanding three-car garage at Shangri-La, and knew there was a reasonable stock of painting equipment and ladders there. “This isn’t for the house, Darc. Just a little side project to keep me busy while you’re deciding on colors. Ah, there’s the white enamel. Two red, two white. That ought to do it for a start.”

“That ought to do what? What kind of little side project?” she asked once they were in the car once more, and heading back to Shangri-La.

“Maintenance,” he told her. “I think that’s what Horry called it. And I’m not even going to charge the estate for my time. I’m such a nice guy.”

Darcie folded her arms and glared at him. “I was right. I don’t know you at all. I never saw this evil streak before. Now tell me what you’re going to do.”

“You’ll see soon enough,” he said, pulling into the small parking lot surrounding an even smaller building advertising sixteen flavors of Italian ice. “Temptation or Silken Mist? Translation, cherry or lemon?”

“I don’t know,” Darcie said, opening the car door. “I’ll go with you.”

She chose lime, which figured, since he hadn’t suggested it. And insisted on paying, which he also should have expected. By the time she’d gotten her change, he'd gravitated toward a low brick wall and was sitting there, waiting for her.

"I feel like I'm playing hookey," she said, hopping up onto the wall. "How long have we been gone?"

"Not twelve hours," he said, watching as she licked at some of the melted Italian ice that had run down over her fingers. He looked toward the horizon, as watching Darcie could be considered hazardous to his mental health. "But I'll admit it, I do keep wondering when Humbolt is going to start showing up with a stopwatch in his hand. Do you think Lily is going to alert him every time we leave Shangri-La? I mean, otherwise, how would he know if we're breaking the rules?"

"Good question," Darcie said, pulling a wad of paper napkins out of her skort pocket and handing him half. "You've got some on your chin. Use your spoon."

"Yes, ma'am. Unless you want to volunteer to lick it off?"

"Not particularly, no," she said, but she didn't look at him. "Can you look at Lily? I can't. I keep thinking about how she and Uncle Horry…you know."

"Better than you do, let me tell you," Cameron said, grinning. "Do you know there's a disco ball hanging from your uncle's bedroom ceiling?"

All right, she was looking at him now. "No. No way."

"And a built-in audio system. Surround sound, remote control on the bedside table. I'm going to check it out later. The man knew how to set a mood. Although, I've got all the windows open up there. The whole place smells like my third-grade teacher, Miss Bodish. Especially the bathroom where, if you can stand the shock, I found a pair of pink bunny slippers."

"They could have been my—no, that's stupid. They're Lily's, aren't they?"

"That's my guess. The slippers and the barber pole."

"Oh, God, I forgot about that. Is it really a barber pole?"

"It could be, if it was shorter, and had been on the Atkins Diet for a few months. It's a souped-up stripper pole, Darc, a good eight feet of it—with mechanized red and white stripes on a revolving cylinder inside the glass casing. Really fine workmanship."

"Oh, God. Are you sure you don't want to switch to another bedroom?"

"Not on your life. The surround sound is also linked to a flat-screen TV over the fireplace, and I already saw the satellite dish on the side of the house. Uncle Horry really knew how to live."

Darcie crumpled the paper cup and eased herself down from the wall. "You do know he died in that bed."

"I'll flip the mattress," he said, crushing his own empty cup and tossing it into the huge oil drum that served as a garbage can. "Okay, I'll buy a new mattress. And box spring." She was still looking at him, one eyebrow raised. "What? New sheets? New bedspread?"

"Good thought. But there has to be another mattress set that will fit, somewhere in all those bedrooms. And bedding, too. I'll look, and then we can make the switch."

"You just want to get into Horry's room and see the disco ball."

"I most certainly do not," she said, easing into the passenger seat. "I want to see the barber pole."

Cameron laughed. "That's my girl. Do you think Lily used to dance around it for Horry? Think about it. Frau Blücher doing the dance of the seven veils, music arranged for pole humping and bunny slippers."

Darcie coughed. Choked, actually. "I…I really don't think I want to know the answer to that one, but I'm trying very hard to believe it's only a decoration, and maybe some wishful thinking on Uncle Horry's part. And don't be crude, even if you are being funny. What I do know is that I'd like it very much if Lily were to take a hike."

"You can't throw her out. Horry said she could stay as long as she wanted, remember?"

"And she's probably acting as Attorney Humbolt's spy, to make sure we don't leave Shangri-La for more than twelve hours at a time."

"Also true. And she cooks."

"I know," Darcie said as he pulled into the long drive, at which time all conversation stopped as the frogs set up their *ribbit-ribbit* alert that probably was in violation of any local noise-pollution ordinance, if Shangri-La wasn't a five-acre estate, far away from the other houses that lined the cliff on Quarry Road.

She stood behind the car and helped Cameron unload the trunk, taking two of the paint cans and carrying them up to the porch. "Hello, Lucky," she said, and patted his head as she sat down, then looked at Cameron. "There's really no way to get rid of her, is there? I mean, I used to think she liked Uncle Horry, but now I'm not so sure. She could have been a…a long-term gold digger?"

Cameron joined her on the porch, setting down the other two gallons of paint and the bag of brushes and complimentary paint stir sticks. "That bunting did come down in a hurry," he said, seating himself on the top step beside Darcie, and as far away from Lucky as he could get.

"And I found the magnolias in the garbage can out back when I offered to empty the kitchen waste can after lunch. Magnolias turn all brown in a hurry. They're very delicate. But she'd ripped the petals off most of them. And she looks at me as if she hates me."

"Oh, don't read too much into that, Darc. I've always thought constipated was Frau Blücher's only expression," Cameron said, then looked at the rocking chair nearest him, as it had begun to move. And the other two rockers weren't moving. And there wasn't any breeze.

"She always treated me like some sort of interloper when I'd visit Uncle Horry. I never said anything to him. It wasn't my place to complain, after all. Thirty years. I wonder why he never married her."

The rocker stopped as if some invisible someone sitting in it had just jammed both feet against the porch floor. "Darc," Cameron said, waving one hand toward the rocker. "Did…did you see—never mind. Look, we can't know why Horry never married her, but he had to have had his reasons. And he did leave her well provided for. Besides, there's the watching-us part of this next month to be sure we don't break the rules thing, not to mention the cooking and cleaning part. She has to stay.

Then, maybe after you get all of the inheritance, you can buy her off or something."

"She does the cooking because she won't let me in the kitchen," Darcie said, looking just a little bit mulish for a beautiful woman.

"Oh, come on, Darc. I had a kitchen. I scrambled eggs, you made ham sandwiches and soup. Our stack of home-delivery menus was three inches thick. And I had a cleaning service. Do you mean to say you've been holding out on me, and you're a gourmet cook?"

"Not gourmet, but I certainly can do more than slap meat between pieces of bread or open a can." She petted Lucky, who had plopped himself on her lap. "I'm sure I can."

"Your mom taught you how to cook? You took classes?"

"My mother didn't know how to cook. She was always more of a hostess."

"But you learned. You cooked for yourself in Pittsburgh?"

She ignored his question. "And cleaning? It's cleaning. Not rocket science."

"You cleaned house for yourself in Pittsburgh?"

"Shut up," she said, pushing Lucky off her lap and getting to her feet. "I'm just saying that we don't really need Lily around here."

"Darcie, sweetheart, I know we don't know enough about each other, but I do know you lived in a house with a full-time housekeeper while you were growing up, and that from that point on you lived in college dorms and one studio apartment, plus whatever you had in Pittsburgh. And my place, where you made the bed once in a while, which was sort of pointless, as we were always in it. Now you're telling me you want to cook and clean and paint houses?"

"In the way of experiments, yes I do. I've already decided I want to rearrange my bedroom upstairs. I…I want to put my *stamp* on Shangri-La. On *someplace.* Is that so terrible?"

"No, babe, not at all. You can put your stamp on me, too, if the mood strikes you. I'm game, as well as one heck of a nice guy, helping you get this house and Horry's money. You know, by and large, thinking about this thing, I'm a real prince."

"Yes, and so modest with it all." She grinned at him. "I don't want to think about Horry's money, but I do want this house. I didn't realize how much, until I started thinking about the thing."

"Makes for a long commute, though, from here to that great career of yours in Pittsburgh," Cameron said, looking at her closely and, yes, seeing the sudden flush of color in her cheeks.

"I…I'll work something out," she said, tucking her hair behind her ears. "Now tell me what you're going to do with this red paint."

"I told you. Maintenance. You take your time over those color samples, maybe look up some Web sites showing Victorian homes, Queen Anne homes, and get some ideas, and I'll amuse myself in the meantime with my maintenance. Oh, and don't forget to find that mattress for me, unless you want to invite me to bunk in with—man, Lucky, that woman can move a lot faster than I gave her credit for," he ended as the front door slammed shut.

Cameron got to his feet, winced as he stretched and the scratches on his back gave him hell, then went off to the workshop built onto the block of garages to look for a screwdriver to open the paint cans, whistling as he went.

"WHAT AM I to do, Lucky? Darcie wants Lily gone," Horry said, still sitting in the rocker, but unable to master talking and rocking at the same time.

"So? I want her gone, too, and I didn't see you getting all concerned then. I'm beginning to seriously doubt your affection for me, Horry, I really am. And I'm so darned cute, too."

"Oh, Lucky, you don't mean that—and, yes, you are. Now help me. How do we get rid of Lily?"

Lucky stood up, stretched his body out to almost twice its usual length, and that was considerable. "I could pee on her mattress."

"Yes, you could do—no! That's ridiculous."

"Sorry. I'm a cat. It's all I got."

"That's all right, Lucky. I made this mess. Blinded by her beauty. It's a man's curse."

Lucky, by way of an editorial comment to that statement, horked up a hair ball that had been bothering him all morning, then resettled happily on the wood.

"Hey," Horry said, suddenly excited. "I'm a ghost. I am a ghost—right? I'll scare her away. Rattle some chains, bang some doors...what else? I could howl because ghosts howl, except I've been trying, and so far no luck there. Come on, Lucky, think. This is important. What else can I do to scare her away?"

"Well…" Lucky said after some thought, and living up to any remark made over the centuries about cats being devious, "you can tickle *my* belly…"

CHAPTER SIX

DARCIE TOOK A DEEP BREATH and knocked on the door to Uncle Horry's former bedroom.

She'd never been inside the bedroom, and had found out when she was fourteen that he kept it locked when she was in residence.

Now she knew why. She also knew why her late father had called Shangri-La Horry's House of Hoochie. Darcie smiled. She'd never realized her intellectual father had harbored a sense of humor. Except, looking back on it, she didn't think her father had been amused.

"Cam? You in there?"

"Just a minute, Darc," he called out, and she heard a series of bangs and grunts before he at last opened the door. His hair was hanging over his forehead, he was breathing a little hard and his grin bordered on evil. "Hi. I've got the mattress and box spring ready to go," he said, then stood back and waved her into the large room.

Both mattress and box spring were leaning against the frame of a very large four-poster bed, with piles of bedding tossed in a heap near the windows.

"King-size. I thought so," she said, sniffing the air. "There's a very nice king-size mattress in the corner guest room. Why do I smell Jean Naté? One of my roommates in boarding school used to wear it, until we told her it was medieval. I can't believe Uncle Horry used it."

Cameron leaned up against one of the bedposts. "I think the smell goes with the bunny slippers. Which, by the way, are now in the kitchen. I figured that would save Lily some embarrassment." He lifted his head, motioning toward the ceiling. "See it? One disco ball, large economy size. You can turn it on with that switch, beside the door."

Darcie tipped back her head and, sure enough, there was the mirrored ball, smack in the middle of the ceiling. "Oh, gawd."

"Wait. It gets better. I didn't see it until I was wrestling with the mattress. Look under the bed canopy."

She looked at him, saw his grin and wanted to deny herself the dubious pleasure, but curiosity got the better of her. Crossing the room, she stood next to him, leaned forward, past the bed drapes, and looked up. "A *mirror?* My uncle slept underneath a *mirror?* Why, that randy old goat! Oh, that's just gross."

"Don't knock it till you've tried it, Darc," Cameron said, pushing away from the bedpost.

"Oh? You've tried it?" And why did that make her so angry?

"No, but far be it for me to be against new experiences. And isn't that what you want, Darc? New experiences, finding out who you are, and all that good stuff? Ladders are dangerous, so hey, we could start here?"

"In your dreams," Darcie said, looking at the mattress

and deciding where to put her hands to help move it. There wasn't a spot that appealed. "Are we going to move this or what?"

"Since I'm betting the *or what* wasn't anything I had in mind, sure, let's do this thing. Are you sure you can handle the weight? It's pretty heavy and clumsy."

"I can do it," she said, hoping she was right. "I'll…I'll take this end."

Cameron grabbed the other end, counted to three, and lifted his end of the mattress a good foot off the floor…while Darcie's end stayed where it was. "Um, Darc? Three. I said *three.*"

"I know, I know," she said, putting all her strength into trying to lift the mattress. "I…I…it isn't moving."

"Yes. I'd noticed that," Cameron said, letting his end drop to the floor once more.

Darcie wanted to kick the mattress but refrained. "Okay, so now we know I'm not Xena, Warrior Princess. Now what?"

He joined her on her end of the mattress. "Plan B. This thing isn't so much heavy as it is unwieldy. At least that's what I'm telling myself. So, this time, I pull, you push?"

Plan C was implemented a minute later, after the heavy mattress fell over, taking out a floor lamp: Cameron pulls, Darcie shouts encouragement and directions.

Plan C worked, at least until they got out into the hallway.

"Now what, boss?"

Darcie, who was caught between the railing and the

mattress, took a deep breath and asked, "Do you think you can lift it over the railing?"

Cameron was bent over, his hands on his knees. He raised his head and glared at her. "Sure. Just let me go eat a box of Wheaties and a can of spinach, and I'll be right with you."

"That heavy, huh?"

"Bulky, Darc. Hard to handle. Yeah, and heavy."

"Well, it can't stay here in the hallway. We can't get around it." And then inspiration struck. "Cam? Look to your left. See? French doors at the end of the hall. Remember? They go out onto a small side porch that has its own flight of steps to the ground. We could get the mattress onto the porch, aim it toward the steps, and let it slide down them?"

And she had another suggestion, having to do with "walking" the mattress onto the hall runner, then using the rug to help slide the mattress down the hall and onto the porch.

Ten minutes and a few choice curse words later, Darcie stood at the head of the porch steps and watched, grinning in triumph, as the mattress slid down the steps and onto the lawn. "Oh, I'm good. Clearly management material, born to supervise. Now all we have to do is do the same thing with the box spring, then get the box spring and mattress from the corner room, and drag those into Uncle Horry's—into your bedroom—make up the bed, and we're solid."

"And would this be before or after you call the paramedics and have them revive me?" He rolled his shoulders, then winced.

"What is it? You hurt your back?"

"No, or if I did, I probably won't feel that until tomorrow. It's the scratches. I'm sweating, and they're starting to burn. Nothing major. Nothing to worry about. At the rate I'm going here, I don't expect a piano to drop out of the sky and hit me on the head until at least next Saturday."

"Oh, you poor whiny baby." Darcie took hold of his arm and led him back inside, closing the French doors behind them. "How about we quit for tonight? You can sleep in the corner room, and we can buy a whole new box spring and mattress and have it delivered and set up?"

"I can do it. The box spring isn't as heavy as the mattress."

"No, but it doesn't bend, does it? And you'd still have to move the other set from the corner room. And then I'd need a new set in there anyway. Just sleep in the corner room, okay?"

"Are you being masterful?" Cameron said, stepping closer to her. "I mean, is this an executive decision?"

"Cut that out. It's an obvious solution, that's all. I should have thought of it sooner."

"But you did think of it now," Cameron said, twirling a lock of her hair around his index finger as she backed up a little, only to feel the wall behind her. "This may come as a shock to you—I know it has to me—but I like you like this. Commanding. Decisive. My take-charge blonde. We ought to try one of those baggy blue suits of yours again, see if it's a turn-on now. Yum..."

"Are you done? All finished?" She bent her knees and ducked down under his arm, before heading back to the bedroom. "That has got to be the most pathetic excuse of a come-on I have *ever* heard. Pitiful. Just pitiful."

She had gotten only far enough into Uncle Horry's former bedroom to realize that she had no idea why she was there, when the door shut behind her.

Darcie turned around to see Cameron grinning at her. "You're kidding, right?"

"Kidding about what? Oh, you think I'm locking you in? Making you my prisoner? That I have seduction on my mind?" He shrugged. "Well, one out of three."

"Cam…"

He held up his hands. "Kidding, kidding. But you have to see this, Darc. I've been checking out all of Horry's toys. Watch."

Because she knew she couldn't run out of the room without looking like an idiot, and mostly because she really wanted to see whatever it was he was going to show her, Darcie remained in the middle of the room, her arms folded at her waist. "You're such a child. So show me."

He grinned at her, waggled his eyebrows a time or two, and then went around the large room, closing all the heavy burgundy velvet drapes against the setting sun.

Next, he pulled a pack of matches from his pocket and started lighting candles. Goodness, there were a lot of fat white candles in the room, at least three on every surface.

"Okay, okay, I get the picture. Geriatric sex by candlelight. You don't have to light them all."

Cameron shook out the third match and retreated to the door. "Step two," he said, and raised the wall switch that set the disco ball turning, its hundreds of mirrors picking up the flickering candlelight and reflecting it all around the room. Little moving squares of light spun around the floor, the ceiling, played across Darcie's body as she dropped her arms to her sides in amazement.

"And now, the pièce de résistance, as I've heard it called," Cameron said, slipping past the propped-up box spring and reappearing with a small remote control in his hand. He pushed a button, and a full orchestra was in the room with them.

"Is that…what's that music?"

"Ravel's 'Bolero,' I think. Music appreciation class was a long time ago, but I'm pretty sure I'm right. I'm telling you, Darc, all we need now is a rose between your teeth, and we'd be in business."

The box spring, that had been leaning against the bed frame, suddenly fell over, slamming to the floor.

Both Darcie and Cameron looked at the thing in some shock, until Lucky casually walked out from beneath the bed, to sit on his haunches and begin washing himself.

"Lucky did that?"

Cameron shook his head. "I'd say no, but then I'd have to tell you that I'm beginning to think that mangy ball of fur has supernatural powers. Maybe Lily's a witch, and Lucky is her familiar, or whatever a witch's cat is called."

"Take some deep breaths, Cam. Obviously you're oxygen deprived from too much exertion. And turn off that music. It's too loud."

"Not yet. One more thing." He clicked the large remote again, and the red and white stripes on the tall, thin barber pole began to rotate, small white fairy lights in the base and top glowing on and off. "I think it must have been custom-made."

There was nothing Darcie could say, so she said nothing. Her late uncle had been a randy old man. A dirty old man. Even prepared, it was a shock. "Turn…turn it off."

"What's wrong, Darc? You're looking a little queasy."

So, okay, she'd say it. "My uncle was a dirty old man, Cam, that's what's wrong. I'm having a little trouble trying to reconcile the silly, childish, fun uncle with…with Medicare's answer to Don Juan. It's a shock, you know?"

Cameron put his hands on her shoulders. "Horry was a man, Darc. You saw him only as an uncle, but obviously he had a life outside of widgets and mechanical toys."

She looked up at the revolving disco ball. "Oh, he had lots of toys." She shook her head. "Wow. That's got to come down before we have the new bedding delivered. The ball, the mirror, the barber pole. I couldn't look the delivery guys in the eye."

"Now, now, let's not be hasty here, Darc," Cameron said quickly. When she narrowed her eyes and glared at him, he added, "Okay, the barber pole goes. I'll agree to that one."

"And the mirror."

Cameron tipped his head side to side, as if weighing the possibility. "Naw, that stays, at least for a while. I mean, aren't you even a little bit curious?"

"No, I'm not a little bit curious," Darcie said, then tried to back away from him as he grinned at her in a way that had her pretty sure what he had in mind was an experiment containing an ulterior motive. "Cam… stop looking at me that way. We agreed there'd be no—Cam, put me down!"

And he did put her down, but only after he'd managed to carry her *and* lever his legs over the high side rail of the huge four poster. So when he put her down, it was all the way down, depositing her on the hardwood floor, then sitting down beside her.

Floor below them, the bed on all four sides, the bedposts holding up the ornate, velvet, draped canopy. *The mirror.* Her reflection seemed vaguely golden, and a little fuzzy, as the mirror would seem to have a soft, golden cast to it somehow. Sort of like airbrushing a photograph so that everything in it looks good.

"This is stupid," she said. "I feel like I'm in a playpen."

"Yeah, I know," Cameron said, putting an arm around her shoulders and then easing them both onto their backs. "Ah, there we are. Wave to you, Darc."

"You're an idiot," she said, but when he waved, and she saw him waving back from above them, she couldn't help herself. She laughed. "We're both idiots. And don't you feel we're like bugs under a microscope?"

"No, I can't say as I do," Cameron said, his arm

still around her shoulders, cradling her neck. She could see as he began stroking her neck. Feel it, see it while you feel it. It was like stroking in stereo, or maybe 3-D.

"What are you doing?"

"I'm testing, Darc."

"Yes, that's obvious. You're testing *Darc*. Testing *me*. Seeing how far you can get me to go. Well, forget it."

"Not even first base? Aw, come on, Darc, just first base."

He was smiling down at her, looking about as innocent as Jesse James on his way to rob a bank.

"What exactly *is* first base?"

"Kissing. Just kissing."

"And second base?" she said, watching in fascination as he turned toward her and began nuzzling just below her ear.

"It differs, depending on where you went to school. My school? Anything above the waist."

"Uh-huh," she said, biting her bottom lip, because his kisses, his teasing tongue, the heat of his breath, were all combining to send pesky little tendrils of arousal throughout her body, looking for places to wrap themselves. "And…and third base?"

He whispered the words into her ear. "Anything below the—"

She lifted her hand and covered his mouth with it. "Okay, okay, I get the picture."

He licked the center of her palm with the tip of his tongue. She allowed it, just for a moment, then dropped her hand to her side, at which point he began nuzzling again and talking.

"A guy got real locker-room bragging rights with third base. That's when it gets interesting, because that's when it goes into degrees of success. For instance, a home run into the seats is sex, period. Upper deck home run means she let you take off all her clothes in the back seat. Then there was the grand slam...but you probably don't want to hear about that, either, right?"

"And you talked about girls like this? In high school, I suppose."

"And college. Men are pigs, Darc. I'm so ashamed. Really." He began kissing the skin exposed by her scoop-necked knit shirt.

She was fascinated. Appalled that she was fascinated, but fascinated just the same. She could see herself, how her eyes seemed to be growing wider. She could see the back of Cameron's head as he leaned over her. She could watch as her breathing became more rapid, her chest moving up and down, up and down.

See. Feel. Watch. React.

Defenses. Crumble. Resolve. Weaken.

Pleasurable? Yes. Smart? No.

She was just about to tell him that the experiment was over, she understood the purpose of the mirror, and he could quit now, when he raised his head slightly, then came at her mouth, his open very slightly as he slanted his lips against hers.

Now she was watching herself being kissed. Being thoroughly kissed.

She felt the front of him pressing against her. She saw the back of him, lying on top of her. She watched her arms rising up without her giving them any conscious command and wrapping themselves around his back, but carefully, gently, so as not to irritate the poor guy's wounds.

Then she closed her eyes and just let the man hit his damn single….

His tongue exploring her mouth. Her sucking on that tongue, drawing it deeper. His teeth, nibbling at her bottom lip. The advances. The retreats, only to advance again. Long, drugging kisses, one after the other, his entire concentration seeming to be on her mouth, only her mouth. Over and over and over again.

She was on fire. She wanted more. She wanted it all.

And yet, she felt…safe.

He'd promised only kisses, and he was delivering only kisses. He wouldn't press her further, because he'd promised not to press her further, and she believed him. She could give herself up to his kisses, enjoy them, without thinking of them as some sort of preamble to what might come next.

How lovely. How very wonderful. His kiss…his kiss.

He kissed her hair, her ears, her eyelids. He ran nibbling kisses up and down her throat. Always, always, he returned to her mouth, and yet another long, intoxicating kiss of exploration.

But he never tried to stretch his single into a double.

She felt…yes, she felt in control. She was setting the ground rules. She would say if they moved on, or kept to those rules. It was the most mind-boggling turn-on she'd ever experienced…right up until the moment she opened her eyes, to watch Cameron a little more, and saw Lily standing at the bottom of the bed.

She dug her fingertips into Cameron's back, which really wasn't a good idea, because Cameron immediately drew back, saying, "Damn, Darc, all you had to do was say no."

"Lily's standing at the bottom of the bed," she whispered as quietly as possible.

"Okay. Or that. You could have said that. That's got the same stopping power." He stayed where he was. "You're kidding, though, right?"

"No," she whispered. "She's still there, just looking at us."

"Okay, okay," Cameron whispered back, easing himself off her. "I'll handle this."

"I'd appreciate that, yes," Darcie said, closing her eyes, as if that would somehow make the housekeeper disappear. That didn't work, the image was pretty much burned into her eyeballs, so she gave it up and opened them again, knowing she was still just *lying* there on the floorboards like so much roadkill.

Cameron was sitting up now. "Lily. Is there something you wanted?"

"I…I…" Lily's gaze shifted to her right, toward the still-lit and revolving barber pole. She drew herself up straight. "I think you people are disgusting."

Cameron pulled up his knees and rested his forearms on them. "Probably. Anything else? Like, do you want some help strapping that pole on your back so you can get it out of here?"

"You have no right! This is not your house."

Darcie sat up, hiding her head behind Cameron's back. "I think she's got you there," she said quietly.

"It's not hers, either," Cameron said out of the corner of his mouth. "Technically, at the moment, it's Lucky's. Where is that cat, anyway? Oh boy, never mind."

Braving a withdrawal from her hiding place, Darcie looked where Cameron was now pointing, to see Lucky sitting on the large white knob of wood at the top of the barber pole, and looking none too happy to be there.

"How'd he get up there? He's too fat to jump that high. Cam?"

"Maybe he flew. I don't put anything past that animal."

"Get down, you miserable beast!" Lily yelled, flapping her arms in a shooing motion, at which time Lucky hissed and dug his claws into the wood.

Except, funny thing, Lucky was not hissing in Lily's direction. He was glaring, and hissing, in quite another direction…toward the writing desk in the far corner.

Darcie tried not to laugh, but the cat looked so amazed to be where he was, so very put-out about the whole thing. "I'll handle this, Lily. And I'll be sure that the…that is, that your property as per Uncle Horry's will is moved to your quarters as soon as possible."

"I don't want it. I just want it out of here." Unbelievably, Lily's chin went even higher, and her feet seemed to be positively stuck to the floor. "And may I ask what is going on here?"

"Nope," Cameron said, laying Darcie back down on the floorboards once more. "You may go."

"Cam," Darcie whispered in horror.

"Shhh," he said, back to nuzzling her ear. "Trust me, she'll be out of here like a shot. Especially if I make a move toward second."

"Don't you *dare* make a move toward—oh, thank God," Darcie said as she heard the door slam. "Now let me up. I've never been so embarrassed in my life!"

"Meow. *Meow!*"

Darcie shot a look toward the barber pole Lucky was still clinging to as he tried to edge his way headfirst down the side of the thing. He moved slowly, inching his front paws down the wooden knob, but then those paws began to slip when they encountered the glass that protected the rotating part of the contraption.

There was a startled yowl, then a quick retreat…a too-quick retreat, that ended with the majority of Lucky's twenty-plus pounds hanging down behind the pole, with only his eyes, ears, and his two front paws still visible…and slowly sliding out of sight.

"Oh, my God, he's going to—oh, poor thing, he fell. Cam? Cameron Pierce—stop laughing!"

"He'll live. He has all that fat to cushion the fall."

"His pride has to be injured." Darcie got to her feet and climbed out over the side bed slats. "Come here, Lucky, you poor little thing. Darcie's sorry."

"I'm not. I owe that clawing machine one, remember," Cameron said, joining her as Lucky lifted his tail and walked to the door, then looked back at them as if to say, "Anytime you feel the urge, you could open this, you know."

Darcie let Lucky out, getting not so much as an ankle rub for her troubles, then stood in the doorway, her hand on the knob. "I'll find some sheets and make up the corner room for you."

"And that's it? We're done in here?"

"Oh, we most certainly are. Although," she said, relenting, "by and large, you were a very good boy."

"Only good?" he asked, grinning. "So, on a scale from one to ten, you'd give me—?"

"I am not going to give you a rating."

"No? Well, what about the mirror? You want to give that a rating? Thumbs-up or thumbs-down? Stays, or goes. Which is it, Darc?"

She stepped into the hallway, slamming the door behind her. Which had to be at least a little more dignified than having to say, "Stays."

"LUCKY, DON'T RUN AWAY from me. Lucky? I'm trying to apologize here."

"Don't hear you, don't hear you, do *not* hear you," Lucky said, bounding down the steps, so that Horry, who'd been wanting to do this again for years, but figured he'd gotten too old for it, slid down the banister behind him.

"It was the only thing I could think of to do," he said as Lucky sat down facing the front door. "And it worked, didn't it? Got Lily's attention? Embarrassed her? Got her out of there? I thought she'd stand there forever until Darcie noticed her. Never thought about Lily as a voyeur. Amazing what all I didn't know about that woman. Not that I wasn't watching, too, but I'm not a voyeur. I'm a ghost, doing research."

"Open...the...door."

"Sure. Sure thing, Lucky. There, door's open. Anyway," Horry said, following Lucky again, "I think things are going very well for Darcie and Cameron. Good boy, that boy, always thought so. He'll bring Darcie to her senses before the week is out."

"Then you'll go away? Because I have to tell you, Horry, you're beginning to wear on my nerves."

"Aw, Lucky, don't say that. We're talking. We're interacting. If the world knew what I know? Cats *talk!*"

"Yeah," Lucky said, mind to mind. "Freaking amazing, isn't it? Try it with that overgrown beagle down the street, and see how far you get. Now, go away, I've got to make my rounds."

"Rounds?"

"Rounds, Horry, rounds. The woodpile, the woods, behind the garages, a little spraying around the front gate just so everybody knows I'm here and this is all mine, a quick check on that calico next door because she'll be in heat anytime now—rounds, Horry. Don't you know anything?"

"Apparently not. You lead an interesting life, Lucky," Horry said, still tagging along, not really paying attention when the frogs on the drive began their *ribbit-ribbit* alarms as he passed by...

...but, Cameron—who'd been looking out of the windows of the turret in his temporary corner bedroom before facing the project of making up the bed with the sheets Darcie had tossed at him before disappearing down the back stairs to the kitchen—did hear the *ribbit-ribbit.*

He'd already been standing there for a full minute, wondering how Lucky got out, again.

And now the *ribbit-ribbit.*

The frogs were a good three feet high, with the motion sensors stuck in their mouths. Lucky was two feet high at the tip of his tail, tops.

So what in hell was setting off the sensors?

"Better question," he mumbled to himself as he turned away from the window. "Do I really want to know?"

CHAPTER SEVEN

DARCIE SLEPT remarkably well for a woman who was pretty sure she'd gone to bed alone and in the wrong bed, and she woke early, to pad barefoot to the window and look out over Shangri-La, take in the view.

What she saw was Cameron, dressed only in a pair of khaki shorts and a Phillies baseball cap with the brim turned to the back of his head, sitting on the lawn beside the driveway, with a paintbrush in his hand.

She was showered and dressed and running down the back stairs in record time, pausing in the kitchen only to pour herself a tall glass of orange juice before heading for the front door.

Then she slammed on the brakes, considering strategy.

She could stay on the porch, and just casually call a good-morning to him. She could just tiptoe out there and sit in one of the rockers to watch him, without saying a word, but just admiring how good he looked, how silly and cute he was, and talk herself into believing that overwhelming physical attraction was more than enough for two people to expect in life.

Or, she decided, putting down her glass, she could not be an idiot and go see what the heck he was doing.

"Cameron?" she asked, careful to stay on the grass and not set off the frog sensors. "What are you doing?"

"Maintenance," he said, not looking up at her.

"But…but that's paint. Red paint. White paint. The flamingos are pink, Cam. And the frogs are—"

"Green, yes, I'd noticed. Do you know these things are custom-made? They're signed by the artist, for crying out loud. Too bad it wasn't Picasso, so they'd be worth more than ten cents a pop. Damn, I smeared it. Hand me that rag, will you, babe?"

Darcie picked up the rag lying beside the paint cans and walked closer, handing it to him as she got her first look at whatever he was doing.

"Oh, Cameron," she said on a sigh. "Tell me you're kidding."

He leaned closer to the flamingo and carefully wiped at a smudge of red paint. "Nope. This is serious work."

"But…but, you're painting *targets* on the flamingos?"

"And the frogs. But only one side—you'll see them coming, but not going. Look behind you, I've already got one done."

She turned, looked at the first frog in the row. Smack on its side, there was a bull's-eye. Red center, ring of white, ring of red, ring of white.

"I'm going to alternate circle colors. This one I'm starting with white, then red, then white, then red."

"Why?"

"I don't know. So I don't get bored?"

"No, you idiot. Why are you painting bull's-eyes on flamingos and frogs?"

"Because we may have guests, and I'm hoping they like a challenge. Because when I cut the grass—there's a nifty riding mower in one of the garages—I might decide to mow them down, too, and the targets will add to the fun. Because I'm losing my mind, but jumping off the cliff seemed too final. Pick a reason, any reason."

"Uncle Horry loved those stupid things. And isn't there something in his will about them?"

"Maintenance," Cameron said, nodding his head. "He talked about maintenance. I'm…maintaining."

"You're defacing," Darcie said, then looked down the length of the curving drive, at the long, double lines of flamingos and frogs that had been her uncle's crowning achievement of silliness. "There are over two hundred of them. This is going to take forever."

"I know. My version of a cold shower."

"Oh, so that's it. You're doing this to annoy *me.*"

He grinned up at her. "And it's working—damn, I'm good."

Darcie looked down the rows of flamingos and frogs. She looked at the bull's-eye Cameron had already painted. She watched as he finished making a very creditable freehand circle of white paint to finish off the bull's-eye on the first flamingo.

"It's funny," she said, smiling. The smile was followed by a giggle, the giggle with an outright laugh. "Oh, God, Cam, it's *funny!*"

"Thatta girl," he said, dragging the piece of heavy canvas holding the two paint cans and a pair of brushes along the grass, to the next frog. "Do you want to help?"

"No, not really. You can go crazy by yourself," she said, shaking her head even as she wiped tears of mirth from her eyes. "I think I'm going to take a walk around the grounds, see if anything interests me."

"Such as?" Cameron asked, already painting in a small white circle.

"I don't know. Gardening? I've never...never *gardened.* I grew up in a Manhattan high-rise, remember? Once Mom and Dad were gone, that was sold, and I lived in dorms and visited here sometimes during school breaks. Not that I paid much attention. I was only outside to work on my tan. Speaking of which—did you put on sunscreen before coming out here to turn my flamingos and frogs into mini Picassos or Dalis or Warhols or whatever you think you're doing?"

Cameron reached for the paintbrush he used for the red paint. He leaned around to talk to the frog. "Aw, did you hear that? Am I wearing sunscreen, she asks. Obviously, the woman cares."

"Okay, I'm out of here," Darcie said, turning away, only to stop when Cameron called her back. "What? We've already had our first-thing-in-the-morning conversation. I think I'm getting to know you better, just as we discussed. I'm getting to know me better, too. Or at least well enough to know that I'm attracted to nut-jobs."

"Nut-jobs, huh? Well then, maybe I shouldn't mention what I was going to mention. Something I think is a little weird. Never mind," he said, waving at her with the paintbrush. "Carry on getting to know you."

"You shouldn't mention what? And if it has to do with Lily, you're right. Don't mention it."

"Lily, huh? Okay, that's one way. She could have opened the door last night, let Lucky out."

Darcie put her hands on her hips. "Is this going anywhere? I left my orange juice on the porch."

"And you're getting your vitamin D out here on the lawn with me." Cameron put down the brush. "Okay. I'm standing at the turret windows in the corner bedroom, right, last night, after you threw the sheets at me?"

"If you say so."

"I say so. I'm standing at the window, looking out over the front lawn—this lawn—and it's getting dark, and suddenly, there's Lucky."

"Lily opened the door and let him out. It seems reasonable."

"Absolutely. Although he could still walk straight, and I would have thought she wouldn't have just opened the door for him, but maybe also drop-kicked him halfway down the drive. Now, to the weird part. Lucky walked down the drive, about a dozen flamingos and frogs worth, before heading off toward those bushes over there. And...and this is the part where you have to promise you're not going to send for the guys in the white coats—the frog sensors went off, each time he passed another frog."

"So? He walked past the frogs and set off the sensors. There's nothing weird about—" Darcie looked at the frogs. She held her hands out in front of her, measuring in the air, first for length, then for height, while considering the dimensions. She looked at the frog again. "He's not tall enough to set off the sensors, is he?"

"And we hope you enjoy your brand-new Frigidaire. Would you like to keep that prize and quit or try for the Wurlitzer CD-ready jukebox?"

"Hush, I'm thinking. So how did the sensors get tripped, or set off, or whatever they do?"

"No, no, Darc, answers, not questions. I've already got plenty of questions. For instance, is it possible Lucky's an alien? A good try by some extraterrestrials, although when they built him, they screwed up on the eye color and settled for one of each?"

"I found Lucky at the ASPCA, remember? He really set off the sensors? *Really?*" Braving the gravel on the drive, Darcie stepped, barefoot, onto the stones, setting off a frog on either side of the drive. She stepped to one side, then bent over, waving her hand in the air at what she considered to be Lucky height. Nothing.

"Go higher, include his tail if he had it sticking up straight," Cameron suggested.

She waved her hand again. "Still not high enough. This is…this is sort of spooky."

"No, spooky's ghosts. We're not talking ghosts. We're talking alien cats here. Don't complicate things."

"I wasn't doing anything. You're the one who's getting me all creepy about Lucky. And he was such a cute little baby, all soft and cuddly."

"Attila the Hun's mother probably said the same thing."

"Enough of this, Cam. I'm sure there's a reasonable explanation. Oh, and that front door latch isn't working right, I don't think. You might want to check on that, unless you think Lucky can open doors. Now I'm going to go drink my orange juice and find something to do. Something *sane* to do."

"Darn. You don't want to rehash what happened last night, discuss every little detail? I mean, they say men don't like that sort of thing, but I'm game."

"Talk to the frog," Darcie told him, and made a break for the porch before she kissed him or something.

CAMERON WAS ON flamingo number eight when he heard a car coming up the drive.

"Nice wheels," he said as, red paintbrush in hand, he headed for the car just as Attorney Humbolt was climbing out of it—operative word being *climbing,* because today the man was driving a low-slung sports convertible that would only help him attract females if he put a bag over his head when he drove it.

"Yes, thank you. I just picked it up this morning," Humbolt said, closing the door, then taking out a large white handkerchief and wiping the area around the handle. "I've always wanted one of these, but the wife wouldn't allow it. But this is worth the alimony I'm going to be paying, let me tell you."

"Recent breakup?"

"I moved out last Sunday," Humbolt said, giving the paint job one final swipe before smiling and sighing at the car—Cameron was beginning to wonder if the man was going to kiss it. "I've been eyeing up this baby for months, and now it's mine."

Knowing there was pretty much nothing left to say about the car, the divorce or the satisfied smile on the lawyer's face, Cameron asked, "Are you here to see Darcie?"

"Actually, you'll do—no need to embarrass the girl. Lily called me this morning. Seems she's got a complaint." He looked at Cameron. "Were you two really messing around with her barber pole?"

"Lily and me? Not that I recall," Cameron said, straight-faced. "But, hey, if she wants to give it a go? No. Sorry, I don't think so."

Humbolt, proving himself to be a man with no sense of humor, just shook his head. "Son, I'm talking about you and Miss Reed. According to Lily, you two were cavorting in Horry's bedroom. And him not in his urn for a week. Lily's threatening to leave."

"Really? Maybe Darcie and I can *cavort* in the kitchen next time, while Lily's making dinner. Thanks for the inspiration."

"No, no, you're not getting my point. I agree, Lily can be a trial, but she was fond of Horry. Stands to reason, seeing as how she was in bed with him when he died. But she can't leave. Who do you think is keeping tabs on you two—that's you and Miss Reed, in case I wasn't clear. I have to be certain you stick to the requirements of the will."

"Okay, I'd already figured that Frau Blücher was your mole. Tell you what. If she promises not to open any doors before knocking and being told to come in, we should be good." With malice aforethought, Cameron then leaned his backside on the front bumper of the Divorcemobile. "Anything else?"

"No…yes…son, will you please not lean on my car? And watch that paintbrush."

Cameron looked to his immediate left, then his immediate right. "Oh, wow, I didn't realize. Sorry, Humbolt." He stood up, then turned to bend low over the bumper. "Boy, I sure hope I didn't get any paint on this. Well, it won't really show up, unless it's the white paint." He gestured toward the car with the wet paintbrush. "The red pretty much matches, though, don't you think?"

Humbolt made a sort of strangled noise in his throat, and dropped to his plaid slacks-covered knees to inspect the paint job. "I see why you and Miss Reed are no longer engaged. You're a considerably annoying person, Mr. Pierce."

Cameron shrugged, thinking it could be fun to slap some red paint across Humbolt's chest so he'd match his car, but only said, "Hey, what can I say? I try."

Humbolt, his beady eyes narrowed, said, "I don't think I like you, Mr. Pierce. You're considering this to be nothing more than a huge joke, aren't you?" Still glaring at Cameron, he pointed behind him, at the house. "Shangri-La is at stake, Mr. Pierce. Horry's considerable fortune is at stake. Or do you really want to see Miss Reed's inheritance taken from her? And, if so, why are you here?"

Okay, so now Cameron wasn't amused anymore. Not even a little. He took two steps toward the smaller man and looked straight down into his face. "I am here, Attorney Humbolt, because I love that woman. I could give two damns right now about this house, the money. Sure, I want her to have both, because she should have them, and because that's what Horry wanted, and we all know that. Do you have any idea how Horry's will has screwed up everything? Do you?"

Humbolt backed up a step, punched at the nosepiece on his sunglasses. "Uh…no."

"Yeah, well, never mind. Are we through here? I've got to get back to my painting."

Humbolt followed him. "Those are bull's-eyes, aren't they?"

"Sharp as a tack, aren't you, Humbolt?" Cameron said, then mentally kicked himself. The guy couldn't help being a fatuous jerk, and he had nothing to do with Horry's stupid will, except that he was guilty of not talking the man out of it.

"Why are you painting bull's-eyes on them?"

"Archery's a hobby of mine," Cameron said, dipping the brush in the red paint once more.

"Oh." Humbolt walked onto the drive to inspect Cameron's work, setting off six frogs. "No, wait. You can't mean you're going to use Horry's ornaments for target practice. I can't allow that."

"Really? Tell me, other than maintenance, what's in Horry's will about these things?"

"Um, nothing," Humbolt said, skirting around a frog and back onto the lawn. "He just left funds for their maintenance. Painting, repair, that sort of thing."

"Painting. Then we're good. Ah, here comes Miss Reed. Let me handle the business about Lily, okay? That's bound to set her off. She's not proud of it, but Darcie tends to throw things when she's mad, and your car looks like a pretty good target itself."

"She wouldn't!" Humbolt all but ran toward his new toy as Darcie walked around it, looked at the interior. "Miss Reed! Good morning! So good to see you again!"

"Mr. Humbolt, hi. What a pretty car."

"Thatta girl, Darc. Sixty-thousand-dollar piece of phallic-symbol, precision machinery, and you call it pretty," Cameron said, having ambled up behind Humbolt. "Now say goodbye, because Attorney Humbolt was just leaving."

Darcie frowned. "Really? Why did you come, Mr. Humbolt?"

"Yeah, Humbolt. Go on, tell the lady why you're here," Cameron said, because he wanted to see the man squirm. Really, once he had some time to himself again, he'd better stop thinking about how Lucky set off those sensors and start thinking about his own behavior, which was, even to him, getting a little weird.

"You want me to tell her? But you said—" Humbolt looked at Darcie, his car, the open paint can Cameron had just *happened* to bring with him from the lawn and then put down next to Darcie's foot.

To Darcie, to the paint can, to his car.

Darcie, paint can, car.

Paint can, car.

Humbolt rushed into speech. "Um...I've just had

word from Horry's half brother. Isn't that *wonderful* news! Happy news!"

Cameron's smile faded, and he swore under his breath.

Darcie seemed delighted. "Really? It's so strange. Do you know, my family never even mentioned him to me. I had no idea I have another uncle. It is wonderful news. Where is he?"

Cameron barely heard Darcie, or her delight, because now he was too busy looking at Humbolt, at the red stain on the back of the man's neck that had a lot more to do with rising blood pressure than the sun…or red paint.

"Mr. Willikins? Um, he's overseas, Miss Reed," Humbolt said, looking everywhere but at Cameron, who was trying to visually bore a hole into the man's brain to find out what kind of maggots lived there.

"You contacted him? Why?" Cameron asked.

"Me? Oh, no, no. He contacted me. Um…you know modern inventions. Mr. Willikins—Mr. Edwin Willikins—explained to me that he often swims the Web, and he saw a notice of Horry's death that mentioned my name. Local newspaper, you understand. Always trying to fill space with anything and anyone. Why, they even mentioned Lucky as being Horry's beloved pet cat."

"*Surfs* the Web, Humbolt," Cameron corrected, just because he wanted to. "And so, just because he called, just chitchatting, the two of you—you told him about the will?"

Humbolt opened his mouth to answer, then closed it

again. Cameron thought he could almost hear the maggots running on the treadmill inside the man's head. "No, of course not. Mr. Edwin Willikins is not a direct beneficiary of the will, and as such, is not entitled, per se, to any information concerning its contents, the beneficiaries, terms or conditions."

"I love it when you talk lawyer, Humbolt. Gets me all excited," Cameron said, lifting his cap and then turning it around before replacing it. It was an idle move, meant only to shade his eyes from the bright sun, but mostly, he'd done it so that Humbolt couldn't see his eyes, or the skepticism in them that probably was easy to read.

"Cameron," Darcie said on a sigh. "Don't you have frogs to paint?"

Humbolt turned to Darcie. "Your uncle will be here in a few days. To pay his respects. And I must say, he's delighted to realize that you're all grown-up now."

"He's seen me? I don't remember. I didn't even know my grandfather had a second wife. Why didn't anyone ever tell me?"

"Yes, yes, family secret, as I understand it. An unfortunate marriage of short duration to a wholly unsuitable, vastly inappropriate woman. A single child together, quickly followed by a bitter divorce. Very embarrassing, all the way around. I imagine your mother and Horry considered the whole thing an episode best forgotten."

"Why didn't you tell us all this the day we learned about the will?" Cameron asked, noticing the trickle of perspiration running down the side of Humbolt's face.

"I didn't know," he said, looking at Darcie. "Your uncle was very vague about the whole thing. Why, it took him a moment to recall his half brother's first name when he was making up the will. But Mr. Edwin Wilkins was very forthcoming. Oh, he's sixty-two, to your uncle's more than seventy years. And your mother was somewhere in between. I do know that your mother married rather late in life. At forty, I believe Horry told me. At any rate, Edwin is, I believe, sort of the black sheep of the family. You've never dabbled in genealogy, Miss Reed? Fascinating subject."

"No, I haven't. I…I thought that when my mother died, and then my father a year later, that Uncle Horry and I were the only ones left. I'm looking forward to meeting Uncle Edwin."

"Me, too. We'll have to find a fatted calf for the prodigal's return," Cameron said, putting an arm around Darcie's shoulders. "Now, is there anything else? Can we offer you refreshments? Maybe you want to talk to Lily about something?"

Humbolt mumbled something about a meeting at his office, and while Darcie climbed to the porch, Cameron hastened to open the car door for him. "Funny, Humbolt, how you told me about Lily, and nothing about Uncle Edwin. And funny how you were going to leave without mentioning him at all, until Darcie showed up. Strange, even."

"There's nothing strange about it, Mr. Pierce," Humbolt said, turning sideways to squeeze himself backward and down into the low leather seat. "You'd warned me not to upset Miss Reed with Lily's complaint, and I was left with nothing to tell her when you said I had wanted to speak to her. Her uncle wished his arrival to be a surprise, and now you've ruined it. I do hope you're pleased with yourself. And now, if you'll close the door?"

Cameron did as he was asked, but then leaned down, his folded arms on the door. "I'm curious, Humbolt. How did old Edwin take it when he found out he gets nothing if Darcie and I live up to the terms of the will?"

"I already told you, Mr. Pierce, I have not as yet apprised Mr. Willikins of the provisions of the will."

"He's just jetting here from Europe or wherever to pay his last respects? After about sixty years, and with no one to see but a niece he probably never met? Oh, wow, Humbolt, I think your nose is growing."

"You're a most obnoxious man, and if you're accusing me of some sort of breach of ethics, may I remind you that I am an attorney?"

"Sure, go right ahead, remind me. And then I'll remind you that obnoxious guys like me don't give a rat's ass who you are." Cameron leaned in closer, close enough to smell Humbolt's mouthwash. "I'm going to be watching you. And the next time you feel the need to come out here—call first."

Cameron stood back from the car and smiled as Humbolt pretty much murdered the transmission, trying to get the sports car into second gear as he turned and headed back down the drive.

Ribbit-ribbit. Ribbit-ribbit. Ribbit-ribbit...

"God. I think I love those frogs," Cameron said, then went to join Darcie on the porch.

"I should have told Mr. Humbolt that Uncle Edwin is welcome to stay here, at Shangri-La," Darcie said as Cameron collapsed into the rocking chair beside hers.

"Don't you want to wait until he shows up before asking him to join the party? For all you know, he comes with a wife and six kids."

"We have room for a lot of kids."

"Yeah, but I'm kind of planning on the two of us supplying the kids."

Darcie ignored that and looked at her thumb. Like it was the only thumb in the world…that's how she looked at her thumb. "I've got a splinter."

Cameron sat up, took her hand in his. "Cripes, that's not a splinter, babe. That's a two-by-four. What have you been doing?"

"I was being stupid, if you must know. I saw the mattress as I was walking around the house, and I thought it should be propped up against the stair railing so it wouldn't crush the grass."

"You're kidding."

"No, seriously." She winced as he lightly touched the skin at the base of her thumb. "I grabbed the mattress by one of those little rope handles its got and held onto the banister for leverage, and my hand slipped. You know, Cam, instead of painting flamingos, maybe you should be sanding that banister."

"It's true, what my dad always said. Wait long enough, son, he'd say, and women will find a way to blame you for everything. Except that porch painting is going to be your job, remember, unless we have to place you on injured reserve. Come on," he said, taking hold of her wrist and pulling her to her feet. "That's got to come out."

"I can do it myself," Darcie said as he let go of her wrist and bowed her into the foyer. "I wouldn't want to take you away from your bull's-eyes."

"It's your right hand, Darc, and you're right-handed. Put a needle in your left hand, you'll end up sticking yourself in the nose."

"Needle?" Darcie did a quick about-face, heading for the door once more. "I don't remember talking about needles."

"Ah-ah-ah," he warned, grabbing her by the shoulders. "Come on, Darcie, sweetie. Be a good girl for Uncle Cameron and when we're done, you might just get a lollipop."

"I don't like needles," Darcie said as he half pushed her down the hall toward the kitchen. She turned to him, looking hopeful, and only slightly desperate. "Tweezers. We can try tweezers."

"Oh, for crying out loud. I just hold a match to a needle, sterilize it, then lift your skin a little and edge out the splinter. It's not major surgery. I never knew you were such a baby."

"And another point to me on the subject of how well we don't know each other. Except that I'm not a baby. I'm…I'm simply not fond of needles, and I'm very sure a match can't sterilize anything. Besides, I'm getting sort of fond of this splinter and might want to keep it. I could name it Woody."

Cameron bit back a laugh. "Is this where I slap you because you're becoming hysterical?"

"Please, Cameron? I've got a tweezers upstairs, in my makeup bag."

"All right," he agreed as she made a run for the stairs, "but if it doesn't work, then we sterilize a needle. Deal?"

"Oh, it will work," she said, leading the way to her bedroom that he noticed, and was amazed that he had not before noticed, was at the front of the house, directly next to the corner bedroom.

While Darcie hunted through a large brocade bag with just her left hand, Cameron worked out the logistics of the room in his head. Two sets of double-hung windows, facing the front of the house. Check. Dark oak paneled door to the left of the room. He opened it. Large, old-fashioned bathroom complete with claw-foot tub; probably once the box room, converted to a bathroom. Check.

That left the only other door as the entry to the closet, except that this was an old house, and lots of old houses didn't have closets in every bedroom. Which would explain the two large freestanding wardrobes in the room…but not the other door, the one on the wall this room shared with his.

This merited checking, as he already knew his room's closet was on the right side of his room. Why put one closet per wall, when two could share ends of the same wall, butting up side by side? Architecturally, it wasn't good design.

"Got it," Darcie said, holding up the tweezers. "What are you doing?"

"Admiring an old house?" Cameron said as he turned the knob on that extra door, opened it just a hair, and looked in on his bedroom. Somewhere the gods were smiling, and the devils were doing a delighted jig. "You know what, Darc? I think this room was probably originally designed as some sort of nursery, or sitting room."

"Uh-huh, that's nice. Cam, my thumb is really beginning to hurt."

He closed the door, pocketing the large skeletonlike key that had been in the lock on her side. "Sit on the bed, Darc, while I open the rest of the drapes for better light."

Then he sat down beside her and took her offered hand in his, accepting the tweezers. "My scratches, your splinter. By the time this month is over, Darc, we're going to need a branch office of the local emergency room set up at Shangri-La. Now don't move."

"I'm really not a baby, Cam," she said, sitting very still as he bent over her thumb, trying to grab the bit of the splinter that stuck out from her skin. "I once got hit in the face playing field hockey, and my nose bled all over me. I didn't faint or scream. As a matter of fact, once the bleeding stopped, I went back on the field. So I'm not a baby."

He closed the tweezers carefully, missing the splinter. "You played field hockey? In those little plaid skirts and knee-high socks? You're kidding. When?"

"In high school and college. You mean I never told you? We were together for over two months, Cam. I can't believe we didn't talk at least a little. Ouch!"

"Sorry. Hold still, I've almost got it. We did talk, Darc. You'd ask where I wanted to go for dinner. I'd ask you which movie you wanted to rent. You'd tell me about your day at work. I know I told you all about the Johnston project. Remember?"

"The one where you and Doug designed that strip mall in Kensington to blend in with the neighborhood? Careful, Cam…the end that's sticking inside my thumb feels really sharp."

"Sorry. See? We did talk."

"About superficial things, sure."

"I beg your pardon. My work is not a superficial thing."

"Neither was…is mine," she said, then gasped when he gave the tweezers one last shot, and the splinter finally slid out of her skin. "Oh! It was *that* big?"

"Goodbye, Woody," Cameron said, looking at the splinter.

But then he looked at Darcie, his expression serious. "I apologized for not understanding that, Darcie, that your job was important. You had just gotten chased out of a job you loved, and I said it didn't matter, just marry me. I know I screwed up. It may have taken me a while to figure out I was being an insensitive chauvinist bovine—"

"Bovine? That's a cow, Cameron, I think. You mean pig."

"I do, but pig is so trite. Not bovine, huh? Then what?"

Darcie shrugged as Cameron took the tweezers over to the wastebasket and disposed of Woody. "Porcine? You know, like Porky Pig? We can look it up later. For now, keep groveling. I think I like it."

"I knew you'd enjoy this. Okay, so I was thick and unfeeling and Porky Piggy about your career, but I did figure it out. And I know this new job in Pittsburgh is great for you, and you're great for it. I'm not cracked up over the idea of it being in Pittsburgh, but I can handle it. I am handling it. Now come on, you need to wash that hand."

"Cam, about the job in Pittsburgh…"

He put the rubber plug in the drain, then turned on both old-fashioned faucets, stirring the water as the basin filled. "I really don't want to talk about that, Darc. I'm trying hard to be the nice guy here, okay? There, warm enough. You need new faucets, Darc, with only one spout. Architecturally, these fit the house, but there are ways around that, designs that are functional as well as decorative. Now, stick your hand under the water. Use the soap, clean the area really well. Oh, here, I'll do it."

"I can wash my own hands, Cam."

"I know." He soaped up his own hands, then took hers in his, working the soap all over her palms, the backs of her hands. Onto each finger, drawing little circles on her palms with the tips of his fingers…

"Cameron…"

"Hmm?"

"Cameron, I think my hands are clean now. My hands, your hands…"

He smiled. "Do you have any other body parts that might need attention?"

She pulled one hand free and turned on the tap nearest her, to rinse her skin. "Damn!" she said, quickly jumping back. "That's the hot water!"

Cameron grabbed her and plunged her left hand into the sink, then pulled the plug and turned the cold water on full force. "Just keep your hand under the water, Darc. I already decided to turn down the temperature on the water heater after I nearly scalded myself in the shower this morning. I love this house, but a person could spend his life working on it."

"Ow, *ow-ow-ow.*" Darcie was tapping one foot on the tile and sort of dancing around as he held her hand beneath the cold water faucet. "This is just great. Splinter in the right hand. Third-degree burns on the left. I'm such a klutz, Cameron. I wanted to know who I am, and now I know. I'm a klutz."

"Don't be silly, Darc, you're not a— Hey, are you crying?" He grabbed a towel from the rack and gently wrapped her hands in it. "Come here." He opened his arms, then pulled her into his embrace when she just stood there, caught between a pout and a whimper.

"Oh, Cam. Can you believe this? Horry's dead. I've got an uncle I never knew existed—that my mother didn't bother to tell me existed. I've got you trying to seduce me with a *mirror,* for crying out loud, when you're not just trying to drive me crazy, much as you're being a really good sport about all of this. I've got Lily and that barber pole. I've got a cat from Mars. I've got…I've got bull's-eyes on my flamingos and frogs. God. I have flamingos and frogs. People shouldn't have flamingos and frogs, Cam, I'm sure of it. And now I'm self-destructing. What next?"

Cameron chuckled low in his throat, then kissed her

hair. "Did it ever occur to you, Darc, that maybe you're trying too hard? Why don't you just relax, step back a little and let me handle all of this for you? I can—"

He stood there, alone in the bathroom, empty arms still hanging in the air, wondering yet again how the woman had learned to move that fast...and when he was going to figure out how to talk without his foot in his mouth.

CHAPTER EIGHT

DARCIE DECIDED she'd mastered one thing since her arrival at Shangri-La. She'd learned how to avoid people. Lily. Cameron. Her own tiny, mixed up mind.

For five whole days after what she'd begun to think of as The Woody Incident—until she decided that might be a bit double-entendre for a nice girl like her—she'd successfully found ways to keep herself very busy.

She'd driven to the local mall and picked up how-to books in the bookstore there, ranging from how to cook, to how to garden, to how to crochet. She'd done research on the Web—did every mattress company name have to begin with an *S*?—before driving back to the mall to order a new mattress and box spring for Uncle Horry's bed, knowing she planned to be far away from Shangri-La the day the set was delivered.

She'd spent three entire days pulling weeds in the backyard...because Cameron was still in the front yard, painting bull's-eyes. He'd worked his way all the way down one side of the drive, and was already three-quarters of the way back up the other, leaving all those bull's-eyes behind him.

Busy days. Busy, busy days.

And lonely nights, because that's when Cameron

took off, damn him, going to Philadelphia to look in at his office, even going to the movies on his own. And she knew he had, because he'd come home with the popcorn box and had the nerve to try to offer her some.

It wasn't that they weren't speaking. They were speaking. They just weren't talking. Just like the first time. Just like before, only this time it was a conscious effort on her part. All she'd have to do was wink in his direction and they could be in bed together, but that wouldn't solve anything.

Because the man still thought he should be the big Magoo, or whatever, and that she should just curl up and let him be in charge. Him Tarzan, her Jane. Him older and wiser, her young and pliable.

Even if he hadn't *really* meant that, either time.

But she'd taken it that way, both times. And that was her problem.

Now if she could only figure out *why* she reacted that way when Cameron was such a good guy, when all he was doing was trying to help.

Maybe it was an age thing? Maybe he was simply too old for her. Or she was too young for him.

And this business about getting to know herself? Pitiful. That she wanted to get to know him better? Ridiculous. There was something deeper going on here, and it was her problem, not Cameron's. He was just getting the fallout, poor guy.

All right, so they'd gone to bed first, started talking later. The big, romantic whirlwind courtship, and all of that. Was all of that really so bad? So terrible? If the world's countries could be as compatible as she and Cameron were in bed, there'd be world peace…piece… no, she had to get her mind away from Cameron the lover, and think about Cameron the man.

So he'd said exactly the wrong thing when she'd had to quit the job she thought would be the first step in proving herself. So he'd looked at her and seen marriage and babies and a house in the suburbs and a full-time wife.

So what? These were bad things?

Darcie pulled at another weed, then realized she'd just yanked out what she was pretty sure was a daffodil that had bloomed last month. The leaves *looked* like a daffodil, like the photograph in one of the gardening books she'd bought. Or maybe those were tulip leaves? That bottom part sure looked like a bulb, that much she did know.

She looked around, praying no one had seen her mistake, then reached for her small trowel and quickly stuck the thing back in the ground.

And got back to thinking…

She loved Cameron. She really, really loved him.

Didn't she?

Darcie remembered—why now, she didn't know—that years ago, in high school, she'd played that "he loves me, he loves me not" game with daisy petals. Could she play the same silly game with weeds—did she love him or love him not?

She yanked at one, yanked hard, and when the long white root finally gave up the fight she landed on her back, legs in the air, dirt raining down from the root onto her face.

"Was that a yes or a no?" she asked the weed.

Using her tongue to *ptui-ptui-ptui* a small bit of dirt out of her mouth, then wipe at it with her forearm, Darcie sat up again and looked down the length of the foundation planting bed—that's what it was called in the gardening book, a foundation planting bed.

To her right, ornamental rhododendrons and azaleas and a remarkably pretty-leaved thing called a something-or-other andromeda were up to their knees in weeds.

Ah, but to the left of her! To her left the plantings were standing there proudly, surrounded by nothing but the rich, dark mulch she'd found in huge bags in the garages, then shoveled around their feet.

What a kick! What a feeling of accomplishment! This was hers, this was something she'd done that you could *see,* something that made a difference in the world, even if it was just her small part of it.

She'd gone to bed early last night after another long day of pulling and digging and shoveling, and awakened this morning sore but happy, and more than eager to get right back to it.

Who knew she could feel so proud of some dirt and bushes?

She was communing with nature, that's what she was doing. And as her hands worked, her mind could relax, expand, think deep thoughts or silly thoughts or no thoughts at all.

The whole world should know about this, she decided, then grinned at that particular thought.

Darcie tried to remember her feelings of accomplishment at work, then compare the two feelings. But there was no comparison, none. What she'd done in her career was move paper while she tried to move herself ahead. She'd worked, worked hard, so she could advance to a higher level, a more plush office, and she'd done it well—but not for the love of the work. Her jobs had been like...been like...been like school with a paycheck. And the paychecks had been like report cards, proof, something she could hold up and say, "See? See? All As."

But here? Here in this garden, with birds singing in the trees, with the sun warm on her back, with the smell of the earth—why, this wasn't work at all. She *loved* this.

She'd spent most of last night, while Cameron was munching popcorn in some mall cinema, drooling over descriptions of prefabricated greenhouses. A person, even a person in Pennsylvania, could grow orchids in a greenhouse.

She was learning the proper names of flowers so beautiful the mere photographs of them had made her want to weep.

She'd even begun drawing up a rough plan of Shangri-La's vast, mostly devoted-to-grass grounds. A small garden here...a sweep of red and white and pink peonies in a sort of elongated half-moon in an area just off the side porch, where what was described as their heavenly fragrance could be enjoyed by those sitting on the porch.

And clematis, dozens of variously colored clematis vines, positioned to climb up the porch posts, where she could train them to wrap themselves around the railings—huge blankets of blooms every spring.

Each page she turned sparked a new idea, provided a new thrill.

A corner office, or her own corner of the world? Faxes and reports and bottom lines and office politics...or sun, and digging your hands into the rich dirt, and making things *grow.* Was there really any comparison?

Suddenly all Darcie wanted was to find Cameron and tell him. Tell him what she'd learned about herself, about a part of herself she hadn't known existed. She was so *happy.* She had set sail on a voyage of discovery of sorts, and she'd actually discovered something!

Tossing the last weed she'd pulled on top of the others she'd loaded into the old apple basket she'd found in the garage, Darcie got to her feet and headed for the front lawn.

"Cam? Cameron?" she called out eagerly as she turned the corner at the front of the house. "You know how I said I wanted to—*omigod.*"

"Darcie," Cameron said, waving her over to where he stood with...

"Uncle...Uncle Edwin?" Darcie asked, shocked to her bare toes.

She was looking at a man, a rather small man. A man with her uncle Horry's twinkling blue eyes and thick shock of white hair. A man with Uncle Horry's smile, Uncle Horry's rather large, protuberant ears, Uncle Horry's silly pug nose. He was Uncle Horry, just smaller. The Shrinky-Dink version of Uncle Horry.

"My dear, dear girl," Edwin Willikins said, advancing toward her, both hands held out to take hers, which she offered, then hastily withdrew, as they were still inside a pair of dirty garden gloves. "There, there, I don't mind a little dirt. Let me kiss your cheek, my dear. You don't look a thing like your mother. What a blessing. Handsome woman, your mother, in her way, but quite intimidating. Close-set eyes, as I remember."

Darcie smiled nervously, tilted her head to the left, which was wrong, because Uncle Edwin was coming at her from her left. So she tilted her head to the right, and they sort of banged noses before he could finally plant a wet one on her cheek.

"Um, thank you," she said, smiling weakly, still pretty much in shock as she looked at the man again. He looked as if he'd just gotten off a yacht, down to his white slacks and shoes, his navy blazer with some sort of crest picked out in gold on the pocket, to the dazzling white shirt open at the collar to expose a…was that called an ascot?

Oh, yeah. An ascot. Giggles, Darcie decided, probably wouldn't help her make a good first impression. "How…how very lovely to finally meet you, Uncle Edwin."

Edwin's Uncle-Horry face reworked itself from an avuncular smile to a profound frown of dismay as he raised a hand to his chest. "And under such tragic circumstances, my dear. Poor Hecuba, aye, we hardly knew ye."

Darcie shot a look—okay, a plea for help—toward

Cameron, who just sort of stood there in his khaki shorts and backwards Phillies cap and grinned at her as if to say, "Ball in your court, sweetheart, just the way you wanted, remember?"

"Um...yes, so very sad. You and Uncle Horry were never close, were you? Something about an estrangement after your mother and my grandfather divorced? To tell you the truth, my own mother never mentioned you."

"Sweet Harriet. Such a delicate-minded old besom. Tarred me with the same brush the Willikinses used on my mother, who deserved all of it, and more, by the way. The woman was a real pisser."

"Cameron! I mean...Cameron, when did my uncle arrive?"

He poked himself in the middle of his bare chest. "Who? Me? You want me to play, too? No, no. I don't want to break up this lovely family reunion."

"Cameron Pierce, get over here," Darcie said, speaking through her clenched-teeth smile. "Uncle Edwin, how silly of Cameron to have you standing out here in the sun. Wouldn't you like to come inside for some refreshments? I'll just run ahead to alert Lily—the housekeeper, Uncle Edwin—and then go wash up and meet you in the living...er, the drawing room?"

"Ah, an executive decision. Am I invited?"

She really was going to have to kill him later. "Yes, Cameron, you're invited."

"Oh, goodie. How about her?" he asked, hooking a thumb over his shoulder toward the house, just as the front door slammed and a female voice trilled, "Found the potty! What a relief that was, let me tell you. Oh, Poobie-bear, you have such a pretty house. *Ouuu,* all these steps. Come help your Pookie-bear."

Just one quick, shocked look toward the woman and several things registered with Darcie. Hair, badly bleached blond. Hairstyle, straw broom in a wind tunnel. Face, Magic Marker on cracking marble. Jiggling boobs that came with their own bar code stamped on them. Cinched-in waist, nonexistent hips. Skintight spandex over flat-as-a-board backside, stick-thin legs, stiletto-heeled gold sandals. Floral scent that preceded her by about six feet.

From the boobs up, a Tootsie-Roll Pop, from the boobs down, the stick.

"Your servant, Pookie-bear!" Edwin hastened to assist the woman down the wooden steps.

Darcie trotted over and grabbed Cameron's arm. "Okay, I'll bite. What in *hell* is that?"

Cameron grinned down at her. "Post-menopausal Barbie?"

"Oh, God." Darcie finally gave in to the giggle, then buried her face against Cameron's sun-warmed shoulder for a moment before daring another look at Uncle Edwin's...Uncle Edwin's *what*? "Cam? Who is she? Wife? Girlfriend?"

"I'm not sure, to tell you the truth. She does sort of look like the for-a-good-time-call-five-five-five-Pookie kind, doesn't she? If nobody painted the men's bathroom walls for forty years, that is."

"That's not nice, Cameron. Possibly true, but still not

nice. When did they get here? And, as long as we're standing here, watching Poopie drool all over Pookie, why didn't you let me know right away?"

"Not Poopie, Darc, Poobie. Poobie- and Pookie-Bear. They just drove on in—you might want to rethink leaving the gates open. And I was just going to go find you, except your uncle was telling me all about how broken up he is about Horry. It was kind of hard to cut and run while the guy was weeping into his handkerchief. Silk, by the way."

"He looks just like a smaller version of Uncle Horry, doesn't he? I mean, it's sort of…unsettling."

A scream that would probably register a seven on the Richter scale ripped through the air, coming from the porch. Darcie and Cameron turned as one, just in time to see Lily rather gracefully crumple into a neat heap at Uncle Edwin's feet.

"Hoo-boy, looks like Lily thinks she's just seen a ghost," Cameron said, having already grabbed Darcie's hand, and they set off for the porch at a run.

"What on earth? Darcie, who is that woman?"

"Uncle Horry's housekeeper, Uncle Edwin," Darcie said as Cameron hauled the still-unconscious Lily to the nearest rocker and, after only three attempts, succeeded in propping her in it. Darcie pulled down the woman's skirts and pushed her bony knees together. That took two tries. "She must have looked at you and thought she'd just seen Uncle Horry's ghost."

"Poor old thing. I'll just go fetch up some water, all right?" Pookie-bear volunteered, climbing the steps in her four-inch heels, her elbows bent at her sides, her fake-nail-manicured hands sort of flapping in front of her as she rushed into the house using small, mincing steps. "Back in a jif. Poobie, hold the fort."

Darcie thought about slapping Lily's cheeks to rouse her, but quickly gave that up as a bad idea, and contented herself with rubbing one of the woman's hands. "Lily? Lily, it's all right. It's only Edwin Willikins. Edwin, Lily, not Horry."

Cameron, standing behind the rocker now, holding onto the back so it wouldn't wobble, said, "I have to get back to my paintbrushes, Darc, before they dry up. But you're in charge, right? Nothing you can't handle. Or maybe not. But, hey, how's a person to know what they can do unless everyone leaves them alone to do it?"

Lily moaned, almost awakened, then sort of slumped in the rocker once more.

Kneeling now, Darcie looked up at Cameron's mocking grin. Oh, yes, it was a mocking grin. She knew a mocking grin when she saw one, and this one screamed mocking grin. In spades. "Revenge can be a terrible thing, Cameron Pierce."

"Right! Good! See? You're already learning. Okay, babe, I've had enough fun. As the saying goes—meanwhile, back at the flamingos… In other words, you're on your own, sister. I'm just the hired help."

"I could seriously hate you," Darcie said as Cameron brushed past her, and she watched as he saluted Uncle Edwin smartly, then headed back to his damn flamingos and frogs.

"Okay, okay, okay, stand back everyone, here comes Pookie!"

Darcie watched, eyes and mouth open wide, as the blonde minced her way out of the house holding Uncle Horry's Tiffany cut-crystal vase, and dumped its contents straight down over Lily's head.

The housekeeper jerked away, flailing her arms as if underwater and making a break for the surface, sputtering and yelping.

"Oh, dear," Darcie said, wiping some water—very cold water, as if Pookie had gotten it from the refrigerator—from her face. She looked at Lily, but only for a moment, because the woman had murder in her eye and was obviously searching out a target.

Then Darcie looked to Pookie, who smiled as she openmouthedly chewed a wad of pink bubble gum and preened at her rescue effort. A quick look to Uncle Edwin didn't reveal much, other than the fact that men in ascots were as useless as men in khaki shorts.

And then she heard Cameron. Heard him, then saw him. He was laughing. Laughing so hard that he was now in the process of bending his knees, one arm stretching down toward the ground, to cushion his collapse onto the grass. Once there, he hung on the first flamingo in the lineup and giggled like a six-year-old boy who'd just heard his first toilet-humor joke.

Which was horrible of him. Funny. But horrible.

Obviously nothing could be worse…that is, until Lucky ambled out from beneath the overgrown bushes surrounding the porch, walked over to Uncle Edwin, lifted a back leg, and proceeded to "mark" the white slacks and shoes as a part of his territory.

"HIGH FIVE, PAL. Come on, high-five!" Horry said as Lucky appeared around the corner of the house.

"Control yourself, Horry," Lucky said, mind to mind, but then gave in and lifted a paw, at which time Horry bent over and gave it a swipe. "There goes the old dignity again, straight to hell. This is trouble, you know, having this guy show up."

Horry stood again, frowned. "What? That idiot? How can he be trouble? Great taste in women, though, I'll give him that. You catch the rack on that babe?"

Lucky sat and began licking his shoulder. "Sorry, no. Not the end I'm interested in. So, why's he here?"

"Why, that's obvious, Lucky. He's here to pay his respects. I'm dead, remember?"

"That's not something I'm soon going to forget. Shouldn't you be sprouting wings and flying away soon?"

"In time, Lucky, in time. Obviously, I'm still here because I led a good and pure life, and the Almighty has decided I can stay around to make sure Darcie and Cameron are all settled."

"Yeah. Right. You really are a prize, Horry."

"No, seriously. I am…was a good man."

"In your dreams. You were good at widgets, period. You've screwed up everything else. There's what you did to Darcie and Cameron, but that's nothing. It's what you've done to me that should get you sent straight to hell. Or didn't you see the way that Edwin twirp was looking at me?"

"You peed on his shoes, Lucky."

"Right. And he *smiled* at me, called me a sterling example of feline beauty. He *knows,* Horry. He knows what happens if I bite the big one."

Horry shook his head. "What happens if you—oh. How did that go again?"

Lucky headed toward the cliff. "Darcie and Cameron take care of me for a month and this place is theirs to divvy up any way they want. I croak, and everything goes to Captain Skippy back there."

"Yes, I remember now. But he can't know that," Horry said, floating after Lucky. He'd gotten the floating bit down pat now, and employed it every chance he could. "Only Darcie and Cameron and Lily and Humbolt know that."

Lucky sighed, quite a feat for a feline. "Haven't figured it out yet? That's okay, I'll wait."

Horry floated from tree to tree along the cliff line and finally settled himself on top of the chain link fence. "Lily? Humbolt? Oh, no, not Lily. She fainted when she saw Edwin."

"When she saw him, sure. But that doesn't mean she never *talked* to him. She could have made a deal, offering him half if she told him what she knows."

"I never thought of that one. Lily, huh? But you thought of it right away. It's true, this stuff they say about cats. You are sneaky. Wily."

"And here you thought I had nine lives. Wrong. We

cats just know how to *survive* with the one we've got. Let me tell you, sport, if it weren't for the shrimp—okay, and the sushi—I'd be in Jersey by now. I've got a bigger target on my back than any of those dummy statues you've got out front."

"No! No, you can't leave. I'm depending on you bringing Darcie and Cameron together. Or do you really want Lily or Edwin to have all of this? Lily, Lucky—remember?"

"So get rid of her. One down, then we can concentrate on sailor boy."

Horry slipped to the ground. "You know I tried. Last night, I tried. Slipped into her room. Leaned over her bed. Blew softly into her ear. Reached right through the blanket and began stroking her belly."

"I didn't hear a scream."

"I know. I held it back when she started smiling in her sleep and making these little sounds, but let me tell you, it wasn't easy. I couldn't get out of there fast enough."

"Sorry I asked," Lucky said, and broke into a run.

HIS HAIR STILL DAMP from his shower, Cameron wandered into the kitchen, following the sounds of banging cabinet doors. "Darc? What's going on?"

She slammed one last door and turned to him… turned *on* him. "What do you think is going on, laughing boy? I'm making dinner here. That's what's going on."

He leaned back against the countertop and finished

buttoning his shirt. "Okay, that's one way. I was wondering how we'd get rid of our guests. That should do it. Where's Lily?"

"She's taken to her bed like some Victorian lady, that's where she is," Darcie said, motioning for him to move himself so she could open and slam more cabinet doors. "Where *is* it!"

"Where's what, Darc?" Cameron asked, enjoying the hell out of watching her.

She looked so good. Her skin had taken on a warm, golden glow from her days in the sun, and he was pretty sure those were freckles on her cheeks and nose. And who would have known that pulling her hair back in twin ponytails could be such a turn-on for him?

"The microwave," she said in some exasperation. "There's none on the counter, so I thought maybe Lily just likes her counters cleaned off and she has a small one and keeps it in a—damn! There's no microwave. How is a person supposed to cook without a microwave?"

Cameron took hold of her shoulders and turned her to the left. "See that? Over there, Darc. Big white thing with the knobs on it? That's called a stove."

She pulled away from him. "Would you just get out of here? I know what a stove looks like. It's just that I bought this cookbook the other night, and—oh, hell."

Following the wave of her hand, Cameron spotted the large paperback cookbook on the table: *101 Easy Microwave Meals*. "Okay, I see your problem. And no microwave pretty much kills any idea of the freezer being stuffed with microwave dinners."

"Ah, a master of the obvious. Go…away."

"I could order out for pizza?"

"No. Absolutely not. Uncle Edwin just flew here from overseas, eating airplane food, and probably jet-lagged. He needs a good meal. I'm the hostess, and I will prepare dinner. I'm considering it a challenge."

"And I'm considering the blue-plate special at the diner down the road," Cameron said, ducking.

"Thanks for the vote of confidence. And if you aren't going to go away, then help me."

"Delegating? Good move, Darc. A good executive knows when to delegate."

"And you can knock it off about this executive stuff, okay? That's not all there is to me, you know."

"Yes, babe, I know. But it's interesting to hear that maybe you're beginning to know it, too. Now come on, what can I do to help?"

She shrugged. "Help me find a cookbook?"

"That's one way. But how about first we check the refrigerator. Maybe Lily already had something planned?"

"Good thought."

"Yeah, I have them occasionally. Good thoughts."

"Don't push, Cameron," she said, opening both doors of the side-by-side appliance and holding onto the handles, looking inside. "O…kay. We've got milk. We've got eggs. We've got green things in a drawer. We've got a dinner plate with a big hunk of raw meat sitting on it."

Cameron looked over her shoulder. "I think that's a beef roast. Lily probably had it thawing in here. Roast beef, Darc. Roast beef, gravy, mashed potatoes, salad, maybe some homemade rolls—no, scratch the rolls, we don't want to do it all in one day."

"I don't want to do it at all." She let go of the doors and they closed over the hunk of red meat sitting in a puddle of its own juice. "We've got to find a cookbook. I can read, therefore I can cook. It's working with the gardens."

"Will these help?" Cameron said, opening the small cabinet above the refrigerator, and revealed about a half dozen cookbooks that had probably been there, untouched, since the Kennedy administration. He selected one. "The Fanny Merritt Farmer Boston Cooking School cookbook. Sounds like a good title."

"Bet your fanny," Darcie said, snatching it from him and opening the fat, hardback book on the counter. She turned to the back and found the index, running a finger down the pages. "Meat…meat…meat…ah, here we go. Beef. That's meat."

God, he could just kiss her. Cameron retrieved two bottles of water from the refrigerator and put one down in front of Darcie. Then he ran the back of one finger up the length of her neck before giving a playful flick to one of her short ponytails. "I don't know how to tell you this, Darc, but watching you in the kitchen is a real turn-on."

"*Shhh,* I'm reading. And don't tickle me."

"Oh, yeah," he said, this time to himself. "Definitely a mutual turn-on. The woman can barely keep her hands off me."

"Oh, damn!"

"Problem, Darc?"

"I don't know," she said, looking up at him. "What time is it? And how much do you think that side of beef in there weighs?"

"Two o'clock, and how the hell should I know? I'm an architect, remember? I could eyeball the thing and give you its square footage…."

"I'll ignore that last part. Okay, so it's two o'clock," Darcie said, heading for the refrigerator once more, all business. She pulled out the plate of meat, hefted it in both hands. "Three pounds? Four? Take away a little for the plate." She shoved the plate back into the refrigerator. "Twenty minutes a pound for well done."

"I like mine medium rare," Cameron said. Not that he cared one way or the other, but it was fun watching Darcie attack cooking like she was costing out a project.

"Tough," she said, counting on her fingers.

"Oh, I hope not. I don't think Uncle Edwin still has all his own teeth."

"Would you shut up? Honestly, Cameron, I never knew how *annoying* you can be. Now go find me something to put that meat in, okay?"

Cameron clicked his sneakers together, saluted and went on the hunt for a roasting pan, because he did know that beef roasts go into something called a roasting pan. He'd watched those cooking shows once in a while, like at three in the morning for weeks after Darcie left, when he couldn't sleep because she wasn't in the bed beside him. He didn't give them up until some clown tried to make him believe cajun squid over rice was a good idea.

The roasting pan, a huge black metal thing with white speckles on it, was located in the pantry, two shelves up from a big plastic bag of potatoes. All right, progress!

Within twenty minutes, the hunk of beef was in the roasting pan and the roasting pan was in the oven, after only a five minute debate on whether or not the lid was necessary. All the potatoes had been peeled. Cam's finger had been bandaged.

"I could grow these," Darcie was saying as she held up a cucumber before lowering it to the cutting board. "These and radishes and different sorts of lettuce. Carrots." She looked at Cameron. "Even tomatoes and peppers. Oh, and herbs! Fresh parsley! There's a great spot for a vegetable garden out back. Lots of sun, good drainage. You'd need a fence, though, stuck well into the ground, to keep out the rabbits and groundhogs and that sort of thing. And spread some dried blood. Deer and rabbits stay away from dried blood."

Cameron snatched a freshly scrubbed carrot from the counter and took a bite. "Hello, I'm Cameron Pierce. Who the hell are you?"

"No, Cameron, don't tease. I'm being serious here. I've been reading, and thinking, and there's just something about *growing* things…I don't know, I can't explain it."

He looked at her. Really looked at her. Standing there with her ponytails and her shorts and top covered with a bib apron that could double as a pup tent. Looked at the freckles, the glow in her eyes, the eager expression on her face.

He compared this Darcie with the tailored Darcie of the French twist and navy-blue power suits. He'd always known there was a *real* Darcie beneath the daytime, corporate Darcie. He'd seen her after hours, he'd held her, he'd made love to her.

But, damn, it was good seeing her in the daylight.

"Tell me more about it, Darc," he said encouragingly. "Please."

She picked up a tomato and began slicing it on the cutting board. "I don't have the words, Cam. It's…it's more of a *feeling.* A *rightness* about being in a garden. I think I sat and stared at one of the roses for twenty minutes. I *cried,* looking at that rose."

"I've given you roses."

"Oh, I know, I know. But this was different, Cameron. This rose was alive, not cut and put in a vase. I looked at it and knew it would close a little at night, when it got dark, and then open itself to the sun again the next morning—I read that, you understand. Flowers *react,* just like people. But it's not just the flowers. The trees, all plants. We get nature on loan, Cam, and we have to nurture it, and protect it, and then it rewards us with…with…"

"Roses?"

She kept slicing the tomato. "Yes! And clean air, and shade from the sun, and food, and—am I making sense?"

He ran the back of his hand down her cheek, feeling

very sorry for himself. "I think so. You've found out something about you that you didn't know before, didn't you?"

She picked up the cutting board and slid the tomatoes onto the large platter, beside the sliced cucumbers. "I told you I wanted to do that."

"And you couldn't have done that with me?"

Darcie, eyes wide, turned to him. "Oh, Cam," she said on a sigh. "You're hurt, aren't you? I hurt you."

He bent his head, scratched at his forehead, more to hide his expression than in any effort to find an answer to that question. Because, yeah, he was feeling a little raw at the moment. "What do I do with the potatoes, now that I peeled them?"

"Cam, please." Darcie put out her hand, saw the paring knife, then quickly tossed it onto the counter. "Cam? I'm doing it with you *now.*"

He lost it. "Right. And you're all done? You've learned all about you and now you're ready to whistle me back, tell me you're ready for me to be in your life again, thanks for waiting, Cam, thanks for putting your own life on hold for nine damn months? Is this it? Nature, is it? All your discoveries made? All your priorities set? Because of a rose? Oh, and not only that, but you expect me to be happy for you. Are you nuts?"

Her expression closed, hardened. "Fanny Farmer says you cut the peeled potatoes into quarters and put them in enough water to cover them, then boil them until they break apart easily with a fork. I'm going to finish the vegetable plate now."

"Good for you. You do that. You can finish the potatoes, too. You can damn well finish all of it. Who knows, maybe you'll have another epiphany, this time about your previously undiscovered love of cooking. Me, I'm going to go to finally take a good look at Uncle Horry's pool. Then, hey, if I'm lucky, I can jump in and cool off."

"No, Cameron, listen to me," Darcie called after him. "I thought you'd be happy that I'm learning that I was wr—"

He didn't hear what else she had to say because he was too intent on slamming the door behind him as he went off to kick himself for being jealous of a damn rose.

"I'VE GOT TO HAND IT to you, Horry," Lucky said, exiting the pantry, where he'd successfully chewed through the bottom edge of a new twenty-pound bag of dry cat food and had himself a midafternoon snack. "Your plan is working like a charm. If you were planning for World War III."

"They'll stop fighting soon," Horry said, not sounding very confident. "They're both very strong-willed people, that's all."

"Uh-huh. That's one word for it, I suppose," Lucky said, hopping up onto the counter to purr and suck up as he watched Darcie quarter potatoes and throw them into a large pot already filled with water.

Cut the potato. Toss the potato. Splash the cat.

"Okay," Lucky said, hopping back down, "that's enough for me. Not getting any sushi out of that woman. Let's go check on Edwin and the bimbo, all right?"

"You really think she's a bimbo?" Horry asked, following Lucky.

"I'm a tomcat. Trust me, I know bimbos."

"Or she's a gold digger, like my Lily-pad," Horry suggested, walking through the wall while Lucky nosed his way against the swinging door that led to the dining room. "Perhaps Edwin has money of his own, although I never heard that he did. Unless she's attracted to his looks. He is a handsome fellow."

"He looks like you," Lucky said, sharpening his claws on the velvet drapes. "Follow the money, Horry, follow the money…."

CHAPTER NINE

THE DINING ROOM at Shangri-La might have been described as *ornate*. As it was, *ornate* didn't quite cut it. *Grandiose* came closer. *Outrageous* seemed a good word, although *flamboyant* might be a tad lame.

Garish. Glaring. Tactless.

Okay, getting closer.

Horry just called it his gargoyle room.

Table, chairs, sideboards, china closets, all had their share of intricately carved gargoyles. Gargoyles decorated the heavy crown molding, with large ones anchoring each corner. One particularly large, fierce-looking guy who looked to be in a really bad mood sat on his haunches in the far corner, a silver tray welded to the top of its homely head.

Darcie would have cut some flowers from the garden to use as a centerpiece, just to draw attention away from the gargoyle population, but since that would be about as effective a camouflage as a training bra on Anna Nicole Smith, she decided not to sacrifice the blooms.

She stood at the head of the large table, counting chairs. "Uncle Edwin, Pookie-bear, Cam, me. We'll sit two a side. If we distributed ourselves equally around the table, we'd have to use bullhorns to talk to each other. How does that sound, Lily?"

Lily leaned against the tall back of one of the chairs. "You called me in here to ask me this? What, you can't count to four on your own? I'm going to get my tea and go back to bed."

The housekeeper's not-so-graceful swoon had seemed to rob her of any remaining civility. Which was sort of okay, because Darcie had lost any remaining awe of the woman left over from her childhood.

"I'm sorry you're not feeling better, Lily, but what I really wanted was to know where the linens are kept, and the good china, the silver."

Lily looked at the china cabinet at the far end of the room, the one behind her. "Guess. Or do you think I keep it in the garages?"

"Oh, I know where it all is, actually. I just didn't want to use anything Uncle Horry particularly treasured, that's all. I'm afraid I don't know the difference between good and priceless, antique. I wouldn't want to—"

"Use the Rosenthal. That cabinet, over there. Bottom door on the left. Silver in a case in the buffet table, linens in that closet. And it's not Horry's stuff. It's yours."

"Well, actually, until the month is up—"

"Fine. Ask the cat. I'm going back to bed. And you'd better have that stove clean by tomorrow, missy. It's still my kitchen. And you wonder why I never let you in there."

Darcie stayed behind in the dining room as Lily, holding on to things as if she was aboard a ship caught in choppy seas, headed back through the butler's pantry, into the kitchen.

Why had she asked for Lily's help anyway? Because the woman had shown up in the kitchen to make herself a cup of tea just in time for the pot of potatoes to boil over, putting out the gas burner, and Darcie had wanted to redirect Lily's attention?

That was a good reason: get the woman out of the kitchen.

Okay. So maybe she was still a little in awe of Frau Blücher. It was picturing her having killer sex—literally!—with Uncle Horry, that's what it was. Darcie was just having trouble coming to grips with that one.

Darcie sighed, then removed the hulking silver centerpiece from the table, along with the pair of gargoyle-decorated candlesticks, before heading for the closet in the butler's pantry.

She loved this house, if not all the furnishings, and one of her favorite spots was this silly little hallway between the kitchen and dining room that was fitted out with floor-to-ceiling drawers and leaded glass-fronted cabinets, plus one full-length closet. The wood was a sort of heavily grained reddish-brown, like all the woodwork, and two of the built-in cabinets held up a black slate counter and a small sink. All the knobs were made of leaded glass. The entire area was something out of the past, a tradition mostly abandoned in modern houses, and an omission she believed a true loss to the world.

She gave a quick, rather worried glance at the built-in wine rack, and decided she'd ask Uncle Edwin to choose the wines for dinner. She'd ask Cameron, except he wasn't speaking to her, and at this point she was only hoping he'd show up for dinner.

Opening the tall closet, Darcie was confronted with a double row of wooden poles, each hung with another carefully pressed tablecloth. Did Lily iron them, or send them to a laundry? Would she, Darcie, want to iron tablecloths? With her income from her parents, on top of all of Uncle Horry's money that would soon be hers, would ironing tablecloths be part of discovering if she had a domestic side—or just plain nuts?

"Just plain nuts," Darcie said, grabbing a snow white linen cloth and carrying it to the table.

"Don't you dare!"

Darcie wheeled around to see Lily standing in the doorway once more, pointing one shaking finger at her.

"I shouldn't use this cloth?"

"Not without putting down the table pads to protect the wood I polish every week. That's an antique table, girl, shipped all the way from Bavaria. You have no appreciation, do you? It's priceless. Table pads are in the kitchen pantry. My God, that Horry should leave this house to such an ignorant child. It's criminal, that's what it is. All my work. All my hard work."

Darcie squared her shoulders. "I thought you were going back to bed, Lily."

"How can I? My kitchen! What have you done to my kitchen?"

"Lucky's kitchen right now, Lily," Darcie reminded

her, brushing past the woman, trying not to look at the mess she'd made. "When he complains, I'll let you know."

It was a fairly good line, but she didn't have time to enjoy it before panic set in. "I smell gas."

Lily gave a sniff. "It's the stove. Didn't you turn off the burner?"

Darcie panicked. "Did I have to? It went out when the potatoes boiled over. I've never used a gas stove."

Lily put down her teacup and lifted a box of kitchen matches out of a drawer, then relit the pilot as Darcie stood back, waiting for the kitchen to explode. "Clean this up, missy, and don't come into my kitchen again."

"Hey, now look, Lily, I—"

But Lily was gone in a swish of ankle-length, pink chenille robe and Darcie was left to look at the mess she'd made.

She'd thrown all the salad and potato peelings in the sink, then realized the homey, old-fashioned kitchen didn't have a garbage disposal. She really had to clean that up, but not yet.

In a moment of madness, she'd decided she could make biscuits, following the directions in the *Fanny Farmer* cookbook, and learned two things: directions could sound easier than they really were, and five-pound bags of flour, when dropped on a slate floor, reveal a basic design flaw somebody really should do something about.

Darcie looked at the wall clock, fashioned like a turquoise cat, with the clock in its belly and its tail serving as a pendulum.

Five thirty.

Set the table. Pull out the roast and let it "rest" for fifteen minutes before carving, during which time mashing the potatoes sounded like a plan. Open a can of corn. Pull the vegetable tray out of the refrigerator. Shower, wash her hair, get dressed for dinner.

Something had to give, and the shower bit seemed the most logical.

And there definitely was no time to sit down at the old, white-enamel-topped kitchen table and have herself a good cry.

Darcie heard the clack-clack of high heels on the slate tile but didn't raise her head until she heard, "Wow, what blew up in here?"

Darcie pasted a smile on her face and turned to look at Uncle Edwin's whatever. "Hi. Dinner isn't ready yet."

"Honey," the blonde said, toddling over to the sink to pick up a dish towel, "I've got eyes in my head. Where's that Lily woman?"

"She still doesn't feel well," Darcie said, getting to her feet, looking around for something to do that she couldn't screw up too badly. "I'm making dinner, Miss—I'm sorry, I never caught your name."

"Oh, just call me Pookie, everybody does. Doubt I even remember my given name," the blonde said, turning on the faucet and wetting a bright aqua sponge. "I'm Pookie, I call all my men Poobie—it cuts down on mistakes, you know? This kitchen sure is out of the Ice Age, isn't it? *Old.* It does smell good in here, though. Rump roast?"

"Could be," Darcie said brightly. "And mashed potatoes and corn and some cut up cold vegetables. And gravy, if I can do it. It's not like there's cans of artichoke hearts in the pantry. Nothing fancy. Uncle Horry liked plain cooking. You cook, Pookie?"

"Oh, yeah," she said with a wave of her hand, before tackling the countertop with the sponge. "Flipped a million burgers in my time. Back in Biloxi. You want I should help? It's no trouble. Poobie-bear's still sawing wood upstairs, anyway. I keep telling him he's too old for nookie in the afternoon. I might as well help out here."

Throwing her arms around her latest house guest and sobbing into her shoulder probably wouldn't go over well, and she certainly had no comment to make about Poobie and Pookie enjoying some afternoon delight. So Darcie just said thanks, then told Pookie she was going to set the dining-room table.

"You do that, honey. Then go take a nice shower and get yourself all pretty for that Cameron boy. I mean it, honey, if I was only ten years younger, I'd give you a real run for your money." Pookie laughed, a fairly grating bray of a laugh, then winked. "Who am I kidding. Fifteen years. Now go on, shoo! Shoo!"

Darcie escaped, too relieved to be ashamed.

"SHE JUST WIPED the counter right through you," Lucky mind-talked to Horry, who was still perched on the counter, a rather dreamy smile on his face.

"Yeah. Twice," Horry said, then sighed. "I think I'm in love."

"I really have to spend more time away from you, Horry. You're scaring me."

"Not true, not true. I'm a friendly ghost. Like Casper."

"You're a horny ghost. Horry, the Horny Ghost."

"Quiet," Horry said, motioning toward Pookie. "I want to enjoy the moment."

Pookie had begun singing as she opened cabinet doors, first locating a bib apron she folded at the waist, then tied around herself—the ties went around her twice—then locating an ancient chrome Sunbeam table mixer and beaters for the potatoes.

Lucky followed her to the refrigerator, wrapping himself around her skinny ankles, but the sushi remained in its Tupperware container as she pulled out milk and butter.

"Come on, lady. Look down here. Isn't he cute? What a precious little darling. Feed the cute kitty."

Pookie sneezed. Then sneezed again.

"Uh-oh, Lucky. Looks like you're out of luck," Horry said, pushing himself off the counter. "I think Pookie's allergic."

Pookie sneezed again, into the dish towel, then glared down at Lucky. "Get out of here, you mangy animal."

"Make me," Lucky said, although it came out as a sort of plaintive *meow*.

"Damn cats. I've always said it. Can't eat 'em, can't wear 'em," Pookie grumbled, opening a drawer and coming out with a long wooden spatula she used to take a swipe at Lucky. "Go on, go on—*shoo!*"

Lucky, the spatula swishing by only an inch above his head, decided retreat might be a better sort of valor at the moment and took off, leaving Horry to enjoy the sight of Pookie-bear bending over to check on the roast beef....

"HELLO THERE, SON," Edwin said, stepping out onto the front porch. "Have you seen my Pookie-bear?"

Cameron continued up the steps to the porch, holding on to the large cardboard box by its built-in handles. "No, Mr. Willikins, I can't say as I have. I just got back."

"Been shopping have you?"

"Pretty obvious, huh? It's a microwave for Darcie."

Edwin sat down in the nearest rocker, shaking his head. "Son. Son, son, sonny-boy. Not scoring any points here. Women do not consider kitchen appliances to be gifts. You do know that, don't you, boy?"

Putting down the box, Cameron grinned at the man, who was now dressed in pink slacks, pink leather loafers and a pink-and-green-flowered shirt. Horry had often dressed with similar flair. Maybe it was something in the Willikinses' genes?

"Yes, sir, I know. This isn't really a gift. Unless the housekeeper recovers by tomorrow night, I'm considering the microwave more in the way of being protection against starving to death." He leaned closer. "Darcie can't cook."

"Well, that's not good. Maybe I can get Pookie to help out. She's a whiz in the kitchen. She's a whiz just about everywhere, if you take my meaning. Oh, and call me Edwin, why don't you, seeing as how we're all going to be living on top of each other for a while."

"We are?" Cameron said before he could stop himself. "I mean…how nice."

"Oh, better than nice. That little niece of mine said we could stay as long as we want, and since my money is all tied up right now—took all I had to get us here, you know—it'll be nice to swim around in old Horry's digs for the next few weeks. Could have been mine, this place, you know, if m'mother hadn't been such a tramp. This was our grandfather's house, you know. Been in the family forever."

Cameron sat down on the top step. "Really? I didn't know that. So you lived here, too? Years ago?"

"That's what they tell me. I don't remember. But it's the Willikins homestead, that it is. Nice place to put down roots or while away an old age, don't you think? Who gets it, anyway? I'm thinking Darcie. Hecuba didn't owe me anything, right?"

"Right," Cameron said, looking at Edwin, who was smiling and rocking and all over pink. The man looked about as devious as a psychedelic cherub. "So it doesn't bother you that Darcie gets the house? And the inheritance?"

"What? Money? I've got plenty of money. Plenty of money." Edwin rocked some more. "Just went and outspent my allowance, that's all. I do that a lot. No head for finance, you know, so I hired a man to run herd on me. Otherwise, I'd probably be living under a bridge somewhere." He slapped his hands against the arms of the rocker. "So? You want to go see if it's time to hang on the old feedbag?"

Cameron got to his feet, picked up the box. "Sounds good to me," he said, following Edwin into the house, just in time to see Darcie coming down the stairs.

Cameron liked the honey glow to her skin, and she'd pulled her hair back into a low-riding single ponytail. Her face was definitely showing a few freckles, along with a fresh-scrubbed look that really shouldn't be doing such naughty things to his libido.

She looked so damn good. This house was beginning to look so damn crowded...

Darcie stopped on the third step from the bottom, pointed to the box. "What's that?"

Edwin held out a hand to assist her the rest of the way. He planted a kiss on her cheek, then said, "Beware of geeks bearing gifts."

"Thanks, Edwin, you're a big help." Cameron put the box on the floor. "It's a microwave. And, as Edwin here has pointed out twice, now, not exactly a great or inspired gift."

"You...you drove into town and bought me a microwave?"

Cameron was just about to hand in his Smart Man T-shirt when Darcie launched herself at him, throwing her arms around his neck and planting a big *"mmm-mmm"* kiss square on his mouth. "So you're not mad, are you? You're not mad anymore and now I'm not mad anymore, and— Oh, Cam, a *microwave*! That's just about the most thoughtful, wonderful..."

"Pitiful," Edwin said, shaking his head. "Absolutely pitiful. I don't know which of you has disappointed me more. I'm going to go find my Pookie-bear. Now there's a woman who understands gifts. Give her a kitchen appliance, and I'd be wearing it."

Cameron slipped his arms around Darcie's waist and pressed his forehead against hers. "This is good. I like this. What happens if I remodel the entire kitchen?"

She laughed, then stepped back. "I don't know. I don't think I'm ever going in that room again while Lily's around, unless I want my head chopped off. Pookie's taken over for tonight."

"Really? Well, it does smell good in here. So you don't want the microwave?"

"You mean, have I discovered that I don't like to cook? No, I think I could do it. Have you really drawn up plans to remodel the kitchen?"

Cameron put his arm around her and led her out onto the porch. "In my head? Sure. I do that wherever I go, it's just automatic. But this place? This place is special. The trick in any remodeling is to maintain the integrity of the house, the style. For instance, I'd keep the cabinets in the kitchen, although I'd have more built to match them. I'd put in a center island that would pretty much mimic that old enamel-topped table that's there now. Big island, because it's a big room. Kitchens were huge when these houses were built. A little later they were smaller, really small. And the back staircase that leads to the kitchen? It isn't weight-bearing, I checked. I'd remove that wall, open it up so the staircase isn't so dark. The stove's good—great, actually—but it needs some work, and the sink has be replaced, and—"

Darcie held up one hand. "Time out. You'd put in a garbage disposal? Add a dishwasher? Or would those corrupt the integrity of the house or something?"

"No, they wouldn't corrupt anything. The idea is to make the house look original, and still function in the most efficient way. I'd really like to build the cabinets myself, and— Oh, hell, I'm sorry, Darc. You should have stopped me, I got carried away."

"No, I think you're adorable."

He pulled her closer. "Well, in that case, how about I tell you my plans for Horry's old bedroom? Okay, okay, I think I know that look. We'll try another subject?"

"Good thought," she said, then stood on tiptoe and kissed him again. Quickly. Then retreated, to walk the length of the porch, lightly dragging her hand along the railing. "You know, you've talked about your work before...when we first met. But I don't think I ever realized how much you love what you do. I think I'm jealous."

"Of my work?" he asked, following her.

Darcie turned to face him. "No. Of how happy you are in your work. You know, I really thought that I was—"

"There you are, you two. Din-din's ready. Come and get it!"

"Thanks, um, Pookie," Cameron said, smiling at the woman even as he wished her somewhere else—like Europe. Then he turned back to Darcie. "You really thought that you were what, babe?"

She shook her head. "Later. Pookie's been so nice, I should go give her a hand."

"When later?" Cameron asked her, following her back across the porch and into the house. "Where later? It's getting a little crowded around here, in case you didn't notice. Come on, Darc, name a place and a time. I mean, I think we're getting close to breakthrough here, and—"

Darcie turned so quickly that he nearly ran into her. "And you want to take advantage of it?" she suggested, running her hands up his chest. "Like, maybe we should find some place to be alone and…get reacquainted? Hmm?"

He used to be dumb. Past tense. The woman was waving a red flag, egging on the bull, and if he took the bait she'd skewer him with one of those pointy sticks. "You think I'm only after sex? Man, Darc, that hurts. I want us to talk. Sex? Sex is the *last* thing on my mind."

Her grin was pure evil. "Ah, Cam, really? That's too bad, because I was just thinking we could maybe bend that rule I made just a little bit, and some sex might be good about now. Well, hey, if it's the last thing on your mind, far be it from me to try to…"

She let her voice trail off.

"You're not nice," Cameron said. "I used to think you were nice. But you're not."

"Nope, I'm not. I am not the pliable, agreeable, of-course-she'll-want-what-I-want Darcie you thought you had nine months ago." She raised her chin. "And I think you should be happy about that."

"Yeah. Delighted. There's going to be handsprings

of joy going on real soon, so you might want to step back, give me a little room."

Her smile faded. "You do know how much I appreciate what you're doing, don't you? You didn't have to agree to Uncle Horry's ridiculous terms. You could have just walked away. You still could. Instead, you're going to paint the house, you're thinking about remodeling the house, you're—Cam? How much do you like this house?"

That one took him a moment, but then he laughed, a short bark of laughter. "Right. I'm here because of the house. Hell, I saw this house before I gave you the ring—maybe I only gave you the ring because I wanted the house someday? Damn, I'm sneaky."

"No! No, Cam, that's not what I meant. I just want to know how much you like this house. Is it a professional sort of liking? Or a 'gosh, I could really enjoy myself, fixing up this place' sort of liking?"

He was beginning to feel better. "That depends. On some points, it's both professional and personal. Starting with the flamingos and frogs."

"You don't like them. You're painting them."

"I'm done painting them, in case you haven't noticed. Now I want to hire a bulldozer and knock them all down. Professionally. Personally."

"Oh, me, too. And then line the drive with ornamental trees. Pink and white dogwoods. Flowering pear. Tulip trees—they're a little messy, but if the entire planting is kept fairly informal, to look like an almost natural scattering of—"

"Yo! Sometime today?"

"Oh, gosh," Darcie said. "We're sorry, Pookie. Here we come."

Cameron watched Darcie run off down the hallway, remaining where he was. "What just happened here?" he asked Lucky, who had wandered into the foyer. "Dogwoods? Tulip trees? *Sex?* I'm more than willing to play the game, God help me, but damn, I wish I knew the rules."

"GARGOYLES WERE originally designed to be functional. Rain ran down the roof to the gutters, the gutters funneled into the gargoyles, then shot out their mouths, away from the sides of the buildings. No two were alike, which is amazing. Churches liked them, as they could be seen to serve as a warning to the Devil to stay away, while at the same time attract pagans to the church. Now, of course, they're mostly ornamental."

Darcie, her chin cupped in her hand, said, "Cameron? Are you saying you like gargoyles?"

"I don't know about him," Pookie chirped, "but that big one in the corner has been eyeing me up all night, like it's got something filthy on its mind. Why is his mouth all propped open, with bars in it?"

"To strain the runoff from the roof," Cameron said, which got a quick "Oh, dis-*gusting*!" from Pookie.

"You're an interesting fellow, Cameron, when you're not buying appliances," Uncle Edwin said, so that Darcie had to quickly cough into her napkin. "So, overall, what do you think of this place, architecturally?"

"Architecturally, it's fantastic. Structurally? It seems Horry was more concerned with the interior of the house, except for changing the exterior color scheme fairly often. Not that the place is falling down, but it needs a lot of work. A lot of very expensive work."

Now why, Darcie wondered, would Cameron feel the need to mention the cost of restoring Shangri-La to Uncle Edwin?

"A money pit, huh?" Uncle Edwin said, using a piece of bread to wipe up the last of the gravy on his plate. "Glad it's not mine. Pookie's my money pit, right, Pookie-bear? Go on, show everybody your new trinket."

Pookie quickly got to her feet. "I thought you'd never ask," she said, pulling up her shirt to show the enormous diamond stuck in her navel. "Poobie calls it the Hope Diamond. Says he's always hoping he'll get to see it. Almost swallowed it last week, right, Poobie? I told him to watch out, or I'd have to call Roto-Rooter to snake it back out of him."

"O-kay," Cameron said, giving Darcie a mild kick under the table. "Unless there's dessert…? Great meal, Pookie. Really."

"Yes, it was wonderful, Pookie," Darcie said, getting to her feet as she picked up her plate. "I can't thank you enough for rescuing me. Now why don't you and Uncle Edwin relax and let Cameron and me do the dishes?"

Cameron shot her a look that told her washing dishes wasn't exactly the sort of after-dinner exercise he'd had in mind. "Yeah, that's good. You two relax—we'll clean up." He even smiled as he said it. But Darcie knew he didn't mean it.

"You really don't have to help, Cam," she said when he followed her into the kitchen and put his plate down next to hers.

"Hey, I said I'd help, and this way you'll get done faster, as there is a method to my madness." He looked around the kitchen. "Damn."

"What's wrong?"

"I forgot. There's no dishwasher."

Darcie, having found them in her earlier search of the kitchen, opened the cabinet under the sink and came up with a square plastic dishpan and a bottle of liquid soap, handing both to Cameron. "Oh, yes, there is. I'll dry."

"I think that's open to discussion," he said, reaching for her. "I mean, getting back to your idea that we've never talked enough, this might be a good time to list our preferences as they pertain to—"

"Nope. Executive decision. We clear the table, you wash, I dry and put away, you put the table pads back in the kitchen pantry. You start with the glasses, then the flatware, then the china, then the—"

He was looking fairly close to panicky, which was nice, because now he could understand how she'd felt when she'd first noticed the lack of a microwave.

"Something else missing?"

"Damn straight something else is missing. I just remembered there's no disposal. Oh, yeah, definitely. The kitchen's top priority, Darc, once this place is yours."

"Unless I decide to sell it, of course," she said, sensing an opening.

Cameron put the dishpan in the bottom of the sink and turned on the taps. "Oh, right. Pittsburgh."

And here it was, that opening, yawning wider than any gargoyle. Her chance to tell Cameron what had happened in Pittsburgh, what had happened to her not only that last day, but how she had changed over the nine months she'd been on her own, trying to prove herself.

She only wished Uncle Horry hadn't died. She'd loved that silly old man, and missed him. But even more, he'd complicated her life. How could she tell Cameron she'd thought of him every day she was in Pittsburgh, every night? How she'd worked so hard because work was the only thing that had kept her from thinking about him…and working so hard had taught her that she was in the wrong place, doing the wrong thing.

"Cam," she said, watching as he squirted soap into the water, then swished at the water with his hand to make even more bubbles, "I want you to listen to everything I'm going to say now, and not jump to any conclusions before I'm finished, because I know it could look sort of bad, even wimpy, and it isn't, not really, so—"

"Coming through, coming through, so move your hands, kiddies, if you've got them where you don't want us to see them! Going for a dip in the hot tub, oh, yes," Pookie trilled, toddling into the kitchen on her stiletto heels.

Darcie blinked. "The hot tub? Gee, Pookie, I don't think there is a—"

"Horry put in a hot tub, Darc," Cameron told her quietly. "Didn't you see it yet? Next to the pool. Their room overlooks the side yard, so they probably noticed it from there. You really didn't know?"

"No, I didn't," Darcie said, weakly waving to Uncle Edwin, who had waved to her as he followed behind Pookie, wearing an unholy grin, his arms stretched out in front of him, as if he was trying to catch her. "I haven't looked at the pool yet, except from a distance. Is that why there's that high fence around it now?"

"Privacy fence, although I can't figure out who Horry thought could see them," Cameron said as the screen door slammed and Pookie and Edwin could be heard giggling outside. "The chain-link fence is still there, but he added the privacy fence. He added a few things."

"Huh, I didn't know, I didn't look, I—wait a minute. They didn't have bathing suits with them." She looked at Cameron, her eyes wide. "Did they? Cam, *they didn't have bathing suits.*"

"Yeah," he said, lowering two water glasses into the suds. "Too bad the new mattress set isn't here yet. They'd have loved Horry's bedroom. Anyway, I don't know about you, babe, but I'm not going out there for a while."

"I may *never* go out there," Darcie said, shivering, then headed for the dining room to gather the rest of the plates. She and Cameron could talk later…maybe once Poobie and Pookie were tucked in for the night.

"COME ON, COME ON, don't throw it all away," Lucky said as Cameron scraped remnants of roast beef into the flip-top garbage can. “Would you look at that? Just look at that. Oh, I can’t look at that. He’s throwing it all away! Hey! Yo! Down here! Ah, that’s better,” he said as some small bits of meat were scraped into his dish. “Horry? Where are you going?”

“Pookie-bear’s in my hot tub. Don’t you listen to anything?” Horry said, floating toward the back door. “Where do you think I’m going?”

“And they say cats have no morals. Are you going to watch these two kids, too, if they ever stop dancing and figure out why they’re here?”

Horry stopped, half in and half outside the kitchen wall. “Lucky! That’s reprehensible. Of course I wouldn’t watch.”

“But watching the bimbo and Captain Skippy isn’t? And you think you’re going to Heaven when this is over? Fat chance, bucko.”

Horry appeared to consider that for a moment before easing himself back into the kitchen, then glared at Lucky, who was happily scarfing down cold roast beef. “What idiot decided I should be able to talk to you?”

“I don’t know. Maybe I’m your conscience?”

Horry’s next statement would probably earn him another decade in purgatory.

CHAPTER TEN

ALL RIGHT, CAMERON THOUGHT, so maybe he wasn't as smart as he'd been telling himself he was, and maybe the mixed signals he was getting from Darcie really meant she was trying to find some way to say "You're a nice guy, Cam. It has been fun. I appreciate the hell out of what you're doing for me, but when this month is up, you're history."

But he doubted it. Was that his ego talking? Some other, baser part of himself talking? Was he reading her right, or reading himself wrong?

She kept trying to tell him something and never quite getting there. Interruptions, inevitably followed by cold feet, a quick excuse and a run for the hills.

Like once they were finished with the dishes.

"You've done enough, Cam. I'll dry these and put them away. Why don't you go see if the Phillies are on?"

"They're in Arizona. The game won't be on until about ten o'clock. You know, Darc, you were telling me something before Pookie and your uncle dashed through here. You want to get back to it?"

Her smile had been bright, but he could see the panic in her eyes. "Maybe tomorrow? I'm really pretty tired."

So here he was, hanging out on the front porch, still trying to figure out how Lucky set off the frog sensors, and wondering how many cold showers a man had to take before he was conditioned into not thinking about dragging Darcie off somewhere and doing his best to hit a home run.

"Croaking frogs. Think about croaking frogs," he told himself, stepping down from the porch to approach the drive. "Frigging big, hulking, ugly ceramic croaking frogs. A frog and flamingo battalion. But, hey, they aren't gargoyles...."

It was fairly dark now, almost nine o'clock, but the day-glo-pink ceramic flamingos and equally day-glo-green frogs were just as ugly by twilight as they were in full sun. The targets, a whim that was now reality, didn't really do much to make them look worse. Then again, not much could. Maybe if he got a pack of paper lunch bags, and put one over each flamingo's head...?

"You're losing it, boy," he told himself, "you're really losing it."

Cameron crouched down beside the first frog on the left side of the drive, waved his hand back and forth about two feet above the ground. Nothing.

He'd corralled Lucky earlier and measured him, paws to the top of his head—just one more bit of proof to prove that, yes, he was a man in serious danger of bending over and having all the marbles drop out of his head.

He'd also measured the cat's tail, then added that to the height. Two feet, give or take an inch, considering that Lucky hadn't been real happy to have his tail pulled on and the measuring had to be quick, followed by a search for the Band-Aid box.

It was impossible. There was no way, no frigging way Lucky could have set off the sensors the other night just by walking past them. None.

"Okay, genius, so what did?" Cameron stood up again, turned to look up at the huge house with its many porches and corner turrets and fancy gingerbread trim. Big house. Beautiful house, once you got past the pink. Not a forbidding house. Not a *Psycho* house. A *nice* house.

Still, it could be considered the sort of house people might think could be haunted…if some people were to believe in ghosts, and he certainly wasn't someone who believed in ghosts.

And yet…and yet…

He'd tried to get rid of the barber pole, but every time he put screwdriver to floor screw, something interrupted him. A noise. A slamming door he'd needed to investigate. An open window slamming shut. Always something.

"Hey," he told himself out loud, "old house. Poorly maintained old house. Bad hinges, broken sashes. A million reasons."

Behind him, the front door opened, and Lucky strolled out—*stroll* not being a really good descriptive word for how cats walked, but for Lucky, it fit.

"Going out for your nightly maul and a movie, big guy?" Cameron congenially asked the cat, who stopped, turned, looked, yowled once, and then dismissed Cameron as if he was a mouse too small to catch. "Be back by midnight, or we'll have to ground you," he called after the cat, then watched as Lucky kicked it up a notch as he ran onto the lawn.

Cameron walked across the porch to inspect the lock on the door, which had closed once more. These were the original, stained, wooden doors; double, but narrow, with glass in the top half. They could be a little warped? Or there had to be something wrong with the lock—it couldn't be catching correctly, not if Lucky could scratch at it and get it to open.

Hmmm. No scratch marks on the wood. None on the brass knob. And the latch seemed in good order. So how in hell—

Ribbit-ribbit, ribbit-ribbit.

Cameron's blood didn't exactly run cold, but his corpuscles gave it a good shot. He whirled around to face the drive.

Lucky was cutting across the drive at an angle, probably heading for the row of oak trees that lined the right edge of the property.

Ribbit-ribbit, ribbit-ribbit.

Cameron watched as the animal stopped, lifted its head, gave two quick, almost angry switches of its tail, would have looked as if it was saying something—if that wasn't impossible—then continued across the drive.

No more *ribbit-ribbit,* which was a good thing, because, otherwise, Cameron knew he'd have to tell Darcie what he'd seen and heard, and then Darcie would pat his hand kindly and smile at him sweetly…until she could find a net.

And, since thinking about Darcie made Cameron want to be with Darcie, he ordered himself to forget everything he'd just seen or thought, and go find her. It was either that, or sit on the front porch humming *do-do-DO-do* until someone came to take him away….

TIPTOEING AROUND her own house. Ridiculous.

Okay, not her own house. Almost her own house. In three weeks her own house.

It was still ridiculous.

Hiding from Cameron until she could figure out some way of explaining that she wasn't taking him as second best, or convenient, because she'd failed in Pittsburgh.

No! She hadn't failed in Pittsburgh, any more than she had failed in Philadelphia. She'd worked hard. She'd done good work. Her *bosses* had failed.

Still, that wasn't the point. The point was, she'd discovered she could do the job in corporate America…she just didn't want to keep doing that job. And that didn't mean she was a quitter. She'd almost convinced herself of that. Almost.

And now Uncle Horry was gone, and his house and wealth were soon to be hers, and she would never have to work again, ever, so she was free to marry Cameron and live in suburbia and raise kids and putter in her own garden and learn how to cook and maybe take a ceramics class and…and be a traitor to the feminist cause.

Darcie rubbed at her forehead as she paced her bedroom, hiding here now because when she'd tried to leave, Uncle Edwin and Pookie had been coming down the hall toward their own bedroom, holding hands, swinging their arms, singing "Wherever you go, whatever you do…"

It must be nice, being that happy, that free and easy with each other. Darcie didn't know that feeling. What she and Cameron had nine months ago had been hot, passionate and kind of scary. They'd still been learning each other, still sort of dancing around each other in some sort of modern-day mating ritual that had a lot to do with where to go, what to do, and very little to do with actually getting to know each other.

And she'd certainly never felt so free and easy about…well, about sexuality. There had been plenty of passion, but they hadn't been able to joke about it.

She hadn't been able to joke about it….

Even that was different this time. Earlier, on the porch, she'd been daring. Sort of daring. Teasing. Definitely teasing.

She flopped down on the bed. "Forget it. Just forget it. You're never going to be Pookie-bear."

"I'll drink to that," Cameron said, and Darcie all but fell off the bed as she sprang to her feet, to see him standing in the doorway to his—wait a minute!

"How did you get the key to that door? Is that what you were doing when you were supposed to be getting rid of my splinter? That's just plain *sneaky.*"

"Not really, Darc. Sneaky is hiding out up here to avoid…exactly what are you avoiding?"

"*You.* And now you know why," Darcie said, putting

some distance between herself and the bed. "We're not supposed to have sex, remember?"

"No. Well, maybe vaguely," he said, advancing on her, his grin positively evil. "I think I've been getting mixed signals. Would you know anything about that?"

"I know. I've been up here, trying to feel bad about that." Darcie wet her lips, looked around the room. "Where are they?"

"Where are who? Oh, Poobie and Pookie? Last time I saw them they were looking through Horry's DVD collection. Horry has everything arranged by content, you know, and I found Pookie looking in the comedy section for *Fatal Attraction.* Now tell me that doesn't terrify you."

Darcie frowned in concentration. "Isn't that the one with the bunny?"

"Right. Pookie told me she fast-forwards through that part. It's the sex scenes she thinks are—what did she say? Oh yeah. *A hoot.*"

Darcie sat in the window seat, drawing her legs up and hugging her knees. "We can't ask them to leave, Cameron. Pookie told me earlier that they expect some sort of memorial service for Uncle Horry. That's why they came here. When I told her Uncle Horry was already installed on the mantel, and didn't want any fuss, she said Uncle Edwin was going to have a cow, so we can't tell him."

She looked at Cameron. "Bottom line, the memorial service is now planned for the day after tomorrow, in Uncle Horry's study."

"You're kidding, right? What kind of memorial?"

Darcie shrugged. She'd been thinking about just that, off and on for the past hour, when she wasn't thinking about Cameron, and how much she wished he'd hunt her down here in her bedroom. "I don't know. I guess we could invite Attorney Humbolt. Lily. Poobie and Pookie. You and me. Uncle Horry lived here, never traveled, never even went into town. Now that I think about it, I don't remember him ever leaving this house. No farther than the porches, a bit of the yard, the pool. He just had everything brought to him. All his toys, his electronics. Everything."

She looked at Cameron. "Why didn't I ever realize that before? Uncle Horry was a recluse. Or agoraphobic? Is that the word?"

"I think so," Cameron said, leaning against the bed. "That could explain a few things. Everything inside the house is in pretty good shape. Out of date, out of fashion, but in pretty good shape. But outside? Other than the paint, that could have been meant to keep people away, now that I think of it, this place is pretty much going to seed. I found some dry rot under the side porch, for one, and I'm sure there's more."

"And the gardens. He used to have some service come here. At least, I'm sure I saw somebody last year when I was here. But nothing's been done this year. I've been pulling weeds for days, and if you hadn't cut the grass we'd be up to our knees. Thank you."

"I asked Lily about that. Horry still has someone who cuts the grass, only the guy broke his hip or something. It wasn't a problem for me, as I seem to share that male fascination for doing wheelies on a riding mower. Whacking down the weeds around the frogs and flamingos? Not quite the same joy."

"I can imagine. But maybe the frogs aren't so funny, after all. Maybe Uncle Horry meant it when he said they were his early-warning sentries? Poor Uncle Horry. It was just him and Lily and his toys. I mean, I visited, but not often, at least not since I went away to college. I didn't even come home for Christmas this past year. Or Easter. Oh, Cam…"

"Hey, babe," he said, pushing away from the bed, "don't beat yourself up. I didn't see it, either, and I was here with you. And you know what? I think the old boy was happy. This was his Shangri-La, not his prison. If he had a problem, he'd learned how to cope with it, even enjoy it. I mean, did you ever think he was unhappy?"

"Uncle Horry?" Darcie grinned. "I think he was the happiest man I've ever met. So different from my parents. So free, so open. Like a child who never quite grew up. You're right, Cameron. He *was* happy here. He never left."

Cameron leaned past her, looked down toward the drive. "Yeah. Never left. He'd been here for so long, it probably would be hard to leave. Darcie?"

"Hmmm?" she said, the fact that he was now belt buckle high to her gaze not lost on her. Could she reach out? Take hold of his belt and sort of *pull* him closer to her? Would that be overt? Oh yeah, that would be overt. Then again, overt could be good.

"Darcie, do you believe in ghosts?"

"Do I believe in—*what?*"

"Never mind," he said, shoving his hands in his pockets. "I was just thinking. You know. Old house? Horry's house that he never left? Wouldn't it be something if your uncle decided to stick around?"

Darcie got to her knees on the window seat and pressed the back of her hand against his forehead. "You did wear sunscreen while you were painting those targets, right?"

"Very funny," he said, capturing her hand and bringing it to his lips, an action that sent a thrill running through her body. "Doug believes in ghosts, you know."

She sat down again, but didn't pull her hand away. "Doug. I didn't think he believed in anything except making money and having a good time."

"You need to get to know him better, Darc. He hasn't let you past the front door yet. He's really a good guy. And if he doesn't exactly believe in ghosts, he does believe old houses have…spirits, or something. We work on a lot of old houses, and I have to admit, they do have their…their idiosyncrasies. Even personalities. Doug says the houses absorb the energies of their owners over the years. He can feel them."

"Really. Can you?"

"I never used to think so, no."

Darcie tugged on his hand and urged him to sit down beside her on the window seat. "But you think so now? You think this house has a personality?"

"Or something," he said, looking out over the drive

once more. "I'd call an electrician out here to check those damn frogs, except they're solar. No electricity. Unless Horry put in an underground backup? You know, that could be it. He put in a backup, and there's a short somewhere. Why the hell didn't I think of that sooner?"

"Cameron?" Darcie placed her hands on his chest, rubbed lightly. Moved a little closer to him. "Are you still trying to figure out how Lucky sets off the frogs? *Now?*"

He turned to look at her in the dim light. Smiled. "I have something else to think about? *Now?*"

She sort of walked her hands up his chest, began lightly stroking his neck, behind his ears. Hooked one leg up and over his thighs. "You don't think we're making some progress? You and I?"

He put his hand on her bare thigh, inched it upward, slid his fingertips under the hem of her shorts. "At least one of us is, yeah. So we're what? Calling a temporary truce? Doing a little research in order to make an informed decision? If this is a test, how will you grade me?"

"You get an A-plus if you shut up right now and just kiss me," Darcie heard herself say—was amazed to hear herself say—and then she couldn't say anything else, because Cameron was kissing her and she was kissing him back.

Ribbit-ribbit.

"I didn't hear that," Cameron said against her mouth, then picked her up and carried her to the bed, her legs wrapped around his waist as she clung to his shoulders, kissing his neck.

Ribbit-ribbit.

"Or that," he said, laying her on the bed, then joining her even as he pulled his shirt over his head and tossed it toward the floor.

Darcie paused, her hands crossed at her waist as she prepared to lift her own shirt up and over her head. "You sure?"

"Positive. It's a short. Lucky sets off a short. It's impossible, but tonight it works for me."

"You're so cute when you're confused," Darcie said, watching as he unbuttoned his shorts. Then she began racing him, pulling off her shirt, her bra, unzipping her shorts.

Clothing exploded into the air, superfluous to the moment, and then Darcie and Cameron were kissing. Kissing. Hotly, deeply. Instantly on fire.

Was this love? Darcie thought so, although she couldn't be sure. Physical attraction could mimic love.

Physical attraction they had. In spades.

He looked at her, and she could almost feel him touching her. He touched her, and she melted. He kissed her, and sanity folded its chair and left the building, whistling for all her self-control to follow.

He kissed her, his hands intimately skimming her body, setting small fires that had laid banked for nine long months. She touched him in return, digging her fingers into his muscled back, pulling him closer so that she could lick at him, bite at him, taste him.

It was fast. It was furious. It was explosive, mind-blowing sex, and when it was over she felt sated…but not complete.

As she surfaced at last, still breathing hard and trembling, her arms still around Cameron as he lay half on top of her, also breathing hard, Darcie knew the sex, as always, had been everything it was supposed to be.

But something was missing. Something important. Something nebulous, untouchable…out of reach, even as he held her, even as she held him.

Their bodies were in tune. Had been from the start. Their months apart hadn't changed that; if anything, they were even hungrier for each other.

Cameron levered himself up a little and they were face-to-face, with his eyes sort of shiny and his hair falling forward on his forehead. So cute. So adorable. "Well," he said, then grinned.

She grinned back at him. "Yes, actually. *Very* well."

"Kiss me."

She grabbed his cheeks and moaned theatrically as she ground her lips against his, finished with a resounding *"Ummmm-wah!"*

"Cute, Darc," he said, still so close to her, his face only inches from hers, his eyes no longer quite so clear, so bright. "How about I sleep in here?"

Panic. Instant, unexplainable panic shot through her. "Um…well, I…"

"Never mind," he said, dropping a quick kiss on her forehead. "It was a truce, I remember. Temporary break in the—hell, in the whatever it is we're doing. Was this a test? How'd I do, Darc?" He shook his head. "No. Never mind. Answers are definitely not on the agenda tonight. Not that they ever are, are they?"

"Cam…"

But he was already out of the bed, picking up his clothes. "No, Darc, don't say anything else. Not while I'm trying to figure out if the fifty bucks goes on my nightstand or yours. Either way, thanks for the sex."

"What a…what a *lousy* thing to say. Cameron Pierce, you come back here!" Darcie called after him, but he'd already closed the connecting door—slammed it—and she was left alone in the dark, to try to figure out why she could have mad, crazy, monkey sex with the man, and still not be able to *talk* to him. Why was it so difficult, so impossible, for her to *talk* to him?

"WHAT ARE YOU DOING?"

Lucky looked up at Horry, and mind-spoke around the bit of yarn tangled in his teeth. "What does it look like I'm doing? I'm on the floor, rolling around tangled in yarn."

"Yes, I can see that, and I think poor Darcie is having enough trouble trying to do whatever it is she's trying to do without you messing up her yarn."

"I know," Lucky said, untangling himself and standing up, intent on leaving the room. "It's demeaning, but they expect it. Ball of yarn. Cat. Cat gets tangled in ball of yarn. Ah, look at the cute kitty. It's a cliché, but sometimes it's important to amuse the humans, maintain the façade."

"You've still got yarn wrapped around your tail," Horry pointed out just before Darcie dropped the *Easy How-To Crochet* magazine and chased after the cat.

"Lucky—stop! Come on, Lucky, you're making a

mess out of—oh, the hell with it," Darcie said, subsiding into the wing chair once more. "I think I can safely scratch crocheting off my list of possible talents."

Horry floated in front of Lucky, who had finally rid himself of yarn and was sharpening his claws on the Persian carpet. "Is that what she was doing? Learning how to crochet? From a *book?* Is that possible?"

"Apparently not," Lucky said. "She's been crying, too. Don't quote me, but I think this one's on you."

"Really?" Horry asked, shooting his niece another quick look, to see her wiping at her eyes with a crushed tissue. "I didn't do anything."

"Right. You pushed those two at each other instead of leaving well enough alone. I'd feel sorry for both of them, but I've got my own problems. Or do you really think your little brother isn't out to kill me?"

"Edwin? He's too busy with Pookie. Besides, nothing's happened to you. You're overreacting."

"Nothing's happened *yet.* And I'm not getting any sushi anymore. You've noticed that? I don't like this, Horry. They're treating me like a cat around here."

"You *are* a cat. Oh, look, Darcie's throwing the magazine in the trash can. I guess she's given up."

"Here you go, Lucky," Darcie said, putting the tangled yarn down in front of the cat. "It's all yours. Go wild."

Lucky looked, sniffed, raised his tail and walked out of the room. "Keep them confused, that's what I say," he said as Horry followed him.

"You're cold, Lucky. Even cruel. Now where are you going?"

"That depends. Where are you going?"

"I don't know," Horry said, opening the door for Lucky. "There's nothing much happening around here today, is there? Darcie crying in my study, Cameron sanding porch railings out back, Edwin and Pookie sleeping late. I guess I'll go to the kitchen and see what Lily's doing."

"In that case, I'm heading outside. Uh-oh, would you look at that?"

Horry stuck his head out half through the doorway, and saw Lily, his Lily-pad, sitting on the ground in front of the second flamingo on the left of the drive, a paint brush in her hand. "What on earth?"

He floated toward her, then paused, appalled, to look at the first flamingo, the first frog. They now had mustaches. Big, black mustaches.

Lucky caught up with him, as he hadn't been in a hurry. He sat down in front of the first flamingo, cocked his head to one side. "You know, Horry," he said after a moment, "I heard one day on *Animal Planet* that cats have a brain about the same size as a peanut. Small. And I still think we've got humans beat, paws down."

Horry hovered over Lily, who was clad in one of her nicest house dresses, her hair piled on top of her head, her face made up with so much eye shadow, rouge and red lipstick that he had a fleeting fear she'd taken a paintbrush to herself, as well. Her eyes were narrowed, her lips in a thin, tight smile. She was humming quietly as she defaced yet another of his beloved flamingos, this time by painting a large, black drooping mustache down either side of the statue's bright-yellow beak. Pancho Villa Flamingo.

"You know what it is, Horry?" Lucky said, keeping his distance. "I think she hit her head when she took that nosedive on the porch yesterday. Shook something loose inside."

"Or she's had a breakdown of some kind," Horry said, wringing his hands. "The shock of seeing Edwin, seeing him looking so much like me. You're wrong. She loved me, Lucky. She really did."

"Yup, definitely smaller than a peanut. *Shelled* peanut. Okay, I'm off—wait. Did she just say something?"

Lily had begun adding eyebrows, chanting as she dipped the brush in the black paint once more: "Hate you, Horry. Hate your stupid flamingos. Hate your stupid frogs. Polish your furniture, starch your shirts, cook your meals. Put that stupid rose between my teeth. For *years.* And for what? For what? To watch that girl ruin my kitchen? My dining room table? This should be *my* house. I *earned* it. God, I hate you, Horry."

"Gosh, boss, tough break," Lucky said as Horry collapsed to the ground, put his head in his hands. "I really could live without seeing you this way, watching all your plans going belly-up, watching your old dead heart breaking and all of that. Darcie, crying. Cameron, hiding out. Lily? Yeah, well, I think I like her better this way. See ya."

"Where…where are you going?"

"Right. I'm going to tell you all my hiding spots? I don't think so."

Horry watched Lucky take off across the grounds, then returned his gaze to Lily, who had moved on to begin defacing a frog. "Lily? Lily-pad? Is this really necessary?"

Lily dipped the brush in the paint and began dotting the frog's back with spots. "Hate your frogs, hate your frogs, hate, hate, hate your frogs."

Placing a hand on her shoulder evoked no reaction. Blowing in her ear did nothing. All Horry could do was stand there and watch as Lily methodically defaced his flamingos and frogs.

"I should have made it a bigger annuity? You didn't really think I'd leave you the house, did you?" he asked plaintively, then shrugged and floated back into the house, all the way into the study, one very unhappy ghost....

"...and Attorney Humbolt," Darcie was saying to Edwin.

"That's it? That's all? What about his friends?"

"Uncle Horry was a very, um, private man. Very content but very private. I looked in his address book this morning, but other than his insurance agent, a few other business numbers and Attorney Humbolt, there were no personal numbers. But that doesn't mean it won't be a lovely memorial. It is the thought that counts, isn't it?"

"It's closure, that's what it is," Edwin said, touching a hand to the gilded urn on the mantel. "You don't just pour him in a jar and not say a few words over him."

"Uncle Horry didn't want a fuss."

Edwin turned to Darcie and grinned. "If he complains, we'll stop, all right? Now, who all is going to speak? You, of course, maybe that young man of yours. The housekeeper. I really didn't know him, so it wouldn't be my place to say anything. I'll just recite a little prayer."

"A prayer would be nice," Darcie said, rolling up the ball of yarn she'd rescued from the floor. "And I could tell about the time I was seven, and Uncle Horry dressed up like Santa Claus for me. It was August, but I couldn't visit him over Christmas. He was…he was such a good…such a—oh, excuse me."

Horry watched as Darcie ran from the room, yet another tissue pressed to her face, then floated himself over to where Bupkus stood guard beside the door. The girl was rather fragile this morning. "Still, it's nice to know you've been appreciated, isn't it, Bupkus? Hey—what do you think you're doing?" he exclaimed, watching as Edwin lifted down the urn, placed it on the desktop.

Edwin lifted the lid of the jar and peeked inside, causing Horry to cover his privates with his hands, as he felt suddenly violated.

"So that's what ashes look like," Edwin said, replacing the lid. "Wonder how you know if you got all the right ones back."

Horry, suddenly panicked, lifted his hands, began patting at his chest, his belly, checking himself over. No. He was all here, and all him. Nobody else was here with him. Those had to be his ashes in that jar.

"What're you doing, Poobie?"

Horry watched as the blonde tottered into the study on four-inch heels, dressed all in clingy knit leopard-skin print, and with her long fingernails painted to match. An amazing woman. A real heartbreaker.

Edwin hefted the urn, placing it back on the mantel. "Nothing, Pookie-bear. Just checking to make sure old Horry's really in there."

"Where else would he be?" Pookie asked, looking around the room in much the same frantic way Horry had just checked himself out. "He is dead, you know. Deader than a doornail."

"I know. And we never talked. What a strange family we Willikinses are. Sad, don't you think, Pookie?"

"Ah," Pookie said, holding out her arms, "come to me, sweetheart. You poor thing."

Horry floated toward her, then realized that she hadn't been beckoning to him, but to his half brother. There was nobody to hold him. Nobody could see him. He could only talk to a cat. His earthly remains were in a jar with a loose lid.

He'd missed his chance to know his brother. That was sad. But that was his family. Nobody ever talked. Ever. Not his father, once his mother died. Not his sister. Bunch of damn clams, that's what they were.

Everybody keeping to themselves, nobody sharing a thought, let alone a kind word. Just achieve; must achieve; never fail; never disgrace the family. A motley bunch of stiff-backed, stiff-necked, closemouthed, emotionless *nothings* who'd rather chew nails than let anyone see a weakness, learn a secret…risk a rebuff.

Horry floated out of the room to find Lucky, while he thought about his niece. "Never talked, never said what was on our minds. But not Darcie. She's not going to make the same mistake. That's why I'm still here. I knew there had to be a reason. Well," he said, smiling sheepishly, "besides having myself some fun, that is…"

CHAPTER ELEVEN

LUCKY HAD COME to the conclusion that he needed a small vacation, away from the humans that were constantly giving him a headache. At least, he thought it was a headache; he hadn't known cats got headaches until he'd opened his eyes the morning after Horry died, to see him standing over him, grinning like a madman as he waved hello.

Now, after eluding Horry, who'd been telling him in boring detail what had happened earlier with Edwin and Pookie, Lucky wandered around the house for a while, checked out his catnip mouse; ate the tail. He scratched at the dining room draperies, checked his dish in the kitchen in the hope the sushi had been put there. It had, but humans obviously didn't have very sensitive noses, because the fish was bad. Bad. He wouldn't deign to eat three-day-old fish. Lucky had his standards.

He exited the house via the cat door Horry had rigged up in the kitchen, the one that played the overture from *Cats* every time he went in or out, then stopped, blinked at the two people who were standing at one end of the porch, their heads close together.

"There he is."

Lucky looked behind him. No one was there. Oh. It

was him. They meant *him.* Big deal, this was his house, he lived here. Why the public announcement?

"We've only got three weeks left."

"I told you. It takes time to get from one place to another. I'm here now. Why didn't you take care of it?"

"I don't know. He…he scares me."

"He's a cat. German shepherds scare people. Pit bulls scare people. Cats do not scare people."

"Good. Then you do it."

"Fine. What makes this any different? But how?"

"Rat poison?"

"Traceable."

"All right, all right, let me think. I know! An accident with the car. Back out, don't see him there…?"

"And how do you get him to stand behind the car?"

"I've got it! Didn't I see an old wringer washing machine in that room just inside?"

"The pantry. It's called a pantry."

"Big whoop. It is a wringer washer, right?"

"Yes. But—"

"So here's the deal. Terrible accident. Terrible, terrible accident. Cat was playing around the washer, the way cats do, curious and all that crap, and he tripped the switch with his paw—*squish!*—sucked right into the wringer."

"Would you look at that? That damn cat piddled on the porch, and now he's running like his tail's on fire. Maybe there's already something wrong with him."

"If not, there soon will be."

CAMERON PAUSED in the act of ripping loose yet another section of lattice and sat back, wiped sweat from his forehead with the back of his forearm.

It felt good to work. Real hands-on stuff he hadn't done since working his way through college. Now he did the thinking, the planning, but never the actual execution. He missed it.

Besides, hiding out on the side of the house seemed like a good idea after the mess he'd made last night with Darcie. What a damn fiasco that was.

It wasn't that Darcie was *flawed*...in the way of "how about we just call this a draw, and you go check out some good psychologist." She was, however, dealing with some problem she wasn't ready to share with him.

Her original idea, no sex, had been a sound one. Falling into bed last night had been a mistake. They already knew where they were compatible, they were supposed to be trying to get to know each other better this month. He already knew every inch of her body, what her body did to his.

And he loved her. Damn it, he loved her. Did a person really have to have a *reason* to love someone else? Couldn't he just look at that person and *know?*

But then he'd rushed her into an engagement. Good intentions, lousy tactics.

This was their second chance, his second chance. An entire month of being together, courtesy of Uncle Horry...to learn about each other, build the base that would sustain the marriage.

After all, man does not live by sex alone. "But we

sure do keep trying," he said to himself, shaking his head in semishame and a bit of wry amusement.

Then there was the problem of all of Horry's money. Cameron made a good living, more than a comfortable living, but some people could think he was going through this stay-a-month thing, the reconcile-with-Darcie thing, for money. As long as Darcie didn't think so…

He picked up the claw hammer once more, then caught sight of Lucky out of the corner of his eye. "Hey, where are you—damn. Didn't know that cat could move so fast."

"He thinks he's Smarty Jones. Hello. Um…what are you doing?"

Dismissing the already departed Lucky, Cameron turned toward the sound of Darcie's voice, looked up at her, shading his eyes in the morning sun. "Hi, babe." He offered her the hammer. "You want to use this on me?"

Darcie went down on her knees in front of him. "Can we just forget last night? It…it was a mistake."

"No kidding. Sure, we'll forget it." But he didn't look at her as he said the words, because she was wearing another one of those belly-showing knit tops and a pair of short-shorts. Her hair pulled back in twin ponytails, her face free of makeup. She was so damn wholesome, he felt like a lech even considering what he knew he shouldn't be considering. "But let me apologize."

"No, no apologies. We were both wrong, and we both know it, right? I…I just hoped you'd be okay with that. I mean, do we really need a post mortem?"

"No," he said, putting down the hammer, wishing Darcie found it easier to talk to him. "I guess not. You asked what I'm doing here. Remember I told you I found some dry rot? Okay, so now I'm looking for other problems. This lattice is only decorative around the bottom of this porch, and it's in bad shape, so I'm pulling it away enough that I can crawl under the porch and look around for other damage."

Darcie leaned forward and looked into the darkness under the porch. "You're going to crawl around in there? But there could be spiders, and thousand-leggers, and…and skunks." She shuddered. "We can hire someone, you know."

"You could. Once the place is yours, you can do anything you want. But I need something to do here, anyway, and I'm enjoying myself. You could have someone else clean up the gardens, and you're doing it yourself. It looks great on the other side of the house now, if I haven't told you."

He'd have to think back, later, decide exactly what he'd said to put such a sparkle in Darcie's eyes, such joy in her voice…because for the next quarter hour, as he ripped lattice, she kept up a running monologue of what she'd done to the gardens, what she planned to do, what sorts of flowers and shrubs do best in the southeastern Pennsylvania climate, the practical applications of having a compost heap, a Web site she'd found that belonged to a local nursery where they sold a huge variety of gazebos, one of which would look fantastic here, how much she'd like her own greenhouse…

"I could build a greenhouse for you," Cameron said at last, when he could get a word in edgewise—it would seem there were some things she could talk about for hours. Just as long as it wasn't *personal.* He'd have to think about that, later. "Same for the gazebo. Get some plans, make a few alternations you might want, customize them, and just build the suckers."

She looked at him as if he'd just told her he'd unlocked the secrets of cold fusion or something. "You could do that? Build them from scratch?"

"I told you I'd worked construction, Darc. What can I tell you? I'm a double threat—plan it, build it. I'm a real catch. You ought to snap me right up."

"I'm thinking that isn't such a bad idea," she said, blinking as tears built in her eyes.

"We wouldn't be rushing this get-to-know-you, getting-to-know-ourselves idea of yours? Where did you come up with that one, anyway?"

She sniffed, lost her smile. "I'm not sure. But I didn't know you could do the sort of thing you're doing here. I thought you just sat at a desk and drew up plans for buildings. I'm seeing a whole new side of you here, Cam."

"And you're liking it?"

"Except for the idea you could crawl around with spiders and act like it's fun? Yes, I'm liking it. I'm liking you."

"All right. Confession. I had no idea you were anything more than my beautiful Darcie, who looks good across the table from me in a restaurant, and drives me wild in bed. I had no idea you'd get such a kick out of pulling weeds, or that you'd look so scared in the kitchen—but still give it your best shot. You're getting more…human to me, Darc, every day. And I'll admit it. I do like it."

She put her hand on his cheek. "There's still so much to learn…"

"We can't know it all at once, Darc. Nobody can."

"True." She sat back on her haunches. "But I am learning a few things about me, been learning them for months, things that probably would have broken us up if I hadn't begun to figure them out. So I'm *glad* we broke the engagement, Cam."

So much for the fantasy. Cameron drew on his leather work gloves once more, picked up the hammer. "So, if Horry hadn't died, pulled this stunt with his will, we wouldn't be having this conversation now?"

"I don't know. You didn't come after me, Cam," she said quietly.

"No, damn it, I didn't. Don't you think I've been kicking myself for that? And you—you didn't even come home for Christmas."

"Christmas? Were you thinking—"

"Horry. Horry told me to wait, wait for Christmas, wait for you to come home. He said I should give you some time to get your head on straight and—"

"Get my head on straight! He said *that*?" Darcie wrapped her arms around herself, maybe so she wouldn't fly apart into a million pieces. "Uncle Horry said that? And that's what you thought, too? That I just needed to get *my head on straight?*"

Hiding the hammer behind his back became a really good idea. "Well, it wasn't just you who'd blown everything out of proportion. I can't just be an innocent party here. I saw you as wanting what I wanted. Dumb, I know. Men don't always say what they mean. Ask Dr. Phil—he's made a fortune explaining us dumb men. We do dumb things."

"Like kissing old girlfriends in their office just as their fiancée is coming to apologize?"

"You…you'd come to the office to *apologize?* Well, shit, Darc, why didn't you say something?"

She got to her feet. "Would that have been before or after you were putting your tongue down that woman's throat?"

"I did not have my—wait," he said, holding up his hands in surrender. "We weren't going to talk about the past anymore, remember? Old arguments, old girlfriends. Gone. We're starting over, remember? And we've been doing pretty damn well, too, until—"

"Until we went to bed together," Darcie told him. "You know what, Cam? It's like we can be lovers, or we can be friends. But we can't seem to be *both.*" She blinked back tears, looked out over the lawn. "Ohmigod! *Lucky!*"

Darcie was up and running across the lawn before Cameron could move, but he was close behind her when she skidded to a halt, dropped to her knees in front of the cat.

"Oh, Lucky, what happened to you?"

"What's wrong, Darc—ah, cripes." Cameron joined

her on the grass as Lucky lay there, looking like he'd been rolled in dirt. "He's just dirty, Darc."

"No, no. He was limping, and then he fell down. Lucky? Come on, sweetheart, walk for me. Get up and walk for Mommy."

"Mommy? Does that make me— Never mind, I don't think I want to go there. Come on, cat, get up and walk. You're scaring Mommy."

Lucky raised his head slightly, then let it drop against the grass once more.

Got them on the ropes. Now to give them the full treatment.

Mewling once, plaintively, Lucky slowly got to his feet, holding his left front paw off the ground as he took three hobbling steps, then collapsed, rather gracefully, on Darcie's knees.

Panache. It was all about panache.

"Do you think something fought back?" Cameron asked as Darcie ran her hands over Lucky's plump body.

"I don't know. He's not wincing when I touch him.

Really? I thought that'd be overkill. Yeah, well, if that's what it takes.

Lucky winced.

"Here, let me check him." Cameron repeated Darcie's examination, marveling at the muscles beneath the cat's fur. "This animal's built like a brick sh—"

"Stop. He winced again. And he's purring. Ah, Cam, he's purring." She went nose to nose with the cat. "Who's the best baby, hmmm? Who's my sweet little kitten?"

"Right. A kitten. A twenty-pound kitten. Come on, Darcie, let's get him up to the house, call the vet or something. But I think you'd better carry him I'm just starting to heal from the last time Lucky and I got close."

Darcie got to her feet, cradling Lucky against her, and the cat purred all the way to the kitchen, where she put him down on the table. "The vet's number is in Uncle Horry's address book. In the study. You watch Lucky, and I'll go call."

Cameron stood there, looking at Lucky, who was watching Darcie's retreat with soulful eyes before turning them to Cameron. He mewled plaintively.

"Don't make like you like me. You know, cat, that's it for you and running around outside. Anything happens to you in the next three weeks, Darcie loses this place. That hasn't occurred to her, because she loves you, but it has occurred to me." He leaned down closer to the cat. "So. How do you feel about a harness and a leash, *mmm?*"

Lucky growled, low in his throat, and Cameron retreated. Who knew cats could growl? Why would he think Lucky couldn't?

"What's going on here? What's Lucky doing on the table? What happened to him? Look at him—dragging all that dirt in here, all over my table. Get him out!"

Cameron looked at Lily, who was glaring at Lucky.

"He came home limping. Dirty and limping. Darcie's on the phone with the vet."

Lily blinked. "He's hurt? How badly? Is he dying? Oh, poor kitty." She leaned down to look at him. "Is he dying?"

Lucky growled again, and his tail began banging against the tabletop.

"He was purring when Darcie held him," Cameron supplied helpfully. "He growled at me, too, but that's no great shock. Still, I thought he liked you."

"Oh, he does, he does. Cats like anyone who feeds them, and Horry had me feeding this animal sushi and fresh salmon and premium ice cream. That cat eats better than most humans. I'm going to go call Attorney Humbolt." She looked at Cameron. "Darcie's in big trouble, you know."

"Right. Thanks for the reminder. But you don't have to call Humbolt, Lily, at least not yet. Can't this wait until we come back from the vet? Lucky probably just took a fall or something. Probably while stalking a deer."

I could, you know, so don't make like that's a joke. Just get me to the vet so he can tell you all I need are love and tenderness and fresh sushi and protection. Definitely protection. I am brilliant. No doubt about it. Brilliant. I am—

"I'll bet," Cameron told Lily, "that he just bruised his paw or something, and all he needs is some rest and a bath. Definitely a bath."

Oh, shit…not so brilliant…

LUCKY YOWLED all the way to the vet and all the way back, while Cameron maintained a closemouthed smile that told Darcie he was a very good person who wasn't considering stopping the car, jumping into the back seat, opening Lucky's cage and strangling him. Really.

The car had barely stopped when Cameron was out of it and reaching into the back seat, extracting Lucky's cage and running it inside, leaving Darcie to sit in the car and look at the small assembly on the front porch.

Uncle Edwin. Pookie. Lily. *Attorney Humbolt.*

She looked again. A concerned looking Uncle Edwin. Pookie, blowing on her fingernails. A smiling Lily.

And a pained-looking Attorney Humbolt.

"Hi," Darcie said as brightly as she could. "Lucky's just fine. Doctor Stanton thinks he may have taken a fall and bruised his paw. Nothing's broken. I should have called from my cell phone, to reassure everyone, but Cameron and I went for some lunch while Lucky was getting a bath, and I— Why is everyone staring at me?"

"Oh, honey," Pookie said as she picked up a bottle of silver nail polish, "its been hitting the fan around here. Tell you what, how about I go get you a nice tall glass of iced tea? Yes, that's what I'll do."

Pookie toddled to the screen door, both silver-tipped hands sort of waggling in front of her, then stopped and looked appealingly at Uncle Edwin, who rushed to open the door.

Humbolt stepped forward. "Ms. Reed? Perhaps you'd like to tell me why I had to hear about Lucky's mishap from Lily here, instead of you?"

"I told you, we went to lunch and— Oh, for goodness' sake. He's *fine.*"

Cameron reappeared on the porch. "She's right, Humbolt. I told Lily to wait." He looked at the housekeeper. "But you couldn't, could you? Just had to tell him the news. I don't know if you forgot, but you don't get this place, or the money, even if Lucky takes a swan dive into a wood chipper before the month is up."

There was a loud *meow* from the other side of the screen door, followed by the sound of clawing paws trying to gain traction on a polished wood floor as Lucky raced for the stairs.

Uncle Edwin—or Admiral Willikins, as he was dressed for a day on the high seas again—raised a hand like a schoolboy and asked, "Excuse me? Am I missing something here somewhere? It's a nice cat, but what does a cat have to do with Horry's house and fortune? It is Horry's house and fortune you're talking about here, isn't it? And what's this about a month?"

Darcie looked to Cameron, who looked back at her, then shrugged, nodded.

"Well, Uncle Edwin," Darcie said, climbing the steps to the porch, "it's like this. Right now, and for the next three weeks, Lucky owns everything and Cameron and I had to agree to live here. When the time is up, we decide between us who gets Uncle Horry's inheritance."

"She does. I get Bupkus," Cameron said, leaning against one of the posts, then frowning yet again as he turned, looked up to where the pillar was attached to the underside of the roof. He gave the pillar a shake, and it moved back and forth slightly. "More repair work before I can paint. At this rate, Shangri-La is going to stay pink for another two years."

"Cam, you're letting yourself be distracted," Darcie

whispered to him. "Or don't you want to tell Uncle Edwin the rest?"

"Let Humbolt handle it," he whispered back to her, giving the pillar another shake. "You watch Uncle Edwin and I'll watch Lily."

"Why?" Darcie whispered out of the corner of her mouth, then smiled at the woman advancing toward her with a tall glass of iced tea clutched in one silver-tipped hand. A silver-tipped hand that matched the silver lamé of her halter top, stiletto heels and the long scarf she'd tied around her head, its fringed ends hanging over one better-uplift-through-chemistry boob. Her skintight black leggings could have been painted on. If the woman could twirl a flaming baton, she could try out for the Oakland Raiders cheerleading squad.

"There you go, sweetie," Pookie said, looking from one face to another. "Did I miss anything, Poobie-bear?"

"No, no, I don't think so. Oh, except that Lucky owns the house," Uncle Edwin said, then grinned. "I really wish Horry and I had gotten to know each other. I really think I would have liked him."

Attorney Humbolt cleared his throat to gain everyone's attention. "I will not get into the particulars of Horry's will, as the principals are all fully aware of the conditions. However, that said, Ms. Reed, Mr. Pierce, you two, as of this moment, are officially on probation. Horry's wish was that you remain here and care for Lucky for the period of one month. Your neglect has already served to injure the cat. If something…untoward occurs and the animal dies within the stated time, the estate is awarded to the alternate inheritor."

"I know," Darcie said quietly. "Nothing's going to happen to Lucky. He was barely hurt, just dirty. I told you, the vet couldn't find anything wrong with him except that he's...limping."

"Limping! Oh, that poor baby," Pookie exclaimed, pressing silver-tipped fingers to her cheeks. "I'm allergic to the little dears, which just breaks my heart because I've always wanted a kitty. Well, we'll all just have to take very good care of him, won't we, so that Darcie and Cameron get the estate. We'll just watch his every single move."

"Poobie-bear gets everything if the cat croaks in the next three weeks."

Darcie, eyes wide, whirled to gape at Cameron, who was smiling as if he knew he'd just dropped a bomb on the porch.

"What...what's that?" Uncle Edwin said, a hand to one ear. "Did I hear you right, Sonny? *I* get everything? *Me?*"

"Mr. Pierce," Humbolt said, "I specifically avoided mentioning—"

"Yeah, yeah, I know," Cameron interrupted. "Shame on me. Edwin, Lucky bites the big one in the next three weeks and this is all yours," he said, shaking the loose pillar yet again. "Oh, and the money. There's a lot of it, as I understand."

"But...but I don't want this house. I used to think I would like it, the family homestead and all of that, but—

but look at it. It's pink, for the love of Mike. And the furniture? It's like living in a museum. No. I don't want this house. And I've got plenty of money. Don't I, Pookie-bear? Here—pull up that shirt and show them the Hope Diamond."

Darcie held up her hands. "No, no, that's okay, we've seen it," she said quickly. "Mr. Humbolt? Exactly what do you mean, we're on probation?"

The attorney pulled himself to attention. "Horry may have talked me into the video will, but I only agreed when *he* agreed to also have a written will, which I did not bother to read to you all because…well, things were slightly strained that day, weren't they?"

Darcie remembered how she and Cameron had been at each other's throats. "Yes. I suppose so."

"Yeah," Cameron said. "What with your tee time and all, right, Humbolt?"

"Cam, hush. What else do we need to know?"

Humbolt straightened his tie. "Horry, because he trusted my judgment implicitly, gave written permission for me to amend the rules and penalties if, in my considered judgment, such broad provisions as he laid down in said video will became, in my considered opinion, not sufficient to the execution of his wishes."

"English, Humbolt," Cameron said, slipping an arm around Darcie's waist.

"You're not taking this seriously," Humbolt said, jutting out his chin. "Therefore, I'm amending the rules covering the feline. From now on, Lily here will phone me twice daily, in the morning, at eight, and in the evening, also at eight—Lily, my cell phone in the morning, please, as I'll be on the golf course most days."

"You do a lot of golfing, don't you, Humbolt?" Cameron asked. "What's your handicap—besides the plaid pants?"

Darcie couldn't help herself. She giggled.

But Humbolt ignored both of them. "If, for any reason, Lucky is not to be found, if, for any reason, Lily reports to me that Lucky is dead, or missing for a period exceeding twelve hours, the estate, in its entirety, goes to Mr. Edwin Willikins. Is that clear enough, Mr. Pierce?"

"Oh, yeah, clear. Crystal," Cameron said.

"No, it's not," Darcie said quickly. "Lucky's an outside cat. He's out all night. You can't really expect us to...to... Cameron?"

"To whistle him home for roll call twice a day," Cameron said, not helping her all that much. "Hey, I've already decided to cut his traveling privileges. From now on, for the next three weeks anyway, Lucky's an indoor cat."

Darcie wasn't buying it. "Yes, but what if he gets out? What if someone opens the door and Lucky gets out? He likes to hide halfway up the stairs, in the shadows, then race down and out when someone opens the front door. After being cooped up, he might not come back for days."

"Oh, don't you worry about that, honey," Pookie said. "We'll all be very careful. Won't we, Poobie?"

"Lily?" Cameron asked.

"Not my cat, not my house, not my worry," she said,

then walked down the steps and stomped, stiff-backed toward the drive.

"Where's she going?"

Cameron laughed. "You haven't noticed? She's decorating the frogs and flamingos. Mustaches, eyebrows, spots. Dimples, I think, on a couple of them. She's got about a dozen done by now. You didn't see that when we drove up?"

"No-o-o, you're kidding." Darcie watched as Lily walked down the drive about twenty yards, then sat down beside a flamingo and picked up a paintbrush. "Is she…has she…?"

"Sprung a leak?" Cameron shot back. "That would be my first guess. My second is that she's really pissed at Horry, and she's taking it out on the statuary."

Darcie rubbed at her forehead. "I…I think I'm going to go lie down for a while, if nobody minds?"

She didn't wait for anyone to agree or object, and escaped to her room, passing Lucky, who was hunkered down on the stairs. "You be *good,*" she told him, and kept moving.

"NOT MAKING ANY FRIENDS, are you, Lucky?" Horry said, watching Darcie run up the stairs—right through him, as a matter of fact. "So, after you overheard them you took off. That makes sense. But why the dirt? The limping?"

"How else am I supposed to get everyone's attention? Slip a note under Darcie's door? Now everyone will be watching me, watching out for me." He jumped off the bottom stair, onto the circular Persian carpet, and began rolling around, to rid himself of the perfumy smell of the shampoo that would make him the laughing stock of the neighborhood.

"The limping was good," Horry said, perching himself on the bottom step. "The dirt might have been overkill."

"Tell me about it," Lucky said, rubbing his neck against the carpet. "And while you're talking, tell me how I'm supposed to stay alive for the next three weeks with those two killers hanging around? Tell me that one."

Horry sighed. "I can't believe it. I never imagined—"

"Yeah, yeah, we already know what you never imagined. Now imagine me, in a wringer washer. I screwed up, Horry. I figured they'd watch my back for me, that's all. But Cameron says I'm locked in the house from here on out, and that makes me a sitting duck…cat. You have any suggestions?"

"Not really, no. Hey, Lucky, speaking of ducks—watch this." Horry retrieved an umbrella from the stand and floated over to where a large yellow mechanical duck was tucked into the decorative cutout at the top of the grandfather's clock. He hit the umbrella sharply against the wall, twice, and the duck began to quack and wave its wings. "Isn't that something? I can do it with the singing mouse in the bathroom, too."

"Yeah. I'm all impressed," Lucky said, then jumped back when the screen door opened and Cameron stepped into the foyer, his gaze already on the still-quacking duck.

"How in hell?" he said to himself, then looked at Lucky. "You made that noise and set it off?"

Lucky limped a few steps, then laid down as if the effort had exhausted him.

The duck had stopped quacking. Cameron stepped closer to the clock and clapped his hands. The duck began quacking and flapping again, as it was sound activated.

Cameron looked at the duck, shook his head. "I'm not even going to think about this one." Then he looked at the screen door, the heavy wooden door. "Guess what, Lucky, old boy. By tonight, both these doors are going to have hook-and-eye locks on them. Way up here, at the top. You manage to open either of these doors again, and I'm going to know you had help. And now I'm going to lock the cat flap in the kitchen door."

He looked around the foyer, into the corners, up at the ceiling. "You hear me, Horry? The cat stays inside."

Cameron headed for the kitchen, mumbling under his breath, leaving Lucky and Horry alone together in the foyer.

"You're not going to listen to him, right? I don't want to be a prisoner, Horry. You're signing my death warrant here. Horry? *Horry.*"

"He knows about me," Horry said, smiling dreamily. "What a bright young man. I knew he was perfect for Darcie."

"Oh, yeah? So he tells Darcie you're a ghost and you can open doors and make ducks quack. Boy, that'll have her racing to the altar."

Horry sighed. "Yes, there is that, isn't there? Still, I will have to find some way to communicate with him."

CHAPTER TWELVE

DARCIE STEPPED OUT onto the porch a little after eight o'clock the next morning, quickly shutting the screen door while determinedly ignoring a plaintive-looking Lucky, who definitely had designs on escape.

"Hi, Uncle Edwin," she said, seeing the man sitting in one of the rocking chairs. "Where's Pookie?"

"Exfoliating," he said, getting to his feet and politely offering her his chair. "I'm glad we can have these few minutes, my dear. To talk about Horry's rather eccentric will. I've thought of nothing else since yesterday. I'm so sorry."

"Oh, don't be—it's not your fault." Darcie sat down, laid her gardening gloves in her lap. "Uncle Horry meant well. You see, Cameron and I were engaged last year, but we...we broke it off. Uncle Horry wrote that silly will as his way to get us back together. I don't think he really meant it, it's just that he may have felt powerless, or something, so he did what he could. He probably meant to show it to us at some point. I most certainly don't think he planned on dying, just to get Cam and me back together."

Edwin also sat. "And yet I don't see a ring on that pretty left hand of yours."

Darcie felt her cheeks growing hot. "I know. We're…we're working things out. I think."

"Poor old Horry. I hope you two do get back together, for his sake. It would be nice if he could have gone out with a bang."

"Oh…well, he did sort of do that," Darcie said, wincing. "That is, I think he died a happy man."

Edwin sighed, shaking his head. "He never had much of a life, you know. I don't think he ever left this place after— Well, we shouldn't speak ill of the dead, should we?"

"No, we shouldn't. But speak ill, Uncle Edwin? That sounds as if Uncle Horry once did something…bad."

"More like something sad. My mother kept me up to date on all the Willikinses until she died, rest her nosy, jealous soul. Her avaricious soul, too, but that's a story for another day. Anyway, Horry used to get around a lot, you know, when he was young. I'm talking his early twenties. In the Air Force, you understand, stationed in Germany. That's where he met the woman. Name escapes me. He was ga-ga over her, told the old man he was getting married, bringing home his bride. Horry had just patented his widget for airplanes, or whatever it was, and our esteemed father knew Horry was going to strike it rich. So he bought off the woman."

"He what?"

"My mother told me all about it. I don't know how she found out, but she still had some friends living back here. She told me, to show me why I wouldn't want anything to do with the old man, as if the fellow had ever so much as blinked at me. Anyway, Horry finished out his time, came home to sell his big idea for a lot of money."

"And shared it with his father...with my grandfather?"

"I don't think so, because my own mother was doing a lot of smiling when she told me her stepson—she called Horry her stepson, which he was, technically—had finally put the kibosh on the old man."

"So he must have known what his father did? About the woman, I mean."

"Maybe. Probably. I don't like to tattle, but I think my mother might have had a little something to do with filling Horry in on that part. Anyway, the old man died maybe six months later, which served him right, and Horry dug himself in here, never left again. I tried to visit him a time or two after my own mother died, wrote to him, but he never wrote back. Your mother guarded him, sicced a lawyer on me as a matter of fact."

"My mother did that?"

"Oh, yes. A veritable tiger she was. And one to see the bad in everyone. Sorry. I know everyone thought I just wanted the money, but that wasn't true. Still, I can take a hint, so I stayed away. If I hadn't seen the death notice on the World Wide Web, I never would have known he was dead. What a waste."

Darcie closed her mouth, that had dropped open somewhere along the line. "But he was happy," she said with conviction. "I mean, he really was happy."

"And alone."

"He had Lily... Oh, never mind."

Uncle Edwin stopped the rocker. "Lily? Oh, you mean the housekeeper. Really? Now that's pitiful. Not a patch on my Pookie. And I've been looking around the house. Horry filled it with gadgets and toys. Part museum, part fun house. But mostly it's a sad house, trying too hard to be happy. You know what it needs, honey? This house needs a family. That's probably why Horry wrote the will. He wanted you and that young man of yours to take over, make the house happy again. Not silly, happy."

Darcie sighed. "One minute I think Uncle Horry was happy, and the next I think he must have been miserable. I loved him very much, you know. I only wish I'd told him."

"We all have our regrets. And those regrets are mostly for the things we didn't say." Edwin stood, bent to kiss Darcie's cheek. "Wouldn't it be nice if you and I got rid of the old Willikins tradition of silence?"

"Yes, it would be, wouldn't it?" Darcie said, smiling up at her uncle. "We're going to have to work on that." She would have said more, would like to think she would have said more, but she heard a vehicle coming up the drive and turned to see a delivery truck pulling to a stop. "Ohmigod, the mattress." She leaped to her feet. "Stall them, Uncle Edwin, please. I've got to go find Cameron."

ONE MORE PULL, and the last bit of lattice would break loose. Just one more pull…

"Cameron? Cam, where are you?"

He looked up at the sound of Darcie's voice, saw her leaning half out of a window on the second story. "Morning, Darc. What's the matter? Is it Lucky?"

"No, no. It's the mattress guys. They're here. First I thought they'd never come, and then they were supposed to call before they came, damn it. Come upstairs and help me. Uncle Horry's bedroom, Cam. *Now.*"

"Help you what?" he asked, but she was gone, the window slammed shut once more. "Yeah, well," he said with one last look at the lattice. "Ours is not to reason why…"

He headed for the kitchen door and the back stairs, found Darcie in Horry's bedroom. She had a large sheet bunched in her hands and was jumping up and down, trying to toss it over the top of the barber pole that was anything but a barber pole.

"Help me," she said when he laughed. "Please, Cam. I can't let anyone see this."

"Oh, right. Can't let anyone see this," he said, taking the sheet from her and tossing it over the pole. Then he stood back, looked at what he'd done. "Looks like it's wearing a condom."

Darcie's wail had him laughing again, even as he tried to tell her he was kidding, just kidding.

But Darcie wasn't listening. She was much too busy racing around the room, gathering up candles and shoving them into drawers. "Did I get them all?" she asked a few moments later, clutching three fat white candles. "I don't want those delivery men getting the wrong idea."

Cameron slapped his hands to his cheeks in mock horror. "Oh, gosh, oh, gosh, you're right! Will a couple of complete strangers be able to see the bedroom? What will they think? I'll never be able to look them in the eye. How embarrassing! Is it dark enough in here with the drapes closed?"

"Oh, stop it. If I'm being ridiculous it's because I, at least, have some sense of modesty, of common decency. Something you obviously don't. I closed the drapes on purpose."

"Yeah, I figured that one out on my own. Here, let's see if this helps," he said, then flipped the wall switch that controlled the disco ball. "There. Better? No. I think we need the candles."

Darcie advanced on him, eyes narrowed. "I could seriously hate you sometimes. Oh, never mind. It's not like I can do anything about that mirror. Just turn off the disco ball, okay, and let me go hide somewhere while the men bring the mattress up here, and—"

"This room? Ma'am? The guy on the porch said he thought it was the first bedroom on the left. This is it, right? Wow. Disco ball. Cool."

"Oh, God," Darcie wailed quietly, depositing the three candles on the bureau behind her, then trying to hide herself behind Cameron's back.

"Too late to ask for divine intervention, babe," Cameron whispered, sliding an arm around her shoulders. Then he said, louder, "Yeah, you've got it right. In here."

The delivery man nodded, then hefted the box spring a little and began backing into the room, to be followed by a short, thin man whose arms appeared to be made out of thick ropes. "Easy, Gus, don't push. I'm trying to guide this thing."

"Can I help?" Cameron asked, holding on to Darcie, who tried to bolt for the doorway when it was clear once more. "The missus asks that you be particularly careful about the mirror. Over the bed, under the canopy. See it? She gave it to me last year, for my birthday." He gave Darcie's shoulder another squeeze. "Didn't you, hon?"

Darcie spoke through clenched teeth. "You do know that at some point you'll have to turn your back to me, right? Beware, Cam. Be very ware."

The box spring was in position now, and Gus and his partner retraced their steps, walking past Darcie and Cameron. Gus saluted.

"Let me go," Darcie said, once they were gone.

"Sure," Cameron said, letting go. She'd gotten almost to the doorway before he said, "Do you think Gus will get a kick out of seeing the barber pole I gave you for *your* birthday?"

She wheeled, glared at him. "You wouldn't dare."

"I would if you leave."

Darcie walked back across the room, stopped approximately one and one half inches in front of him. "Why? Why are you doing this? Exactly what point are you trying to make here?"

He looked down at her. "I never noticed that before. Darc? Do you know that your nostrils sort of quiver when you get mad? No, seriously, they do. I think it's cute."

"You're embarrassing me so you can see my nose twitch?"

"No, that's a bonus. I'm embarrassing you, Darc, because you're so easily embarrassed about what is, at the heart of it, a basic, human activity. S-e-x. You know, that thing we do, used to do, but never talk about?"

"You think...you think I'm *embarrassed* by sex?"

"No, I don't think that at all. I just think you think it's something separate from the rest of us, a part of us that goes into one compartment, while friendship goes in another. Then there's this whole other area, we'll just label that one Personal, Hands Off, that you keep under lock and key. I don't know how to say this, Darc, but the more I get to know you, the more I know I don't know you at all. I just know parts of you, the ones you let me see."

"So you turned on the disco ball and pointed out the mirror. Sure. That makes sense. Cameron Pierce, you are out of your tiny mind."

"So you're not embarrassed to be known as a sensual creature? In the daylight, that is? I won't just have my tigress at night, and the uptight businesswoman in the day time? I'll get to see the whole person, all at once?" He grinned. "Here they come, babe. Prove it."

Darcie made a low, angry sound in her throat, relaxed her hands, the ones she'd drawn up into fists, and stepped back three paces. Turned, nervously smiled at Gus and company as they levered the mattress on top of the box spring.

"You're really daring me?" she asked out of the corner of her mouth.

"Oh, yes. Definitely daring you. Double-Dutch daring you. Come on, Darc, let loose a little. Have some fun. Make old Gus's day for him."

She looked at him as if to say, Okay, just remember, you asked for it. Then she squared her shoulders and gushed, "Oh, Poobie-bear, I'd forgotten how big and soft and cushy our new bed is. I just can't wait to put the sheets on and try it out. Here, let me get this—oops."

"Darcie," Cameron said quietly, worrying if maybe he'd gone too far, daring her that way.

Holding the sheet she'd just dragged off the barber pole, Darcie giggled, blinked at Gus. "Oh, dear, I forgot. Silly Pookie. I wasn't going to give this to my Poobie until tonight. Isn't it fabulous? Here, watch."

She grabbed the remote control and turned on the pole, so that the lights winked, the red-and-white-striped center pole began to rotate behind its glass covering.

Then, as Cameron watched, wondering what sort of monster he'd created, she linked her fingers together around the pole, leaned back far enough to be able to look at him, and said, "Happy new bed, stud muffin."

"Here...here you go, boys," Cameron said, quickly pulling two twenties out of his pocket and handing them over without looking at either man. "Thank you."

"Oh, no, sir. Thank *you,*" Gus said, still gaping at Darcie, who was still holding on to the pole. "Man..."

Cameron closed the door behind the delivery men, switched off the disco ball and turned on Darcie, who was now posed beside the barber pole, her legs pressed close together, her hands folded in front of her. "Poobie-bear? Stud muffin? What in *hell* was that?"

"*That*, Mr. Pierce, was me showing *you* that you were wrong."

"Oh, yeah, you did that. I think I now have full bragging rights in the boys' locker room. Feel better?"

She frowned, thought about it. "You know, I think I do, now that you mention it. Not that I'd ever do anything like that again, but it was sort of fun. Uninhibited. Different."

"Uninhibited certainly is different for you. In the daytime, that is. So? What's next? I'm game for anything."

"Are you, Cameron? You were looking pretty inhibited and uptight a few moments ago."

She was right. He'd wanted her to loosen up a little, but, damn, not that much. "Okay, you've proved your point. Lesson learned. Neither one of us, thank God, is Poobie or Pookie. I apologize for egging you on. Now, what's next?"

"I don't know. Does something have to be next? Oh, okay, something did happen, the sort of thing I guess you'd want to know, discuss. Something about Uncle Horry. Sort of."

"Is it a state secret, or are you going to share?"

"Share. I'm learning, Cam. I'm sharing. I was talking to Uncle Edwin, before the delivery men came, and he was saying that it's a Willikins trait that nobody talks to anybody about anything important."

"Give that man a cigar," Cameron said, leaning against one of the bed posts. "Go on."

"I am, I am," she said, her back to him as she used the remote to switch off the barber pole. "I…I also think he's right. I think we're, we were, a pretty uptight family." She shook her head. "I have a lot to tell you, about Uncle Horry. But, mostly, I realized when Uncle Edwin was talking to me—I don't know why, it just suddenly occurred to me—that I never saw my parents kiss each other. That's not normal, is it?"

"No, babe, it's not. My parents used to kiss, say I love you…right up until the day they started screaming at each other. At least your parents never divorced."

"Oh, they wouldn't. That would have been totally out of character. You start something, you'd damn well better finish it, that was the credo. But maybe they should have divorced. Unless having me show up so late, and so unexpectedly, made that even more impossible for them," she said, then pressed a hand to her mouth.

"So you feel guilty now?"

"No," she said, blinking at him. "No, I don't. Not today, anyway. I really, really don't feel guilty."

"Right. It was their problem, not yours. So you never saw them kiss? Never saw signs of affection? Really?"

"Really."

"What about with you? Were they openly affectionate with you at least?"

"They always let me know how they felt, what they expected." She shrugged. "You know what, Cameron? I'm going to go check on Lucky. And yesterday you said you were going to put hook and eye locks on the front door, remember? Although I don't know what good they'll do, because you can't use the door, then lock it behind you, can you? Or did you already think of that, because you didn't do it?"

"A person could get whiplash, the way you change the subject. But you're right. Stupid idea. I'll just nail the big door shut. That'll stop him."

"Stop Lucky," Darcie said, nodding.

"Yeah, right. Stop Lucky. That's who I meant."

Right.

"But you know you can't really nail the front door shut."

"I know." Cameron scratched a spot behind his ear. "Yeah, well, we'll just have to keep watching him, like Humbolt said. Speaking of which, I was watching Lily out there yesterday, while Humbolt was doing his song and dance, and you were supposed to be watching Edwin, but we haven't talked about that yet, about what we saw. I can tell you, as far as Lily goes, that is one seriously pissed-off woman. What about Edwin?"

"I think he was genuinely shocked about the will. And I don't think he's happy about it, either. Now tell me why we had to watch them. Do you really think one of them tried to hurt Lucky? That is what you're hinting at, right? Isn't that a little far-fetched?"

"So you don't think this house and Horry's millions appeal to anybody?"

"They appeal to Lily, obviously," she said, sighing. "But if something happens to Lucky, she still doesn't get anything."

"No. Unless she contacted Edwin, told him about the conditions of the will, about Lucky, and now Edwin's here, helping plan Lucky's demise. Do you think she went for a fifty-fifty split, or maybe seventy-thirty, with her also getting Shangri-La?"

Darcie's eyes widened. "I never thought of that. But...but Uncle Edwin seemed so shocked to hear the conditions of the will. And he sounded very sincere when he said he didn't want this place, or need the money."

"Which of course explains why he hit me up for a hundred bucks to take Pookie-bear out to dinner last night."

"He *did?* Wow."

"He said he's got enough money, but he wants to ration it out until some allowance thing is due. A grown man, with an allowance? I'm not buying it."

Darcie gnawed on a knuckle for a moment. "I don't know. It is Uncle Edwin. He's...different."

"Okay, let's keep moving, then. What if it isn't Lily? What if *Attorney Humbolt* told Edwin about the will? After all, nothing happened to Lucky until your long-lost uncle got here. Those two could be working together."

"You're still saying half of this, if there *is* a this, is Uncle Edwin. Can't it be *just* Attorney Humbolt, and maybe, somehow, Lily?"

Now it was Cameron's turn to frown. "Humbolt did just ditch his wife and buy a sports car. The man could think he's about to come into some major money."

"And Lily doesn't get anything, anyway, and he did speak with Uncle Edwin on the phone, as I'm sure you were about to remind me. He told us so. Anyone could be out to get the estate. But I like Uncle Edwin. I refuse to believe he's only here for the estate. And besides, you haven't convinced me that anything's going on at all. Lucky hurt himself, period. Is there really any big reason for all these conspiracy theories?"

"I don't know, Darc. Did Lucky, or did Lucky not show up yesterday, looking like a cat that had been just tossed over a cliff?"

"Oh, that's it. I'm going to go find Lucky and keep him next to me."

"Night and day for the next three weeks?"

"If I have to, yes," she said, leaving him alone in the bedroom, then sticking her head and shoulders back around the doorway to add, "Mattress pad, sheets, pillows and blankets are in the linen closet at the end of the hall. Thanks!"

"Who's sleeping in here? You? Me? *Us?*" he called after her, but she didn't answer. "Damn."

But as he made up the bed, Cameron smiled, realizing they'd had a couple of breakthroughs. Darcie had let her hair down a little, shown herself to be able to joke, to tease, to—in a way—show affection somewhere outside the bedroom.

And she'd talked about her family. Her screwed-up family, that was not his screwed-up family, but proved that neither of them really had much experience with *normal.*

"First time around, we knew nothing about each other, except that we couldn't get enough of each other. This time, less thinking with the glands, Cam," he told himself, "and more thinking with the heart, the mind. We'll talk, we'll really communicate, we'll learn about each other. We'll work it out as we go," he said, grunting as he tugged on the corner of the contour sheet. "And if we do it right, that should be half the fun."

HORRY HOVERED a few inches above the grand piano in the music room as Lucky paced the carpet, his tail flicking, his ears flat against his head.

"Out. I've got to bust out of stir. The screws, the lousy food. Go get some sheets and tie them together for me."

"Ha! What's the matter, Lucky?" Horry asked. "Do you feel like you're in Al-*cat*-traz?"

"Not funny. You hear me, Horry? I need *out*. You have to help me, I'm going crazy here. I've got to make my rounds. I've got to show myself. And the calico—she'll be in heat in just a couple of days. There's a new tomcat about a mile from here. I know he's thinking he'll take over my territory. I've got to get out."

"And you've got to stay away from—"

"Don't remind me. I've been hiding out in here all morning, until I figured they could slam the top of the piano down on me and call it an accident." Lucky paced some more, stopped. "And a fat lot of help you've been. What have you been doing, because you sure haven't been here, holding my paw."

Horry lowered his head. "Trying to scare Lily. She stopped defacing my frogs and flamingos—ran out of black paint, thank goodness—but now she's sneaking around with a big green plastic bag, stealing all my toys. I never knew she disliked them. She already put one whole bag in the garbage. My Power Rangers. Jeff, from *The Wiggles*. He was always my favorite. My entire collection of Pokémon cards, not that they're not worthless now. I couldn't even sell them on eBay last year. Oh, and the duck. Duck's gone. I tell you, she goes within five feet of Bupkus, and there's going to be hell to pay. I *can* be dangerous."

"You're a ghost. You can't do anything. You started all of this, and now you can't do anything. You know what, Horry? I'm outta here, washing my paws of you, this whole place. Just as soon as I can figure out *how*."

AS IT WOULD APPEAR Lily had gone on strike, Darcie drove into town after leaving Cameron to make the bed, or not make it, although a part of her secretly hoped he would.

She'd shopped a little, at a pet store, at a local nursery, then picked up pizzas, steak sandwiches, French fries, and a half-dozen garlic bread knots, figuring that would make a decent lunch for everyone. Later, after the memorial service, she could look through the microwave cookbook and come up with something for dinner.

Cameron had taken one of the steak sandwiches—with everything, plus extra hot peppers, just the way she knew he liked it—and two slices of pizza, carrying them back outside, mumbling something about a caulking gun. The mumbling ended in a moan when she called after him that he might soon want to think about showering and dressing, as the memorial service was scheduled for two o'clock.

She watched him go, already missing him. He'd stripped to just his shorts, sneakers without socks, his red Phillies hat, worn backward, and a white T-shirt shoved half in and half out of one back pocket, a cold can of soda in the other one. His skin was getting tanned, his hat had pushed his hair front into silly, adorable bangs, and he smelled of sun and grass and man-at-work.

Jumping the man's bones was becoming more and more of a necessity.

He was so sweet when he was worrying about the house. Her house. Maybe their house?

"You want to run after him and take a great big bite, don't you, honey?"

Darcie jumped slightly, turning to see Pookie grinning at her from the kitchen doorway. "Oh, hi. I didn't see you."

"Because you only have eyes for him, right?" Pookie said, padding into the kitchen on bare feet, her toes propped apart by cotton balls, her nails painted poor-circulation blue. "I smelled the pizza from upstairs. I'm famished. This keeping myself gorgeous isn't easy, you know. I've been at it for hours."

Darcie looked at Pookie. At her white-blond hair that no longer showed dark roots, at her freshly painted blue fingernails, her freshly makeup-slathered face. The woman was dressed in a knee-length red satin robe cinched tight at her waist and, Darcie was pretty sure, nothing else. "I'm sure Uncle Edwin appreciates all your efforts."

Pookie gave a limp-wristed wave of her hand as she rummaged in the French fries, picked up a dark one. "Oh, they do, they do. I had one once who used to paint my toenails for me, but he went home to his wife. I don't miss him a bit, but I do miss the pedicures. What's wrapped up in here? Oh! Cheese steak! They don't make these in the Bahamas, let me tell you that."

"The Bahamas?" Darcie got Pookie a soda from the fridge and sat down across from her at the table. "So that's where you and Uncle Edwin were when you learned about Uncle Horry. I thought you were overseas."

"Mmmmf…mmmf…" Pookie mumbled, nodding emphatically as she chewed on a large bite of cheese steak. "Oh, heaven, pure heaven. Yes, that's where we were. Monaco. And then a quick stop in the Bahamas, on our way here. Touring, you know. Poobie doesn't like staying long in one place. I'll bet we'll be out of here as soon as his allowance shows up. It should have been here by now, but it was already on its way to Monaco when we were heading here. The Bahamas just about cleaned him out. Where's the salt?"

"I'll get it," Darcie said as Pookie, careful not to smear her fingernails, nudged a bit of chipped steak back in her mouth. Darcie was fascinated, in spite of herself. She could watch this woman for hours; Pookie was so open, so free, so without inhibitions. She put the salt shaker down in front of the woman. "How long have you and Uncle Edwin been…um…together?"

"Bed buddies, you mean?" Pookie smiled as she turned a piece of pizza nearly white with salt, then held the shaker, stared into the middle distance. "Let me see. I was in Branson, with Georgie—that's in Missouri. Then Vegas, with Tommy. Then—January? Yes, that's it, January. I took one look, and had to have him. You know how it is? Poobie-bear is the *bomb.*"

Darcie bit on the insides of her cheeks, swallowed with some difficulty. "Uncle Edwin? He's the bomb?"

"Oh, yes. Older men? They're *so* grateful, if you know what I mean? Gotta go. My curlers must be hot by now. I'll take this upstairs to finish it. And the rest of the pizza, if you don't mind? Poobie's in the tub, but I know he'll want some. Well, men always want *some,* if you know what I mean, but all he's getting is pizza. We're leaving for Atlantic City as soon as the memorial service is over. Don't bother to keep a light on for us, we won't be back until tomorrow afternoon."

Darcie got to her feet. "You're going to the casinos?"

"Not half so posh as Monaco, I know, but a slot machine's a slot machine. What we won in Monaco we left in the slots in the Bahamas, but I know my luck's about to turn. Oh, and in case I don't get to see him? Thank your Cameron for the...well, he'll know."

"He will?" Darcie took one last bite of steak sandwich, then headed for the side of the house. "Cameron? Cam, where are you?"

"Under here. I was hoping you'd show up—ow! Damn it, stop that!"

"Who are you talking to?" Darcie got down on her knees in front of the gaping opening under the porch. Tipping her head, she could see the soles of his sneakers about ten feet away, but not much else. "What are you doing? Did you put your shirt on, at least, before you went crawling in there?"

"No. Need it. Just…just hang on. Stay there, and get ready for—son of a—!"

"Cam? What's—" But he was coming toward her now, sort of wiggling himself toward her, feetfirst, until at last she could see the white of his T-shirt.

The next thing she knew, Cameron was out from beneath the porch, holding onto a T-shirt stuffed with yowling, wriggling cat.

"Here—reach for the halter. I got the halter on him, got him connected to the leash you tied around the old hitching post—and the next thing I knew, he was running past me."

"Oh, Lucky," Darcie said, finding the blue harness. "I've got it," she said, and Cameron let go.

Lucky's one green and one yellow eye both seemed to glow red as he worked his head out from the tangled T-shirt. He yowled at Darcie.

"Damn cat," Cameron said, sort of working his shoulders as he brushed dirt from his arms, tried to get a look at his own back. "You've got a good hold on him?"

"He won't get away. This harness is pretty strong. Oh, but look, Cam—the metal loop thing you use to connect the leash to? It's all bent out of shape. Do you think Lucky could really…?"

"Pull hard enough to bend metal? That's a rhetorical question, right?" He got to his feet. "Just hold on to him, Darc, and I'll go get the *c-a-g-e*."

Darcie was still kneeling on the grass, Lucky's body pushed between her thighs, both her hands wrapped around the harness—one at the neck, one at the second strap that went around the cat's belly. "You're spelling cage?"

Lucky yowled. Lucky hissed. Lucky leaped a good foot into the air with Darcie still hanging on with both hands.

"Oh, that's it," Cameron said, and a minute later Lucky, wrapped cocoonlike inside the T-shirt, was deposited in the study, the door closed behind him.

Darcie looked at Cameron.

Cameron looked at Darcie.

"You're a mess," they said at the same time.

"We both need showers," Darcie pointed out as they made their way toward the stairs.

"True," Cameron agreed. "But do we need *two* showers?"

Darcie paused at the top of the stairs. "We've got to get ready for the memorial service, remember? Besides, I've got questions."

"You already know how Lucky got out. I was feeling sorry for the miserable bastard and thought we'd try out the halter and leash you picked up for him. Last favor I do that cat, let me tell you. What else?"

Darcie looked down the hall, then pulled Cameron into her bedroom. "Uncle Edwin and Pookie are leaving after the memorial service. They're going to the shore—to the casinos. And you gave them the money to go, didn't you?"

"They're going to stay overnight, not be back until late tomorrow afternoon."

"And that's your reason?"

His grin curled her toes. "I needed a better one?"

"But we…we've decided to—I mean, not that it isn't a…a *lovely* idea—"

"Darcie. Babe. Stop it. I think we need an evening alone, that's all. You. Me. The two of us."

"To talk."

"Absolutely."

Panic? Fear? Anticipation? Something. Definitely something—and anticipation pretty much fit how she felt. "Maybe we can go out to dinner first? Then come back here and…talk."

"Leave Lily with Lucky? No, not a good idea, not while I'm feeling this paranoid. We'll order in."

Darcie nodded. "And then we'll…talk."

"Talk." Cameron kissed her forehead. "Lots of talking. If we're really good we may talk all night."

She giggled as he smiled at her, then sort of backed himself out of the room….

CHAPTER THIRTEEN

CAMERON FIGURED this time he'd gotten it right, choosing casual slacks and a light blue dress shirt, sans tie, for the memorial service, and then realized he'd packed his black dress shoes, but had left them in the trunk of his car.

His mind was on the memorial service, at least some of it. The majority of his mind was on waving goodbye to Poobie and Pookie, so that he and Darcie could be alone. Alone. Blessedly alone.

He was rudely shocked out of his fairly erotic daydream when he stepped onto the porch to hear: "Not quite two weeks in suburbia, and that's your idea of a fashion statement? But I think it's white socks with black shoes, not black socks with white sneakers. Then again, don't quote me on that, I could be wrong. Not as wrong as those sneakers, but wrong."

"Doug?"

"Last time I checked, yes. Hello."

Amazing. There he was, all more than six feet of Doug Llewellyn; his longish black hair not moving at all in what was a pretty stiff breeze. His gray eyes hidden behind dark glasses, his Armani suit clinging to his body in gratitude. The man was *GQ,* but with more style. Seeing Doug Llewellyn voluntarily in suburbia was about on a par with a penguin sighting in Miami.

"And hello to you, too." Cameron held up his car keys. "Forgot my shoes in the trunk," he said, heading for his car. "What happened? Philadelphia announced a city-wide casual-dress day, and you've evacuated?"

"Not quite. But *Shee*-la wants your input on a few changes I've made in the pool plan. I'm insulted, definitely, but it seemed like a good excuse to come check up on you. Last time I saw you, you were not a happy man. So? Should I have brought a bottle of scotch? Or have you two worked it out?"

Leaning against the rear bumper for balance, Cameron pulled off his sneakers, tossed them in the trunk and slid on his shoes. "Not now, Doug. We're making some progress, and I don't want to jinx it. What kind of changes? Are those the plans?"

Doug looked at the cardboard tube in his left hand. "Now you want me to comment on the obvious?" He turned his attention to the house. "I've been standing out here, trying to figure this place out, for about five minutes now. Nothing you've ever said has done it justice. Let me guess. Uncle Horry was color-blind?"

Cameron closed the trunk. "Good thought. But, no, I don't think so. The pink matches the flamingos, and if you tell me you didn't notice them, or the frogs, I won't believe you."

"Oh, I noticed. Nice sound effects. Money doesn't buy good taste, does it? And, speaking of *Shee*-la…"

"Bad?"

"Excruciatingly bad. She's decided the addition should be modern, like their new beach house in Avalon. Which, before you ask, was a four-million-dollar project we did *not* get. Thank God."

Cameron grinned at his friend and partner. "You know, only a guy who was born with a full set of silver spoons in his mouth could say something like that, could afford so much artistic sensibility."

"I've brought photos she gave me. See the beach house, then tell me about my artistic sensibility. Place looks like a pregnant Tinkertoy. One good thing, she's decided I'm not her type. She's chasing the interior decorator she hired to work along with us. *Ralph.*"

"Poor Ralph. You know, Doug, the more you tell me, the less bummed I am over not handling the project. A modern addition on a fieldstone colonial built in 1812? Let me see the plans."

"Later. And they're minor changes. When we started to excavate, we found an old foundation, about fifty feet from the house. Springhouse, I'm figuring, so I decided to reconstruct it on the same footprint, and incorporate it into the overall design. No biggie. Fortunately, the guy writing the checks agrees with me. Just tell me more about this place. And then tell me how you can stand those frogs."

Cameron motioned for Doug to follow him down the drive, to the first frog. "How do you like the bull's-eyes?"

"Saw them. The paint looks fresh. Your creation?"

"Therapy," Cameron said, turning to look back at the house.

"Sure, you could try that. I think our health insurance covers it. And now you're painting mustaches on flamingos?"

"No, the housekeeper was doing that, but she ran out of black paint. Mine was therapy, hers, I'm pretty sure, are in the way of revenge. But, the artwork to one side, what do you think of the house? Fantastic, isn't it?"

Cameron watched as his friend and partner visually examined the front of the house, then walked toward the side where he'd been pulling off the decorative lattice.

"I see you've been busy."

"The place needs some repair. But it's got great bones, Doug."

Doug nodded. "That it does. Victorian, definitely, in the Gothic Revival mode. Those elaborate bargeboards, the gingerbread. Reminds me a lot of Stephen Decatur Button."

"You really think so? That would put the house in the late 1800s. I think that fits."

"Button designed homes like this for a lot of years. My favorites are in Cape May. A lot of those have been fully restored, several with some pretty elaborate paint choices."

"You know, I forgot that. Darcie and I could drive down to the shore, tour Cape May, take notes. We're going to paint, you understand."

"Ah, then it's not true. Love isn't blind." Doug hunkered down, carefully hitching up his pants legs at the knee, and peered into the darkness under the raised porch. "What have we here?"

"You name it, it's there. If we'd been called in on this house, we'd be taking out our calculators about now, figuring our profits."

Doug straightened, headed for the front of the house once more. "But we're not, are we? You're going to do this on your own. Don't deny it, Cam, I can see it in your eyes. May I volunteer my services? With the inspection, the plans, not the work. But you knew that."

"I'd be honored. I'm already considering adding some closets, working in another bathroom downstairs, a few other things," Cameron said, taking his sneakers out of the trunk and slamming it shut. "Hey, how about a tour of the place? A tour, some talk about a few other ideas I've had...and a memorial service. You're dressed for it."

Doug lowered his sunglasses a fraction and looked at Cameron over top the lenses. "You're kidding. Shouldn't the funeral have been last week?"

"The cremation was last week. Horry didn't want a fuss, but his half brother showed up a couple of days ago, and he expects a memorial service. Nothing fancy, just a small gathering in Horry's study. I'm saying a few words."

"*You* are." Doug grinned. "You know, that's almost enough to make me say yes. But not quite. Not unless there's going to be a chorus line." The screen door slammed and he turned to look up at the porch. "My God," he said, "I need darker sunglasses. What is that?"

Cameron knew he didn't even have to look. "My bet is that's your chorus line," Cameron said. He looked.

"Yup, Pookie-bear. That, I think it's safe to say, is her idea of the perfect all-day outfit, one that takes you straight from funerals to casinos."

"I never realized I lead such a dull life. Introduce me," Doug said, leading the way to the porch, one hand held out in front of him. "Madam, good afternoon. What a vision you are."

Cameron followed, shaking his head. Well, at least she was wearing black. The parts of Pookie that were covered in rhinestone-decorated black satin, that is—which weren't a lot. The Hope Diamond was in full view, as were most of Pookie's stick-thin thighs; from the knees down, she was wrapped in black patent leather high-heeled boots. With silver spurs. Big hair, big boobs, skinny everything else. She looked like Dolly Parton on Slim-Fast.

Pookie, to Cameron's dismay, giggled and limply held out her hand, which, to Cameron's shock, Doug bent over without hesitation. When you got right down to it, Doug really was a good guy.

"Pookie," he said, "please allow me to introduce to you my business partner, Douglas Llewellyn. Doug—Pookie."

"Charmed, madam," Doug said, stepping back.

"Ooouu, you look good enough to eat, don't you?" Pookie said, winking at Doug. "Are you here for the memorial service?"

"Doug's here to see me about some business," Cameron said. "I'm afraid he's already told me he can't—"

"I would be delighted, Pookie," Doug said quickly. "I never met Mr. Willikins, but I do believe I'm getting to know him better by the moment."

Pookie giggled, not a pleasant thing to hear in a fifty-something woman with a diamond stuck in her navel. "I'll just go tell Poobie. He's been worrying that there aren't enough of us."

As Pookie toddled back into the house, Cameron leaned against one of the porch posts. "That's not the housekeeper, Doug, if that's what you were thinking. That's Uncle Edwin's girlfriend. Lily's the housekeeper, Horry's former bed partner. We're pretty sure Lily thought she'd inherit everything, so if you see any spit-balls being shot at Horry's urn during the service, you'll know who they came from."

"Okay. It sounds like I'm not going to know the players without a scorecard. How about you get us both some iced tea or water or something, and then you fill me in."

"All right, that sounds reasonable," Cameron said, already heading for the door. "I'll tell you about Poobie and Pookie and Humbolt. How we've put Lucky into protective custody until the month is up. Oh, and about Horry maybe being a ghost now. You might want to hear about that, too."

"Make that two cold beers," Doug called after him.

DARCIE STOOD behind Horry's desk, rubbing her hands together as she surveyed the scene in front of her. She had enough chairs, except that there were so few chairs, so few people coming here to talk about her uncle.

It was nice of Doug to agree to stay, although the man was looking a little too amused to suit the expected solemn tone of the service.

"And that's what's wrong!" Darcie slapped her palm to her forehead as the realization hit her. "Everything about this is *wrong.*"

She sprang into action. Down came the black crepe bunting she'd hung at the bay window behind the desk. She opened the drapes, letting in the afternoon sunlight.

She ran to the butler's pantry and grabbed one of the neatly pressed tablecloths she'd seen hanging in the long closet: the blue one, with the Looney Tunes motif.

Back in the study, she cleared Horry's desk, then covered it with the cloth. And there they were—Bugs, Daffy, Porky, Elmer: "My name is Elmer Fudd and I own a mansion and a yacht." Uncle Horry used to repeat that line to her all the time.

Darcie giggled, worried if it was a hysterical giggle, but then got back to work. Solemnly, and praying she wouldn't trip or something, she took down the gilt urn and placed it smack in the center of the desk.

Now all she needed were a few of Uncle Horry's friends.

She headed for the foyer to get the duck. It wasn't there. Okay, maybe it broke, and she hadn't realized it was missing. "The mouse!" She went looking for the mouse. Not there. The hula-girl lamp. Gone. Horry's Dora the Explorer sing-along cassette player. Also among the missing.

The gorilla that played the cymbals—that had been sitting on a table beside the baby grand piano, *that* she was sure of. But the table was bare.

The clown on roller skates. The slightly naughty dancing teddy bear. The talking Jeff doll from *The Wiggles.*

Not here, not here, not here.

"Lily?" Darcie called out, entering the kitchen, to find the woman dunking a teabag in a large white mug. "Where are all of Uncle Horry's toys?"

"Why?" she said bitterly. "He wants to play with one of them?"

Darcie took a step back. Lily was getting meaner by the day. "No, I want them for the memorial service. Did you pack them away?"

Lily sniffed. "You could say that. I have to live here, you know, and I refuse to live one more day with those stupid toys. They're out behind the garages, waiting for the garbage man." She looked up at the wall clock. "Unless he showed up already."

"Who gave you permission to— What *right* did you have to— Oh, God, I hear a truck!"

Darcie flew out of the kitchen, kicked off her heels, and ran for the garages. "Wait! Wait!"

EDWIN WILLIKINS joined Cameron and Doug on the front porch just as Cameron had finished a fairly sheepish explanation of ghostly occurrences he'd begun to attribute to Horry and was waiting for Doug's response.

Looking on Edwin as a rescue boat arriving just before the shark could open its mouth, Cameron all but leaped to his feet to introduce the two men.

"Forgive the tuxedo, gentlemen," Edwin said. "I'm afraid it's the only black I brought with me."

Cameron took in the wide lapels, the satin stripes down the outside of the legs, the black-and-silver-tapestry vest, the standup collar shirt with a black, choke-me bow tie. "You always travel with a tuxedo, Edwin?"

Edwin frowned. "Why, of course," he said—the "doesn't everyone?" only implied. "But this one's my favorite. Lots of pockets, see?" He then proceeded to show off the pockets, those hidden inside the jacket, the vest. He stuck his hands into the outside pockets, and came up with three flat, yellow-banded circles that looked very much like— "Well, would you look at that? Oh well, I'll cash them in if I ever get back to Monaco."

Doug, who had been sipping from his beer can while this was all going on, leaned closer to Cameron. "I don't know if the colors are standard everywhere, but those, my friend, could be one-thousand-dollar chips."

"You're kidding," Cameron said quietly, watching as Edwin casually slipped the chips back in his pocket, then ran to open the screen door for Pookie. "And he hit me up for cash? Something isn't making sense here."

"Besides you, you mean," Doug said, watching as Edwin and Pookie made a production number out of leaning their faces toward each other, puckering up and carefully kissing each other's lips. "She really calls him Poobie? You know, she looks like a gold digger—a little over the hill, but then, so is Poobie—but she seems genuinely fond of the guy. Yes?"

Cameron nodded. "I don't think she knows Edwin could be out to get rid of Lucky, no, if that's what you're asking. Then again, Darcie is convinced her uncle is innocent of any ulterior motives. To tell you the truth, I am beginning to think I overreacted when Lucky got hurt and I started seeing bogeymen everywhere."

"And ghosts everywhere else."

"Only one ghost, and I told you, I'm not married to the idea. Ah, here comes Humbolt. At the reading of the will, I wore a suit, and he showed up in plaid golf pants, so I figured what I'm wearing today strikes a happy medium. Or I did, until you showed up in the Armani and Edwin in the tux."

"Also an Armani, or didn't you notice? About ten years old, but a very distinctive cut. I didn't know you worried about being overdressed or underdressed, Cam. It's a whole new side of you."

"Actually, I was just trying to go one up on Humbolt. I don't like the guy."

"Nice wheels, though I wouldn't have gone for the red. Too desperate."

"Humbolt," Cameron said as the attorney climbed the stairs in his lime-green golf shirt and green-yellow-and-pink-plaid slacks—ha! got him! Making quick work of the introductions, he then asked everyone to come inside, as Darcie had asked that they begin the memorial service at two o'clock.

The sooner the service began, the sooner it would be over, the sooner Poobie and Pookie would be on their way to Atlantic City, the sooner he and Darcie would be alone…

…good God!

Cameron stood just inside the doorway of the study, amazed. Speechless.

The room was packed with toys. Horry's toys. Christmas elves and reindeer and Santas to the left; bunnies and ducks and pink and blue baby chicks to the right. Everything else on the desk, including the guest of honor.

Dining room chairs were lined up in two short rows, and Cameron motioned for Doug to precede him into the longer second row, leaving the first for Darcie, Edwin and Poobie.

Doug sat down, hooked a thumb to his immediate left, said in suitably hushed tones, "Who's this?"

"Bupkus," Cameron said, trying to keep a straight face. "He's one of the mourners."

"I had to ask. That'll teach me. Where's the uncle?"

"In the big gold gilt urn on the desk. Right next to Buzz Lightyear."

"Who's—never mind, I don't want to know."

"Good choice. Okay, here comes Lily. And doesn't she look happy to be here."

Cameron watched as Lily, carrying her teacup, looked toward the desk, sniffed, then pulled a chair from the second row, moving it away from the others, and sat down.

"*That's* the bed partner? She's...um, she's—"

"Yeah, I know," Cameron said. "And *that's* Lucky."

Both he and Doug watched as Lucky sauntered into the room with the grace of a well-fed tiger ignoring a field of gazelles, then singled out Pookie in the front row and began winding himself around her boot-clad ankles.

Pookie sneezed, and Cameron saw her shoot out her right foot, none-to-gently nudging Lucky in the gut. The cat meowed, looked at Cameron, meowed again.

"It's talking to you," Doug told him. "Does it run on batteries, too, or is that the real thing?"

"Funny. Oh, here comes Darcie. I'll let her know we're ready."

Cameron got to Darcie before anyone else saw her, took hold of her elbow and pulled her back into the hallway. "I adore you," he said with some feeling, then kissed her, kissed her until he felt her arms wrapping around his shoulders and she kissed him back.

"What…what was that for?"

"That was for that room in there. It's perfect. Doug's suitably impressed. I sat him next to Bupkus. Nice of you to include him, by the way."

Darcie peeked into the study, then grinned at Cameron. "What did he say?"

"Bupkus? You know how it is, Darc. Bupkus doesn't talk much."

"No, I meant—oh, Cameron, do you really think I did the right thing? Uncle Horry didn't want anything, but this seems…this seems to work. As long as nobody gets all solemn or anything."

"I've already seen the rest of the guests, babe. I'm pretty sure you don't have to worry about that. Uh-oh, Edwin's getting up. I think we've started."

Cameron took Darcie's hand and led her to her seat beside Pookie, then rejoined Doug, just as Edwin stepped behind the desk.

Edwin coughed into his hand, adjusted his cuffs and then picked up the urn, holding it in front of his face. "I planned to say a prayer, but something else has come to mind. Something from the great Bard himself. 'Alas, poor Yorick!—I knew him, Horatio; a fellow of some infinite jest, of most excellent fancy; he hath borne me on his back a thousand times.' Well, enough of that. Let's get to the good part." He hefted the urn higher. "'Where be your gibes now? your gambols? your songs? your flashes of merriment, that were wont to set the table on a roar?'"

He put down the urn and smiled at the assembled and fairly astonished, company. "Sorry. I've always wanted to do that. *Hamlet,* you know. But in truth, alas, poor Horry, I knew him not, my friends. I would have liked him, I'm sure of that, but I didn't know him." He looked at the toys. "These were all his?"

Darcie got to her feet, to stand beside her uncle. "Yes, these are all Uncle Horry's. He loved toys…gadgets."

"She's not kidding. You should see his bedroom," Cameron whispered to Doug, then quickly added, "on second thought, no, you shouldn't."

Attorney Humbolt got to his feet, motioned for Edwin to sit down and let him speak.

"Hecuba Willikins was a fine man. An honest man. He paid his bills on time. A man of pure heart and with a child's curiosity." He pointed to Lucky, who had managed to stretch out across the desk without knocking over a single toy. "And he loved this cat. If anything—*anything*—happens to this cat, I will come down on you all like thunder."

"Well, I'll be damned," Cameron said to no one in particular. "That almost sounds like the man cares."

Humbolt glanced at his watch, then looked around the room at the small gathering. "All right. Tee time in less than an hour. So that's it. Amen, may he rest in peace. Gotta go."

"A little," Cameron added as Humbolt left the room. "He might have cared a little."

"Well, that was rude, wasn't it?" Pookie said, having turned in her chair to watch the lawyer go, then got to her feet, waved at Edwin. "Poobie? May I be excused? The limo will be here in ten minutes, and I still have to go tinkle."

Doug looked at his watch. "That's it? That's the memorial service? I'm pretty sure I clocked it at four minutes."

"I know. Pitiful, isn't it? Darcie?" Cameron asked. "Did you want to speak?"

She shook her head. "No, I think Uncle Horry was right. I'd really like to remember him the way I last saw him. Happy. He would want us to remember him in our hearts, not give speeches about him."

"Well, I've got something to say!"

Cameron watched as Lily advanced none too steadily on the desk, Edwin stepping back so as not to be trampled.

Lily rested her palms on the edge of the desk and leaned forward, looking around the room. "See this? Mine. Everything else? Mine. I *babysat* this man here for thirty years. Thirty years! Polished his furniture. Washed his windows. Turned his dirty socks right side out. Cooked his meals. Put up with his damn toys. And for what? So I could live here until I die, cleaning this house, washing these windows, cooking meals? No! This is mine! I *earned* it. You hear me, Horry?" she yelled, going nose to lid with the urn. "I *loathe* you, Horry Willikins. And I hate these stupid *toys*!"

Darcie reached for Lily, but wasn't quick enough, as the housekeeper lifted her fists, then brought them down hard on the desktop.

Now, it would seem that Horry's collection of toys most fascinated him because they moved. They made noise. Many of them, most of them, were sound activated…and the ones that hadn't been had been modified by Horry himself.

Lily's desk banging, therefore, set a chorus of toys into motion and sound.

The duck quacked.

The monkey banged his cymbals.

Jeff from *The Wiggles* began playing: "Wake up, Jeff…"

The clown roller-skated off the edge of the desk.

Chicks cheeped. Santas ho-ho'd. On the corner of the desk, a bunny laid an egg.

The teddy bear suggested, "Come on, honey, let's hibernate."

And, in the midst of it all, Lucky stood up, yawned, stretched, and with great dignity, proved that salmon and his digestive system didn't always get along. It was a silent killer that was unleashed, but deadly, and everyone evacuated the room before the last chick cheeped.

Curled up on the window seat, an invisible Horry Willikins laughed until invisible tears ran down his invisible cheeks. "Now *that's* what I call a send-off!"

DARCIE STOOD ON TIPTOE on the front porch and kissed Doug's cheek. "Thank you so much for staying for the...the service." She winced. "Terrible, wasn't it?"

"Not to me, no," Doug told her, squeezing her hands. "As a matter of fact, consider yourself hired to arrange this year's office Christmas party."

"Coming through, coming through!" Pookie warned as she exploded from the house in her distinctive hands-wagging totter. "Hurry, Poobie, the limo's here," she called back through the screen door.

Cameron watched as Edwin used his elbow to push open the screen door, his arms loaded with two leather suitcases and a suit bag. He held the door, offered to take one of the suitcases. "I thought you were only staying overnight?"

"These are Pookie's," Edwin told him. "She needs her beauty potions."

"And yet only two suitcases," Doug said quietly as Edwin handed off the suitcases to the limo driver. "I would have thought five, minimum."

Darcie giggled, then told him he wasn't nice. "And now, if you'll excuse me? I really think I should check on Lily. She really doesn't look well, does she?"

"If I were lacing my tea with hundred proof, I'd look pretty bad, too," Cameron told her. "I checked the cup after she ran out. But it's pretty clear why she stuck around for thirty years, and it wasn't true love. She really did expect to inherit everything."

"I know." Darcie sighed. "Maybe I won't go see how she's doing. But I will go clean up the study. I don't want her near Uncle Horry's toys again."

Cameron watched her go, then walked Doug to his car. "Yeah, well, partner, can't say we don't know how to entertain here at Shangri-La. Do you want me to look at those plans now?"

"No, you've got enough problems." Doug looked up at the house again. "Can't you just hire someone to take care of this?"

"I could, I suppose, but then Lucky would have to sign the checks."

"Oh, right, I forgot about that," Doug said, sliding behind the wheel of his car. "God. So this is what love does to a man, huh? Good thing I'm immune."

Cameron held on to the open door. "Doug? Be honest with me here, okay? Do you think I proposed to Darcie because I love her, or because she just happened to be around when I decided to do the marriage thing?"

"Well, that one came out of left field, didn't it? You mean, you met Darcie at the right time? Maybe even saw this monstrosity at the right time? Subconsciously she, and this place you had to be pretty sure would be hers someday, kind of blended into a good idea?"

"Yeah. That."

"Cameron, if you were just wanting to get married, settle down—God, just saying that gives me the shivers—you'd be married to someone else by now. Instead, you've spent the last nine months moping and sighing and generally being a pain in my ass. Don't think too much, old friend—it only complicates things."

Cameron grinned. "Thanks. I think." He closed the car door, then stood and watched and listened as Doug drove off down the drive, following the limo.

"The limo. How much did I pay for that limo?" he asked himself, then wandered off to skim the pool and check on the hot tub. Because he had plans.

Oh, yes. Definite plans.

HORRY WATCHED as Darcie loaded toys into green plastic garbage bags, stopping every once in a while to sniff, to smile, to wipe her eyes.

"She's such a good girl," he told Lucky, who had cornered one of the fuzzy little yellow chicks and was holding it down with his front paws. "You do know that's not real, right?"

"I know. I like it. Hey, I can be a cat if I want to, you know. There's no law against it."

"No, I suppose not. I checked on Lily—she's passed out on her bed, snoring like a drunken sailor. She's snapped, hasn't she?"

Lucky rolled over, taking the chick with him. "What was your first clue, Sherlock?"

"Oh, I don't know why I talk to you," Horry said, floating over to sit down beside Bupkus, who was the lone remaining mourner. "Or you."

Darcie left the room, returning a minute later with a few large boxes for the lighted reindeer.

"Busy, busy, and paying absolutely no attention to the cute little kitty innocently playing with the chick," Lucky mind-talked around the chick in his mouth. "Horry, follow me. It's time I make a break for it."

Horry floated after the cat, who was already halfway to the foyer. "You can't do this, Lucky. You're safe right now. And you heard Humbolt. Down like thunder, he said. Oh, I wish I'd never written that will. Stupid! Stupid, stupid, stupid!"

Lucky pushed at the screen door with his head, knowing just where to push to get the latch to slip. "Oh, come on, Horry, take a walk with me while I check the perimeter. Cool your brains."

"But I…you really shouldn't…oh, okay, if you promise to come back home before dark. Maybe, with our heads clearer, we can come up with a plan? Some way I can warn Cameron?"

Lucky walked down the drive, Horry following, and the frogs *ribbit-ribbited* as they went.

CHAPTER FOURTEEN

ONE THING OFTEN LEADS to another and then another. At least, that's how it worked for Darcie when she returned the cymbal-banging monkey to its accustomed perch on a table beside the baby grand piano in the music room, because she needed *something* of Uncle Horry to be where she could look at it, smile at it, from time to time.

She'd stood back, admired the effect, then stepped forward, moved the monkey an inch to the right, stood back again, stepped forward and placed the monkey on top of the piano. Stood back, admired the effect.

"Better," she told herself.

Encouraged by this small victory, Darcie leveled a measuring look on the arrangement of sofa and two flanking chairs. A rather formal arrangement, and anyone sitting on the love seat in front of the window would have to have X-ray eyes in order to see through the piano to anyone sitting on the couch. And the lighting was really inconvenient for anyone who might want to curl up in here with a good book. And should the piano really be facing that way, with the open end visible to everyone instead of the beautiful wood of the raised top. What did they call the top of a grand piano, anyway?

And why was she even thinking about this, when all her life she had been the sort who adapted to her surroundings, rather than adapting her surroundings to her? She was pretty sure she'd not so much as moved a vase in either of her furnished apartments, and God forbid she touched anything in her parents' house, even in her own room.

But she wasn't in her parents' house, was she? She wasn't in a furnished studio apartment. She wasn't even in Cameron's apartment. This was Shangri-La, and this, bless her Uncle Horry, was soon to become *hers*.

Darcie felt almost giddy.

An hour later, breathing heavily after pushing the love seat to the west wall, changing places with a long table that now sat in front of the bay window, Darcie stood in the middle of the room, admiring her work.

The heavy velvet draperies were in a heap on the floor, and only the rather lovely lace sheers still hung at the window, really lightening the mood of the room.

"The *space,*" she reminded herself. "Rooms are called spaces now. Which is fairly ridiculous."

All she needed to do now was rearrange the lamps, rehang the landscape so it was centered over the love seat, and turn the piano around. That one could wait for Cameron's help.

But the music room did look better. More inviting. More…more *her.*

Darcie smiled.

More her? Yes. Yes! More *her.*

"Oh, wow, this is probably some sort of epiphany,"

she said, hugging herself. "I had no idea I could do this, and *like* doing this."

Next up, the living room, or the Indian drawing room, as Uncle Horry had called it. She'd call it the living room; there would be no *spaces* in her house, only wonderful, lovely, welcoming *rooms.* And she already knew what had to go—the spinning wheel. It didn't fit with all the darker wood, the intricately carved wooden screen, the, she was pretty sure, Victorian couches. Neither did the elephant's foot table, but at least that had some character.

Tired, but marvelously excited to have learned something else about herself—she *did* have opinions of her own, damn it!—Darcie began stripping the yellowed lace doilies from the arms and backs of the couch and chair, planning to remove those and the draperies to the attic before moving on to tackle the living room.

"Just what do you think you're doing?"

Darcie turned, startled, to see Lily charging into the music room, murder in her eyes. She grabbed the doilies from Darcie and began placing them back on the furniture.

"I just took those off, Lily."

"And I'm just putting them back on! These doilies are here for a reason, missy. Hair oil, that stupid man insisting on eating potato chips in here and then wiping his greasy fingers on the arms of the chairs? I'll not have my couches ruined, do you hear me?"

"*Your* couches, Lily?" Darcie was trembling, and angry with herself for trembling.

"My couches, yes. Or did you vacuum them every week? And that table belongs over there. It has *always* been over there. Things should stay where they're put."

And Lily's just put you in your place. Come on, Darcie, that's what she's saying, and you know it. The question is, what are you going to do about it?

"I think the room looks better this way," Darcie said, wishing she could sound more emphatic. "The furnishings are formal, I'll give you that, but this arrangement is more…more friendly. I've already got some ideas for the living room, too."

Lily glared at her. "This is not your house. This is not your say-so."

"Right, Lily, you've got me there. It's Lucky's house, isn't it? At least for another few weeks. Then the chances are pretty good that it's mine. You will live here, Uncle Horry made that provision for you, but it will be my house. And there will be changes."

There. That sounded pretty firm.

The housekeeper's fingers closed around the doilies she held in each hand as she advanced on Darcie. "Don't count your chickens, missy," Lily said fiercely, then stomped out of the room, nearly knocking down Cameron.

"Whoa, what set her off? Hey, it looks nice in here. What did you do?"

Darcie took a deep, steadying breath, attempted a smile. "You really think so? It looks nice?"

Cameron walked around the room, inspecting it, then gave it his seal of approval. "Yeah. It's lighter, brighter.

If you don't mind a suggestion, I'd say we turn the piano around, but that's up to you."

"I thought it should be turned around, too," Darcie said, pushing the unpleasant interlude with Lily to the back of her mind. "What's the part of the piano that sticks up?"

He shrugged. "I don't know. The whole ball of wax is called the case, I think, but that's all I know. Is it in tune?"

He sat down at the keyboard and experimentally plinked on a few keys.

"I've always wanted to learn how to play," Darcie said, sitting down beside him on the bench. He looked good here, in this room, in this house. Like he belonged. "Did you ever have lessons?"

"Five years' worth," Cameron said, playing the scale—at least, Darcie thought it was the scale. "And I hated every minute of it, especially at Christmas, when my mother insisted I play 'Silent Night' for company. I've forgotten everything I learned. Piano lessons, by and large, probably shouldn't be wasted on kids who'd much rather be outside hitting a ball around."

Darcie leaned her head against his shoulder. "I never knew you took piano lessons. You learned how to work the pedals, and everything? Play 'Silent Night' for me, Cam. Please?"

He smiled at her, and Darcie's stomach did a small flip.

"I have a better idea. I'll teach you how to play 'Chopsticks.' That one I remember."

She sat up straight, nervous, eager, her hands held over the keys. "Show me."

He took hold of her right hand, moved it over what he informed her was middle C. "First lesson, raise your wrist a little. Good. Poise and posture, that's how I remember Mrs. Grimwald saying it. Now, just relax, and I'll play down an octave lower, and you follow along here." He looked at her. "Ready?"

HUMMING THE TUNE to "Chopsticks," and sounding almost as badly out of tune as the piano in the music room, Cameron made his way through the local supermarket, gathering everything he needed for their Night Alone. Night Sans Poobie and Pookie. Alone Night. Just The Two Of Us Night.

Talk night.

Talk night?

Yeah. Right. That was going to happen.

Not.

They were getting along fine. Great. Terrific. Even better than the first time.

Talking might ruin all of that.

Let the past stay in the past, that was his new motto. They'd started over, the day after the reading of Horry's will, and they were doing all right, better than all right. Whatever they'd had before had only gone underground for nine months, and it was back in full force now. With a bonus he hadn't expected. His passion was just as hot, but he liked this "getting to know ourselves better" experiment. He liked Darcie better. Bed was good, but wanting to be with that same person all day, all year, all of their years? That was special, and they had that now. He was sure of it.

Pittsburgh? That would work out.

Learning about each other? They had their whole lives for that one.

Like this afternoon, in the music room. That had been fantastic. More than fantastic. Just the two of them, sitting together, the smell of Darcie's freshly washed hair, the feel of her body close beside his as she bent over the piano, so adorably intent on learning the right notes. Nothing sexual—oh, okay, so he had thought about it. But he hadn't acted on his thoughts, deciding to enjoy the moment for what it was. Just two people, compatible. A couple. The *right* couple.

And a serious student. She tried so *hard.* Everything she did had to be perfect. It had taken him a while to get her to relax enough to laugh at her mistakes, to for God's sake stop *apologizing* for each mistake.

When he'd finally left her to run his secret errands, she was sitting by herself at the piano after discovering an ancient *Piano for Beginners* lesson book inside the bench, and was picking out middle C with an intensity that he was pretty sure would have had Mrs. Grimwald sobbing in ecstasy.

Cameron stopped humming. "She tries so hard," he said quietly as he reached for a pack of note paper. "Why does she always try so damn *hard?*"

Maybe they should talk. He'd said they'd talk. Promised they'd talk.

Maybe they should talk…

"Tomorrow morning," he told himself, and pushed the cart to the next aisle. "We've got a good thing going here right now, and I'm not about to screw it up with logic."

DARCIE WALKED OUT of her bathroom after her second shower of the day, still rubbing at her damp hair with a hand towel, to see a note on her bedspread.

She looked left and right, realized that wasn't doing her any good, didn't explain anything, and picked up the note.

Cameron's precise, block-print handwriting:

Who: Frau Blücher
What: outta here
Where: at the movies
When: ten minutes ago
Why: you have to ask?
How: blatant bribery
Continued on next note.

"Next note? Where?" She turned over the sheet of paper, grinned.

Who: you and me
What: dinner
Where: follow the clues
When: five minutes ago
Why: still asking questions?
How: see Where

"See where? Oh, see *Where.* Clues. Follow the clues." Darcie made a face, turned the paper over, and over again. Nothing. "What clues?"

And then she saw it. Her midnight-blue bathing suit was hanging from the doorknob to the hallway. On it was a small note: "Optional."

"Oh, yeah, right, in your dreams, Cameron Pierce," she said, crumpling the note. "And we *will* discuss exactly how you found this suit."

She dropped her towel and pulled on the suit, then returned to the bathroom to comb her hair, pull it into a damp ponytail. Lipstick, a little waterproof mascara. Frowned at what looked to be an addition to the crop of freckles she'd been sprouting since beginning the gardening. "You're about as sexy as Strawberry Shortcake. Okay. Next?"

Thinking it the obvious thing to do, she opened the door to the hallway, stepped out, and nearly tripped over the can of pineapple. And another note: "Sorry. No fresh ones available. Just consider it a clue."

"Pineapple? This is a clue? He's planning a luau?"

She picked up the can and moved on to the head of the stairs, where she found two gorgeous, cellophane-wrapped T-bone steaks. Raw.

"Okay, that's a relief. At least he's not roasting a pig on a spit."

Bottom of the stairs: a basket.

"Good thought," she said, depositing the can and the steaks in the basket, and headed down the hall toward the kitchen, picking up two foil-wrapped potatoes, four already shucked ears of corn and a bag of marshmallows along the way.

She found the bottle of wine, two glasses and a corkscrew on the kitchen table, along with another note: "Outside, take the first right, meet you at the second palm tree. Be there or be square."

"A luau beside the pool. Sort of," Darcie told herself, swinging the basket as she headed out onto the porch, then ran down to the grass, turned right and made a beeline for the fence-enclosed pool area.

She hadn't been in for a swim yet, but she had inspected the area, so she already knew that Uncle Horry had, once again, outdone himself.

The pool had been there for ages, and was a pretty standard in-ground pool, but the hot tub he'd added since her last visit was pure Uncle Horry.

Darcie pushed open the gate on the six-foot-high redwood fence that concealed the huge hot tub, which was mottled pink fiberglass with all the trimmings. Fake palm trees, complete with coconuts. A three-sided hut and actual straw roof surrounding the hot tub. A water feature sporting fake lily pads, equally fake water grasses, and a waterfall (that part, thankfully, was real). Even the koi were fake. A real (or not so real) maintenance-free slice of Shangri-La.

A glass-topped table fitted with a bamboo-looking base and matching chairs was already set for two, and over there, reading the manual for the enormous, shiny chrome propane grill that could possibly pull double duty as a control panel at NASA, stood Cameron. Her hero.

"I had no idea you could be...whimsical," she said, tapping him on his bare shoulder, for he wore only a pair of dark green swim trunks. "And you forgot the salad."

"Hi, babe," he said, a little distracted. "Salad's in the fridge. Fridge, in case you're wondering, is under here," he went on, opening one of the doors in the grill. "You wouldn't know how to work this thing, would you?"

"Not a clue." Darcie leaned closer, looked at the open booklet. "You don't know how to turn it on?"

"I don't know *where* to turn it on. This thing has more knobs than a pipe organ—and don't ask me why I said that because I don't have the damnedest idea. It just shot into my head." He lifted the domed lid, pressed a button rather obviously labeled *Ignition*. "Stand back, we may have lift off."

"You're doing the cooking?" Darcie asked, sitting in one of the two sling-back canvas chairs beside the hot tub. "And, no, that wasn't really a question. The question is—has the strain gotten to you, do you think? I mean, canned pineapple?"

"To go with the fake palm trees, the whole grass-hut motif Horry has going here. I thought it was inspired."

"I know. And I think you're cute."

Cameron laid the foil-wrapped potatoes on the grill top, followed them with the steaks, then turned to look at her. He wasn't smiling. "Darc...I had this all figured out. Poobie and Pookie gone, Lily gone, the two of us here, alone. Alone together. A little food, a little wine, a little hot tub, a little talk…a lot of not talking."

Okay, so she hadn't imagined it. Cameron was trying to be light and romantic and everything, but something, some indefinable something, was just a little… off. "I think it's a lovely idea, Cam. All of it. Very romantic."

"Yeah. Romantic. My thoughts exactly." He adjusted the heat on the grill, lowered the hood, then picked up two soda cans and sat down beside her. "And then the telephone rang."

"It did? I didn't hear the phone. I must have been in the shower."

"Probably. It doesn't matter. I took the message for you."

"The message for me. The phone call was for me?" What was wrong?

Cameron nodded. "A Clive Blackwell. He asked me to tell you that the Hastings merger is back on and he wants you to reconsider, come back, since you're the resident whiz kid on the project. He'll up your salary by twenty percent, dating from the day you quit, and throw in executive-dining-room privileges."

He looked at her, his gaze seemingly trying to bore right through her. "'The day you quit,' Darc."

Darcie closed her eyes, felt her stomach drop to her toes. "What…what did you tell him?"

"That I'd give you the message."

"Oh." She opened her eyes, looked past him, out over the clear blue water of the swimming pool. The one she could seriously consider drowning herself in. "I…I was going to tell you."

His voice was low, his tone mild. "Really? And when were you going to do that, Darc?"

"I…I might have, that first day. The day we learned about the will. But…but then we sort of…*argued*…and then I felt I had to prove my point and—oh, God. I should have told you. I've been wanting to tell you. There just didn't seem to be a good time, you know?"

Cameron stabbed his fingers through his hair. "I've been telling myself I could handle it. Find a way to handle it. It's five or six hours to Pittsburgh by car, about an hour if I fly. I could do it, work with you while you climb the corporate ladder, get the experience you want, set yourself up in a position where you could pretty much name your own job if you wanted, when you thought you were ready to come back here, get married. Maybe not five years, but I'd give it my best shot."

He looked at her. "Because it was important to you. Really important to you. And because you're important to me, I was ready to bend myself six ways from Sunday, to make things as easy as possible for you, for us."

"You'd have done that?" Darcie worked at the pull tab on the soda can, snapping it but not opening it. Staring at it. "I'm so sorry. I didn't know how to tell you. But now you know. Twice. I've failed twice in two tries. It…it's not something I wanted to tell anybody."

"Failed? What do you mean, failed? The guy was calling you to ask you to come back. You quit, right?"

She could smell the steaks, the aroma that would, at

any other time, have whetted her appetite. Right now, at this moment, she was pretty sure she'd never want to eat again.

"I wasn't fired, if that's what you mean. Okay, I did quit, right after Blackwell asked me if I wanted him to chase me around the desk."

There were silences that vibrated. This silence had echoes.

"He what?" Cameron asked at last. "And I was polite to the son of a bitch? Damn it, Darc, how does having an idiot for a boss turn into *your* failure? I don't get it."

She popped the can at last, took a few gulps of ice-cold soda. But she still didn't look at Cameron. "I met Blackwell at the second interview. I should have known, I should have seen something, picked up on a vibe, something. I should have done the same thing the first time, in Philly. I…I didn't do it right."

Cameron laid a hand on hers. "Don't look now, Darc, and please don't take this the wrong way, but I think one of your squirrels just fell off the wheel. Tell me, did you do your job right? Both jobs? Were you ever written up? Were you ever called on the carpet for screwing up?"

"No. But that's not the point. The point is—"

"The point is, some men are jerks when they see a beautiful woman, and a beautiful woman with brains just doesn't compute for these guys. There are more qualified applicants out there than there are good jobs, you know. They assume you know your looks sealed the deal, got you the job over everyone else, and they figure they know why you want the job—so you can fool around with, maybe even marry, the boss. Mostly, they figure you'll be grateful. *Really* grateful."

Now she looked at him. "No way."

"Wanna bet? I'm a man, remember. I talk to other men. Not all of them are princes. You just happened to have had the bad luck to run into two jerks. Now tell me you haven't been kicking yourself about the first job, about this last one. Tell me you don't think you're a failure."

"He really wanted me back?"

Cameron shrugged. "That's what he said. So you had to have been doing something right with that merger thing."

Darcie rolled her eyes. "I worked my tail off," she said, then put a hand to her mouth to stifle a giggle. "Bad choice of words, huh? I worked really hard, Cameron. I know Hastings's company cold. I know his soft spots, where he's vulnerable. I know exactly what it will take to get that company and none of its drawbacks."

"And?"

Her grin was so wide it almost hurt. This was it, the perfect time to tell Cameron what she'd discovered—that she'd already been pretty sure she was good at what she did, what she'd studied so hard to learn how to do...she just didn't want to do it anymore. Why had she thought it would be so difficult to tell Cameron what she'd discovered? Why had she thought he'd think she'd failed?

"Darc?"

She took a deep breath, let it out slowly. "And Clive Blackwell can just damn well go find himself another dumb schmuck who's willing to work sixty hours a week *and* weekends." She looked at Cameron. "I am *vindicated*. I'm good. I'm really, really good, damn it. I am."

"And you're gorgeous and sexy and definitely desirable," Cameron said, his smile slow and definitely seductive. "It's a curse for you, I know, but if you don't mind, I'll enjoy it anyway."

Darcie's eyes went wide.

"What? What's wrong? I—oh, shit!"

Darcie watched as Cameron threw back the lid to the grill, waving away the thick smoke that had the distinctive aroma of burnt T-bone.

"YOU KNOW," Darcie said, pausing to swallow, "if you ever wanted to give up being an architect, I think you've got a great future as a short-order cook. You make the *best* scrambled eggs."

"Yeah?" Cameron said, leering at her comically. "And you can fry my bacon anytime, babe."

"Stop that," she said, and blushed. He liked it when she blushed. He liked being able to make her blush.

"What's the matter, Darc? It's not dark out yet?"

"And you're insinuating...what?"

He picked up both their plates, stood, and headed for the sink...the sink still minus a garbage disposal, which he'd forgotten again, so he'd have to scoop a half-dozen eggshells out of the damn thing before he could wash the dishes. "I'm not insinuating anything. Darcie Reed doesn't make love until the sun goes down. That's all."

"I'm a prude. That's what you're saying?" she asked,

advancing on him with the skillet smeared with congealing bacon grease. The woman couldn't look domestic if she tried, and the skimpy bathing suit wasn't helping.

He held up his hands in self-defense. "Not a prude, definitely not a prude, and I'm a happy man to say that I know this from personal experience. After dark, or very, very early in the morning—when it's still dark, come to think of it."

"Oh, that is so *wrong*," she said fiercely, then stopped, frowned. "Isn't it?"

He took the pan from her, placed it on the counter. "Is it?"

Still frowning, she waved her hands at him. (That had been a good move on his part, getting rid of the frying pan.) "Hush. I'm thinking."

"Oh, good. Then I'm not still smelling burnt steak and potatoes."

"Pushing. You're pushing," she warned, then began to pace, biting at her bottom lip. She held up one finger as she paced, moving her hand for emphasis as she appeared to be mentally counting off times, places…moments.

"Let me help," he said, trying to figure out what to do with the bacon grease, and failing. How did people exist without garbage disposals? "There was that Sunday morning we'd decided to stay in, read the papers, and I sort of made a move, there in the living room, and you told me, and I quote, "Oh, not now, Cam. It's ten o'clock in the morning."

She stopped pacing, leaned against the counter. "I

don't remember that." She looked at the floor, then looked up at him again. "Really. I don't—okay, I remember that."

"Good. Onward? Yes, onward. Then there was that party at my office, remember? I tried to be affectionate, and you gave me that same line—oh, not now, Cam. A kiss, Darc, I wanted to kiss you. In public. I kept waiting for you to say something like it wasn't *proper,* or something. It's just an observation, babe, not a complaint. You just seem to keep it all for the bedroom." He grinned. "After dark."

He watched, part amused, part worried, as she scratched at her head, pressed a hand to her cheek, looked around the kitchen as if in search of some sort of outside inspiration.

"I never saw my parents be affectionate," she said at last. "We've covered that, right?"

"Yeah, we've talked about that. My parents were, until they decided to hate each other's guts. So that's it?"

"It could be. I guess. We weren't exactly a touchy-feely kind of family. I just don't…don't feel *comfortable* showing physical affection, I think. Showing any emotion, actually, except maybe anger. Definitely anger. Which is pretty ridiculous, isn't it?"

Cameron could see Darcie pulling in on herself, berating herself, and that wasn't the point of this conversation. But he was pretty sure he now knew the problem, and it could be summed up in her parents. Who never showed love, but obviously were pretty good at showing anger. Interesting. Sad, but interesting.

"You know what?" he said, taking her hand. "There's probably a twelve-step program to rid you of all these inhibitions."

She squeezed his hand. "Let me guess. You're volunteering to help me with this problem?"

"I'm nice that way. One of the genuine good guys," he said, tugging her hand, pulling her along with him, out onto the back porch, down the stairs…breaking into a bit of a run, still holding her hand, aiming them toward the pool enclosure. With the sun still hanging low on the horizon, beyond the far side of the quarry.

He stopped once inside the fence as the gate slammed shut behind them. "Hot tub, primed and ready." He let go of her hand and walked over to the control panel he'd discovered earlier, pushed several buttons. Fairy lights appeared in the palm trees, in the straw of the three-walled hut, along the edges of the pool. Small colored lights accented the waterfall in blue, pink, green and yellow. Don Ho's "Tiny Bubbles" began playing from hidden speakers in the palm trees.

The lights didn't make a lot of impact, not with the sun still visible, but it wasn't bad, either.

"Welcome to Shangri-La," he said holding out his hand to help her into the hot tub.

"This…this is silly," Darcie said. But she took his hand, let him help her into the foaming hot tub. She sank onto one of the seats, the water coming up to the tops of her breasts. "Do you think Poobie and Pookie found that control box?"

"Truth?" he said, settling himself beside her. "I'm

trying to forget they've ever been here at all. Now," he added, sliding an arm around her shoulders, "are you comfortable?"

"Yes, I'm comfortable," she said. "Stop looking at me like I'm some sort of junior-high science project."

"Right, you're relaxed," he teased, leaning in to nuzzle the soft skin of her neck even as he began playing with her left shoulder strap.

"I can't help it, Cam. This is stupid. It's not as if we've never made love. Why am I so nervous?"

He whispered into her ear. "Because I can see you, I think. Because you can see me. In public, it's because other people can see us, if we were to hold hands, if we were to kiss."

"I hate to see people pawing each other in public."

The strap was off her shoulder now. "I agree. But for two people? Just the two people involved? Why would you want to keep expressions of affection to a timetable? No lovemaking until the sun goes down?"

"That is stupid."

"Not stupid. You just didn't grow up seeing displays of affection, and you took your cue from that."

"Oh, good. Blame the parents," she said, smiling weakly. "That doesn't seem fair."

Second shoulder strap, gone.

"I don't blame them. I thank them, come to think of it. They raised a lady. A very proper lady with hidden fires. I think it makes you even sexier. The Darcie Reed the world sees, the woman in my bed. I get the best of both worlds. We'll get to the showing-anger part in our next lesson. But, for now, it's just us, Darc. Time to relax the rules."

She took a deep breath, let it out slowly. "Cam, we're outside. Anyone could see us. I'm just not...comfortable."

"So much for my overwhelming sex appeal blinding you to your surroundings," he said, once more nuzzling her neck. Didn't the woman feel their wet bodies touching? Wasn't her temperature rising in the warm water? Didn't the caress of the foaming water from the jets add to the moment? Did her libido really run on a time clock? "Come on, Darc. First base."

"Kissing. I remember. Oh, this is silly. Here!"

She cupped her hands on his cheeks and laid a big wet one on him. His feet slipped off a ridge in the tub and he sank, taking her with him.

They came up laughing, sputtering, and it was only when Cameron's gaze zeroed in on her breasts, which had escaped the suit, that they stopped laughing.

The setting sun washed over her bare shoulders and breasts, her wet skin glistened. Her nipples puckered in the cooler breeze of the air.

Cameron forgot to blink.

She moved to pull up the suit, slide the straps back over her shoulders, and he would have stopped her...but she stopped herself, rested her hands on his shoulders instead.

"You're lovely, Darc. *Beautiful.*"

He watched, mesmerized, as the flush of color washed over her, whether from the heat of the hot tub or embarrassment, he didn't know. He was too fascinated to care. She was here, she wasn't moving away from him.

It was a voyage of discovery, that's what it was. Just as if they hadn't made love before, nearly every night they'd been together in his apartment. This moment, here and now, was so different. Somehow, so much more personal.

He looked at her, slowly smiled at her, and then dipped his head, capturing one pebbled nipple in his mouth.

Her grip tightened on his shoulders, and the soft moan she breathed on a shaky exhale urged him on. Braced so that they wouldn't slip off the seat again, he clasped her rib cage as he worshipped her breasts; tonguing her nipples, sliding his mouth over her warm water-slicked skin, feasting on her even as she slid her fingers into his hair, pulled his head even closer to her breasts, urged him on…and on…and on…

"*Pigs!* Filthy pigs! What have you done to my kitchen? How dare you—*stop that this minute!*"

Darcie pulled so hard on Cameron's head that he had to almost pry her hands off him, at which time she sank below the foaming water. He could see her desperately trying to pull up her suit and hoped she wouldn't let herself drown if the suit refused to obey her frantic tugging on it.

Meanwhile, he had to get rid of Frau Blücher. Burying her under the porch held some appeal.

"Lily," he said, standing up in the hot tub, "you still haven't learned about opening closed doors, have you? Or, in this case, gates," he said, speaking through clenched teeth.

Clearly the woman didn't embarrass easily. While Darcie resurfaced, bathing suit back in place, to turn her back to the housekeeper, Lily advanced across the brick patio, murder in her eyes.

"Back off, Lily," he said. "And why aren't you at the movies?"

She sniffed. Snorted, actually. There was not a lot about this woman that appealed to Cameron. Nothing, actually.

"As if I go to movies. I took your money and went to the mall."

"Probably to buy a new broomstick," he whispered to Darcie out of the corner of his mouth and, hiding behind him, she giggled.

Lily began shaking one long, skinny finger at them. "I knew what you wanted, young man. You wanted to be alone, have sex. That was bad enough, but you've destroyed my kitchen. You're not allowed in my kitchen!"

When he had time, later, at his leisure, Cameron felt he should reflect a little more on the knowledge that while Darcie had trouble showing affection unless it was dark, she didn't seem to have many reservations about showing her anger; night, day, twilight, you name it. None, when you got right down to it. She was really *good* at showing her anger.

"Okay, that's it, party's over," Darcie said, steadying herself against Cameron's shoulder as she climbed out of the hot tub. "What is it going to take to get you out of here, Lily? Huh? That's what this is all about, right? You don't want to stay here any more than I want you here, do you, and you're making sure I want you gone. So, all right. You win, you're obnoxious and I know it. Name a figure, and once the month is up and I have access to the money, I'll pay it. But if you want me to pay what you want, you'll stop being such a pain in my neck, starting *right now.*"

Cameron considered a rousing cheer, but didn't want to interrupt, because Darcie seemed to be on a roll, bless her.

As Darcie advanced on the older woman, Lily backed up a few paces, but then stopped, drew herself up to her full, bony height. "This is not your house, missy. You're so smug, so sure of yourself. Moving my furniture around. Messing up my kitchen. Having sex with that man so that he'll give you everything. Does he know you're playing along, just to get the house, get Horry's money? Huh? Does he? You tossed him over once. You'll do it again. You're a Willikins."

Darcie's next pithy suggestion to Lily totally blew the ponytail, the freckles, the whole "good girl" thing right out of the water, and Cameron punched a fist in the air several times, celebrating as Lily turned on her orthopedic-shoe heels and retreated.

"That's my girl," he said as he climbed out of the hot tub, then tried to take Darcie in his arms.

She held him off. "Oh, Lord. Did I *say* that? Did I really say *that?*"

"Oh, yeah, you said that. Really good enunciation, too. Another first, Darc?"

She swallowed with some difficulty. "You could say that. Ohmigod, I have to go apologize."

"Over my dead body," Cameron told her, picking her up and heading for the house. "Come on. We've got her on the run, we can't stop now. Try to look like we can't wait until we get upstairs to my room, okay?"

He carried her up the steps to the rear porch, then pushed open the door…setting off the overture from *Cats* as the cat door swung back and forth.

Cameron stopped in his tracks, cursed under his breath.

Talk about a bucket of cold water being thrown over your head; where Lily had failed to break the mood, had even lent some new spice to it, the music had triumphed.

"What?" Darcie asked, picking up her head, which she'd previously had burrowed into his shoulder, probably so she wouldn't have to look at Lily as they made their way through the kitchen.

"I locked that," he said, putting her down as he bent to inspect the cat door. "I damn well know I locked that. Where's Lucky?"

"Lucky," Darcie called, racing from the kitchen, not paying the least attention to Lily, who was wiping the sink with a damp sponge. "Lucky! Here, kitty-kitty! Yum-yums, Lucky. Come get some yum-yums."

Cameron stood once more, looked at the housekeeper. "Let me guess. Your work, Lily?"

"She doesn't deserve this house," Lily said, tipping up her chin. "She didn't work for it."

Darcie burst into the kitchen once more. "He doesn't come when I call him," she said, peering under the table, then running into the pantry, coming back out again, frowning. "He must have gotten out. Cam? You take the front yard, I'll take the back. Then we'll look in the woods, okay?"

Then she was gone, a pair of hastily put-on sneakers untied on her feet.

"Clock's ticking," Lily said, running the sponge under the faucet. "No more than twelve hours for you two to be away from Shangri-La, no more than twelve hours for Lucky to be away from Shangri-La—" she pointedly looked at the clock "—starting now. And now I'll go phone Attorney Humbolt."

"Not one of my better days," Cameron muttered under his breath as he raced up the back stairs to his room, to get a shirt and his own sneakers. "Horry?" he called out quietly as he moved through the house, stepped out onto the front porch. "Horry, this was all your stupid idea. So, a little help here, okay?"

HORRY PEERED under the porch, where Lucky's mismatched eyes glowed eerily in the last rays of sunlight. "They figured out you're gone. You have to go home," he said. Pleaded. "You promised to be home before dark, remember?"

"I did go home, but my personal door was open, and what goes in can go out again. Besides, cats don't make promises, Horry," Lucky mind-talked around the mouse in his jaws. "Watch this." He opened his jaws, and the mouse made a break for it, only to have Lucky slam a fat paw down on its tail, trapping it again.

"Stop teasing that poor little rodent. You know you aren't going to eat it. You eat eight-dollar-a-pound sushi."

"I know, but this is good practice. A cat's got to keep in shape. Oh, all right," Lucky said, lifting his paw. The mouse took off like a shot. "Happy now? But I'm not going back inside again. Not yet. I have my reputation to think about, you know. I'm no dog to come running, tail wagging, when somebody calls. When they shut up? Then I'll go home."

Horry tipped his head, to hear Darcie's voice coming from the large backyard. A moment later Cameron's deeper voice could be heard, both of them calling for Lucky.

"He'll look under here," Horry pointed out. "It's the first place he looked last time."

Lucky got up, stretched and walked out from beneath the porch. "Good point, Horry, thanks."

"So you'll go up on the porch and wait for them to see you?"

"Always the optimist. No, Horry, I'm going to my secret place."

"What secret place?"

"Yup, the optimist. Look, I want Darcie to have this place, too. I'd be nuts not to. I'll be back by morning, so bug off, stop following me around. And start thinking of a way to get rid of—"

"I know, I know. It's just so disappointing. Are you absolutely sure they're—"

"Planning ways to fricassee me? Oh, yeah. Oops; here comes Darcie. The smart-ass won't be far behind her. See you around, Horry. Gotta go…."

CHAPTER FIFTEEN

DARCIE WOKE SLOWLY, winced as she stretched and then came instantly alert, remembering. She was lying on the larger couch in the living room. The windows were open, the better to hear Lucky if he came home, since Cameron had locked the kitty door in the kitchen again. Nobody wanted Lucky to come in and then go out again.

"What time is it?" she asked herself as she levered her feet to the floor, sat up, tried to wake up. She and Cameron had hunted Lucky until after midnight, shining their flashlights into the trees, under the house, anywhere they could think of that the cat might be hiding.

Then Cameron had gone off on his own, and Darcie could have sworn she heard him talking to himself in between his calls for Lucky. Not that she blamed him; she'd felt like talking to herself, too.

Neither of them had gone to bed before three, with Darcie insisting on dragging her pillow and a blanket down here while Cameron finally bailed and went to his room. She didn't blame him for that, either.

After all, Lucky was her problem, when you got right down to it.

She picked up her sneakers, pillow and blanket, and

headed upstairs to her own room, to see that it was already seven o'clock. Showering, she dressed quickly and ran back downstairs, out onto the porch, her hair wet and hanging onto her shoulders.

"Miss Reed."

"Attorney Humbolt," Darcie said, skidding to a halt as the lawyer climbed out of his bright red babemobile. "A little early, aren't you? Let me guess. You have a tee time, and want to disinherit Cameron and me now, then head for the golf course?"

"Lily phoned me last night, yes. But I was hoping to arrive to hear that Lucky has returned, safe and unharmed. Horry loved that cat, remember." He looked at his wristwatch. "We don't know how long Lucky, in actual fact, has been missing, but taking the twelve hours from eight o'clock last night, when Lily apprised me of the situation, I'd say you have forty-five, no, forty-four minutes to produce the cat."

"Ah, look who's here, the psychedelic turkey vulture, circling hopefully around the soon-to-be deceased," Cameron said, appearing from the side of the house. He climbed onto the porch, to put an arm across Darcie's shoulders. "In case you haven't noticed, Humbolt, you're about as welcome as your slacks."

"There's no need to be personally insulting. I take no joy in any of this, Mr. Pierce," Humbolt said stiffly. "As I've said before, I made a serious attempt, *several* serious attempts, to dissuade Horry from drawing up such an absurd will."

"And we thank you for that," Darcie said quickly, because this wasn't helping anything. She turned to Cameron. "I thought you were still in bed. What have you got in that wrapper, anyway? You smell like fish."

"It smells? Bite your tongue, woman. This, Darcie, is the finest, freshest sushi in fifty miles, if I want to believe the guy I bought it from this morning. Remember 'Hansel and Greta'?"

"'Hansel and Gretel,'" Darcie corrected, smiling at him indulgently. He looked so tired, and so cute in his morning beard. "But I think I've got the point. You've been laying a trail of *sushi?*"

"Exactly. From the tree line I've seen Lucky duck into, to the front porch. I stopped when I heard Humbolt's car drive up—Humbolt, you might want to consider a tune up—but now I'll go back and lay the rest, leading right here. Excuse me."

Not really all hot to stay with Humbolt, Darcie volunteered to help, and went with him. They both stopped short when they turned the corner.

"Lily. Put…the…sushi…*back,*" Cameron said, slowly and distinctly as the housekeeper tossed a strip of sushi into a kitchen pot.

Darcie got an instant flashback to the night she and Cameron had watched a video of *Young Frankenstein.* They'd loved the movie, and had quoted lines to each other for a week. He had said the wrong words just now, sort of, and it hadn't been Frau Blücher's line, but it was all so "Put…the…candle…*back,*" that it wasn't easy to contain a shout of laughter, even as she wanted to strangle Lily.

Insane. The world, at least their small corner of it, had gone insane. Stupidly, absurdly insane.

All three of them stood very still, frozen in a strange "gotcha" tableau, as if waiting for someone to yell, "And, *action!*" in order to say the next line.

"What's going on here?" Clark Humbolt asked from behind them, breaking the spell.

"Frau Blücher's sabotaging my sushi trail," Cameron said.

He made this accusation with all seriousness, obviously affronted, upset. Pissed, actually.

And Darcie, maybe from worry, maybe from lack of sleep, maybe from Cameron's *Young Frankenstein* reference following so close on her own recollections, sat herself down on the grass and laughed until tears rolled down her cheeks.

"This...this is *ridiculous,*" she managed to say. "Cam laying a trail of sushi, of all things, and Lily following after him, picking it up again. We should all be locked up in padded rooms."

And she was off again, laughing, crying, knowing she was losing it but unable to control herself.

"I was trying to help, babe," Cameron said, sounding hurt. She looked up at him. He *did* look genuinely hurt.

Which set off another round of near-hysterical giggles.

She looked at Lily, still in a dressing gown and those horrible pink bunny slippers, matching pink rollers in her hair, and still holding a pot in one hand, a strip of sushi in the other. That didn't help; Darcie hugged herself as she sat there, because her sides had begun to ache.

"Darcie. Darcie, shut up," Cameron said, waving a hand at her. "Listen!"

Darcie clamped her lips between her teeth for a moment as Cameron helped her to her feet. "Listen to what?"

"The frogs. I hear the frogs." He kept hold of her hand. "Come on."

"Oh, Cam, not the frogs again. We already proved that Lucky isn't big enough to—Lucky!"

And there he was, strolling up the drive without a care in the world (really, how many cares can a cat have?) the frogs doing their *ribbit-ribbit* routine yet again.

"Oh, Lucky, you've come home! And you're not even limping anymore!" Darcie exclaimed, running toward the cat, then dropping to her knees beside the stone drive, at which time Lucky calmly climbed up on her and let her hug him.

"Chalk up one for Horry," Cameron said, standing beside her. "Thanks, old man."

Lucky yowled, began to struggle in Darcie's arms.

"Now see what you did, Cameron?" she said, getting to her feet, hanging on to Lucky for dear life. "You shouldn't say that name. Lucky misses him. And don't start that ghost stuff again, okay?"

"Right," Cameron said as he followed her up onto the porch, holding open the door for her so that when Lucky broke free, and leaped, he ended up on the foyer floor, the screen door closing behind him. "You give it your explanation, and I'll give it mine. Where's Humbolt? I'm in the mood to gloat, even if you don't buy my ghost stories."

"Humbolt is only doing his job, Cameron. It's Lily I want to strip naked and tie down on an ant hill."

"That works for me—except the stripping her naked part," Cameron said as they walked to the side of the house, to see Clark Humbolt deep in conversation with a belligerent-looking Lily Paige. "Uh-oh, get the hose, Darcie, we may need to separate these two."

"Oh, no. She's *mine,*" Darcie said, any humor she'd found in the bizarre situation long gone. "Attorney Humbolt, please," she said, rubbing her hands together as she advanced on the pair. "Allow me."

Lily's eyes went wide and she gave a little cry, dropped the pot, then turned and fled, leaving one bunny slipper behind.

"You'll get her next time, babe," Cameron told her as he walked up behind her, putting his hands on her shoulders, to give her a quick, bracing massage, as if she were a boxer between rounds, and he was her corner man. "Only promise I can be there."

Humbolt turned to look at Cameron. "There's no need for violence. I reprimanded Lily. I have no idea why she's behaving so badly, considering it's Horry's half brother who will inherit if the terms of the will aren't met. I pointed that out to her, but she seems so, well, so consumed by hatred of you two, that I don't think she cares who gets Cliff House or the money, just as long as you don't."

"But why? I don't get it. I was never anything but nice to that woman," Darcie said, feeling her temper heat up once more.

"Because you didn't work for it?" Cameron suggested, shrugging.

She turned on him. "And what does *that* mean?"

"Damned if I know, but it seems to me that Lily likes to ride the I-did-all-the-work train, right? How long did she work for Horry? Thirty years? Worked for him… and the rest of it," he added quietly. "Then you, just because you're blood, you waltz in and get everything, and she gets to live here for the rest of her life, probably cleaning and cooking for *you*. I mean, looking at it through Lily's eyes, I can see her point."

"Well. Gee. Thanks," Darcie said, stung. "As I remember the thing, Uncle Horry gave her some kind of annuity a while ago, plus the money that goes to her from his estate. It's not like he gave her a cheesy gold watch and told her, 'Thanks for everything, now take your barber pole and hit the road.' He provided for her. Right?"

"Right. But you have to admit that the way he *did* do it, for Lily, for all of us, wasn't exactly what any sane person could call helpful. Or even fair."

"Uncle Horry knew what he was doing," Darcie said tightly. "It's not up to us to judge what he did, or why he did it."

"He made me a part of this, Darc, so I can damn well judge what he did."

"Oh! I can't do this now! Does *no one* in my family do anything right, according to you? Lord knows *I* can't, that's for sure."

"Oh, cripes. That isn't what I meant, and if you

weren't always so damn quick to fly off the handle, you'd—"

"If I might interrupt?"

Both Darcie and Cameron turned to him in exasperation, growling in unison, *"What?"*

Humbolt, who'd had one arm raised slightly, raised the other one, too, pretty much an action of self-defense, and stepped back. "Perhaps…perhaps I can explain, um, your uncle's, um, motivation?"

"We already know his motivation," Darcie said, wishing the subject dropped, and quickly. She was overtired, had expended way too much worry over Lucky, her love life was just starting to get interesting, damn it, and she hadn't eaten since last night's scrambled eggs and bacon. She'd definitely used up a lot more energy than she'd gotten from a couple of eggs and part of a pig. She wanted to go somewhere and cry, and maybe have a bologna sandwich with lots of mustard. Mostly, she wanted to get away from Cameron before either of them said something lethal.

"We do know his motivation, yes. At least we can agree on something," Cameron said, shooting her a not-very-loverlike look. "Horry wrote the will to get Darcie and me back together again. It couldn't be more obvious."

"Yes, yes. And he was going to show it to you, when he could get you both here, together. He was counting on the Fourth of July, as I remember it. What he didn't count on was dying, did he? But a last will is just that, the last, the legal will. So now you're stuck with it. We're all stuck with it."

"The Fourth of July? Damn," Cameron said, scratching at his head. "Okay. I'm starting to get it now. The Fourth of July."

Darcie, however, was still doing a slow boil, and wasn't real happy that he was seeing the light, or whatever he was doing. "And are we going to share with the rest of the class?"

"Sorry, babe. Horry and I spoke on the phone, at least three or four times, after you ran away to Pittsburgh."

"Correction. I did not *run away* to Pittsburgh!"

"You say *tomato,* I say—Let's just forget that, okay? The point is, I wanted to go after you, and Horry talked me out of it. He told me the worst thing I could do was to push a Willikins, whatever the hell that meant. He said you'd come back on your own, and if you didn't, I could give you until the Fourth of July because by then you'd either be ready to see reason or at least not want to kill me anymore."

"Nice. Real nice. Go on."

"I'm going, I'm going. I was going to fly to Pittsburgh on the Fourth of July, but I'm thinking now that Horry had other plans, some way to get you here, and me here."

"To show us the video will. Oh, that's *so* Uncle Horry." Darcie was beginning to understand. "He meant to sort of shock us? He did that bit with the Looney Tunes stuff to help prove he wasn't really serious about the will, just that he wanted us back together?"

She turned to (turned *on* might be a better description) Clark Humbolt. "And you *helped* him? Didn't it occur to you, to either of you, that Uncle Horry could have died with that will in effect?"

Humbolt's cheeks turned an unflattering red. "How was I supposed to know the guy was boinking Lily?" He clasped his hands in front of himself, shook them. "I didn't say that. I didn't mean to say that. I…I'm sorry I said that. Mixed company, you know."

"We get the point, Humbolt," Cameron said. "Right, Darc?"

She nodded. Talking just didn't seem like a good idea.

Cameron picked up the slack. "So, that takes care of the provisions and, come to think of it, how sort of off-hand Horry was about everything going to Edwin if we wouldn't go along with the deal. He didn't put a lot of thought into that part of the will, because he never saw any of it as happening. But that doesn't explain Lily, does it?"

Humbolt sighed. "He joked about that section, actually. Something about rewarding the loyal retainer, something like that. But no, I don't think he meant any of it. In his previous will, written about fifteen years ago, he'd given her a more substantial sum of money and—oh boy."

"Oh boy what?" Darcie asked, because now Humbolt's cheeks, his entire face, was sort of gray.

"And the house. He willed her Cliff House," he said quickly, looking in the direction Lily had gone earlier. "Do you suppose he ever told her?"

"Pillow talk, you mean?" Cameron nodded. "Oh, yeah, he told her. He had to have told her. No wonder she's all bent out of shape. She must have seen you as the enemy every time you showed up here, as you got older, and Horry began to see you as an adult, not a child. I know he was crazy about you. He was probably going to change his will in your favor, anyway, or the idea of the video will never would have occurred to him. Lily had to have been worried about him changing the will, no matter what, and then we broke up, Darc, you move away, and, bam, sure enough, she loses the house, anyway. At least, that has to be how she sees it."

Darcie was feeling mulish, as her father had often described her. "Yeah, well, too bad for Lily. I know that sounds cruel, but this house is the best present Uncle Horry could have given me. Not the money, Shangri-La. I always liked this house, but I love it now, for what it is, for how it makes me feel. And I won't let her ruin it for me."

"You can't evict her, you know. I agree that she's behaving badly, but she's done nothing illegal," Humbolt pointed out. "And now, I really do have to run. Nothing you can prove, in any case. May I suggest you lock up the cat?"

Darcie waited until Humbolt had turned the corner before looking at Cameron. "You wanted to come after me?"

"I told you that. I did tell you that, right?"

"I don't remember," she said honestly, sighing. "To tell you the truth, these last few days have pretty much melded into a blur. As a matter of fact, I think I'm mad at you right now. And you're mad at me."

"True. But we'll get over it, use our special brands

of amnesia to forget it. We always do," he said, smiling. "So. Now we know who's out to get rid of Lucky and lose you the house. We're not counting the money. Since Humbolt says we can't kick her out, what do you want to do? Put Lucky in a cage?"

She shook her head. "He'd be a sitting duck in a cage. Besides, he wouldn't like it, and he can be pretty vocal when he doesn't like something. We'll just have to watch Lily, that's all."

"Watch Frau Blücher. Terrific. Just the way I want to spend the rest of the month. And, just to make our lives even happier, I'm still not convinced Poobie isn't here to get rid of Lucky so he gets everything, and by everything, I mean the money. I don't think he wants the house. Humbolt says he didn't tell him the terms of the will before he got here, but I believe that about as much as I'd believe Plaid Boy could break ninety on the golf course."

They walked back to the front porch. "And I still think you're wrong. Uncle Edwin is not that kind of person. Lily's the one, the only one, and not because she'd inherit, because she won't, but just because she's mad."

Cameron held open the screen door, glaring at Lucky as if daring him to try to make a break for it. "How about we compromise? I'll buy Poobie as innocent, if you'll agree with me that Horry could still be hanging around Shangri-La. He's the one who brought Lucky home, you know. *Ribbit-ribbit?*"

Darcie rolled her eyes, picked up Lucky and headed for the stairs. "We'll discuss that after I lock Lucky in my room and we go somewhere for breakfast, since there's no way I'm going near that kitchen right now. Your treat."

"YOU'RE HERE TO LET ME OUT? About time. A cat could get mad and start clawing some clothes, you know. A cat might have already started. And why do you only have your head through the door? That's fairly revolting, you know."

Horry turned his head from side to side, made a face, tried to push himself completely into the closet. Nothing. He couldn't get in, couldn't get through. This probably wasn't a good thing, a loss of ghostly powers or something, so he wouldn't tell Lucky.

"She locked the door and took the keys. And I think she's right. Darcie means well, Lucky. Besides, they'll be back soon. Or do you want Lily to find you?"

"Please, don't mention that woman's name. Even money she picked up all that sushi and flushed it. Miserable woman. How you could go sniffing her tail every week makes me wonder about you, Horry. It really does."

Horry hunched his shoulders and gave one last push. Nothing. "I'm paying for that particular sin. Now listen, Cameron's begun to figure it out, with Humbolt's help, of all people. But I still have to find some way to communicate with him. After all, he's only got the half of it."

"The ghost half," Lucky said, sharpening his claws on the woven side of Darcie's suitcase.

"Right, I didn't count me in there, did I? Okay, so

he's got two-thirds of it. You're a picky feline. He's got the ghost part, he's got the Lily part. But none of that means anything if he doesn't get the rest of it. The *why* of it."

"Which you don't know, either," Lucky pointed out, because he could, and because he was getting pretty sick of feeling like he was in a bad movie. A bad movie titled *Get Lucky. Get Lucky Dead.*

"We know who. We don't have to know why."

"Wrong. We know who. Cameron and Darcie have to know who. *And* why. To *prove* the who they need the why. Are you sure you can't find a way to talk to him?"

Horry sighed, shook his head. Again, this probably wasn't a good time to tell Lucky he'd been hiding out lately as, one by one, he'd realized he also couldn't open doors anymore or knock on walls. He couldn't even tickle Lily. Then again, who else could he tell? "Lucky, I have some bad news. Now, be brave."

"Bad news? Worse than being locked in a closet while people are trying to kill you? Somehow I doubt that, Horry. Sock it to me, I can handle it."

"All right. I'm losing my ghostly powers. I think...I think I'm fading. I think I'll be gone soon."

Lucky's ears went flat against his head. "While I'm still in trouble? That's not funny."

"I know, I know. But I'm also hearing heavenly music once in a while, so that's good, right? It means I'm going up, not down."

"Yeah, yeah, yeah. How nice for you. So that's why

you aren't in the closet right now? Because you can't get all the way in?"

Horry nodded. "And there's a draft out here. I can only go in and out if someone opens the door and I can slip through. No more walking through walls. It's all rather embarrassing. Lucky? Will you miss me?"

"Oh, yeah. Sure. I'm getting all choked up here, Horry. *Are you nuts?* You can't go anywhere yet. And you think you're going *up?* After what you did to me? Fat chance! Not unless you fix this, Horry. Now think. *Think!* You have to fix this!"

"SO," CAMERON SAID, leaning against the porch railing as Darcie sat in one of the rockers. "Have you figured out how we're going to keep from starving to death for the next two weeks, since neither of us wants to go near Lily's kitchen?"

"It's not her kitchen. And, no, I haven't. And we can't go out to eat, not for every meal. We can't keep leaving Lucky."

"I think I've got the grill mastered, and it does have a small refrigerator, remember? That's damn near an entire kitchen out there. Between that and takeout, we should manage. Then you get the money, we pay her off and get her out of here."

"You're forgetting Poobie and Pookie, Cameron. They have to eat, too. Besides, that woman is not going to lock me out of the kitchen. That's ridiculous."

"Maybe, but I don't want to eat anything she cooks for us," he said, having already given the subject some thought. “I don’t want her feeding Lucky, either. She’s not just being mean, Darc. She’s being *nuts* mean. Picking up the sushi? That’s just not rational.”

“But laying a trail of sushi is?” She smiled. “It was cute and adorable, that’s what it was. Thank you, Cam.”

“Yeah,” he said, pushing himself away from the railing. “That’s me, cute and adorable. How about a reward?”

“Meaning?”

“*Not* meaning, ‘Oh, Cameron, it’s barely noon and someone might see us.’”

“Oh.”

He grinned as she stood up, smoothed down her skirt. Held out his arms. “Ready?”

“Give me a minute, I’m warming up to the idea,” she told him, the mischievous twinkle in her eyes having a pretty nifty effect on his used-to-be-tired body. “Okay, I’m ready.” She held her arms out, as well. “Come and get it, big boy.”

Cameron didn’t wait for her to ask twice, and a moment later they were wrapped in each other’s arms and he was tasting maple syrup on her mouth as she ground herself against him.

He slid one hand down her back, to cup her buttocks, meld her more closely to him as he slanted his mouth this way, that way, and she slid her tongue into his mouth.

Instant arousal. He was Pavlov’s dog when it came to Darcie’s kisses. Reacting to her stimulus. Hell, he’d roll over and beg for her stimulus, and he wasn’t ashamed to admit it.

Her fingers lightly explored the back of his head,

sliding into his hair, skimming over his ears, caressing his jaw before moving lower. She was rubbing her thumbs over his nipples now, through the thin knit of his shirt.

Pulling her down into one of the chairs, on his lap, began to seem like a good idea. Picking her up and carrying her up to his room a better one.

But, no. That was the point, wasn't it? That they could show affection anytime they wanted to, even in the noonday sun? Everything did not have to lead to the bedroom…or any convenient flat surface. Kiss her, kiss her, just kiss—oh, where's her hand going now?

He had to do it. He broke the kiss, pulled her against his shoulder. "I think this is the part where anybody who saw us would tell us to just go get a room. You don't do anything halfway, do you, babe?" he asked her, trying to regulate his breathing even as he kissed her hair. "A real overachiever."

"I've always believed in giving my best effort," she said into his chest. "Happy now?"

"That depends. Have we proved anything here?"

She pushed herself slightly away from him, grinned. "What do you think?"

"I think," he said, as the frogs began to *ribbit-ribbit,* "that either I sit down right now and pull the entire Sunday paper over my lap, or Pookie is going to say something really embarrassing."

Darcie leaned to her right and looked past Cameron's shoulder. "They're home already? I didn't think they'd be back until closer to suppertime."

"Checkout's at eleven at the Borgata, and that's where they went. My guess is they lost, or they would have just checked their bags and stayed a few more hours. Okay, I don't need the newspaper. I can handle this."

"Someone was handling it a moment ago," Darcie said, then pressed a hand to her mouth as if she'd just shocked herself, when he was pretty sure she hadn't. "You know what it is, Cam? You're a bad influence on me, that's what it is."

"Hey, what can I say? We both believe in giving our best effort. Okay, now smile, because here they come."

Both he and Darcie watched as the chauffeur opened the passenger door and Edwin climbed out, still dressed in his tuxedo. He was followed by Pookie, a vision in gold lamé and silk leopard skin.

"That wouldn't even look good on Britney Spears," he grumbled quietly.

"And you'd know this how?" Darcie asked him as Edwin peeled several bills from a fat roll he pulled from his pocket and handed them to the driver, who then raced to unload the trunk with the sort of speed that announces: "Big tipper! Big tipper!"

"There you are," Edwin said as he and Pookie headed for the porch. "How nice, a welcoming committee. Oh, the time we had! Pookie-bear, tell Darcie about the time we had while Cameron and I do a little business. Cameron?" he said, then walked to the corner of the porch.

"What's up, Edwin? You got hit hard at the Borgata?"

"On the contrary. My first visit, I grant you, but by the time we left this morning those lovely people had comped our suite and erased our dining bills from my account. Comps, Cameron. A gambler's fringe benefits. We would have gotten more, I'm sure, except that I forgot to show my card—they give you identification cards—to the pit boss, so only Pookie's play was registered on the slot machines. Pookie does love the nickel slots. Now let me pay my debt."

Cameron held out his hand when Edwin gestured for him to do so, and watched in fascination as the man peeled hundred dollar bills from the roll, counting out ten of them for him.

"Here you go, son, thank you again. Put that back in your piggy bank."

"That's too much, isn't it?"

"The limo, boy. It was quite costly. Remember when I had you come to the phone and read off your credit card number? You're really a good boy, you know that? Very trusting. You probably ought to be careful about that," Edwin said, tucking the still-fat roll back in his pocket. "But don't worry, I'm flush now until the first of the month, thanks mostly to Pookie. Then I get my allowance, you understand. I have to watch myself. I've been outspending way too often lately."

"Okay, if you're sure," Cameron said, still wondering about that allowance business. "Tell me something. I've been to the casinos a time or two myself, and I pretty much know what they give you. How do you get a casino to comp a suite and meals by playing nickel slots?"

Edwin laughed and patted Cameron's shoulder. "You

can when you play them the way Pookie-bear does. A multiline slot, playing the maximum on each line? I'm talking ninety nickels a spin, son, and sometimes she has three machines going at the same time. She had some not-so-little crowd standing around watching her play one of those bonus rounds when she ran one of the machines up to thirty-eight thousand points. She does that a lot. Either loses in a hurry, or hits it big. Go Big or Stay Home, that's Pookie's motto."

Cameron did some quick mental math. "She wins that much? On a *nickel* machine? I didn't think that was possible. Why doesn't she just play the dollar machines?"

"That's my Pookie-bear. She says the nickels are more fun," Edwin said proudly. "We've been having so much fun, too, traveling, seeing all the casinos. I tell her I'm dug in at the blackjack tables, but the truth is, I spend most of my time in the lounges, sticking close so I can check on Pookie. She stays up all night, so I stay up all night. Gambling's all right, but I don't get quite the thrill she gets. Still, a new experience is a new experience, right?"

Cameron tried to digest this. "A new experience, Edwin? So when did you start going to casinos?"

"Oh, I dabbled a time or two in my day, but nothing as intense as this until I met Pookie," he answered, looking past Cameron, waving in Pookie's direction. "Almost six months now, I think. I probably should think about something for our six-month anniversary. Any suggestions? I mean, after the Hope Diamond, where does a man go?"

Cameron considered this. "Six months. That would be about, what—January?"

Edwin nodded. "Excuse me. Pookie's handing out the gifts. Lovely shops at the Borgata, Cameron. You really should take Darcie." He winked broadly. "Show the girl a good time, if you understand what I mean?"

Cameron stayed where he was, watching as Pookie opened one of the suitcases and began pulling out bags, looked in them, handed one to Darcie.

"Yoo-hoo, gorgeous! Come get your present."

He walked over to take one of the bags, thanked Pookie and then looked at Darcie, who was holding up a magnificent, pale-blue negligee she gaped at, then quickly stuffed back into the bag.

"Wow. Thank you, Pookie."

"Don't look now, Cameron, but that was supposed to be *my* line," Darcie whispered, stepping closer to him. "Open yours. And stop leering at my bag."

Cameron unrolled the top of the bag, peered inside, then pulled out two pairs of silk boxer shorts, one midnight blue, the other black. "Uh…thanks?"

Pookie gave a wave of her limp-wristed hand. "Don't mention it. Boxers help the little swimmers, you know."

"Really?" Darcie said, tipping her head and looking at Pookie, looking so innocent Cameron wanted to clap a hand over her mouth before she said anything else. "Could you please explain that, Pookie? Little swimmers?" Too late.

"Knock it off," Cameron warned her quietly out of the corner of his mouth as he stuffed the boxers back into the bag. "You know damn well what little swimmers are."

"Well," Pookie began with another limp-wristed gesture, "little swimmers are—oh, look who's here. Lily. Don't look so sour. Come here, come here, come here. I've got something for you, too, sweetie. I wouldn't forget you."

Lily, who had stepped onto the front porch, once more dressed in her funereal black, minus the magnolia, took her time looking at everyone, one person at a time, her expression murderous. At last she looked at Pookie. "A present? And I suppose I'm supposed to thank you?"

"No," Pookie said gaily, obviously a woman who wouldn't allow herself to be insulted. "But it is of a rather *personal* nature, wink, wink, sweetie. How about we go up to my room, and I'll show you. Poobie? You wouldn't mind postponing your nappy-poo for a while, would you?"

"Nope, not me," Edwin said, waving the two women on their way.

"She gives you a negligee and me boxers for my swimmers, but she's giving something too *personal* to Lily? Do you think we even want to know what it is?"

"I know I don't. I don't even want to think about it," Darcie said.

Edwin sighed as Pookie disappeared into the house, then turned to smile at Darcie. "How's the cat, my dear? Not giving you any trouble, is it? I'm still quite upset with Horry, for dragging me into this, you know."

Cameron listened closely, but didn't hear any hint of insincerity in Edwin's words. Maybe Darcie was right. Maybe Edwin was just what he was and nothing more. Being Edwin certainly seemed to be enough for anybody.

As Darcie launched herself into a shortened, and considerably funnier story of what had happened with Lucky while Edwin and Pookie were in Atlantic City, Cameron was free to think about the Very Odd Couple. Not Edwin and Pookie. Pookie and Lily.

They didn't compute. They were a Mansard roof paired with a contemporary ranch. They were gingerbread on a Midwest Craftsman home. They were…interesting.

Ribbit-ribbit. Ribbit-ribbit.

Cameron whirled about to look down the drive. The empty drive. "Son of a—Darcie? Did you hear that?"

Ribbit-ribbit. Ribbit-ribbit.

"Hear what, son?" Edwin asked.

"The frogs, Uncle Edwin," Darcie said quickly, glaring at Cameron. "There's a short in the frogs. *Isn't that right, Cameron?*"

"Right," he said, responding to Darcie's newest twist on *Not now, Cameron.* "Definitely a short somewhere. Excuse me, I'm going to go look for it again."

"Good thought," Darcie said, shaking her head. "Now, Uncle Edwin, let me help you get these suitcases upstairs, all right?"

Cameron had gotten to the bottom of the steps before Edwin said, "About taking my suitcases upstairs to my room, my dear, and I thank you for the offer, you're a sweet girl. I happened to peek inside Horry's old bedroom yesterday, before we drove off to the shore. Would you perhaps not mind if Pookie-bear and I moved into the room? It's so much…larger than our bedroom."

Darcie looked at Cameron, then at Edwin. "Well, I suppose there's no reason to—"

"*No!*" Cameron winced, knowing his quick answer was a little over the top. But, damn it, he had *plans* for that room, and they didn't include trying to erase a mental image of Pookie-bear barber pole dancing to "Bolero." "That is, I mean, no, Edwin. I'm sorry, but I'm afraid I've found a problem with the bathroom floor. A leak of some kind that rotted out the subflooring," he invented quickly. "Sit in that bathtub, sit anywhere in that room, and the next thing you know, you'll be in the kitchen with Lily. So—" he spread his hands "—it really wouldn't be safe." Oh, he was going to hell. He was going straight to hell….

"All right," Edwin said, nodding and smiling. "It was only a thought. I think I'll go upstairs and see if I can boost the ladies out of my room. I'm not the night owl I was twenty years ago, you know. I need to take my heart medicine and have myself a little lie-down."

"Your heart medicine, Uncle Edwin?" Darcie put a hand on his forearm. "You have a heart condition?"

"Nothing too serious, a part of my diabetes, both controlled with the proper pills, they assure me, if I take care of myself. I've given up sweets, smoking, strong drink, caffeine, red meat…"

"Sex?" Cameron added, climbing back up onto the porch.

Edwin looked at him as if Cameron had just asked the man if he knew he had a chicken on his head. "Be reasonable, son. Sex? Me, give up sex?" He turned for the door, chuckling. "You *have* seen Pookie-bear, haven't you?"

"Cameron?" Darcie said once Edwin had gone inside. "Uncle Edwin has a heart condition. Diabetes."

"That's what he said, babe." Cameron shook his head. "I'm trying to remember if he's sticking to his diet the way he says he is. I don't think so."

"You'd think Pookie would take better care of him," Darcie said, looking worried. "Well, that's it. I know enough about diabetes to know he has to have his meals on time, the proper meals. I'm going upstairs to go on the Internet, learn what I can. And then I'm going to kick Lily out of the kitchen. This is *my uncle.*"

"Go get 'em, tiger," Cameron called after her, then shoved his hands in his pockets and headed for the lawn once more. As he walked, he ticked off his problems:

Lily, being a royal pain in the ass.

Lucky, also a royal pain in the ass, squared.

Clark Humbolt, an enigma wrapped in plaid slacks.

Pookie, who seemed to care more about having fun than about her Poobie-bear.

Edwin, who was either too good to be true, or very good at being bad.

He wandered onto the drive.

Ribbit-ribbit.

Oh, yeah, and Horry. Can't forget about Horry.

"I have to be in love with the woman. I'd be a thousand miles away from here by now, if I wasn't…."

CHAPTER SIXTEEN

"LILY?"

The housekeeper turned away from the kitchen counter, hiding something in the hand she'd pushed behind her back. "You."

Oh, boy, this was going to be fun. Not.

Darcie walked to the refrigerator and pulled out a can of ginger ale she really didn't want. "Lily, we have to talk."

"I have nothing to say to you."

"Okay. But I have something to say to you. I have several things to say to you. Let's start with Lucky."

"I didn't know your lover was dropping the sushi all over the place. I was only cleaning up a mess."

Darcie smiled. "Is that all you could come up with since this morning? Sorry, that doesn't work. Attorney Humbolt told me that Uncle Horry had an earlier will, one that left this house to you, along with a lot of money. I don't know what Attorney Humbolt considers a lot of money, but I don't think Uncle Horry gave you as much this time. Am I right?"

"How would I know. I washed his socks."

It was probably a good thing Cameron hadn't come to the kitchen with her, because he would have laughed at that one, seen it as a euphemism for another "service" Lily had performed for Hecuba Willikins. Men, even her Cameron, could be so crude. Then again, she'd thought of it, too.

"So you never knew about the earlier will? You weren't shocked when you heard the new one? You didn't go from the grieving woman I met when I showed up to the woman who ripped up the flowers and tossed them in the garbage because Uncle Horry changed his will? You know, Lily, if I liked you more, I might try to believe that. But I don't."

"I didn't ask you to like me."

"Then you aren't disappointed. Good." Darcie popped the can top and took a drink, because her throat was really dry. Scared dry. But she wasn't going to back down. "Now, here's the deal."

"I'm not agreeing to any deals, missy," Lily said, searching, one-handedly, in one of the drawers, coming out with an old, creased, brown paper bag. She turned her back, shoved whatever she'd been holding into the bag, then turned to face Darcie once more. "You're still here?"

"I meant what I said last night, Lily. The minute this place is mine and the money is released, quote me a figure and I'll pay it, within reason, if in return, you get out of here. You don't want to be here with me any more than I want to be here with you. And I am going to be here, Lily. I am."

"'There's many a slip 'twixt the cup and the lip,'" Lily said, her smile positively evil.

"Huh? Oh…oh, okay. You want to be cute? Let's be cute. You touch one hair on Lucky's head—coat—and

I'll have you arrested, you got that? Attorney Humbolt knows now, not just Cameron and me, so you'd better hope Lucky is still fat and sassy and very much here at the end of the month."

"I told you, I didn't know why that sushi was all over the ground. I keep a clean house. I'll tell anyone that. I never hurt that cat. If he dies tomorrow, nobody could say I killed him. Nobody."

Darcie blew out an exasperated breath. "Warning delivered, subject dropped," she said, putting the soda can on the counter. "Now, on to the next thing. This kitchen. It is not yours. Everybody here has to eat."

Lily sniffed. "Then everybody here can learn how to open a soup can. And clean up after themselves. I'm not the housekeeper anymore, I'm living here because Horry said I could. And now I'm going to my room."

She grabbed the paper bag from the counter. There may have already been a tear in it, or perhaps it caught on the metal lip of the counter. Maybe Lily had been sniffing the cologne when Darcie came into the room, and not closed it tightly enough, so that it had leaked and made the bag weak and soggy. No matter what or why, the bag ripped enough that its contents dropped to the floor.

Lily was on her knees in an instant, picking up fifty-dollar bills and a bunch of twenties, as the contents of the now smashed bottle of cologne soaked the money and puddled on the floor.

"I'M TELLING YOU, Cameron, I kept expecting her to clutch all the money to her chest and scream, 'Mine,

mine, all mine!' It was the weirdest thing I've ever seen."

Cameron was still checking the scratches on his arms, the ones he hadn't bothered covering with Band-Aids. The next time someone asked him to put that halter on Lucky, he'd have a better answer ready than, "Okay, hand it over, I'll give it a shot."

But here they were, walking around the grounds of Shangri-La, the three of them. Darcie. Him. And Lucky, who obviously had yet to understand the concept of a leash. Or maybe he did.

"So, babe, what do you think is going on?"

"I said I don't know. The bags Pookie gave us were plastic, remember? This was paper, Cameron, and I watched her get it out of the drawer. The cologne might originally have come in the plastic bag. Cologne is the sort of gift Pookie might give a housekeeper, right? Lily might have left the bag upstairs, in Pookie's room. But when I showed up in the kitchen, probably while Lily was counting her loot, she picked up the cologne and the money and stashed it all in the same bag. So where did she get the money?"

"I don't know, Miss Marple, where did she get the money?"

"Funny. Real funny. From Pookie?"

"I thought you might be going there. I don't have any other ideas."

Lucky collapsed his bulk on the grass. Cameron gave a tug or two on the leash, then gave it up as a bad idea.

He was still trying to figure out how he'd ever explain taking a cat for a walk if anyone were to see him.

"So we both think the money came from Pookie. What I'm not getting is *why*."

Cameron gave another tug on the leash. Lucky rolled onto his back, grabbed the leash between his front paws, and glared at Cameron while he bit on the thin blue woven cord.

"Lily could have slipped Pookie money for the slot machines, and Pookie was returning the winnings. Lily did show up on the porch, remember, when she's been doing a pretty good job of avoiding everyone. She might have come checking on her investment."

"There had to be five hundred dollars there."

"Chicken feed, to hear Edwin talk about Pookie's gambling winnings. They comped them their suite."

"I don't know comps, so let's not go there. But that's it? Lily slipped Pookie some money to gamble for her, and Pookie brought back the winnings. Okay. Since I can't think of anything else, I guess I'll have to buy that one. But I am *not* buying that 'just picking up the sushi' business. So now what?"

"So now we give the prisoner, here, some fresh air twice a day and watch him like a hawk the rest of the time." Cameron clicked his sneakered heels together, saluted and said, "I'll take the first watch, Captain, while you get some sleep."

Darcie pursed her lips, sort of shifted those pursed lips from side to side as she looked at him. "I'm getting the feeling that one of us isn't taking this seriously enough."

"That could be because one of us keeps trying to get to second base," he reminded her, grinning.

"Yeah, well, good luck on that, okay? I'm going to go look up more diabetic meals on the Internet, then go shopping for ingredients." She didn't click her heels together, but she did salute, with her left hand. "Take over, Sergeant. Remember, there could be a medal in this for you."

"Not exactly the reward I'm looking for, here!" he called after her, then glared down at Lucky. "You're laughing at me, aren't you? You don't have trouble getting women. You're *Lucky*. And I'm pathetic. Come on," he urged, tugging on the leash once more. "The only thing dumber than walking a cat has to be standing here like a complete jerk. So, Lucky, what are your thoughts on a custom-built cage? Big sucker. Grass under your belly, chicken wire on the top and all four sides? Sound like a plan?"

Lucky yowled.

THEY WERE ON THE BACK PORCH again, and Horry had slipped outside with them when they'd pushed open the screen door.

"You nearly blew it, didn't you?"

"It wasn't that bad. They aren't that smart."

"Oh, yeah? *That* was smart?"

"We knew we couldn't plan everything. It all just happened faster than we thought. And I still don't know why you're complaining."

"That's because *you're* not that smart."

"Don't do that. Don't you do that. You always do that!"

"I always have a *reason* to do that!"

Horry floated out of earshot as fast as he could, as he had always been the sort who didn't like messy scenes.

This was all getting complicated. This all had to be over. Soon.

If only he knew how to fix this grand mess he'd made.

He floated to the fence, tried once more to float over it, to hang over the quarry, which would have to have been fun. Except he couldn't seem to get past the property line here any more than he could in the woods.

It hadn't taken Lucky long to figure out that one, either, which was why he hadn't been able to watch his friend as closely as possible.

So, after looking wistfully out at the world he'd never been all that interested in visiting since his days in the army, he floated to the side of the house that held his study, where he'd spent so many hours, thinking his thoughts, dreaming his dreams and talking to Bupkus, who had been such an uncritical listener.

But when he slid his head through the wall, it was to see Clark Humbolt standing in front of the fireplace, staring at the large gilt urn.

What is he doing in here? Alone?

"Horry, do you remember those old Laurel and Hardy movies? The ones where everything good goes to hell and Ollie says to Stan, 'Well, that's another fine mess you've gotten me into, Stanley'?"

Humbolt rubbed at his chin, continuing to stare at the urn. "Well, this is another fine mess, Horry. And I let you get me into it with your dumb ideas. Word of this gets out? Anyone finds out how I let you talk me into that will? I'll be a laughingstock, and still cleaning up after you, damn it."

Then he opened the middle drawer of the desk, pulled out a manila folder Horry knew contained nothing but his checkbook and the folder of monthly bills, and left the room. Horry had wondered who would pay the light bill once he was gone. Now he knew. Clark was a good man.

But he should have thought about being a laughingstock before he bought those slacks, Horry thought to himself, then grinned. *That was funny. Wow, even dead, I can be funny. Where's Lucky? He'll get a kick out of that one. Before he bought those slacks! Ha!*

EDWIN PUSHED HIMSELF BACK in the porch chair and unbuttoned his slacks. "Now, that's what I call a meal," he said, smiling at Darcie. "And you fixed that all by yourself?"

"With a little help from some recipes I found, and some frozen microwave foods, yes," Darcie said, watching Cameron devour a dietetic Popsicle. "Only forty calories and none from fat," she told him.

"Don't. I'm enjoying this. Let me think it's real."

"Sorry." She subsided against the porch railing, finding it difficult to keep from looking at Cameron as he licked the Popsicle, sucked on it when it began to melt, then bit it in half.

Gosh, she couldn't get comfortable. Maybe she'd

take a walk. Go somewhere away from Cameron and that Popsicle. That seemed like a good idea.

But, like a lot of her ideas, this one rapidly became a bust, because it started to rain. One of those not-here, then suddenly here rains; soft rain, coming down so straight it looked as if someone had starched every drop to make sure it stayed in line.

Almost instantly the air smelled of rain, of the freshly turned earth where she'd begun weeding and mulching the foundation planting areas in front of the porch, even if Cameron had warned that the lattice there was also pretty bad, and the gardens could be messed up when he had to work there to replace the wood.

The rain fell harder, bouncing off the stones of the drive, but still there was no breeze, no lightning or thunder. The sun was still struggling to shine, and there was going to be a beautiful rainbow somewhere out there, very soon. At this moment, in this place, it felt as if they were all on their own private island.

Beautiful. Romantic.

"Man, I hope the roof doesn't leak," Cameron said, standing beside her, also looking out at the rain.

So much for romance.

"Do you really think it might?"

"I don't know. Horry wired this place for the twenty-second century, it's that up to date. But other than that? I already told you what I found under just one porch. And you saw the kitchen."

"I've *worked* in that kitchen, *work* being the operative word here. And I don't care how much the roof leaks. The kitchen gets overhauled first."

"I agree," he said, then leaned closer. "I'd agree to anything if you can figure out how to get rid of Poobie and Pookie for the night. I've made plans, if I can get you alone."

Okay. The romance *was* back. This was a good thing. Lord knew she hadn't been able to think of much else since Lily interrupted them last night than what might happen tonight.

"Any suggestions?"

"None. I already tried sending one person to the movies, and we know how that worked out. You?"

"Not a clue. But I'm pretty sure Pookie isn't the sit-around-the-kitchen-table-on-Saturday-night-and-do-jigsaw-puzzles type, so maybe she's got something planned."

Cameron slid his hand along the porch rail, twined his fingers in Darcie's. "I know I've got something planned."

"You keep saying that, as if it's something really special." Darcie tried to look stern—and failed, badly. "Our no-sex rule got lost somewhere, didn't it?"

"I'm not looking for it, if that's what you mean. But that's honestly not what I'm talking about right now, Darc. What I'm talking about is *talking,* period. And not about Lucky, or this house, or any of that. I hate admitting it, but I don't think we can go too far forward, unless we take just one more look back. Damn. Did I just say that?"

"You said it before I could say it," Darcie told him, leaning against his shoulder. "You remember how we were talking about my job in Pittsburgh, and how you found out I'd quit, and how I said I wouldn't go back?"

"I remember. And you'll remember I was very reasonable about the whole thing. That you hadn't told me. So now you can trust me, tell me anything. Right?"

"Okay." She took a deep breath, swallowed. "That's half of it, what you already know. There's more than me just not going back to Pittsburgh. It's that I don't want to—"

"Rain, rain, go away, Pookie's all dressed up and wants to *play!*"

"Hold that thought," Cameron said, dropping a kiss on the tip of Darcie's nose, then turned toward the house. "Oh, wow, somebody really is all dressed up."

"You like?" Pookie asked, hands on her hips as she struck one pose, then another. She was wearing familiar-looking black patent, knee-high boots (with silver spurs), a crotch-skimming black leather dress…and a deeply fringed, black leather jacket appliquéd in more leather, this leather white, with hands of cards, all picked out in what Cameron hoped were rhinestones and fake rubies and emeralds.

"It's…it's a…and doesn't it fit you well!" Darcie said brightly, while Cameron decided the smartest thing he could do was chew on his Popsicle stick and otherwise keep his mouth shut.

"My Poobie-bear got this for me yesterday when we zipped over to Harrahs for a few hours. They have just the *best* clothes like this in their casino shop." She turned and bent from the waist (Darcie had a hand slapped over Cameron's eyes before he could even think about looking) and kissed Edwin on both cheeks, crooning, "Didn't you, Poobie-bear, my sweet little Poobie-bear. Now, come on, Poobie. Time to go."

"Hot damn," Cameron whispered to Darcie. "Where do you think they're going, with her dressed like that?"

"Church social?" Darcie answered, then giggled.

Edwin was on his feet now, trying to button his waistband.

"You aren't going to believe this one," Pookie told Cameron and Darcie. "I was reading the newspaper in the library—the potty, you know—and I saw an ad for this little club not more than thirty miles from here. Poobie? Thirty miles, right? Okay, thirty-five. You'll never believe who's there tonight." She sucked in a breath, grinned. "*Joan Jett.* Can you believe that? Joan Jett! I just *worship* her."

Darcie frowned for a moment, then remembered. "'I Love Rock 'N' Roll?"

"Right. A classic, I tell you, a classic. Although, when was the last time anyone was able to put another *dime* in a jukebox? Edwin, have you asked Cameron, here, if we can borrow his car?"

Cameron had his keys out of his pocket before Edwin could open his mouth. "You might want to get on the Northeast Extension of the Turnpike, Edwin," he suggested. "Wait, I'll get you two umbrellas, help you into the car."

Darcie watched, more than a little amused, as Cameron held one umbrella over Pookie's head (the woman was wearing leather—did cows need umbrellas?) then stood with the umbrella over his own head as he waved the two of them on their way.

Ribbit-ribbit. Ribbit-ribbit. Ribbit-ribbit...

"Do you even know if Uncle Edwin has a driver's license?" she asked once he was back on the porch, closing the umbrella and stamping his feet to shake off the water beading on his sneakers.

"Do I even *care* if he has one, you mean. All-righty, then, sweetheart. Poobie and Pookie are outta here, Lily's locked in her room sticking pins in her Horry doll, Lucky's caged up in your bedroom with the door locked, and all's right with the world. Let's go." He grabbed her hand and pulled her into the house.

"Where are we going?" she asked as he motioned for her to precede him up the stairs. "My room?"

"Cat. Kitty litter pan. Definitely not your room."

"Your room."

"Better. Horry's room."

Darcie stopped at the top of the stairs. "Really? I don't think I...I mean, I thought we were going to talk, and...I don't think that's quite my thing, you know. Horry's room? Just not my thing..."

"A couple of days ago, kissing in public wasn't your thing, and you got over that pretty well," Cameron reminded her, motioning for her to precede him down the hall.

"But we're going to talk," she said, opening the door,

then stopping dead once more, her eyes adjusting to the dimness inside. "You…you've already set this up?"

"A man can live in hope. I set it up last night, too."

She walked into the room, looking at the fully made-up bed. Walked over to touch the top of the wine decanter, sitting on a silver tray with two glasses and placed on the hassock between the club chairs in front of the cold fireplace.

Out of the corner of her eye she noticed that he'd turned on the disco ball, and now he was using one of those pistol-like propane do-hickies to light candles on the tables and dressers. The mirrored ball began to reflect their light a thousand times over, small spots of light dancing in circles around the room. He'd closed all the heavy drapes, so even at not quite nine o'clock, the room would have been very dark, otherwise, once he'd closed—and locked—the door.

"That disco ball still amazes me. And you forgot the cheese and crackers," she told him, sitting down.

"Picky, picky," he said, sitting in the facing chair. He leaned forward, rubbed his palms together. "Now. Alone at last. Talk to me."

Darcie squirmed uncomfortably. "You turned on the disco ball, but you forgot the spotlight, and I think the question is 'Where were you on the night of the fourteenth?'"

"Okay, okay, you're right. I just wanted this to be perfect—and over with, to tell you the truth. You want some wine?"

"Two gallons, yes, thank you," she told him, because she was no less nervous than he was. What if they talked, and found out they really, truly didn't belong together? "What am I supposed to talk about?"

He handed her a full glass, poured one for himself. "You know what, Darc? I've been giving this some thought, and I think I want to talk about your parents."

That one threw her. "My parents? Why?"

He grinned over the rim of his wineglass. "If I knew that one, I wouldn't need to talk about them, would I? Look, I'll start. My parents married straight out of college, produced me, built houses, spent money, started to hate each other, divorced. I was about sixteen, and didn't get to ask a lot of questions, but Doug suggested something to me that made me start seeing some of the problems they might have had."

"Doug." Darcie sat back in her chair, folded her arms under her breasts. "Oh, this ought to be good. Go on, I'm all ears."

"I called my mother the other day and asked her why they'd gotten the divorce. You see, Doug said it might have had something to do with that marrying-right-out-of-college thing. You know, my mother never getting to work in the real world, use her degree, or whatever—we're talking the late sixties, early seventies here—maybe starting to resent never spreading her wings a little. That kind of thing?"

"And that was Doug's idea? That maybe their marriage would have been happier if your mother had—what was that?—spread her wings a little?" Darcie sipped on her wine, pretty sure she knew where this was going. "Uh-huh. So? What did she say?"

Cameron grinned. "She said she found out my dad was having a midlife crisis and sleeping with his secretary, so she threw him out."

"You forgot napkins, too," Darcie said, wiping at her blouse after spraying a bit of wine. "So...so Doug was wrong?"

"Yeah. Dead wrong. I can't wait to tell him."

"I've never met your parents."

"We were pretty wrapped up in each other last time around. But I would like you to meet Mom."

"What are they each doing now?"

"Mom's still in Philly, still the social butterfly, I guess you'd call her, and spends a lot of her time traveling, her winters in Florida. And Dad's in Chicago, fairly well out of my life. Neither of them married again. So that's it. I'm the child of a broken home, but I'm pretty much over it. Now, on to you. Your parents."

Darcie shrugged. "There's not a lot to say that you don't know. They were both professional people in New York City. They married late, had me even later, and they're both gone now, dying pretty much one after the other while I was still in college." She concentrated on slowly twirling the now-empty wineglass between her fingers. "We...we weren't a particularly *close* family. Or a very communicative one. I didn't even know about Uncle Horry until my early teens, I think. I told you that."

"No family vacations? No great memories of Christmas morning around the tree? There had to be something, Darc."

"Arguing. There was arguing. They could argue

about anything, and after a while they let me join in, although they never let me win one. Cameron, I really don't want to do this. I want to tell you what I learned in Pittsburgh."

"In a minute, babe. That was it? Arguing?"

"And goals. God, let's not forget the goals." She blinked back unexpected tears. "It wasn't their fault. They hadn't expected me to come along. I don't think they knew what to do with me. They probably should have gotten a divorce, but then one of them would have had to take me, wouldn't they? Wow, I just realized that one."

Cameron pulled out a white handkerchief and handed it to her. "I'm sorry, Darcie. You never let on. You never said anything."

"Because there's nothing to say. They had me, and they turned me into a project, I guess. School, school and more school. Even in the summer. Dad? He picked the schools. He picked the courses. He even picked my interest groups." She smiled weakly. "If you ever want to know anything about the history of the stock market or need all the presidents named in order, I'm your girl. I did get to play field hockey, though, because my mother had played field hockey. There was that."

"Sounds pretty gruesome," Cameron said, pouring more wine into her glass.

"You have no idea," Darcie said, her tongue feeling looser. "You hear that stuff about someone getting all As in school, and one B, and the parent asking where the heck the B came from? Look up the quote, they cite my dad as the source. Then there was Mom."

"Better?"

"Different," Darcie said, wishing she could shut up, but she'd never talked about any of this to anyone, not even Uncle Horry, who'd seemed to have known, anyway, and now she couldn't seem to stop herself.

"Mom was one of the trailblazers, a big-time feminist. One of the first to get the good job, get the better job, hit her head on the glass ceiling. She told me it was my *duty* to join the corporate world, carry on the torch her generation had first lit, keep the fire burning, all that good stuff. There was no way, according to her, that her generation had fought that good fight just to have my generation lose the ground they'd gained. Anything less than success was being an ungrateful female who refused to live up to her potential. I always wanted to ask her if she'd burned her bra."

"So she was preparing you? Getting ready to send you off to war?"

"You could say that, yes. There was never any question. She was a business major, so I was a business major. Dad approved of that. They both approved of me setting the world on fire, following in their footsteps—all of it. You must have goals, strive toward them, never quit, never fail. Oh no, no failures in the Reed family, let me tell you. Failure, as they say, was *not* an option. Not in anything." She lifted her glass. "Cheers!"

Cameron put down his glass, took her hand in his. "Darc? Has it ever occurred to you that you might be doing something you don't like because they wanted you to do it? They expected you to do it? Maybe even demanded you do it?"

She looked at him, hiccuped. "Gee, you think? Yes, Cameron, I'm pretty sure that's what a lot of my life has been about. Pleasing people. Living up to expectations. And not dropping the ball." She leaned forward and whispered, conspiratorially, "It doesn't work. Trust me. It does...not...work. We don't all fit into the same slot."

"But you still can't take being what you think is a failure, can you?"

Darcie sat back again. At last, she would say what had to be said. At last, she wasn't afraid to put herself first. Cam, with his love, had given her that freedom, that gift.

"I'm reworking my definition of failure. I've decided I'm good at what I do, I just don't like what I'm doing. That's what I've been trying to tell you, trying to find a way to tell you. I don't want to be in business. I don't want to climb the corporate ladder just because someone else thinks I should. I mean, what did any woman march for, protest for—if it wasn't so every woman had a choice? I don't want to have anyone else tell me what to do. And I don't want to feel guilty because I'd rather dig in the dirt than climb some corporate ladder."

Now Cameron frowned. "Dig in the dirt?"

She nodded, grinning. She'd leapt a hurdle, a big one, and it hadn't been as painful as she'd feared. Cameron understood. "I think it could be great, Cam," she said in her new excitement. "I'd need some schooling, but I could maybe do that nights, and work at a nursery or landscape place or something during the day. A few years, lots of hard work, and then maybe I could open my own landscaping nursery. I've got the business training, I can handle the business part, but I'd really want to be in on the design, the choosing, the planting."

"You do know you're an overachiever, right?" Cameron asked, grinning.

"I never said I didn't want to work. But a person should like what's she's doing." She got to her feet. "I've already done some planning for Shangri-La, on this computer program I found at the electronics store at the mall. I mean, we both know the flamingos and frogs have to go, all but one of each, at least, and those two I've worked into the plan. Let me go get my laptop."

Cameron also stood, and took hold of her hands. "Whoa, babe, whoa. I believe you. I mean, I can see it in your eyes. You're really jazzed, aren't you?"

"Oh, yes," she said, not really noticing as he redirected her toward the bed. "And I know I'm going too fast, but I've already thought that someday we could even work together on a project. You know. You designing the house, me the gardens? But also working independently. Making my own decisions."

Cameron turned her back to the bed, lifted her onto the mattress, laid his hands on her shoulders. "I was doing that, wasn't I, Darcie? Just what your parents did? Telling you what to do? Making decisions for you?"

She put a hand on his cheek, loving him so much. "You didn't mean it. You were trying to protect me, if you're talking about saying I should just quit the job and marry you. That night? It just felt like, well, like here I go again, letting everyone else plan my life. I got mad. I got…loud."

"We both got loud, babe," he said, pushing her down on the bedspread. "And then the next morning in my office, I got stupid."

"And I saw it when I came to apologize," she said as she sat up, maneuvered the bedspread down, pushed at it with her feet as she repositioned herself on the crisp white sheets, kicked off her sandals. "I could have cheerfully killed you that morning, do you know that?"

"I sensed that, yeah," he said, lying down beside her. "And I hereby promise to never tell you what to do again. Ever." Then he grinned. "Now lie down."

Darcie laughed, a little nervously. "It's not just that I'd like to get my way once in a while, call the shots once in a while…"

"It is, too," he said, kissing her hand. "You're dying to call the shots. Admit it."

"Okay, maybe I am. Once in a while. The only time I get to give orders is when I call for takeout. Even then, they always talk me into breadsticks."

"I'm in bed with the woman and she's talking breadsticks. I do love you, Darc."

"I love you, too. And we can spend the rest of our lives getting to know each other. You were right about that."

Cameron sat up, stripped off his shirt. "Tell you what, Darc. Tonight's your night. Tonight, you're in charge. Totally in charge. One hundred and fifty percent, in charge."

"What—what do you mean? You mean *here? In bed?*"

"It's where we are, yes," he said. "Come on, Darc, tell me what *you* want. Even if what you want is to go downstairs and watch TV. I mean it."

"Oh boy," she said, closing her eyes. "I never meant...this isn't what I...I don't...kiss me. That's it. Kiss me."

"It's a start," he whispered. "Where?"

She opened her eyes. "What do you mean, *where?* Oh, for pity's sake, on the mouth. Kiss me on the mouth."

"Tongue or no tongue?"

She glared at him. "There might be a good movie on TV, you know." Then she felt herself blushing. "Tongue."

She'd say one thing for him, he was the obedient sort.

He probably would have kissed her forever, and she probably would have kissed him back just as long, except that people still do have to breathe.

"My...my clothes," she said, gasped against his shoulder. "I want to get out of my clothes."

"May I help?"

She thought about that, for nearly an entire second. "If you want to...I mean, yes. Help me out of my clothes."

He moved away, marginally, and began unbuttoning her blouse...which was when she first looked up and saw the mirror. She'd forgotten about the mirror.

She saw Cameron. The back of his head, actually. His bare upper torso. His khaki slacks, one long leg insinuated between hers.

His fingers, sliding her buttons free.

Saw herself watching herself watching Cameron.

She remembered doing this before. Memory of those moments sent sensation slamming into her, so that now she saw her own legs moving, sliding across the sheets as lying still no longer remained an option.

Not when her skin was burning, on fire. Not when the bits of reflected candlelight from that silly disco ball were so intriguing to watch as they danced across their bodies.

Especially not when Cameron opened her front-closing bra and kissed the straps down over her arms.

She pushed herself up, so he could remove both the blouse and the bra…and waited.

"You want something, sweetheart?"

He really meant this. He wasn't going to do a thing, unless she told him to do it.

"Help me out of my blouse. And my bra."

He did, and she collapsed against the mattress once more.

"You…you could touch me?"

His breath was warm against her ear. "Where?"

Darcie swallowed with some difficulty, looking up at the mirror, seeing herself naked from the waist up, unable to not notice that her nipples were puckered in anticipation.

"You could touch me…you could…second base?"

He kissed her neck. "How?"

She should be angry. Incensed. Certainly frustrated. But she wasn't. She was excited. And getting more excited by the moment. "Your hand."

Still nuzzling her neck, he slid one hand across her midriff, then moved up to cup her breast. She watched in the mirror, trying to control her breathing, as he gently squeezed her, then wet the tip of his index finger in his mouth before touching it to her nipple.

She closed her eyes. Opened them again when he began lightly pinching her nipple between his thumb and forefinger.

Now it seemed she had begun giving orders to herself, because she only watched from "somewhere else" as she raised her right hand and began guiding Cameron's head toward her right breast, urging him on. "With…with your mouth. Your tongue. Please."

With her splayed fingers dug into his hair, she watched as he kissed her breast, teased the other with his fingers. Watched, as her chest rose and fell with her rapid breathing.

Forever. She could stay this way forever, feeling the sensations, watching him love her.

There was a growing tightness between her legs. A blossoming yearning.

All right, maybe not forever.

Her free hand working the button on her shorts, she gasped out, "Third…third base. Please."

My, he was good at this, because both of them were naked in short order, and she'd pulled him close for more kisses, even as she moved his hand low on her belly.

Lower.

She wanted to watch. She had to watch.

"Touch me, Cameron," she said, bending her knees, allowing her legs to fall open. "Touch me."

"Like this?" he asked, and Darcie moaned as she watched his hand slide between her thighs, tensed as his fingers opened her, found her.

"Yes…yes. Touch me."

He was on his side now, meeting her gaze in the mirror above them. She could tell when he redirected his gaze to his hand, still moving between her thighs. "Like this? Do you like it like this?" His breath was ragged, his breathing as tortured as her own. She felt his fingers spreading her even more, his thumb lightly rubbing at her very core. "Or more like this?"

Her blood was roaring in her ears.

"Oh, please, Cam. Just shut up and kiss me!"

His slow grin reflected back to her, and then his concentration was all on the reflection of his hand, moving so expertly over her most intimate, sensitive skin. "Where?"

Darcie closed her eyes for a moment, then slowly lowered her hand, placed it on his.

He kissed her mouth first, his tongue plunging as his fingers mimicked the motion, driving her past all inhibition, all ragged remnants of modesty, then dragged his mouth down over her breasts, to her belly. And lower.

How very strange, to watch what you feel. To see your hips raised, held. To watch as well as feel as your thighs are caressed, kissed; as warm breath teases you; as a hot, moist mouth claims you in the most intimate kiss; as a tongue begins to move…to move…to move …

Take. Take. Give. Give.

Burn…flower…watch…feel…tense…release.

Release.

Darcie forgot the mirror, forgot the rules, forgot the world still existed outside this room, beyond Cameron's touch.

She reached for him, barely able to breathe his name, and he came to her, came into her, came with her.

That, Darcie decided as she slowly floated back to earth, looking up at the mirror to see herself wrapped in Cameron's arms, was the way she wanted them always to be. Together.

WHAT WAS THAT? Ah, the door. The door was opening. Freedom. Sweet Freedom!

Hot damn!

But Lucky wasn't stupid.

He padded to the slightly open door. Slowly stuck his head out into the darkened hallway. Looked left. Looked right.

And never saw the muzzle somebody slipped over his head, so that he couldn't even yowl for help as he was tightly wrapped in a blanket and then carried away….

CHAPTER SEVENTEEN

CAMERON STEPPED OUT onto the front porch, raised his arms above his head and stretched. Life was good. Life was better than good. Life, as a matter of fact, was pretty well damn near perfect.

Shangri-La looked good, even great, with the grass still damp from last night's rain. The sky was washed a clear, bright blue. The white petunias and some pretty red flowering plants Darcie had planted below the front porch almost made him forget that, behind him, the house was still pink.

He could forget a lot this morning, because that would leave him more brain space to remember last night, he thought, grinning, and, he thought, probably looking like he'd gone a little slap-happy.

He didn't care. He was in love, and love didn't hurt. Not anymore. Love was good, love was great. Life was good, life was great. Darcie was...*magnificent.*

And magnificent women shouldn't have to prepare breakfast for a houseful of guests the morning after the best night in the history of the world. Sunday morning doughnuts from the local shop? Yeah, that sounded like a plan. Edwin could eat a plain bagel or something.

Cameron reached into his slacks pocket for his car keys, then remembered that Edwin had taken them, and his car. He looked to his left. Okay, the car was back. But when he checked, the keys weren't in the ignition. Nor were they on the table in the foyer.

He heard footsteps on the stairs and saw Darcie's long legs appearing below the ceiling line. "Darc? We've got two choices. We wake up Edwin and ask him where the car keys are, or I make my famous scrambled eggs. Oh, wait, your car's in the garage. I forgot that. So, your choices are— What's wrong?"

He stepped away from her when she got to the bottom of the stairs, looking as if she was going to cry. "Oh, no. Uh-uh, Darc. Don't say anything. Not a word. This is a perfect morning. We have a perfect morning going here."

"Lucky's gone."

"Damn it," Cameron said, smacking the side of his fist on the banister. "What did he do? Find your nail file and dig his way out?"

"I showered in Uncle Horry's bedroom, then went to brush my teeth. My bedroom door was unlocked, and Lucky was gone. I threw on some clothes and came to find you. Somebody let him out, Cameron. *Lily* let him out."

"I'll say one thing for the woman—she doesn't give up easy. Now what?"

"I don't know. Do we call Attorney Humbolt?"

Cameron lightly pressed the back of his hand against Darcie's forehead. "Nope. No fever. But I think I have a better idea. Let's dismantle all the phone wires, so *nobody* can call Humbolt."

Darcie looked at him disapprovingly. "I don't think so, no. Attorney Humbolt knows Lily's doing this. He can't start the countdown again, knowing Lily's doing this. It wouldn't be fair."

"No fever, but still delirious. Amazing. He's a lawyer, Darc." He took her hand. "Come on, let's see if Lucky left us any clues."

"Clues? Now who's delirious?" But Darcie allowed him to drag her upstairs with him, down the hallway to her bedroom. She stepped inside, sniffed the air. "Does odor count? Let go of my hand. I've got to scoop the litter."

"And I'll open the windows. What does that cat eat, anyway?"

"You don't want to know." Darcie disappeared into the bathroom with the scooper, and Cameron heard the toilet flush before she washed her hands, then returned to the room. "No ransom note, I'll bet?"

"You mean, as in Lily knows we know, and now she's kidnapped Lucky? Keeping you from getting everything isn't enough for her anymore? Now she's looking for a profit?"

"Like that, yes," Darcie said, then shook her head. "No, she'd never get away with it. I guess I'm still having trouble believing anyone could be that vindictive, that hateful."

Cameron leaned against the window wall. "I don't like to say this, but I'm having the same problem. It would be one thing if Frau Blücher gets everything if we screw up, but she doesn't, Edwin does. Unless she's worked out a deal with him?"

Darcie had gone back into the bathroom, and now walked back into the bedroom, her hair scraped back into a ponytail, her mouth full of toothpaste, to shake her toothbrush at him. "I refuse to believe Uncle Edwin has anything to do with this. He's too nice."

"He's also still the logical choice," Cameron reminded her, following her into the bathroom, to find that, even with Lucky missing again, he was in love enough to get a real kick out of watching Darcie rinse and spit. "Admit it, babe. He's the only choice, when you get right down to it."

Darcie splashed water on her face, grabbed some kind of bottled soap, and worked a lather between her palms. Turning to him as she scrubbed her hands over her face—he liked watching that, too; he was definitely a lost cause—she said, "Not really. Maybe Uncle Edwin is actually very much in the way. Did you ever think of that one?"

Cameron squinted as he looked at her bent back, for now she was splashing water on her face again. "Meaning?"

"Meaning, keeping to the idea that Lily is guilty as sin, and believing that she can't be working on her own, not if her motive is more than just trying to screw up my life—maybe she's working with Attorney Humbolt. Yes?"

She lightly spread some kind of cream on her skin, something that gave that skin a soft, clean glow, then reached for her lipstick. Cameron stayed her hand. "Don't. You don't need anything else. You're beautiful."

She went on tiptoe, kissed him. "Thank you. You're

wrong, but thank you. Come on, let's go walk the grounds, and talk about Humbolt while we look for Lucky. Because it really could be him."

They were quiet until they were outside, walking along the lawn, holding hands. "How so? Humbolt, I mean. And keep calling for Lucky while we talk about this."

"Well, what if he was stealing from Uncle Horry all these years? It's possible, you know. Uncle Horry only cared about his toys, all his electronic stuff. And television. He loved television. He never left Shangri-La, never really talked to people. It would probably be very easy to…to rip him off."

"Possible. And Humbolt just separated from his wife and bought that sports car. But that proves what? That when Horry died, Humbolt figured out that you might choose another lawyer? I don't know how large Horry's estate is. Humbolt says it's big, so there would have to be some sort of accounting made for the government, that kind of thing. I'd like to say I know about this stuff, but I don't. But I'm pretty sure whatever Humbolt did, if he did anything, would be discovered."

"Oh. You're right. Even if everything went to Uncle Edwin, and Uncle Edwin sure doesn't seem like the type to pay much attention, Humbolt would be found out. Even if he killed off Lucky, then killed off Uncle Edwin. So we're back to just Lily."

"Or Lily working with Edwin. She takes care of Lucky for him, he gets the house, the money, and he gives her the house. He doesn't seem to want it, although he could be faking that, along with the sweet-old-guy bit. I'm sorry, Darcie, but it's too much of a coincidence, Edwin showing up here after all these years."

"He explained that. He saw Uncle Horry's death notice online."

"And we bought it. He's such a nice guy, we bought it. You know, we should have asked Humbolt just how much money is involved here. *A lot* is too vague. Comfortable a lot? Or I'd-do-something-illegal-to-get-it a lot?"

They had circled the house, talking, calling for Lucky, and were heading back onto the front porch. "I still say it's just Lily, and this time I'm going after her, and I'm not going to be polite about it!"

"No more Ms. Nice Gal, huh? Should I duck for cover?"

"You should search the house while I go put the thumbscrews to her."

"Go get her, tiger," Cameron said, and headed for the living room, to play, yet again, the crawl-around-on-the-floor-and-look-for-Lucky game.

"YOU LOST HIM AGAIN, didn't you?" Lily said smugly as Darcie entered the kitchen. "I heard you two out there, calling for him. So I called Attorney Humbolt. He'll be here any minute now."

The woman couldn't have looked any happier if she'd been dancing around with a rose between her teeth, she was so obviously proud of herself and delighted in Darcie's misery. Darcie, in her current very bad mood, said so. "Don't you dance around me with a rose between your teeth!"

Lily's eyes went wide. Really wide. Wide enough that Darcie could see white all around her irises. Her breathing got deeper, faster, her nostrils quivered. "Who told you?" she asked, advancing on Darcie. "Who—" And then she backed off, relaxed her posture, smiled again. "You don't know anything."

I know you're a whack job, Darcie thought to herself, rethinking her idea of going head to head with the woman. "It won't work, Lily. We all know you've done something with Lucky. You let him out again, and he won't be home for days. Attorney Humbolt will understand."

"Will he?" Lily said, then turned and headed for her bedroom off the kitchen, sort of swaggering as she went, leaving Darcie to realize that she had no idea what Attorney Humbolt would say.

Exasperated, and more than a little desperate, she looked up at the ceiling and said, "Uncle Horry? Uncle Horry, if Cameron hasn't just been teasing me, if you're here—*help.*"

"I'M SORRY, MS. REED, but a will is a binding legal document, and I, as executor, am bound by the terms. The video will, as I said, didn't mention this, but there is a clause stating that if Lucky is gone for—"

"Yeah, yeah, we know," Cameron said, squeezing Darcie's hand. They'd been over the house twice, attic to cellar, and no Lucky. "Lily didn't hide him somewhere—she let him out. He'll be back tonight, tomorrow morning. But that's too late. We know the drill."

Edwin sat on the edge of one of the couches in the living room in his sailor suit, doing a good imitation of someone wringing their hands. "Unless the poor animal has been done away with somehow. Are you sure you've looked everywhere?"

"There, there, Poobie-bear, don't worry," Pookie said, patting him on the back as she sat thigh to thigh with him. "He'll show up. He showed up last time." Then she blew her nose, for she'd picked up a cold somewhere, and her nose kept running, and her eyes were red-rimmed beneath her mascara. "Oh, that's the last time I think it's romantic to walk in the rain at midnight. Poobie, I don't know how you talked me into it."

"Pookie's right, Darc, he will show up," Cameron whispered to Darcie. "In the meantime, this place is feeling too much like we're holding a wake. I'm going to go look for him outside again, okay?"

Darcie nodded, then smiled wanly at Pookie as that woman told her how fond she was of Lucky. "If I weren't so allergic, I'd just scoop him up and snuggle him close to me and..."

Cameron looked at Pookie, then shook his head. No. That was just ridiculous.

Almost as ridiculous as going on a hunt for Horry, but that's where he was heading.

"Horry?" he called quietly, heading up the stairs. "Horry? Knock if you hear me...."

"WELL, IT'S ABOUT TIME! Do you know how hot it is up here? Do you? Do you, huh? Almost as hot as it's going to be where you're heading if something happens to this poor little kitty cat."

"I'm sorry, Lucky," Horry said, his head struck through the roof of the crawl space over the garages. "Can't you get out?"

Lucky's mismatched eyes glinted in the weak rays of sunlight that filtered down through the roof vent. "Oh, sure. Anytime I want. I like being up here. *Are you nuts!*"

"You don't have to yell, Lucky. I wish I could help, but it took all I could do just to float up this high. They're looking for you, you know. Darcie and Cameron. Maybe if you yowled?"

"I heard them, earlier, and I did. Did they hear me? Gee, let's guess. *I'm still here!*"

Horry tried to push himself into the crawl space. Nothing. Maybe part of one shoulder, but that was about it. "I'm so sorry, Lucky."

"Oh, well, then, that's all right, isn't it? You're sorry. A big fat lot of good that does me. You know what's going to happen, don't you? It's going to get hotter up here. Hotter. No water, no food. I'm a dead cat. And *you* killed me."

"I know, I know," Horry said, growing frantic. "Oh! Wait! Yes...yes, that's Cameron. Do you hear him, Lucky? He's calling your name. No, wait. He's calling *my* name."

"And you're still here because...?" Lucky said, his question ending in a cross between a growl and a whimper. "Here's your big chance, Horry. Tell him where I am. And tell him why, darn it, because this locking up the kitty and trying to kill the kitty is getting pretty old, you know?"

"Yes, but how? You know I can't—"

Lucky made a run at Horry, hissing, and the next thing Horry knew, he was on his back on the ground. "Wow, he really means it," he told himself, and got up, dusted himself off and floated after Cameron.

"Horry?" Cameron called, his voice low, but carrying. "Horry, I'm looking like an ass out here. Come on, or I'm going to have to believe I've been making you up."

Horry tapped him on the shoulder.

His finger went straight through Cameron.

He floated in front of Cameron, stuck his fingers in his ears, and stuck out his tongue.

Nothing.

Cameron kept walking and, dejected, Horry floated along behind him, his toes dragging on the ground. He was definitely losing altitude ability here. Time was running out.

"Lucky!" Cameron called loudly. "Where are you, you damn cat? Horry?" he added more quietly. Then he said something else, but Horry preferred not to believe Darcie's nice young man said those words, so he ignored them.

Ribbit-ribbit. Ribbit-ribbit.

Ribbit-ribbit. Ribbit-ribbit.

Cameron stopped dead on the drive, so Horry stopped, as well.

"Okay, that was me, I set off the frogs," Cameron said. "The first pair. I set off the first pair, but I didn't get to the second pair yet. So the *first* pair went off twice. Ah-*ha!*"

Horry floated backward as fast as he could go as Cameron turned around, glared straight at him.

Ribbit-ribbit. Ribbit-ribbit.

"You," Cameron said, waving his hands in front of him, cutting straight through Horry at about waist height. "You're here somewhere, right? I'm not nuts—you're here. I have to tell you, Horry, you were a nice guy, but we've got some serious problems right now, and they're your fault, so how about a little assistance here?"

"Yes, yes, I know. I'm sorry. And Lucky's in the crawl space over the garages and he's really not happy about that and you have to save him and you have to—oh, this isn't working," Horry ended, defeated. "You can't hear me, can you? Cameron? Son? Why are you smiling?"

Cameron put his hands out again, as if he was a crossing guard halting traffic. "I've got it! Stay here, Horry. Stay here, don't move. Just don't go anywhere. I'll be right back. *Don't move.*"

Horry watched as Cameron ran for the porch. As he opened the screen door he was calling Darcie's name.

DARCIE STOOD where Cameron had told her to stand, wondering if the strain would get to her soon, too, the way it had gotten to Cameron. "Cam, you can't possibly believe—"

"Just wait, Darc, okay," Cameron told her, "give this a chance. Horry? You still here?"

"You're expecting an answer?"

"Not yet, Darc, no. Just hang on. Horry? Okay, here's the plan. I'm going to ask you a question, and you're going to answer."

"Oh, my God…"

"Darcie, please. Now, Horry, the way you're going to answer is to step in front of one of the frogs. Or wave your hand in front of one of the frogs. Something in front of one of the frogs." He put his hand on one ceramic green frog head. "This one, okay? I ask the question—a yes-or-no-question—and you step in front of the frog once for yes, twice for no. You've got that?"

Silence.

"How about a glass of iced tea, Cameron?" Darcie asked him, putting her hand on his back. "It is hot out here."

"No!" Cameron said, staring at the frog. "This is going to work. He just didn't know I wanted an answer just now."

"I see," Darcie said, trying not to take any of this too seriously. "Uncle Horry thought it was a rhetorical question. I can see that."

"You're really not getting into the swing of this, Darc. Okay, Horry, once more. One wave in front of the frog for yes, two for no. And here's the question, Horry. Are you here?"

Darcie closed her eyes. Poor Cameron. Maybe Shangri-La got to everyone, sooner or later. Look at Uncle Horry, poor man. Look at Lily.

Ribbit-ribbit.

"Ha!"

Darcie's eyes flew open as Cameron slapped her, none too gently, on the back.

"You hear that? You heard that, Darc, you know you did."

"I had my eyes closed. You did that," she said, not as sure of herself as she'd been a moment earlier.

Cameron put his hands behind his back. "You ask him a question. Go ahead. Ask him something."

"This is ridiculous. Impossible." Darcie looked at the empty space all around the frog, then took a deep breath. "Uncle Horry? How old are you?"

"He can't answer yes or no to that, Darc. Try again."

She shot Cameron an exasperated look. "Uncle Horry, do you know where Lucky is?"

Ribbit-ribbit.

Cameron punched his fist in the air. *"Yes!"*

"I...uh...I think I want to sit down," Darcie said, and did just that. Sat down on the grass. "You, um, you ask him something."

"Right. Horry? Is Lucky all right?"

There was silence for a good thirty seconds.

Ribbit-ribbit.

Darcie looked up at Cameron. "I think that means he isn't sure. That's not good. Find out where Lucky is."

"Horry? Is Lucky outside?"

"That's pretty broad, Cam."

Ribbit-ribbit. Ribbit-ribbit.

"He's not outside. This isn't easy, Darc, with just yes-or-no-questions. Horry? He's inside?"

Ribbit-ribbit.

"Oh, good, he's inside the house," Darcie said, getting to her feet. "We must have missed him. Come on, Cameron. Uncle Horry, we'll be right back."

Ribbit-ribbit. Ribbit-ribbit. Ribbit-ribbit. Ribbit-ribbit.

"Hang on, Darcie, Horry's upset about something. Horry? Is Lucky inside the house?"

Ribbit-ribbit. Ribbit-ribbit.

"But he is inside?"

Ribbit-ribbit.

"But, Cameron, the house *is* inside. There's nowhere else that's—the garages? Cameron? I thought you said you checked the garage."

"I did, I checked. Horry? Lucky's in the garage?"

Ribbit-ribbit.

"Yoo-hoo! What are you two doing out there?"

"Uncle Edwin," Darcie said under her breath, as if it was a secret.

"I heard him," Cameron answered just as quietly. "Get rid of him."

"How?" Darcie said as Uncle Edwin called to them again.

"I don't know. Just do it. Horry, I'm going to go find Lucky. Will you be here when I get back?"

Ribbit-ribbit.

"Great. Darcie, go tell Edwin we were trying to figure out where the short is on these frogs, and then keep him busy. Keep them all busy. Once I find Lucky, your uncle and I are going to have a little talk."

"A yes-or-no talk?"

"Okay, maybe a long talk, not a little talk. I know, take everyone out for breakfast. Horry and I should have everything figured out by the time you get back."

"Even Lily?" Before he could answer, Darcie turned to call to her uncle, "We're looking for the short, Uncle Edwin. How about we all go out to breakfast?"

"No, not Lily. If I have to, I can handle her. Now go, okay?"

Darcie waved at her uncle Edwin again, then looked at the frog…because there was nothing else to look at. "You'll really be here, Uncle Horry?"

Ribbit-ribbit.

"I love you, Uncle Horry," she said, then turned and headed for the porch.

CAMERON WAS SITTING on the porch, nursing a well-deserved beer and two new scratches on his forearms, Lucky back in his harness and connected to his leash, when his car and Humbolt's car pulled into the drive.

Ribbit-ribbit. Ribbit-ribbit. Ribbit-ribbit…

"God, I love that sound. We're definitely keeping some of those frogs. Some flamingos, too, since Horry liked them so much," he said, getting to his feet as everyone piled out of the cars and watched as Darcie walked toward him. "Hi. Nice breakfast?"

She's rolled her eyes. "How about I ask you a question instead? What's the difference between a three-ring circus and a family diner?"

Cameron shrugged. "I don't know."

"Neither does Pookie," Darcie told him, sort of hanging on him, using him as a banister to climb onto the porch. "Uncle Horry?"

"Still out there, far as I know. Wave to him."

"I still don't really believe this. Okay, I'll wave."

Ribbit-ribbit. Ribbit-ribbit. Ribbit-ribbit.

"Scratch that," she said, her bottom lip trembling. "But if this were anyplace but here, I'd think you had a remote control in your pocket."

"But it's Horry's Shangri-La, and I don't think we have any choice except to believe it. Now say hello to Lucky."

"Oh, I didn't see him!" Darcie dropped to her knees, to take Lucky's face between her hands, kiss the top of his head. "Are you all right, baby? You look so sad. Who did this to you?"

"Uh-uh, Darc. Don't ask the cat, ask the frog. Except I already did. I don't have all of it, but Horry and I had a pretty good man-to-frog talk. By the process of elimination, I know who tried to misplace Lucky."

"Lily, right? We already know it's Lily."

"We also know who else."

"Who else? Oh, God, tell me it isn't Uncle Edwin."

"Nope, not him. Lucky tried to tell me who it is, the day of the memorial service, but I didn't get it then. Horry had to tell me. Stick here with me, because I'll need you. Yes-or-no answers don't do much when you don't know the questions, so we're going to have to wing this a little."

Cameron took a step forward and stuck his fingers between his lips, whistled. Edwin, Pookie and Humbolt, who had been deep in admiration of the attorney's sports car, all turned to look at him.

"If I could have your attention, please? I found Lucky."

Edwin grabbed Pookie by the shoulders and gave her a smacking kiss on the mouth. "Isn't that wonderful, Pookie-bear? Congratulations, boy!" Then he ran up the steps and hugged Darcie.

"Where did you find him?" Attorney Humbolt asked, joining Cameron and Darcie on the porch.

"Right where somebody put him. In the crawl space over the garages. Pookie? Care to join us?"

"No. It's *her?*" Darcie whispered, goggling at Cameron, who nodded his head slightly. Oh, yeah, she was goggling. God, Cameron loved this. This was *great.*

"Sure thing, sweet buns," Pookie said, doing her high-heeled wiggle as she toddled up the porch steps. "Such good news!"

"Yeah, it is. What do you say we go tell Lily? She's waiting for us in Horry's study."

Cameron held open the screen door as everyone passed in front of him, then grabbed Darcie, holding her hand as they followed along to the study…where Lily was waiting, tied to Horry's desk chair with her own clothesline.

"Get me loose!" she screeched the moment they'd entered the room. "Call the cops! Arrest that madman!"

"You tied her up? You've lost it, haven't you?" Darcie asked Cameron. "There's been a lot of stress, a lot of nutziness, and you've lost it."

"It was the only way I could figure out to get everyone in the same place at the same time. Just hang in, Darc, and help out if you can."

"You mean, like making sure you get a good lawyer and reasonable bail?"

"Funny."

Cameron clapped his hands as Humbolt untied Lily. "Now that we're all here? Lily? You staying? Yeah, I guess you are, at least until Humbolt gets that last knot."

The housekeeper glared at him.

"I don't know what you're doing, son, but this is illegal, you know."

"Yeah, Clark, I had a feeling it was. But Lily wanted to leave, and I really didn't want her to go. Did I, Lily?"

"She was the one trying to hide Lucky again, so the terms of the will were broken," Darcie said, looking at Cameron, who gave her a quick thumb's-up. "And...and Pookie helped her!"

Cameron winced. That might have been a bit fast on the trigger. After all, he didn't have any proof except Uncle Horry.

"You *idiot!* You *told* him?"

But, then again, he decided, maybe it had been perfect timing.

"Grab her, Cameron!" Darcie yelled as Pookie lunged toward Lily, her arms outstretched, her inch-long nails looking a lot like talons.

Lily scrambled to her feet, tried to hide herself behind Humbolt. "Keep her away from me!"

Edwin sat down on one of the chairs, looking blank. "I don't understand. Pookie?"

Cameron didn't understand, either, but now that the ball was rolling, he'd give it another push. "You're right, Pookie. Lily told me everything."

"Oh, yeah? And I'll bet she told you it was all her idea, too. She never had an idea in her life. Look at her!"

Now Lily went on the attack, and Humbolt had his hands full. "You always do that, Thelma. *Look at her, look at her. She's the plain one. I'm the pretty one.* I *hate* you!"

Cameron was having a rough time, holding on to Pookie by her elbows. "Now, ladies…"

"Shut up!" they shouted in unison.

Edwin looked around the room, his gaze landing on Bupkus. "I'm confused."

Of all people, Clark Humbolt took charge at that point. "Am I to understand that Lily here, and Pookie, are responsible for the problems with Lucky?"

"Pookie, my ass. Thelma. Her name is *Thelma.* Isn't that right—*sis!*"

"They're sisters?" Darcie said, and Pookie turned her head to glare at her.

"Cute, sweetie. Now, stop acting like you don't know. That bigmouth over there told you everything. *Yes,* we're sisters. Oh, let go, handsome. I've been around the block a few times. I know when it's over. Besides, nothing happened. No harm, no foul."

"You're the one who grabbed Lucky this time, aren't you?" Cameron asked, letting go of the woman. "That's why you said you have a cold. You don't. Lucky stirred up your allergies."

Pookie toddled to a chair, sat down, crossed her legs at the knee and hooked a thumb at Cameron. "Listen to him. We've got our own Secret Squirrel here. Yeah, I took him. She'd already screwed it up." She put her hands on the arm of the chair, leaned forward. "You *always* screw it up."

Lily growled, and Humbolt prudently shuffled around the desk, away from her.

"Oh, I'm scared, I'm scared," Pookie said, rolling her eyes. "Okay, bottom line, so we can get out of here. She's my sister, which is my bad luck. I'm the good-looking one, so I had it pretty easy, but she had to take the faithful-companion route. Does sort of remind you of a schnauzer, don't she? Yeah, well, tough beans, sis, I'm telling it like it is."

Lily sat down.

"Anyway, there I was, having my usual good time with one of my Poobies, when she calls me, all hot and bothered. Horry changed his will. Everything she'd worked for had gone straight to hell, and she needed my help. I mean, face it, she was lucky to have Horry. And she's way too ugly to be squatting on another old man, starting from scratch. But you guys already know this."

"I think I'm going to be sick," Darcie said, leaning her forehead against Cameron's arm.

Lily roused again. "I cared for him."

"Sure. Right. You *loved* him."

"I didn't say that, and you know it. Like you loved any of them."

"At least I show my geezers a good time. What do you do, Lily? Cook a nice pot roast? Clean a mean toilet?"

Cameron watched as Edwin pushed himself out of his chair and left the room.

"Okay, let's stick to the facts, ladies," he said as he nudged Darcie, pointed to Edwin, and she quickly followed her uncle out of the room. "Lily found out about the new will, called you, and you decided to find Edwin Willikins, arrange things so he inherited."

Pookie shrugged. "It was time I thought about settling down. A girl could do worse than an old guy with lots of money and a bad ticker. Lily's problem came just at the right time for me. He was giving me an engagement ring, you know. Any day now. We break the will, I talk him into giving sis the house, and she's off my back. Even if the whole thing fell apart, I've still got my hooks in Poobie-bear. Win-win for me. I get the best of it, but she never figures that stuff out, do you, sis?"

Cameron kept pushing for details. "So maybe Edwin found out about Horry's death because you pointed it out to him on the Internet."

"Bright boy. That man doesn't know the Internet from a fish net."

Cameron looked at Humbolt. "And you, Clark, you said you tried to talk Horry out of the new will, that you tried *several* times. One of those times—did you ask Lily to help you?"

Humbolt hung his head. "I thought she could help dissuade him."

"Instead, she started making plans. Even played the

grieving housekeeper when we showed up for the reading of the will, then played the screwed housekeeper—no pun intended," he ended, wincing. "Pookie here was already in place, and having herself some fun, and you got the ball rolling."

"Except," Pookie said, getting to her feet, "dumb-shit over there never did figure out that all I did was check out Poobie-bear, find out how rich he is, and zero in on him. She really thought I was going to help her. I'm only here because, what the hell, it sounded like a giggle, once that Horry guy bit it."

"And because I was going to tell Edwin all about you if you didn't come help me if Horry died," Lily said. "And now I'll tell you something else, Thelma. I never said *word one* to that boy. They had *nothing* on you, until you told them. You dug your own hole, with your own mouth. Now you've lost another sugar daddy, and I've still got my annuity. I've thought about it. What do I want with this old house, anyway? I'm sick of cleaning it. My God, it doesn't even have a garbage disposal!"

"I hear you, sister," Cameron said quietly, then stepped between the women, because it looked like Pookie was going to go on the attack again. "Humbolt? We don't want to deal with this, do we? I mean, nobody looks good in this. Horry. Edwin. *You.* How about we just tell the ladies to pack up and be out of here in an hour?"

"Well, it's…there are probably several crimes in here somewhere and…then again, as the, um, as the lady said, no harm, no foul. Leave a forwarding address, Lily?" He looked at Cameron. "It would be easier just to give her the money Horry willed her. If she promises to go away?"

"Sounds like a plan to me. Now, if we're done here, and I know I, for one, would really like to think we're done here, I think I should go find Darcie and Edwin. And let Lucky off that leash, if he hasn't already chewed through it."

Humbolt looked from one hotly glaring sister to the other and broke into a near trot. "Good idea. Let me come with you!"

Cameron, feeling pretty damn brilliant, bowed to Lily and Pookie. "Thank you, ladies. You've been a big help. We couldn't have solved any of this without you."

Fortunately, the paperweight Lily threw missed him....

CHAPTER EIGHTEEN

"I AM SERIOUS, Uncle Edwin. Uncle Horry is still here," Darcie said, holding the man's hand as she walked him toward the drive. "Cameron figured it out. Oh, Cameron, here you are. What's it like in there?"

Lucky, newly released, trotted past them all to stop, three frogs down on the drive.

"I'm not sure. They're either both in their rooms, packing, or they've killed each other. Hey, Edwin, I'm sorry. Pookie was a gold digger. It happens."

Edwin nodded. "Don't I know it. My mother was one. Where do you think I got the money? I inherited everything she wormed out of four husbands, and then made the same mistakes they did. Three ex-wives, you know. Pookie-bear thought she'd be number four, but I finally got smart about ten years ago and handed my money over to a manager. Real bugger, that guy, about following orders, and my orders were to put me on an allowance and give every last penny to charity if I was ever dumb enough to take another trip to the altar. I…I was trying to find a way to tell Pookie…"

"Did you hear any of what went on, Lucky?" Horry mind-talked to the cat. "I was poking my head in the window of the study and heard it all. Lily and Pookie are sisters. No wonder I was so attracted to Pookie. Although, sad to say, it seems both of them are gold diggers. I was nothing but a sex machine to Lily, a boy toy."

Lucky, always tactful, coughed up a hair ball. "A money machine, you mean. And what are you still doing here? I thought you were fading away, heading upstairs. So go already. I don't like saying this, Horry, but you're a ghost. Gives me the creeps."

"Shh, I'm going, I'm going. That heavenly music keeps getting louder. Aren't you going to miss me?"

Lucky didn't say anything for a few moments, then tried to rub himself against Horry's legs. It didn't work, he went right through him, but the thought was there, Horry decided.

"Thanks. I'll miss you, too."

Lucky, being Lucky, gained control of his cat emotions. "Yeah, yeah, but I get the funny feeling I've seen the last sushi I'm going to see around this joint."

"Shhh! What's Edwin saying now? He sounds sad."

"...but I was fond of her. We did have us some fun. So I'm a fool, Darcie, Cameron. An old fool, at that."

Darcie's heart was aching for him. She kissed his cheek. "It doesn't matter, Uncle Edwin. I'm just so glad you came here, no matter how it happened. You're my family now, you know. We're each other's family."

"And Horry," Edwin said, his eyes twinkling once more. "I'm really going to be able to talk to him?"

Cameron squeezed Darcie's hand. "I asked him, earlier, if he's going to be here forever, and he said no. Bottom line? I think we're lucky if he's here for the afternoon. So, how about we let Darcie talk to him first, okay, Edwin? Go on, sweetheart. He's probably standing next to Lucky."

She took a step forward. "Uncle Horry? Are you there?"

Ribbit-ribbit.

Darcie, caught between a grin and a sob, took a deep breath, squared her shoulders, and went to say goodbye to Uncle Horry.

CAMERON AND DARCIE STOOD arm in arm, watching the limo's taillights disappear down the drive before Cameron hit the remote control, closing the gates on the fading *ribbit-ribbit* chorus.

"As they say in the movies, babe, alone at last."

"He promised he'll be here for our wedding," Darcie said, at last turning to reenter the house.

"Oh, good. Did he happen to say when that is?" Cameron asked, holding open the screen door. "I have a passing interest."

"I thought we'd work it out with your mother," Darcie told him, "when you take me to meet her. And probably before I start horticultural classes in the fall. So, pretty quick."

"Is that so? You've got it all figured out, do you?"

Darcie took his hand and led him toward the stairs. "I've figured out that Uncle Horry's will pretty much says we're going to be alone here together for the next two weeks or so. So, should we just share custody of Bupkus?"

"Sounds good. He always liked you best, anyway."

"And Lucky. We'll share him, too."

"Please, I was having a moment here. Don't ruin it." But Cameron smiled as he said that.

"Okay. Back to us being locked up here together until the end of the month. Does that give you any ideas, big boy?"

"A few," he said, pushing her so she'd move faster, until she ran ahead, into Uncle Horry's bedroom.

No. Their bedroom. They'd had Horry's blessing, and the torch had been passed. Shangri-La was theirs now, lock, stock and frogs.

"Oh, good. Tell me your ideas. Was one of them learning more about ourselves?" Darcie asked him, stopping him by holding on to his shoulders, then beginning to open his belt. Her smile was positively wicked, and he was liking this better and better. "Because there's still so much I want to learn. For instance," she said, unsnapping his slacks, "I want to develop my taste in furniture. You're an architect, you must have studied things like that. What's that piece? Over there?"

Cameron, busy with the buttons on her blouse, looked to his left. "What? That? I don't know, Darc. Ugly. It's ugly. Is it important?"

"No, not really," she said, helping him as he slid her blouse off her shoulders. "Although, I have been thinking I'd like to redecorate the house. You know, you take care of the outside and I'll take care of the inside?"

"You want to get rid of the bed? The mirror?"

"I believe in ghosts now, Cameron. But that doesn't

mean I'm entirely nuts. That bed stays, if we have to rebuild the entire house around it."

"That's my girl. What about the barber pole?"

"Oh, that goes. That definitely goes. When Attorney Humbolt finds out where Lily is, we'll ship it to her."

"Okay, one out of two. I'm not complaining," he said as she began walking backward, toward the bed, crooking her finger at him so that he'd follow her.

"Just hold that thought for one more second," he said, and crossed to the door. Closed it. Locked it.

"Cameron? Why did you lock the door? There's nobody here but us. Nobody but Lucky."

"I know, babe." Cameron pulled his shirt off over his head, smoothed his hair as he looked at her, reached for her. "There's just something about that cat..."

* * * * *

AUTHORS AT SEA
www.authorsatsea.com
Join top authors for the ultimate cruise experience. Spend 7 days in the Mexican Riviera aboard the luxurious Carnival Pride℠. Start in Los Angeles/Long Beach, CA and visit Puerto Vallarta, Mazatlan and Cabo San Lucas. Enjoy all this with a ship full of authors and book lovers on the "Authors at Sea Cruise" April 2 - 9, 2006.
PRICES STARTING AT $749** PER PERSON WITH COUPON!
Mail in this coupon with proof of purchase* to receive $250 per person off the regular "Authors at Sea Cruise" price. One coupon per person required to receive $250 discount. For complete details call 1-877-ADV-NTGE or visit www.AuthorsAtSea.com
MIRA®
HQN™
Carnival.
The Most Popular Cruise Line in the World!

Carnival Pride℠

April 2 - 9, 2006.

7 Day Exotic Mexican Riviera Itinerary

DAY	PORT	ARRIVE	DEPART
Sun	Los Angeles/Long Beach, CA		4:00 P.M.
Mon	"Book Lover's" Day at Sea		
Tue	"Book Lover's" Day at Sea		
Wed	Puerto Vallarta, Mexico	8:00 A.M.	10:00 P.M.
Thu	Mazatlan, Mexico	9:00 A.M.	6:00 P.M.
Fri	Cabo San Lucas, Mexico	7:00 A.M.	4:00 P.M.
Sat	"Book Lover's" Day at Sea		
Sun	Los Angeles/Long Beach, CA	9:00 A.M.	

ports of call subject to weather conditions

TERMS AND CONDITIONS

PAYMENT SCHEDULE:
50% due upon booking
Full and final payment due by February 10, 2006

Acceptable forms of payment are Visa, MasterCard, American Express, Discover and checks. The card-holder must be one of the passengers traveling. A fee of $25 will apply for all returned checks. Check payments must be made payable to **Advantage International, LLC and sent to: Advantage International, LLC, 195 North Harbor Drive, Suite 4206, Chicago, IL 60601**

CHANGE/CANCELLATION:
Notice of change/cancellation must be made in writing to Advantage International, LLC.

Change:
Changes in cabin category may be requested and can result in increased rate and penalties. A name change is permitted 60 days or more prior to departure and will incur a penalty of $50 per name change. Deviation from the group schedule and package is a cancellation.

Cancellation:

181 days or more prior to departure	$250 per person
121 - 180 days or more prior to departure	50% of the package price
120 - 61 days prior to departure	75% of the package price
60 days or less prior to departure	100% of the package price (nonrefundable)

US and Canadian citizens are required to present a valid passport or the original birth certificate and state issued photo ID (drivers license). All other nationalities must contact the consulate of the various ports that are visited for verification of documentation.

We strongly recommend trip cancellation insurance!

For complete details call 1-877-ADV-NTGE or visit www.AuthorsAtSea.com

For booking form and complete information
go to www.AuthorsAtSea.com or call 1-877-ADV-NTGE

Complete coupon and booking form and mail both to:
Advantage International, LLC,
195 North Harbor Drive, Suite 4206, Chicago, IL 60601

Prices quoted are in U.S. currency.

AAS05B